DATE DUE

THE
LOVE KNOT

THE
LOVE KNOT

Elizabeth Chadwick

ST. MARTIN'S PRESS ❧ NEW YORK

ISBN 0-312-24407-X

First published in Great Britain by Little, Brown and Company

First U.S. Edition: December 1999

10 9 8 7 6 5 4 3 2 1

THE
LOVE KNOT

CHAPTER 1

FOREST OF DEAN, GLOUCESTERSHIRE, SUMMER 1140

Oliver Pascal drew on Hero's rein and sniffed. 'Smoke,' he said.

Gawin de Brionne, his companion in arms, halted his own mount and inhaled deeply. 'There's only the hunting lodge at Penfoss nearby. Aimery de Sens holds it for Earl Robert.'

Oliver grunted and shifted his position to ease his aching buttocks. New saddles were always hell, and this one was scarcely a week old, purchased from a craftsman in Bristol. It would take at least a month to mould it into a comfortable shape. What Oliver wanted to do was cross the Severn at the ferry and ride on to the Earl's keep at Bristol where he was assured of a hot meal and a safe place to sleep. With civil war raging through town and shire as King Stephen and his cousin Mathilda fought tooth and nail over England's throne, opportunities to sleep sound were rare.

A man more inured to the depredations of this particular war might have ridden on, but Oliver was still tender to the game of raid and counter-raid, of pillage and slaughter which was becoming so commonplace that men's morals and sensibilities were bludgeoned from existence. For most of the conflict, he had been absent on pilgrimage, dragging a burden of prayers for his dead wife's soul over the stony ground to Jerusalem's Holy Sepulchre. It was only in the last six months that he had returned to a burning, bleeding land, and discovered that, like so many others, he was now a landless man.

Gawin, five years younger at one-and-twenty but a world more experienced, slackened the reins and made to turn away. 'Like as not it's a charcoal burner.'

'You believe that?'

Gawin shrugged. 'There is nothing we can do. It isn't wise to become embroiled.'

Oliver shook his head. 'Perhaps not, but we cannot just ride on.'

The younger knight sighed, his blue eyes weary within the shadows of his helm. 'Your conscience is a millstone around your neck.'

Oliver compressed his lips. Unlike most of his contemporaries he was clean-shaven, for in contrast to his flaxen hair, his beard, when permitted to grow, was a blazing fire-red that made him feel like a freak. 'You leave my conscience to drag me where it will and search your own,' he said coldly, and swung Hero towards the smell of burning.

Gawin hesitated for a moment and then, with a roll of his eyes, spurred after his companion.

Within half a mile the wafts of smoke were stronger, removing the hope that the source was a domestic, controlled fire, and they thickened significantly as the men struck the main track to Penfoss. The horses grew restive and difficult to handle, forcing the two knights to dismount and continue on foot.

Penfoss was enclosed by a stockade of sharpened oak stakes cut from the surrounding forest, with entrance gates of the same, lashed together with hemp ropes. These now hung askew, and beyond them the thatch of the lodge and outbuildings was obliterated by licks of flame and churning black smoke.

Cautiously, swords drawn, Oliver and Gawin abandoned the cover of the trees and approached the stockade. A man's body sprawled across the gateway. There was a gaping wound in his throat and he had been stripped of every garment but the loin-cloth that he had stained in his death throes. A large black hound lay nearby, its breast split open.

Gawin grimaced and looked around nervously. 'Best leave. There's nothing we can do here, and whoever did this must still be close.'

Ignoring him, Oliver entered the compound. Smuts of soot soared on a fire-wind and gusts of heat belched at him. Bodies were strewn haphazardly across the courtyard, butchered in flight to judge from the number of wounds to the back. The armed and the unarmed; men, women and children. Fluid filled Oliver's mouth and he tightened his grip on the hilt of his sword. It was either that or hurl the weapon as far from himself as he could. 'Not in three years of wandering amongst the wildest places on God's earth have I ever seen such as this,' he said hoarsely.

'Better grow accustomed then.' There was a quiver in Gawin's voice that gave the lie to the callous words and his free hand groped for the cross around his neck.

Oliver moved on. A shining mass of golden hair drew him to the body of a woman. She lay on her back, her legs flung wide. Her eyes were open, staring blindly; her cheekbone was swollen and her lip was puffed and split, but she was still breathing.

'God's mercy!' Oliver fell to his knees at her side. 'Amice, Amice, can you hear me?'

'You know her?' Gawin's voice was appalled.

'From a long time ago,' Oliver said without looking round. 'She was one of Earl Robert's wards at the same time as my wife. If circumstances had been different, I might have married her instead of Emma. Jesu's pity, I do not believe this!' He closed her legs and pulled her gown back down over her stained, bloody thighs.

The woman turned her head and focused on Oliver, but there was no recognition in the dark sapphire eyes.

Gawin tugged at the close-cropped beard edging his jaw. 'How badly is she hurt?'

'I don't know. Knocked down and raped as far as I can tell. We can't leave her here. Go and fetch the horses.'

Her vacant stare was unnerving. Oliver well remembered their first meeting for it was inextricably bound up in his memories of Emma. It had been the spring of 1129 in Earl

Robert's garden when he had encountered the girls – two giggling cousins of fourteen and fifteen – playing with a ball. Amice, the older, had a sheaf of golden hair, ripe curves, and a way of looking through her lashes that turned a man's blood to steam. Emma, his future wife, was tiny and fey with a smile that lit up her little pointed face and made it quite beautiful. He had been fifteen too, a gangly youth in no hurry for the marriage that his family was foisting upon him, but Emma had changed all that. Now she was in her grave with the still-born daughter whose three-day bearing had been her death.

The year of their wedding, Amice had become one of old King Henry's concubines and had borne him a lusty son. It was the last Oliver had seen of her, if not heard, until now.

'Go on, Gawin, damn you, stop gawping and bring the horses!' he repeated on a ragged snarl.

When Gawin still did not move, Oliver raised his head and looked round, his lungs filling with a bellow. Then he too saw the young woman standing against the well-housing, a wooden bowl in her hands. Her gown was of tawny-gold wool, worn over an underdress of contrasting green-blue linen. Both the cut and the colours of the garments proclaimed her noble status. Two heavy braids of raven-black hair hung for a full twelve inches below the end of her wimple. She had been creeping backwards but, realising that she had been seen, turned to flee.

'Wait!' Oliver cried. 'We mean you no harm!'

Gawin started after her, but had run no more than a dozen yards when a familiar whirring sound cut the air and he was stopped in mid-stride by an arrow, which punched a hole through his mail and lodged in his collar-bone.

Oliver shot to his feet and stared wildly around, his hand flashing to his sword hilt.

'Throw down your blade!'

The voice was so cold that it should have belonged to a hardened warrior. Instead, Oliver found himself confronted by a lanky boy of no more than nine or ten years old. The bow in the child's hand was drawn taut and the arrow was aimed straight at Oliver's breast.

'We're not raiders, we want to help.' Slowly, Oliver lowered his sword. His heart was thundering in his ears, reminding him how swiftly it could be stopped. To one side Gawin was clutching at the shaft protruding from his mail and swearing.

The boy's face was ashen. 'Get away from her,' he spat. 'Get away from my mother!'

'Your mother?' Oliver dared not take his eyes from the lad to look at Amice. This then must be the son she had borne to King Henry. 'I know Lady Amice, lad, she's an old friend.' He made a calming gesture. 'I'll take you both to safety, I swear.'

The boy's arm trembled. In a moment he was going to release that arrow, and in all likelihood this time he would kill. Oliver took his chance and charged, weaving from side to side as he ran. The arrow shot from the bow and whined past his ear like a hornet. The next shaft was already nocked as Oliver struck. Man and boy rolled over in the dust and Oliver discovered that he was wrestling with an adversary as slippery as a Severn eel. A sharp elbow jabbed his ribs, drawing a grunt of pain; a fist flailed in his face and connected with his eye socket. The fingers uncurled and gouged. Oliver ceased being gentle, hit the lad with his fist, forced him down and sat on him.

'God's teeth!' he panted. 'The only safety you need is a cage!'

The boy lay rigid beneath him. Gingerly Oliver relaxed his grip, but remained alert to tighten it again if needful. 'I spoke the truth,' he said in a breathless but less fraught tone. 'I do know your mother and I can help.'

The stiffness remained a moment longer, then the battle-light left the boy's eyes which filled with the glitter of unshed tears. A lump was swelling on his temple where Oliver had cuffed him.

'I was out hunting squirrels with my bow,' he said jerkily, 'and I saw the knights in the forest riding away from here with bloody swords. I ran home and I found . . . I found . . .' His throat worked and the words strangled.

'All right, all right, go gently, lad.' With a feeling of guilt for his own violence, Oliver rose off the boy. Small wonder that the child had reacted as he had. Great wonder that he was not reduced to a cowering huddle.

Gawin came up to them, the boy's arrow now in his hand.

'Are you hurt?' Oliver looked from the flight to Gawin's white face.

'Stung more than anything, thanks to decent mail,' Gawin said with a grimace. 'It's not a full-grown man's barb or I'd be dead, but it's still made a nasty nick. The repair to my hauberk will cost the best part of half a mark.' He pressed the upper edge of his quilted gambeson against the wound to stanch it and gave the boy a jaundiced look. 'I told you we should have ridden on.'

'Put your morals before your mouth for once,' Oliver snapped. He jerked his head at the blond woman lying in the dust, alive but lifeless. 'That's his mother. Look around you. What would you have done in his place?'

Before Gawin could respond, the boy leaped to his feet and sprinted across the compound towards the other, younger woman who had stopped in mid-flight when he attacked the knights. 'Catrin,' he sobbed and she swept her arms around him and hugged him desperately, burying her cheek in his hair.

Gawin looked puzzled. 'I thought you said yonder was his mother.'

'She is.' Thoughtfully Oliver returned to Amice and, removing his cloak, laid it gently over her. Her eyes were now clear, and this time they widened in recognition.

'You missed the festivities, Oliver,' she whispered with a bitter half-smile.

'I missed them more than ten years ago, Amice. Look, we have horses; we'll take you to tending and shelter.'

The sinews tightened in her throat and she folded her knees towards her belly and clutched with rigid hands. 'It is too late for that!' she gasped.

The other woman hastened over, the boy in pursuit. 'I knew this would happen,' she said grimly as she flung herself down beside Amice. 'It's been threatening for days now, and after what they did to her . . .'

'Knew what would happen?' Oliver demanded.

'She's with child, but not carrying well. For the last month she's been spotting blood. That's the father over by the gate, Aimery de Sens. They slaughtered him like a Martinmas hog and raped her as he died – one after the other, turn upon turn. Richard, go and bring me some water.' She gave the boy the wooden bowl and spared Oliver a look from clear, amber-green eyes. 'I thought you were scavengers come to pick over the bones.'

Oliver watched the boy trot away to the well and shook his head. 'We were on our way to the Severn ferry when the smoke guided us to you from the main track.' He looked at her curiously, for her French accent bore a lilting inflection. The boy had called her Catrin, which he thought might be Welsh. 'How came you to escape this carnage?' He gestured around.

'I was in the woods gathering oak bark for dyeing, but close enough to hear the commotion – and see what the whoresons did.' She leaned over Amice. 'What quarrel did we have with anyone?'

'We have to get her to safety.' Oliver's gut was queasy. He would rather face the entire hoards of hell single-handed than deal with a woman in childbirth. It was worrying too that a band of raiders should be abroad in the heart of Gloucester's territory.

'No. If she is moved, she will bleed to death. I have only a little knowledge, but that much is certain.' She sat back on her heels and regarded him sombrely. 'Her only chance is to remain completely still.'

'Is there no midwife nearby?'

'Dead,' she said with a grim gesture at the bodies strewing the compound. 'And the nearest settlement is more than ten miles away.'

He swore beneath his breath. Jesu, Gawin was right. They should have tarnished their consciences and left well alone.

Walking carefully so as not to spill a drop, the boy returned with the bowl of water. Catrin took it from him and gently raised Amice enough to drink.

'I'll go and make camp,' Oliver said abruptly. He felt as helpless as a straw cast upon the surface of a raging flood. 'Come, lad, you can help me.'

The boy hesitated, but at Catrin's nod and his mother's forced smile followed Oliver.

It was a little beyond full dark when Amice's child came still-born into the world, drenched in its mother's blood which continued to trickle and seep despite all Catrin's efforts. The afterbirth that followed the baby was torn, and Catrin knew that when such a thing happened the mother either bled to death or died within a few days of a suppurating fever.

Sitting at Amice's side, her hands red to the wrists, Catrin uttered a small sound of frustration. The fair-haired knight had given them his own portable shelter for the night and had built an open fire before it. Then he had made another camp across the compound for himself, his companion and Richard, giving the women a modicum of privacy. For much of the time Catrin had been aware of his presence in the corner of her vision as he moved among the dead, straightening and composing, murmuring prayers. Between the labour pangs, Amice had told her his name and a little about him. What she had said had made Catrin even more aware of his quiet, deliberate movements.

'It is no use, Catrin,' Amice said in a reed-thin voice. 'There comes a time when death will not be cheated.'

'My lady, I . . .'

'Be quiet, there is no time to argue.' Amice licked her parched lips and Catrin helped her to sip from the bowl of water. 'Bring me Oliver Pascal. I need to speak with him – hurry.'

Catrin rinsed her hands and, drying them on her gown as she walked, approached the men's fire. Richard was staring into the flames, his hands wrapped around his upraised knees. He raised his eyes to her face, then slid his gaze over her bloodied clothes. Catrin wanted to cry. Instead, her voice wooden with control, she delivered Amice's summons to Oliver.

'How is she?' The knight rose swiftly to his feet, his expression full of question and anxiety.

Catrin compressed her lips and shook her head. 'There is

nothing that anyone but God can do. She has lost the baby and there is too much blood.'

He flinched, but Catrin was too busy containing her own emotions to notice. Sinking to her knees beside Richard, she drew him into her embrace.

Oliver crossed the compound. Behind him, a pattern of glowing embers marked the place where half a day since buildings had stood. From what the child had told him, Oliver understood that Aimery de Sens was a man of few ambitions beyond the bedchamber and even fewer personal enemies. Penfoss had simply fallen foul of a random raid. It was destruction for destruction's sake, and someone had derived warped pleasure from the deed. Oliver shivered at the thought and wondered how men managed to live with themselves.

Reaching the shelter, he stooped inside and crouched beside Amice. His dark cloak covered her from throat to feet, making her resemble a corpse on a bier. Her skin was waxen, her eye sockets the dark hollows of a skull. To one side there was a pile of bloodied rags made from a torn-up undershift.

For a moment his inner eye exchanged these cramped surroundings for the well-appointed bedchamber of his brother's keep at Ashbury, the fire built high, the huge walnut-wood bed dwarfing Emma's pale, still form. Her cold hands were wrapped around the cross that the priest had given her to hold in her dying moments and had it not been for the drained complexion, the bluish tinge in socket and cheekbone, she might have been asleep. Five years had passed, but the memory was still unbearable.

'Amice?' Kneeling, he held her hand.

Turning her head, she forced her lids apart. Her fingers twitched and Oliver felt the cold strike through his own warm flesh.

'You know that Richard is the old King's son,' she said in a thready whisper.

'Yes, of course I do.' And what a scandal it had been at the time. A girl of sixteen and a man old enough to be her grandfather. People said that the troubles in England now were God's payback for Henry's fifty years of lechery.

'It has been so long. I do not know the roads you travel

these days, but I ask . . .' she swallowed. 'I ask you to take Richard to his kin at Bristol.'

'I serve his uncle, Earl Robert, and I'm bound there of my own accord. You need not worry about the lad. I'll deliver him safe.'

She gave him the ghost of a smile. 'I know you will. You were always steadfast, whatever the temptation.'

He winced. She did not know how close he had come to yielding to that temptation.

'Emma saw it in you. I was jealous of her.'

He cleared his throat and looked away; he did not want to think about Emma. 'It is in the past.'

'It is as fresh as yesterday,' she contradicted.

Oliver fought the urge to leap to his feet and stalk away. What she said was true. Despite the passage of time, some memories remained as sharp as glass. If Amice had been jealous of Emma, how much more had he envied Amice her life and her healthy child. Both might have been his had he chosen differently. Now, in place of envy there was weariness and the all-too-familiar sensation of guilt.

'There is one more boon I must ask of you while I yet have breath,' Amice whispered.

Oliver clenched his jaw to withhold the snarl gathering within him. When he spoke, it was with great gentleness, his hand smoothing hers. 'Name it, and it is yours.'

'Find a place at Bristol for Catrin too. She is a widow without family and she has been a loyal companion to me.'

'As you wish.'

'Nothing is as I wish.' Amice smiled bitterly. 'Yesterday was better.' She closed her eyes. 'In the garden, Emma and I . . .'

Oliver set his hand against her throat. The pulse still beat there, but erratically. Her breath stirred the guard hairs on the wolfskin border of his cloak; then it didn't and her mouth fell open. Oliver released her hand and gently crossed it with the other one upon her breast. *In the garden.* Was that a reference to the past or where she was now?

Taking his cloak, he returned slowly to the fire where the living were gathered.

Catrin rose from her place beside the boy and hurried to meet him. Her eyes went from his face to the cloak draped over his arm and he saw the small shudder run through her body.

'I will tell the lad,' he said quietly. 'Go and prepare her so that he can look at her if he wants.'

Her gaze filled with hostility. 'It is not right. You are a complete stranger to him.'

'Sometimes it is better that way. You will still be here to give him comfort, won't you?' He nodded towards the small shelter. 'I'm sorry.'

'Don't be!' she snapped. 'You know nothing about us!' Her face started to crumple and she pushed blindly past him.

Oliver frowned and smoothed the fur on his cloak. Perhaps his regret was for not knowing until it was too late. After a brief hesitation he went to the fire and took Catrin's place beside the boy.

'You don't need to tell me,' Richard forestalled him. 'I know she's dead.'

'Weep if you want.' Oliver extended his hands to the flames, drawing life and warmth back into his body. Across the fire, Gawin poked the burning wood, sending flickers of yellow heat into the night sky.

'I don't feel like weeping,' Richard said stiffly.

'It will come.' Oliver took the flask of ginevra that Gawin stretched out to him, gulped a burning mouthful and passed it on to the boy. 'Sooner or later everyone has to weep.'

Richard took the flask, drank, then choked on the fiery brew; but when he had ceased coughing, he put the flask to his lips and took a second, longer swallow. 'She is better dead.'

Which was not the kind of remark for a ten-year-old to make about his newly deceased mother.

'Why do you say that?' Oliver retrieved his flask before the boy could avail himself again.

Richard shrugged. 'She always had to ruin what she had,' he said moodily.

When nothing else was forthcoming, Oliver broke the silence by murmuring, 'I knew her before you were born, when Earl Robert was her guardian.'

'Did you lie with her like all the others?'

Oliver's palm flew, but he stopped it just short of the boy's ear. Richard did not flinch, his stare blank and dark with misery. 'Christ, boy, what sort of question is that?' Lowering his hand, Oliver wrapped it around his belt and drew a steadying breath. 'No, I did not lie with her,' he said evenly. After all, it was the truth, no matter how easily he could have joined the ranks of 'all the others'. 'She was my wife's cousin and childhood companion. Last time I saw her was at your father's court when you were a tiny baby.'

'We didn't stay there long,' the child said in a savage voice. 'Did you know that she wasn't married to Aimery de Sens? He's just my most recent "papa", but of course he's dead now too.'

Oliver's fingers tightened around his belt. He made a conscious effort to relax them. The boy's pain was a raw, open wound, hence the provocative tone, but what he said was probably true. Amice's nature had been inconstant and wanton as he had cause to know. Had she been male, she would have been granted a modicum of leeway, but as a woman she was damned as a whore. It was unfortunate if the boy had been a witness to the darker machinations of adult behaviour. 'No, I didn't know,' he said, 'but it makes no difference to me. She was a friend, and she was kin by marriage.'

Richard frowned and toyed with the frayed end of one of his leg bindings. 'What will happen to me now?'

'As to that, I do not know. I told your mother that I would take you to your half-brother, Earl Robert, at Bristol. You will be cared for, I promise.'

'Promises are easy.' The boy's tone was far too adult for his years.

Oliver sighed and rubbed his hand over his jaw where the prick of red stubble was beginning to replace the morning's smoothness. 'Not to me,' he answered, 'and not of this moment. I swore to your mother that I would see you safe, and do so I will. Catrin too.'

'What if I don't want to go?'

'Since I promised your mother, I suppose I would have to tie you to my saddle.'

The boy threw him a look to see if he really meant it. Knowing that he was being tested, Oliver returned the look for long enough to impose his will, then rose to his feet. 'Do you want to see her?'

Richard silently shook his head.

Oliver rubbed his jaw again in thought, then turned and stooped. 'Here,' he said gruffly, 'roll yourself in my blanket and try to sleep. It will be a long journey on the morrow.'

When Richard did not move, Oliver draped the blanket around the boy's shoulders himself and then went to check on the horses before walking a circuit of the burned-out settlement.

Kneeling beside her former mistress, all signs of the bloody struggle cleared away, Catrin sniffed and knuckled her eyes. She had been fond of Amice, who had taken her in, a soldier's widow with nothing more than two silver pennies and a roan mule to her name. For almost three years Catrin had sheltered beneath Amice's generous, mercurial wing, turning a blind eye when a blind eye was required, being a companion and confidante, sometimes a scapegoat, but always needed – if not by Amice, then by Richard. What would happen to her and the boy now she did not know; she could only hope that Robert of Gloucester would have the compassion to take them in, penniless dependants as they were.

A shadow passed between Catrin and the fire. She glanced up in alarm, then breathed out in relief as she saw it was the knight, Oliver Pascal.

'I didn't mean to frighten you,' he said, and crouched at her side, adding when she did not speak, 'I'll keep vigil now while you go and rest. I'm taking you and the lad with me to Bristol on the morrow and it will be a long ride.'

Catrin eyed him warily. 'I suppose Amice asked you.'

'She did, but I'm bound there anyway. I serve the Earl and I've to report to him.' He looked at her curiously before leaning over to replenish the fire. 'Amice said you are a widow without kin, but surely you must have had a home once?'

Catrin watched him select and arrange the split logs. In all the earlier conflagration it was ironic that the wood pile had not been touched. 'Chepstow, I suppose, since I was born there, but there is no one left in that place to welcome my return,' she said with a shrug. 'My mother was Welsh, my father a serjeant of the Chepstow garrison, but they are both dead. My husband was also a soldier there.' She compressed her lips, her mind filling with a vision of Lewis's thin, dark features and blazing smile. 'And he too is dead.'

'I'm sorry.'

The predictable response. She had heard it from so many lips by now that it was irritating and meaningless, a stepping stone to buffer the discomfort of others. 'Amice came to Chepstow a six-month after my husband's death,' she said, eager to have done with her story. 'When she left, I begged to go with her rather than dwell alone with my memories.'

He positioned the last piece of wood and dusting off his hands, rested them on his thighs. 'I too am a soldier, one of Robert of Gloucester's hearth knights,' he said after a while, 'although not by choice. My family lands lie close to Malmesbury and my older brother lost them, together with his life, when he declared for the Empress Mathilda. I'm his heir – his dispossessed heir.'

'I'm sorry,' she said in the same polite tone he had used to her, paying him back in the same coin. Then felt honour-bound to add, 'And I'm sorry about your wife. Amice told me about her.'

He gave her a long, level look. 'Sorry doesn't help, does it?'

Catrin blinked and turned away. Mary Mother, she was not going to weep in front of this man. 'I must go to Richard,' she said and started to rise.

Oliver grimaced. 'Be warned then; he was angry – with her, not me – and because of the anger, the grief is trapped within him. He asked me if I had lain with his mother like "all the others".' He glanced grimly at the dead woman's shrouded figure, the red shadows licking the hem of her gown. 'How many "others" were there?'

'Because it matters to you or to him?'

She saw the twitch of his brows, the knotting of muscle in his jaw. 'Obviously it matters to him,' he said stiffly. 'I am not about to sit in judgement if that is your fear.'

'I do not fear your judgement,' Catrin snapped angrily. What else was he doing but sitting in judgement? 'Yes, she liked the company of men, yes, she took them to her bed when she would have been wiser to abstain, but Richard was always well cared for. Her heart was too soft and she sought for love in all the wrong places, but if that is a sin, then more than half of us are damned!' She drew an unsteady breath that caught across her voice in distress.

He stared at her, his mouth slightly open in a surprise that might have been comical under different circumstances. The fire spat and a burning ember flared in the space between them. 'And the rest either find it or go without,' he rallied as the blossom of wood dulled to grey, but his gaze held poignancy and regret rather than challenge. He made a rueful gesture. 'Go and take what rest you can. Tomorrow will be a long day.'

That at least was not something to be disputed. Catrin had neither the heart nor the sharpness of mind to spar any more tonight. Glancing at the weary set of Oliver Pascal's shoulders, she thought that neither did he.

CHAPTER 2

The morning dawned overcast, with a whisper of drizzle in
the air. The stink of smoke had seeped into clothing, hair
and skin. Every breath tasted of it and everyone was eager
to leave the remains of Penfoss behind. It was impossible to
take the dead with them or, with just three adults and a child,
to dig graves here. Only Amice's body was going to Bristol.
As Earl Robert's former ward and Richard's mother, it was
politic to bring her for burial at the church of Saint Peter.
The other corpses were laid out in the compound and covered
with green branches cut from the forest by Gawin's war axe.
Oliver prayed over the bodies as a mark of respect but he did
not linger. A priest and burial party would come from Bristol
within the next few days to perform the necessary rites.

The pack horse's load was redistributed to accommodate
the burden of Amice's body. Gawin's dun bore most of
the displaced supplies, and there was just enough room for
Richard's narrow frame to ride pillion. Oliver watched as
Gawin settled the boy on his mount's tawny rump. Richard's
features were composed this morning, shunning all contact,
but the anger still bristled visibly within him. It was a position Oliver understood all too well, and only hoped that the
comforting security of Bristol Castle and the nearness of kin
would help to break down those brittle barriers before they
shattered inwards.

From his conversation with Catrin the previous night, he
thought that she understood too. This morning her eyes were
red-rimmed and puffy and he did not believe that it was all
the result of smoke. She, at least, had learned to weep.

Oliver swung into the saddle and leaned down, offering his hand to her. 'Set your foot on mine,' he commanded, 'and pull against my grip.'

'I know what to do,' she said brusquely, and drew a section of her skirts through her belt. 'My father and my husband were soldiers, and I could ride before I could walk.'

Oliver tightened his lips on the urge to grin and make a light remark. He could see that she hated being made dependent on anyone.

The hand she slipped into his was cool and work-roughened with short nails. Two rings gleamed on her heart finger, one at the base, the other at the first knuckle joint. Both were of engraved gold. Her husband, it seemed, had been that rare entity, a rich soldier. Most scraped by, affording food and weapons with only small coin for luxuries.

He drew her up behind him and she settled – not side-on as a lady of gentle birth would have ridden but directly astride like a man.

Oliver could suppress his grin no longer and it broke across his face, brightening his dark grey eyes and setting two deep creases in his cheeks.

She glared at him. 'Something amuses you?'

'No, no. It is admiration, not amusement,' he replied, his grin not diminishing in the least. Her hose, he noticed, were of a wonderful, frivolous shade of red and enclosed a shapely ankle and calf.

Seeing the direction of his gaze, she made to tug her skirt down, then drew back and straightened instead. 'Gawp if you want,' she said disdainfully, 'but don't let your eyes pop from your skull before you have delivered us safe to Bristol.'

'Thank you, and I'll try not to,' he said gravely, refusing to be cowed. 'You must blame admiration again, not so much of your hose, fine though they are, but of your mettle.'

She gave him an irritated look. 'Spare your compliments, not the horse.'

Still grinning, Oliver faced his mount's ears. 'Grip my belt,' he said, 'I know you're a horse-woman born and bred, but if you fall off, you'll tear more than just your fetching hose.'

He could almost feel her scowl deepen, but the interlude

had given a moment of light relief to a grim situation and Oliver was not contrite. He gathered up the reins and Hero sidled and attempted to buck. Oliver heard a stifled oath behind him and suddenly two hands grasped his belt.

'You did that apurpose!' she accused furiously.

'I swear I did not!' Oliver protested, but marred his innocence with a smothered chuckle. He half expected her to snatch away her hands, but they remained, together with a stony silence, as the small party rode out of the gates and left the burned-out husk of Penfoss behind.

At first, Catrin sat behind Oliver and nursed her anger in a pet of determined self-indulgence. He neither fed her ill-humour nor sought to cajole her out of it, but left her in peace to brood.

A twelve-inch from her eyes, his mail-clad spine swayed with the rhythm of the horse. Through the riveted links she could see the quilted linen gambeson beneath and the dark streaks that the steel had smudged on it. The belt she clutched was of high-quality buckskin incised with a pattern of oak leaves. At regular intervals, small pewter pilgrim badges had been punched through the leather. She recognised the cockle-shell of Saint James, the sword of Saint Foy and the palm branch of Jerusalem. Catrin decided that he had probably visited each place and tomb himself, for his skin was weathered beyond the capabilities of the English climate.

As they rode, her anger began to evaporate. She reviewed the moment when she had straddled the horse and his eyes had widened on both her posture and her scarlet hose. Her mouth twitched with grudging amusement as she saw the humour in the situation. Lewis would have laughed too, she thought. Then he would have slid his hand up her leg and . . . Catrin tightened her fingers in Oliver Pascal's handsome belt and mentally shook herself. Scarlet hose as may be, such imaginings were not for now.

He must have felt the sudden grip against his spine, for he half turned to look at her. Catrin quickly lowered her lids, avoiding all eye contact, and so did not see the glance he cast at her scarlet legs, or the smile that he swallowed before facing forward again.

The drizzle ceased and the clouds began to shred, allowing peeks of sunlit blue between. Catrin gazed at her surroundings. There were so many shades of green in the early summer forest that they dazzled her eyes; in addition to the individual hues of each variety of tree the play of light and sunlight altered their leaves from pale gold to dark emerald in the passing of a cloud.

A flash of a barred blue wing and the harsh shriek of a jay made her jump. Somewhere a cuckoo sought a mate, the two notes of its song monotonous and sleepy, and a woodpecker drummed for insects beneath the bark of an ash tree. She glanced sidelong at Richard, bumping along behind the other knight's saddle, and saw that he too was observing the woods with an air of concentration.

Last night in the darkness he had curled up against her in a tight ball and her throat had ached. When she had wept, it had been as much for him as his mother. In defending Amice, Catrin had told Oliver the truth whilst withholding the facts. Amice had indeed cared for her son, but as she would care for a puppy or a special trinket. He was petted, loved and cuddled, until something distracted her – usually a man – and then cast aside until the distraction had lost its novelty. Catrin had done her best, but knew that her steadiness had made Amice's whims all the more bewildering to the child. Small wonder if he was angry.

And in Bristol the unknown awaited in the form of his royal kin. What kind of welcome were she and Richard going to receive – if any? It was not impossible that they would be cast out to beg for their living among the camp followers and whores who serviced Gloucester's troops. She supposed that they could travel to King Stephen's camp. He was, after all, Richard's cousin, and Catrin had no strong feelings against him. It mattered little to her who ruled the country, just as long as there was peace. Her mind filled with images of yesterday's slaughter and she squeezed her lids together to make them go away. When she opened her eyes, an expanding shimmer of light obliterated the corner of her vision and, with dismay, she recognised the onset of a debilitating headache.

Ever since the first bleed of her womanhood she had been burdened by the affliction. It came upon her without warning, but usually when she was tired or upset. The headaches were so excruciating and left her so drained that she dreaded the first flickering glimmers. Sometimes in high summer, the sparkle of sun on water would leave its reflection on her eye and she would panic, believing one of her megrims was imminent. The flood of relief when she realised her mistake was enormous. But today there was no reprieve. The shimmer spread inwards, obscuring her vision, and her stomach began to lurch with each stride of the horse. Pain flickered delicately across her brows, probing for a place to settle. When she closed her eyes, the shimmer turned black with frilly, silver edges. Her heart thundered in her ears, each beat driving needles into her skull. Despite her clenched teeth, saliva filled her mouth.

'Stop!' she gulped at Oliver. 'Now!'

He drew rein and slewed round in the saddle. 'What's wr . . .' he started to ask, but Catrin had already bolted from the grey's back and was braced against a tree, retching violently.

Even after she had been sick, Catrin felt little better. Pain surged over her in great rolling waves, crushing her skull like a shell against a rock. All she could do was huddle over herself and gasp.

Frozen by shock, Oliver stared at her and wondered if she was in the grip of some contagion that would bring sickness to all who had contact with her. Spotted fever started just like this. There had been an outbreak in the crusader port of Jaffa three years ago and hundreds had died.

'What ails her?' Gawin's voice and widened eyes held the same fear that Oliver was silently entertaining.

'I don't know. If she has a contagion then it is too late to keep our distance now. Either we'll catch it or we won't, at the whim of God.' Somewhat abruptly, filled with self-irritation, he dismounted.

Richard wriggled down from his perch behind Gawin.

'It's only one of her headaches,' he said scornfully. 'There's nothing to fear.'

'One of her headaches?' Oliver repeated, and felt ashamed as the boy went to Catrin and put his arm around her.

'She gets them sometimes, and then she has to lie down in the dark to make them go away. A leech told her that if she cut open a frog while it still lived and placed its entrails on her brow, they would draw out all the evil humours, but she wouldn't do it.'

'And no blame to her either,' Oliver said with a grimace. Turning to his horse, he unfastened a deerskin bag from a thong on the saddle. The bag, stained and worn, had travelled as far as Oliver in the past four years. It contained a tourniquet cord, linen swaddling bands to make bandages and slings, a small pair of shears and needle and thread. There were also various dried herbs in small linen pouches, their identity separated by different coloured woollen strands tying the necks of the pouches.

'Make a fire,' he commanded Gawin. 'A tisane of betony and feverfew might help her. Ethel always swears by it.' Opening one of the pouches, he crumbled some dried stalks and flower-heads into a small cooking vessel fetched from the supplies on the pack pony. Then he walked a short distance into the forest and returned with the leaves and flower-heads of a wood betony plant. This too went into the pot. He covered the herbs with water from his leather flask and set the mixture to infuse over the fire that Gawin had made out of tinder and a swift collection of dry twigs.

Catrin leaned against the trunk of a young beech, her complexion made greener than ever by the reflection of the leaf canopy.

'How often is "sometimes"?' Oliver enquired, as the liquid began to steam and the water turned deep gold.

Richard shrugged. 'I don't know. Whenever there was trouble, I suppose.'

'The priest used to say that I had devils in my head,' Catrin mumbled, her eyes tightly closed. 'He said that they should be beaten out of me, but Lady Amice refused to let him try.'

'When I was in Rome, a chirurgeon told me that the best

cure for devils in the head was to shave off the victim's hair and make a hole in the skull to force the demons out,' Oliver mused. 'Loth as I am to doubt the word of a learned man, I prefer to use the betony and feverfew myself. They certainly work for me on the morning after a night with the wine.'

Catrin shuddered delicately and half opened her eyes. They were cloudy, as if she had just woken from sleep, and although she tried to focus on him her gaze slipped away. 'If you so much as go near my head, I will kill you.'

'My knife's blunt anyway,' he said cheerfully as he removed the pot from the fire with a folded wad of his cloak and poured the brew into his drinking horn. While he blew on the tisane and swirled it round to cool, Gawin stamped out the fire and went to the horses.

'Here, drink.' Oliver knelt beside Catrin.

Her nose wrinkled at the smell carried in the steam. 'You bastard,' she whimpered, but nevertheless took the cup from him and raised it shakily to her lips, almost missing them. The taste was as foul as she had expected and made her gag, but somehow she forced it down.

'I know it tastes vile, but I promise it will ease the pain,' he said with such optimism that she loathed him. 'Can you remount, or shall I pick you up?'

Catrin swallowed. Her sight was now obliterated by ripples of swimming light and whether or not the tisane would remain in her stomach hung in a very delicate balance.

'I can manage,' she said through her teeth. Forcing her will to overcome the agony, she accepted his hand to rise and staggered over to the grey. The stallion's flank seemed like the wall of a huge cliff. She watched Oliver gain the saddle in one easy motion, his foot scarcely bearing down on the stirrup iron. To one side, Gawin and Richard were already mounted and waiting.

Catrin closed her eyes, put her foot where she thought Oliver's should be, and felt the muscular tug of his arm as he hauled her up. She landed across the grey's rump like a sack of cabbages and grasped Oliver's pilgrim belt for dear life as the horse snorted in alarm and bunched his hind quarters.

Oliver soothed his mount with a murmur, then let out the

reins to ease him forward. 'It isn't as far as it seems,' he said, by way of reassurance. 'We'll cross the river at the Sharpness ferry then ride on down to Bristol.'

Catrin moaned softly. Any distance was too far just now.

After crossing the Severn, it took another five hours at a gentle plod to reach the city of Bristol. Oliver could have covered the ground in half the time, but he schooled himself to patience and let the warmth of the emerging sun soak into his bones. He talked to Richard of the kin to whom he was being taken: Robert de Caen, Earl of Gloucester, and his wife, the Countess Mabile. He described their great household and the magnificent new keep that dominated the fortifications of Bristol castle. The boy said little, but now and again Oliver would see the lift of an eyebrow or a brightening half glance that told him he was not talking entirely to himself. Catrin went to sleep, leaning against his back. Occasionally she gave a soft little snore but did not awaken, even when he paused to drink from his water flask and eat an oatcake from his travelling rations. She had been sick again at the ferry but not as badly, and a little of her colour had returned.

'Will Catrin be allowed to stay with me?' Richard demanded as he washed down his portion of oatcake with a swig from Oliver's flask.

'Of course she will.'

The boy gave him such a hard stare that Oliver was moved to cross his breast and swear on his honour.

'But you have to do what they say.'

Oliver pursed his lips. 'I have sworn an oath to the Earl of Gloucester to be his man, and to the Empress Mathilda that I will uphold her as my rightful queen, but my oath to your mother to see you and Catrin safe is equally as binding on my honour.' He risked tousling the boy's dark hair as he retrieved his flask and looped it around the saddle. 'Don't fret. I promise I won't wash my hands of you the moment we reach Bristol's gates.'

The hard stare remained, and as Oliver clicked his tongue to the grey, he remembered Richard saying by firelight that promises came easily.

*   *   *

Catrin was woken by someone bellowing in her ear. 'Avon eels, mistress! Fresh caught, not an hour old!'

Her eyes flew open to be confronted by a glistening, slithering mass that filled a rush basket not a foot from her face. The raucous voice belonged to a stout woman clad in a frayed homespun gown, who was thrusting her wares at passers-by and extolling their virtues. Catrin shot upright and recoiled. Pain lanced through her skull and her stomach turned at the sight and smell of the fish.

'Avon eels, master, straight from the river!' The woman ran alongside the stallion, shoving her basket beneath Oliver's nose.

Catrin stared round, first in the dazed bewilderment of the newly awakened, and then in the dawning realisation that they had arrived in Bristol. The noise and bustle of the port and town that Robert of Gloucester had made his headquarters struck her like a physical blow. She rubbed her forehead. Her cheek was numb, and when she touched it her fingertips discovered the circular indentations left by hauberk rings.

'Find a basket to put them in and I'll have a dozen,' Oliver told the woman and glanced over his shoulder at Catrin. 'Awake I see. Did the potion work?'

'My head is like a bell tower after Easter Sunday and I could still sleep for a week,' Catrin replied, 'but at least I can think again.'

'Are you capable of holding a basket of eels?'

The woman returned in triumphant possession of a small rushwork pannier in which she deposited twelve shining, slippery bodies.

'Do I have a choice?' Catrin asked as he paid for them.

'You could refuse.'

Catrin cast her eyes heavenwards and grabbed the pannier. 'Give them to me.'

'God bless you, sir, and your lady wife. Them eels'll make a dish fit for a king!'

Oliver thanked the woman with amusement in his voice and rode on. Catrin avoided looking at his purchase and averted her head so as not to inhale its essence.

Oliver laughed darkly. 'Those traders,' he said. 'The wonder is that they ever live to tell the tale. Did you hear what she said?'

Catrin's face burned. 'Yes, but she just made a mistake.'

'A mistake?'

'About us being husband and wife.'

'Oh, that.' He gestured dismissively. 'No, I was talking about the eels. Old King Henry died after gorging himself on a plate of bad ones. They weren't just "fit for a king", they killed a king and started this entire bloody war. You could even argue that a dish of lampreys cost the Pascals their inheritance, since my brother Simon was overthrown and killed for supporting the Empress Mathilda.'

'And you still want to eat them?'

He pulled a face, acknowledging her point. 'They're a gift for a friend,' he explained. 'But yes, I'll still devour them, despite the ill-fortune visited on me and mine. Etheldreda makes the best eel stew in Christendom – there's no resisting.'

'Oh,' Catrin said. She was filled with a mixture of relief and disappointment to discover that there was a woman who cooked and cared for him at Bristol. The way he had spoken last night at Penfoss, she had thought him still alone.

The sounds, sights and smells of the city engulfed her as they rode single-file through its narrow alleys towards the castle. The last time she had visited Bristol was with Lewis in the first year of their marriage. He had bought her a brass circlet and a square of raw silk to make a veil. He had kissed her in the street, his dark eyes laughing, and she had thought herself the luckiest of women. Now she was riding down the same street, bumping along behind a man she barely knew, a basket of mud-smelling eels in her hands, her head pounding fit to burst, and her mistress's body tied in a blanket across a pack pony's withers.

The ghost of Lewis watched her ride past and did not recognise her. Her gaze on the castle walls and the bright gonfanons flying from the battlements, Catrin thought that she did not recognise herself either – except perhaps for the scarlet hose peeping in defiance from beneath her gown.

CHAPTER 3

Bristol Castle was overflowing with hired soldiers. In the space
of five minutes, Catrin heard as many different tongues, as
Oliver led her and Richard to the keep, leaving Gawin in
charge of the horses and the eels.

There were men of every variety and rank, from half-
naked footsoldiers and poor Welsh bowmen to toughened
mercenaries and well-accoutred knights with swords at their
hips. The gap between the ragged and the rich was not as
vast as it seemed, for all soldiers, whatever their rank, wore
the same expression of hungry expectation. Oliver walked
among and through them with ease, now and then smiling
a greeting to those he knew, but Catrin felt great discomfort
at being in the midst of such checked voraciousness. Beside
her, Richard grasped her hand and she saw his blue eyes
darken. To reassure him that these men were allies stuck in
her throat, for they looked no different from those who had
torched Penfoss and murdered its occupants.

Their presence, their stares, the sight of weapons and
grinning mouths in hard faces seemed to go on for ever like
the antechamber to the hall of hell. The image was clarified
in Catrin's mind by the sporadic camp fires which threatened
rather than comforted her.

One soldier held two huge mastiffs on a chain and as she
passed, they lunged, growling. Their owner yanked them
back, laughing at her frightened eyes.

'Got yourself a tasty one there, Pascal!' he yelled, making
an obscene gesture with his free fist.

'Go swive yourself, de Lorys!' Oliver snarled, with a gesture of his own.

The soldier smacked his lips over his stained teeth. 'I'd rather swive what you've got!'

Oliver's hand descended to his sword hilt and his tormentor recoiled with a show of mock terror.

Expression grim, Oliver quickened his stride.

'I see how safe Bristol truly is,' Catrin said with asperity. Both heart and head were thundering.

'Wherever fighting men gather, there are always those who are all mouth and no chausses.'

Catrin shuddered. It was not such soldiers of whom she was afraid although, God knew, they were unpleasant enough, but others of their ilk, who followed up their words with barbaric deeds of rapine and slaughter. Wherever fighting men gathered, there was always that kind too.

She passed women in smoke-grimed dresses – soldiers' wives and followers with gaunt, lithe bodies and weathered faces. She saw one young woman suckling a baby by the fire while two older children played near her skirts. Not a dozen yards from her, a whore plied her trade, offering her own breasts to be groped and suckled. Catrin pulled Richard closer, using her body to shield him from the sight.

Oliver appeared indifferent; all this must be commonplace to him, Catrin thought. But to her and Richard, it was a nightmare. She stumbled in a wheel rut and almost fell. Oliver grabbed her and bore her up. She felt the power in his arm, the bruising strength of his fingers and, although grateful, was also made uneasy.

'Not far now,' he encouraged. 'The camp is always the worst part for newcomers.'

She freed herself from his grip and dusted her skirts, noting with dismay a large, damp stain where the eel liquor had leaked from the basket. It made her realise that she must appear no different from the camp women. Sisters in the bone. There but for the grace of a fickle God. 'Then I am glad,' she said, 'for I do not think I have the stamina to endure much more.'

He gave her a brooding look in which she could see male

exasperation mingled with a certain anxiety. It was clear to Catrin that he wanted her to stay on her feet until he had delivered her and Richard into Earl Robert's household and he could wash his hands of the responsibility. Then he would be free to go and eat his eel stew with his 'friend'.

The quality of the tents and shelters began to improve; there was more mail in evidence, and the accents became mainly French. The drab greys, browns and tans of the perimeter were now brightened with flashes of expensive colour and decorative embroidery. There were plenty of stares, but no one shouted out or tried to intimidate. To one side, a grey-bearded soldier was teaching some younger men how to defend themselves against the thrust of a spear, and everyone appeared to be gainfully employed.

On reaching the keep at the heart of the defences, they were challenged by fully armed guards. Oliver answered smoothly. Obviously he was a well-known face, for they were passed through into Earl Robert's great hall without demur.

Catrin stared round at a simmering bustle that offered small respite to her ragged wits. There were clerks seated at tables, busy with quill and ink; there were groups of soldiers talking, gaming, fondling hounds. Two women tended a cauldron set over the fire, their children playing a boisterous game of chase among the trestles which were being assembled for the late afternoon meal. Servants scurried to and fro with baskets of bread and jugs of ale. Near the dais, four minstrels tuned their instruments. On the dais itself, a retainer was spreading an embroidered linen cloth on the board and setting out cups of exquisite, tinted glass.

A slender, elegant man wearing a blue tunic halted in mid-stride and swung around to approach Oliver's small group. 'Do you have business here?' His nostrils flared fastidiously.

'With the Earl, yes,' Oliver answered, his expression taut with controlled irritation.

Catrin was all too aware of the man's disparaging gaze as he took in the dishevelled appearance of herself and Richard, but it was beyond her energy to return his look with the scorn it deserved.

'The Earl never sees anyone before he has dined,' he said haughtily. 'I might be able to find you a place at the bottom of the hall on one of the spare trestles if . . .'

'You're his understeward, not his spokesman,' Oliver said coldly. 'He will see me, I promise you that. Now, you can either send someone to announce me, or I will go above and announce myself of my own accord.'

'You cannot!' A look of horror crossed the steward's face.

'Then do something about it or lose your living.'

The servant drew himself up, but Oliver remained the taller. When the man's gaze flickered towards the off-duty knights, Oliver caught it and drew it back to his own. 'Have me thrown out,' he said on a rising snarl, 'and I will cut out your voice and cast it to those hounds. Earl Robert's hunting lodge at Penfoss has been destroyed by raiders, and the only witnesses are this woman and the child, who just happens to have royal kin. If it affects the Earl's digestion then I am sorry, but my own belly is full to the gorge!'

Heads turned. The steward licked his lips. 'A moment,' he said and, with his head on high, stalked away in the direction of the tower stairs.

'Conceited arsewipe,' Oliver muttered. 'He thinks because he sees to the placing of the salt and the finger bowls in the Earl's hall that he has dominion over all else.'

Catrin said nothing. The steward's attitude had only served to compound her fears about the kind of welcome she and Richard would receive from Earl Robert.

'Do you want to sit down?' Oliver indicated the benches running along the side of the hall.

Catrin shook her head. 'If I do, I won't rise again – not for an earl or anyone else.'

The steward returned, very much on his dignity, and his nose, although out of joint, still up in the air. 'It is your great good fortune that the Earl has agreed to see you,' he said with obvious disapproval, and beckoned to a boy with a shining mop of chestnut hair and a peppering of sandy freckles across his snub nose. 'Thomas will conduct you to his chamber.'

Hands behind his back in a manner of attentive respect,

the boy acknowledged the steward's command with a deep
bow and addressed him as 'my lord.'

Somewhat mollified, the steward departed to chivvy the
servant who was setting the table on the high dais. The boy
wrinkled his nose at the turned, blue back and, unclasping his
hands, produced the chunk of bread he had been hiding.

'It's for Bran, my pony,' he confided as he tucked it down
inside his tunic. 'Old Bardolf will whip me if he finds out.'
He jerked his head in the steward's direction.

'Are you whipped often?' Oliver asked with amusement.

Thomas shook his head. 'I'm too fast,' he said confidently,
and led them out of the hall and up the stairs to the private
living-quarters on the floor above. Now and again he cast an
inquisitive glance at Richard and Catrin. It was plain that he
was bursting with a curiosity which manners made impossible
to satisfy. Instead he told them about himself. His name was
Thomas FitzRainald, and he was the bastard son of Rainald,
Earl of Cornwall, who in his turn was the bastard son of the
old king. He was cheerfully proud of his ancestry. 'And my
Uncle Robert is fostering me in his household and teaching
me to become a knight,' he finished with a triumphant look
at Richard as they halted before a solid oak door bound with
wrought-iron bands and guarded by a soldier in full mail.

'Steward Bardolf said to bring these guests to my lord,' he
announced in a confident treble.

The guard thumped on the door with his fist. 'You are
expected,' he said to Oliver and, with a wink, wafted his
spear at Thomas. 'Go on, shaveling, away to your dinner.'

The boy wrinkled his nose again, but this time in play, no
insult intended. He bowed beautifully to Oliver, Richard and
Catrin, then ran off towards the stairs.

The guard hid a chuckle in his beard and, at a command
from within, opened the door and ushered them inside.

To Catrin, it was like entering a page from an illuminated
tale of romance. Embroideries clothed the walls in opulent
shades of crimson, green and gold and, where there were
no hangings, the walls were painted with exquisite murals of
scenes from the four seasons. Dried river-reeds strewn with
sweet-scented herbs and slivers of cinnamon bark carpeted the

floor, while all the coffers and benches wore the melted-honey sheen of mellowing oak. Candles of the costliest beeswax had been lit to augment the light. Their scent stroked the air, mingling with that of the herbs as they were bruised by her footsteps.

The man who rose from his high-backed chair and approached them was a little above average height, his stocky build emphasised by his costly tunic of embroidered maroon wool. He had receding dark hair and pleasant, plain features. Had he been wearing ordinary clothes, no one would have given him a second look, but he was King Henry's first-born son, the man whom many said should have been king at his father's death despite the stigma of his illegitimacy. He had rejected the crown in support of his wedlock-born sister, Mathilda, and was now her staunchest supporter against Stephen of Blois, the man who had stolen her kingdom.

Catrin curtseyed and almost fell. Regaining her balance, she locked her knees. At her side Oliver bowed, and Richard copied his example, dipping quickly like a bird at a pond.

The Earl glanced between them with eyes deep set and shrewd. 'Best be seated before you fall down,' he said to Catrin, and gestured to one of the carved benches which was strewn with beautifully embroidered cushions. 'Sander, bring wine.' He summoned a squire who had been standing unobtrusively in a corner.

Catrin was furnished with a brimming cup in which the wine was the colour of blood. Its taste was rich and metallic and her stomach recoiled. She knew that if she drank more than a sip, she would be sick.

'Do I understand that Penfoss has been destroyed?' demanded the Earl.

'Yes, my lord,' said Oliver. 'Looted and burned. Myself and Gawin de Brionne came upon the aftermath on our way to the Severn ferry. Lady Catrin and Master Richard are the only survivors.'

While Oliver relayed the close details of the happening in a voice succinct and devoid of emotion, Catrin stared at the wall, trying to immerse herself in the painted scene of two young women playing ball in a garden. One girl's gown was a vivid shade of blue and her hair was a loose tumble of gold that reminded Catrin of Amice. Her companion wore daffodil-yellow and her hair was black.

'You have no idea who did the deed?' Earl Robert leaned forward, cutting off Catrin's contemplation. 'No one who wished your mistress or master ill?'

'No, my lord. I am not aware that they had enemies. I recognised none of the soldiers. Some wore mail, others were clad in little more than rags, but they were enough to overrun us. They took what they wanted and torched the rest.' In her own ears, her voice sounded as dispassionate as Oliver's, but that was not how she felt inside. Deep down, too far to be dug out, there was hurt and fury. She could have struck out at Robert de Caen just for asking the question, just for being a man, safe in his opulent chambers, guarded and served by men little different from the wolves who had destroyed Penfoss.

'Would you recognise any of them if you saw them again?'

Catrin rubbed her forehead wearily. 'The reason I survived is that I saw the raid from the trees outside the compound. They were of a kind . . . it is hard to remember. Their leader, if you can call him that, rode a chestnut horse with four white legs and a white face.'

'Was there a device on his shield?'

Catrin shook her head. She did not want to draw her mind close to the horror. 'It was green, I think.'

'With a red cross,' Richard added, and outlined the shape on the palm of his hand. 'And his saddle-cloth was made of black and white cowhide.'

Robert of Gloucester sighed. 'Lawless bands are multiplying like flies in a dungheap. Even in my own heartlands I constantly hear of atrocities like this. It is too easy for them. They raid, then slip across the border into Wales, or into another territory where my writ does not run. Three times in the last month I've had farms burned by Stephen's mercenaries raiding out from Malmesbury.'

The war had made it too easy for them, Catrin thought. In King Henry's day, there had been peace, with few outlaws and the King's writ both feared and respected. Now, it was every man to his own gain, and devil take the hindmost. 'So you have small hope of capturing them?' she asked.

'I will do what I can – increase patrols and alert all my vassals and tenants. Like as not they're Malmesbury men.' He tightened his fists, and his gold rings gleamed. 'They will be brought to justice, I swear it.'

Well, that was true if he was referring to judgement-day. 'Thank you, my lord.' Once more she stared beyond him at the mural of the women in the garden. Oliver glanced at it too, but his gaze did not linger and he turned his shoulder so that the wall painting was not in his direct line of vision.

'I have brought Lady Amice here to Bristol in the hope that she might lie in the chapel and be vouchsafed a grave here,' he said. 'It was her dying request that you grant refuge to her son, and to her companion, Mistress Catrin of Chepstow.'

The Earl rose from his chair to pace the chamber. At the window embrasure he stopped and looked out over the narrow glimpse of the river Frome and the lush green cow pasture beyond. Then he turned round. 'Dying requests should not be ignored.' There was a slight frown between his eyes, deepening the lines of habit. He paced back across the room and, halting in front of Richard, tilted the boy's chin towards the light. 'Do you know who your father was?'

'Yes, sir, King Henry.'

'Then you must also know that I am your kin, your half-brother.' He gave a slight grimace as he spoke. The age difference of forty years was a telling reminder that their father's carnal weakness had not diminished with the passage of time.

Once more Richard nodded. 'Mama said I should remember that I was a king's son because I might have need of it one day.'

Robert looked vaguely surprised. 'I never thought her capable of looking further than the next summer's day,' he murmured, more than half to himself.

'She did the best by her lights for Richard.' Catrin spoke up in her dead mistress's defence, as again she heard undertones of judgement in a masculine voice.

'The best by her lights,' Robert repeated, looking at her and stroking his dark beard. 'Then I suppose it behoves me to do the best by mine. Let her be laid out in the chapel and the proper rituals observed.' He gestured with an open hand. 'I will provide both you and the boy with a place in my household. Sander, go and find out if the Countess has returned from the town.'

The squire bowed and left.

Catrin murmured dutiful thanks. Just now she cared not where her place was, only that it was quiet and dark and solitary. A prison cell would have been ideal, she thought wryly. A sidelong glance showed her that Oliver had drunk his wine to the lees. When the Earl turned to pace the room again, she tugged the cup from his hand and quickly replaced it with her own full one. After the first moment of resistance and a blink of surprise, Oliver let her have her way.

The Earl paused beside a gaming board and shuffled the agate pieces at random. 'Pascal, I want you to head the burial escort to Penfoss.'

Oliver took a deep gulp from the second cup of wine. 'When, my lord?'

'On the morrow. Take Father Kenric and as many foot-soldiers and serjeants as you deem necessary. Report back to me as soon as you return.' He waved his hand in dismissal.

'Yes, my lord.' Oliver swallowed down the rest of his wine and started towards the door, but before reaching it swung round to Catrin and Richard. 'I'll come and plague you with my presence,' he said, ruffling Richard's dark hair. 'I told you, I keep my promises.'

The boy gave him an enigmatic look and the smallest of nods that said he was not prepared to trust beyond the day.

Catrin produced a wan smile, the merest stretching of her lips. 'Thank you for what you have done.'

'I doubt it is enough,' he answered heavily. 'Let me know if you are in need and I will do what I can.'

She nodded, her smile warming.

As Earl Robert raised his head and stared, Oliver bowed and left the room.

*   *   *

A clear summer dusk had fallen by the time Oliver emerged from the keep. Grey-winged gulls clamoured in the skies over the Frome and the Avon, escorting fishing craft to their moorings. Others plundered the midden heaps and gutters, arguing raucously over the scraps.

Oliver breathed deeply of the evening air, uncaring that some of the scents were less than delightful. He would far rather the aroma of fish guts, smoke, and boiling mutton fat from the soap-makers' establishments, than the more civilised atmosphere of Earl Robert's private solar. It was not the Earl to whom he objected, he would never have given his oath of loyalty if he had; it was the room, and that mural of the two women in the garden. Although stylised in the court fashion, it had been painted from life more than ten years ago when Amice and Emma had dwelt here. The painter had been taken with their dissimilar beauty – Amice statuesque, golden-haired and blue-eyed, Emma fey and dark – and had used them as his models for that particular scene.

Oliver had visited the Earl's solar on several occasions since swearing him allegiance. He tried not to look at the mural, but it always taunted the corner of his eye and made everything else seem insignificant.

As the dusk deepened, Oliver supervised the conveyance of Amice's body to Earl Robert's chapel, and there saw it laid out decently before the altar, but he did not linger. He had sat in vigil the previous night and said his private prayers and farewells. Others would pray over her now and give her a fitting burial. Two girls in a garden and both now dead, one in childbirth, one in miscarriage. But their images still danced unchanged on Earl Robert's wall.

His thoughts strayed to the other young woman he had left in that room. Like Emma she was dark of feature, although not so fey of build or sweet-natured. He knew that she must still be suffering from a severe headache. Such maladies did not just disappear, and he admired the way that she had pushed her will through the pain. A vision of the red stockings filled his mind, and of the set of her jaw as she tugged the eel basket out of his hand. Without being aware, he started to smile, the grin deepening as he remembered how she had exchanged their goblets and made him drink both measures of wine. It burned in his blood now, making him a little giddy, for he had not eaten since a hasty noonday meal of stale oatcakes.

In the hall, the Earl's household would be sitting down to a feast of at least three courses – twice as many on the high table. Oliver could have claimed a place at a trestle and eaten until he burst if that had been his will. His will, however, took him not to a bench in the hall, beneath the pompous gaze of Steward Bardolf, but through the camp, between the tents and woodsmoke fires, until he arrived at one shelter in particular.

There was no sign of Gawin, but his dun stallion and Oliver's grey were tethered nearby, their noses in feedbags. An elderly woman was crouching by the fire and stirring the contents of a cooking pot. Her gown was of homespun wool, plain but clean. Deep wrinkles carved her face, and her expression was set awry by a slight dragging of the muscles on the left side. Whiskers sprouted from her chin and the corners of her upper lip, but her bones were fine and there was a lively gleam in her eyes.

'I'd almost given up on you, my lad,' she announced in a firm voice that had weathered the years better than her flesh. Holding a bowl over the cauldron, she shook in the chopped, skinned eels. 'Gawin's gone to find a dish more to his taste in the town – her name's Aveline.'

Oliver snorted. 'It was Helvi last week. Gawin's sown enough wild oats to cover a five-acre!'

'Aye, well, this war makes folks live their lives all in a day lest they don't see the next sunrise.' She gave the cooking pot a vigorous stir. Her hands were straight and smooth, with short, clean nails, and showed small sign of her seventy-four years, except for her favouring of the left one. Until a recent seizure in the winter, she had dwelt in excellent health.

Oliver had known Ethel all his life. She had delivered both him and his brother Simon into the world, and had held a prestigious position in the Pascal household as nurse, wise-woman and midwife to the women of castle and village. Ethel it was, who had fought tooth and nail to save Emma and the baby too large to descend her narrow pelvis, and when she had failed had grieved deeply. There had been no more infants to deliver after that, for Simon's wife was barren. When the Pascal family were disinherited of their lands, Ethel was branded an English witch by the new lord's Flemish wife, and forced to flee before she was hanged. It was a common tale and Bristol was full of such refugees.

Oliver sat on a small stool and looked at the steam rising from the cauldron's surface. 'Did Gawin tell you what happened at Penfoss?'

'Aye, he did.' Ethel shook her head and sucked on her teeth. Most of them were worn to stumps by a lifetime of eating coarse bread made from flour adulterated with minute grains of millstone grit. 'And it's right sorry I am. Nowhere is safe any more. If you stay in your village, the soldiers come plundering, and if you flee to a town, either they burn that too, or the cut-purses take your last penny and leave you in the gutter to starve. Don't suppose you know who did it?'

Oliver shrugged. 'A band of routiers led by a man on a chestnut stallion. Could be one of a thousand such.'

'Aye, and that makes me right sorry too,' she said with a sigh, then cocked him a bright glance from beneath her brows. 'Gawin also spoke of the woman and boy you brought out o' the place. Old King Henry's last bastard whelp, eh?'

She ladled the eel stew into two bowls and, while they ate, Oliver told her about Richard and Catrin. Ethel's expression grew thoughtful as she listened. She nodded her approval at his use of the betony and feverfew tisane, and the humour lines deepened around her eyes when he mentioned the scarlet hose and the way Catrin had straddled the grey.

'Sounds an uncommon young woman,' she remarked, watching him scrape the bottom of his bowl. 'Is she married?'

'Widowed.' He sucked the spoon. 'She lost her husband three years ago.'

Ethel absorbed this with a sympathetic murmur. 'You won't just abandon her and the lad now that you've delivered them safe, will you?' She tapped his knee with her spoon.

'No, of course not!' He looked at her with indignation. He still rose to her bait, although he knew that Ethel's badgering did not stem from doubt in his morals, but from long habit and her need to see decency in a world gone morally awry. 'My duties permitting, I'll visit as often as I can until they're both settled.'

'See that you do,' she said in a tone that made him feel as if he were still in tail clouts. But then she abandoned her attack. There was a gleam in her eyes that made him suspicious, but of what he did not know. Ethel was a law unto herself – half the reason why Ashbury's new Flemish lord had hounded her out of the cottage she kept against the castle wall.

The meal finished and respects paid, Oliver rose to leave. As he stretched his arms above his head to ease a kink, one of the castle's young laundry maids approached out of the shadows. She had a round, freckled face, ample proportions and chapped, red hands.

Noticing Oliver, she hesitated, and half turned to leave. Ethel held up a forefinger and, bidding her wait, rummaged in the copious leather satchel beside her stool. From it she produced a knot, woven from three colours of double-strand wool. There was also a scrap of linen tied in a small pouch with a twist of scarlet thread.

'I ain't saying this will work, Wulfrune, it don't always, but I've had more successes in my time than failures.'

The girl looked sidelong at Oliver as she exchanged a coin for the objects in Ethel's hand.

'Mind and make sure you ask the blessing of Saint Valentine before you use them,' Ethel said sternly. 'And don't forget to rub that cream I gave you into your hands.'

The girl nodded a promise and with another swift glance at Oliver hurried away.

Ethel chuckled and folded her arms. 'There's a lad she's after – sells charcoal by the postern gate.'

'And you think she'll catch him with love knots and other ensorcelments?' Oliver gave her a disapproving look.

'Mayhap she will, mayhap she won't. Even with help the course of true love's about as straight as a dog's hind leg.' Ethel stowed the coin in a leather pouch around her neck. 'It does no harm,' she added, as he continued to glower, 'and it earns me enough to eat.'

'What about the fact that you were harried from your home by accusations of witchcraft?'

'Why do you think I warned her to invoke the help of a good Christian saint?' she sniffed. 'Besides, it's tradition. Every wise-woman worth her salt knows about knot magic and love philtres. You can buy 'em anywhere. Show me a single sailor that don't have a herb-wife's knot in his sea-chest to control the winds, or a housewife who don't have one of scarlet thread for stanching nosebleeds.' She patted his arm. 'I keep within the bounds of what's permitted. That whoreson, Odinel the Fleming, chased me from my home because I would not acknowledge him as Lord of Ashbury, God rot his ballocks to a mush.' Her eyes gleamed.

Knowing better than to argue with her in one of her incorrigible moods, Oliver used the excuse of stabling his horse to make his escape and set about untethering the grey. His fingers were clumsy on the knot and he swore to himself, for his difficulty almost seemed like a portent. The skill of weaving cords, threads and rope into intricate knots was an ancient one, rife with superstition. At the making of the knot, a charm was spoken three times, thus binding great power into the curves and twirls. And when they were released, so was the power of the charm – for good or evil. He had no belief in such magic, or so he told himself, but he was glad when the tether slipped free.

Ethel waved him on his way with a smile, and called out her thanks for the eels. Then she sat down again beside her fire and, delving in her satchel, took out three spindles holding yards of thread – white, red and black. With patience and dexterity, despite her weaker left hand, she began to braid and tie, all the time murmuring to herself.

CHAPTER 4

Mabile FitzHamon, Countess of Gloucester, was tall and
gaunt-boned, with an unfortunate resemblance to a plough-
horse, made all the more cruel by her large, yellow teeth. Her
eyes were her saving grace, being large and soft brown with
thick, dark lashes. Just now they were fixed upon the washed
body of Amice de Cormel, lying in state before the altar in
the castle's small private chapel.

'What a waste,' she murmured over her clasped hands.
'She could have led such a different life.'

Kneeling beside her, Catrin inhaled the smell of incense
on the cold chapel air and watched the candles fluttering in
the darkness. The ache in her head was now no more than a
dull pulse, but it had spread throughout her body. She was
numb with exhaustion, her eyelids so hot that she felt as
if someone had scattered their undersides with particles of
burning grit.

Lady Mabile was kind in a brusque, impatient sort of way.
She had welcomed Richard and Catrin into her household,
found them sleeping space for the night amongst her women,
and promised to give them fabric from her coffers to make new
clothes. They had been given food and drink, their immediate
needs tended, all with great practicality and small warmth.
Now Richard was asleep on a narrow straw pallet squeezed
into a corner of the maids' chamber, and Catrin was paying
her respects to the dead.

'How well did you know her, child?' asked the Countess.

'I served her for three years, my lady, and in all that time
she was kind and generous to me.'

'I am sure she was, but that was not my question.'

Catrin turned to face the brown, equine gaze, and found its shrewdness disconcerting. 'I knew her very well, my lady.'

Meaning passed between them without words. The Countess sighed. 'Then you will realise why my husband never sought to pin her to a husband for all that she was his ward. His own father, the king, took her virginity. When Henry's interest waned, she turned to other men for affection and it became a deep-rooted canker. She would have made a cuckold of any man she married, and in short order.' The Countess dabbed a spot of moisture from her eye and looked at her wet fingertip. 'And yet, I was fond of her; she meant no harm. A waste. May the blessed Virgin look kindly on her soul.'

So the waste was what Amice had made of her life, not what those vile soldiers had done to her, Catrin thought with a flash of anger.

'And you yourself are a widow?' the Countess continued.

'Yes, my lady.' Catrin kept her eyes on her clenched knuckles lest she reveal her irritation. Richard needed her and she could not afford to be dismissed. 'My husband was killed in a fight with a Welsh lord. I still mourn him deeply.' She bit her lip.

There was silence for a moment, then the Countess gently touched Catrin's shoulder. 'That is a grievous pity,' she said compassionately. 'Life is always difficult for a woman alone. You are welcome to remain in my household. Another pair of hands is always useful.' Mabile crossed herself and rose to her feet. 'Come, child, it is late. She will sleep peacefully here with the priest until dawn.'

Murmuring her thanks, Catrin rose and followed the Countess. She could raise no enthusiasm for the prospect of remaining in Mabile's household, but at least it was a roof over her head, and a relatively secure one at that. There was nowhere else to go.

If Amice's slumber in the chapel was deep and peaceful, the same could not be said of the Countess's ladies. In the blackest part of the night, when the single candle left burning had begun to gutter in a puddle of wax, Catrin and the other women were wakened by Richard's terrified shrieks. The sound tore across the room and was made all the more terrifying by sleep-fuddled wits and the depth of the hour.

With pounding heart, Catrin staggered up from the bed she had been sharing with three others and hastened to soothe him.

'Hush, Dickon, hush. It's all right, nothing but a bad dream.' She stroked his damp brow. His eyes were wide open but unseeing, and his chest rose and fell in rapid gasps for air. Beneath her touch, his breathing calmed, and after a moment his lids drooped and he turned from her on to his side, sucking his knuckles in his sleep.

One of the women had kindled a fresh night light from the old one. She held it aloft, the cupped flame reflecting light on to her thick plait of dark red hair. Her name was Rohese. She was a skilled embroideress with a voice and skin like silk, and a nature as sharp as a tapestry needle.

'What's wrong with him?' she demanded, her tone making it clear what she thought of the matter.

'What's wrong is that he saw people butchered and his mother raped by a dozen soldiers,' Catrin retorted angrily. 'Wouldn't you have nightmares too?'

Rohese sniffed and declined to answer. 'I hope he does not make it a habit,' was all she said and, ramming the new candle down on the iron spike, stalked away to her pallet. The other women followed her example, some with sour looks, others more sympathetic, but all less than sanguine at having been roused from sleep in so frightening a fashion.

Twice more that night the Countess's women were disturbed by Richard's screams. Forewarned, Catrin was able to calm him more swiftly than the first time, but not before everyone had been thoroughly woken. If Rohese had been hostile at the outset, she was positively venomous by dawn.

Richard had no recollection of his nightmares and was bewildered by all the furious glares cast in his direction. Catrin protected him fiercely from the others. Yesterday's headache still throbbed behind her eyes and she felt almost as exhausted as when she had retired.

'It is not his fault,' she said, as the women dressed and

prepared to go down to the great hall to break their fast. 'He needs time to settle, that's all.'

'Well, I refuse to have him sleep in our chamber another night!' Rohese snapped.

'Surely that is for the Countess to say.'

Rohese gave her a glittering look through narrowed lids. 'I doubt she will oppose my request when I tell her about the kind of night we have all passed.'

Catrin returned Rohese's glare and was sorely tempted to slap the sneer from her haughty face. 'Then ask her and see what she says. I think that you forget this child is her husband's half-brother, and the old King's son.'

'And his mother got herself banished for whoredom. Her nickname was Amice le Gorge-Colps – the sword swallower; we all know the story.' She looked around at her companions for support. A blonde-haired girl tittered, and an older woman sucked her teeth and nodded.

'As you choose to see it, without knowing Amice,' Catrin said heatedly, and was appalled to feel tears gathering at the backs of her eyes. The urge to lash out was almost unbearable.

From the corner where she had been braiding her hair, a freckle-faced young woman spoke out. 'This all seems to me a storm in a pitkin,' she said. 'Are we so feeble-minded that one disturbed night sours us beyond all charity?'

'It is not *my* mind that is feeble,' Rohese said with a pointed glare at Richard, as he emerged from the curtained-off latrine built into the angle of the wall. She terminated the conversation by stalking from the room, her nose in the air.

The young woman left her corner and approached Catrin. 'Pay no heed to Rohese,' she murmured, laying a sympathetic hand on Catrin's sleeve. 'She likes to play queen, and your arrival has tilted her crown.'

'Mine?'

'Well, yours and the boy's. A son of the old King outranks an embroideress any day, no matter that she's a knight's daughter. I'm Edon FitzMar and my husband is one of the Earl's hearth knights.' She clasped Catrin's hand. 'Never fret, you'll soon be at home here.'

Catrin doubted that very much. The bower walls hemmed her in. She knew that this was the way many women of noble birth lived their lives – shut away in the castle's upper chambers, their days occupied by weaving, spinning and needlecraft. It was an enclosed world, seething with under-currents and tensions that had few outlets. The occupants fed upon each other. Amice had spoken often of that kind of life, and never with longing or affection. But since Edon FitzMar had offered the hand of friendship, Catrin kept her misgivings to herself and returned the clasp with a smile and a palliative murmur.

'I suppose,' Edon said to Richard, showing her kindness further by including him in the conversation, 'that you will become a page in my Lord's household. That's what happens to most of the boys fostered here.'

Richard nodded and looked at his feet. 'I would like that,' he mumbled.

'He's a good teacher, Lord Robert. Geoffrey – that's my husband – says that no squire could have a better start.'

Richard mumbled again. His eyes flickered from the ground to the prominent swell of her belly. Seeing his glance, she laughed self-consciously and laid her hand across her midriff. 'My first,' she said to Catrin. 'Due in the autumn. Geoffrey's that proud, he's been puffing out his chest and crowing to all the others like a cockerel. They're all sick to death of hearing about it.'

'My mother was with child too,' Richard said. 'Aimery crowed to all the other men, but he's dead now . . . and so is she.' Whirling from a startled Edon, he ran to the door and banged out of the room.

'I'm sorry, I never thought . . .' Edon looked aghast. 'And after last night too, I should have known.'

'It isn't your fault,' Catrin said quickly, not wanting to lose the tentative friendship that had sprung up. 'He's liable to take off at the slightest thing just now. I have to go after him. Explain to the Countess if she asks for me.' Gathering her skirts, Catrin ran from the bower in pursuit of Richard. Behind her, the women looked at each other, their expressions ranging from disapproval to sympathy for the afflicted.

It was difficult to run down a turret stair in a gown and by the time Catrin reached the foot, Richard had disappeared. Cursing to herself she asked around, but no one had seen him. A running child was of small consequence in a household as large as the Earl of Gloucester's. A running woman, however, was cause for raised eyebrows and more than one murmur about lack of propriety.

Catrin searched the hall then hastened outside. In the bailey she found the young squire, Thomas FitzRainald, breaking his fast on a large oatcake smeared with honey, whilst polishing a piece of harness with a soft cloth. He was only too happy to abandon his task and help her find Richard. While she headed for the outer bailey, Thomas went off to search the kennels and the mews.

A party of horsemen was preparing to ride out, among them a priest. Strapped behind his mule's saddle were a travelling chest and a small case made from boiled leather, shaped to hold and protect his mitre. At the head of the group, Oliver was swinging lightly astride the grey. His face wore the fresh gleam of a sound night's sleep, and he was smiling at something that Gawin had said to him.

Through her anxiety, Catrin was suddenly aware of her own slatternly appearance. The clothes of the last few days still itched on her back because they were the only ones she possessed – travel-smirched, smoky and dirty. She could not have smiled had she tried.

Oliver twisted in the saddle to adjust his shield strap, but when he saw her he stopped, and the residue of the grin faded from his lips. 'Mistress Catrin, what's wrong?'

'Richard's run off.' She told him what had happened in the bower.

His lips compressed. 'Poor little sod.' Raising a forefinger to Gawin, bidding him wait, he dismounted. 'Come, I'll help you look. He won't have gone far.'

'What about your journey?'

'Another half candle-notch won't make any difference. The living matter more than the dead.' He spoke the last sentence with a wry shrug, as if he did not quite believe in the words. Then he shook his head and grimaced. 'Rohese de Bayvel should be tied to that post yonder and whipped. It's not the first time that she's caused trouble in the bower.'

'Then why doesn't the Countess stop her?'

'Because Rohese is probably the best needlewoman in England, and when she tries she can be sweetness itself – and no, that is not a remark made from personal knowledge. I would rather kiss the hand of Medusa than become embroiled with that shrew. I'll go and investigate the guardrooms, shall I? You ask over there at the bread oven.'

Earl Robert's favourite alaunt had given birth to a litter of four pups in the spring. Now, seven weeks later, they were energetic bundles of tawny fur, their coats wrinkling comically on their loose-knit bones. From his corner, Richard watched them tumble over each other and indulge in mock fights, already establishing an order of dominance. Their mother lay nearby, her limbs relaxed but her gaze watchful.

Richard made no attempt to touch any of the pups. It was enough just to observe. His mother had always been promising him a dog, but somehow the promise had always remained as 'next time', or 'another day'. Aimery de Sens had owned an alaunt, but it had been huge and black, with a snarl to threaten anyone who came within touching distance. When Aimery had wanted to lie with Amice, he made the beast guard the bedchamber door so that they wouldn't be disturbed.

Well, they were all dead now. There was a treacherous stinging sensation at the back of Richard's eyes. 'It's all my fault,' he told one of the pups as it left the rough and tumble to investigate him. 'I wished them dead.' He picked it up and cuddled it with a deep longing for the feel of something soft and warm against his skin. The pup wriggled and licked him with a swift, pink tongue. Richard buried his face in the tawny fur while the forces gathered inside him.

'Found you!'

Richard jerked his head up, his eyes wet, the sob locked in his throat as he glared at Thomas FitzRainald. 'Go away!' he snarled.

The other boy did exactly the opposite and came closer.

'They're looking for you. That nurse of yours, Catrin is it? She's running around like a scorched cat. Oliver Pascal's hunting too.'

Richard inhaled the pup's fuzzy coat. 'I don't want to be found.'

'You should have hidden better then.' Thomas crouched down, and the young dog wriggled away from Richard to explore the newcomer. 'Why have you run away?'

'I haven't, I just wanted to be on my own, that's all.' Richard drew the back of his hand across his eyes, and challenged the other boy to remark on it with a brimming scowl.

Thomas raised his chin to avoid the pup's eager pink tongue. 'Is it true that you're the Earl's half-brother?'

'Yes, what of it?'

'Well, that makes you my uncle, because my papa is your half-brother too.' Thomas giggled at the thought. 'Uncles are supposed to be older than their nephews.'

'How old are you?' Richard demanded, curiosity winning out over defensiveness.

'I was eleven at the feast of Saint John.'

'I won't be eleven until Christmas.' The puppy clambered back into his lap and he cuddled it again.

Thomas eyed him. 'We're more of an age to be brothers or cousins. Can I call you cousin?'

Richard shrugged. 'If you like,' he said indifferently, but he was pleased. Essentially he was a gregarious child, who had been forced by circumstances to dwell overmuch in his own company.

Thomas eyed him, as if trying to decide whether the response was an acceptance or rejection. 'You'll have to let them know where you are,' he said. 'Otherwise they'll turn the place upside down and you'll be in worse trouble than ever.'

Richard wriggled his shoulders. 'I don't want to go back to the women,' he said. 'Most of them don't like me anyway' He gazed around the space surrounding him, the comfort of open sky and fresh air.

Thomas eyed him. 'You don't have to stay with them. Ask if you can sleep in the same dorter as the other squires.'

'But I'm not a squire.'

'You will be soon. What else is Lord Robert going to do with you?'

Richard chewed his lip. He thought of the red-haired woman who had scowled at him, and the sympathetic pregnant one who had made him face something that he wanted to banish from his mind. 'What's the dorter like?'

'I'll show you.' Rising to his feet, Thomas wiped his pup-licked hand on his tunic. 'Come on. We'll tell your nurse you're found, and you can stay with me the rest of the day, if you like. I've a heap of saddlery to polish, and four hands are better than two.'

Richard deliberated a moment longer. He was not accustomed to giving his trust, but time and again over the last two days he had been asked to do so by complete strangers. 'All right,' he said, and he too rose, although with a lingering reticence. The pup rolled on its belly demanding to be tickled, and he stooped to oblige before tearing himself away to follow his 'cousin'. 'Catrin's not my nurse, I'm too old for one now,' he added in a defensive tone. 'She was my mother's companion.'

Catrin's anxiety for Richard's safety had almost reached fever pitch when she saw the two boys across the bailey. She had envisaged discovering him among the dregs of Earl Robert's army, his throat slit, or washed up on the estuary, drowned. Or not found at all. To see him unscathed filled her with relief and the rage of relief. She ran across the bailey, not knowing whether to shout at or cuddle him first.

In the event she did neither, for the look on his face brought her up short.

'I shouldn't have run off,' he forestalled her quickly, 'but I couldn't stay.' His eyes were wary and she could see that he was braced for a thorough scolding.

'I know you couldn't,' she said in a gentler voice than she had first intended, 'and I know you were upset, but what you did was not only thoughtless, but dangerous. This camp is huge and you scarce know any of it. People have been looking for you, and I have been worrying myself sick!'

Richard looked at the ground and shuffled his feet. 'I'm sorry,' he muttered.

Catrin's anger melted. She wanted to grab him and fold him in her arms, but with Thomas looking on and the bailey full of witnesses, she abstained for the sake of his tender pride. 'If you need a moment alone, I expect you to go no farther than this bailey, understood?'

Richard nodded, then raised his head. 'Thomas wants to show me the boys' dorter. Can I go?'

Catrin pursed her lips.

'I'll look after him, I promise,' Thomas said, his eyes wide and earnest. 'After that, he can stay with me, if he wants, and help me clean the Earl's harness.'

Richard nodded again, this time vigorously, and looked pleadingly at Catrin. She had a protective impulse to tuck him under her wing, but that was caused by her own anxiety. It would be the worst thing she could do to take him back amongst the Countess's women. Better to let the friendship develop between the two boys. 'I don't see why not,' she said, and was rewarded by one of Richard's rare smiles.

She watched the boys run off together and, between the worry and the relief, felt quite drained. Halfway across the bailey, they bumped into Oliver. He stopped and spoke to them. Catrin saw Richard gesture over his shoulder in her direction, and Oliver glance across. Sending the boys on their way, he walked over to her. His stride was long, she noticed, with a slight downward dip on the right side.

'You found him then?' he said.

'No, Thomas did.' She pulled a face. 'I feel foolish now for my panic, and I've held up your journey for nothing.'

'It would not have been a nothing if he truly had taken to his heels.' Oliver gazed across the bailey at Thomas and Richard, their heads close in conversation as they walked. 'But it seems to have worked for the best.'

'Yes.' She bit her lip.

'He'll be all right.' He touched her arm in reassurance.

'You would not say that if you had heard him last night.'

'It would be strange if he did not have nightmares. After Emma died, I did not sleep unbrokenly for more than a year.'

He folded his arms. 'There are herbs he can be given to help him sleep without dreams.'

'And you know them all?' she said, thinking of the tisane he had made to ease her headache.

He smiled and shook his head. 'By no means, but I know someone who does.'

'Oh yes, Etheldreda of the eel stew.' She rubbed the stain on her gown. 'Did you enjoy it?'

'It was delicious,' he said gravely. 'Look, I'll ask her to make a sleeping potion for the lad in case he needs it.'

Catrin thanked him, then frowned. 'But you'll be gone at least two nights and Richard needs it now.'

'I'll have a word on the way out and tell her to bring it to you. She'll be curious to meet you.'

The sentiment was mutual, Catrin thought. In her mind's eye a picture had formed of an alluring witch-woman, with an abundance of wild, dark hair and snapping black eyes set on the slant. 'So you told her all about me?' It was a disquieting thought.

Oliver tilted his head. 'Not everything,' he said with a slow smile.

Catrin's stomach leaped and her face grew hot. When Lewis had been alive, she had enjoyed flirting, the banter of voice and body language. It had kept his eyes from straying to pastures new. Three years later, with several hard life-lessons beneath her belt, the art had grown rusty. Nor, with memories of how easily her husband's eyes had wandered, was she inclined to play the game with another woman's man. 'I must go,' she said. 'They'll be wondering about me in the bower.'

'So must I, else it'll be nightfall before we arrive.' Inclining his head in farewell, he turned from her and set off in the direction of the outer bailey. Catrin watched his retreating figure, the confidence of his stride, the way he spoke cheerfully to an acquaintance as he went on his way. In the three years since Lewis's death she had come to terms with her loss and it had diminished to a dull ache at the back of her mind. Now, once more, it was a clear, sharp pain that took her breath. She was aware of standing in the bailey, alone amongst all the vigour and bustle, her figure small and insignificant. She doubted that anyone would care deeply, or even notice, if she were suddenly to vanish.

Then Catrin clucked her tongue impatiently. What did it matter if no one cared, as long as she did herself? Relying on others was a dangerous way to live, and frequently a waste of time. Drawing herself up, she returned to the keep, prepared to face whatever the day held.

CHAPTER 5

'You can have these,' said Countess Mabile. She had been rummaging in the depths of an oak coffer and now emerged with a length of unbleached linen and another of sage-green wool. 'You're neither tall nor buxom. There should be enough for an undergown and dress.'

'Thank you, my lady.' Catrin took the fabric with gratitude. The wool in particular was of excellent quality and, despite Mabile's words, there was plenty to make a dress and probably enough for some panels in the sides and modest hanging sleeves. All she had to do was cut and sew them – and as quickly as possible, given the state of her current garments. She had discarded the tawny overgown because it was just too stained and obnoxious to be seen in polite company. Her blue-green undertunic clung flatteringly to her figure, but there was a large patch near one of the seams where moths had caused damage, and a couple of burn marks on the skirt from leaping embers.

The Countess looked her up and down. 'You'll need some-thing for now as well,' she said, and went to plunder another coffer. It was her own personal one and more ornately carved and inlaid than the other. Her face was animated, a pink flush to her cheeks. Catrin could see that Mabile was enjoying herself greatly making a silk purse from a sow's ear.

'I'm sure one of my daughter's old gowns is in here. She left it after a visit – she was pregnant at the time and it wouldn't fit her any more. Ah, here we are.' From the chest, she drew a dress of dark crimson wool. It was in the fitted style, tight to the waist, then flaring out to an almost circular hem. There was gold thread woven into the braid at cuff and throat and the matching waist-tie. Catrin had never seen a gown so fine, and stared in disbelief as the Countess handed it to her.

'My lady, I cannot!' she gasped, feeling overawed.

'Don't be foolish,' Mabile snapped. 'It's lain here for three years as it is. If it stays any longer, the moths will make use of it beyond repair. Put it on and let me hear no more.' She thrust it into Catrin's arms and turned back to the coffer. 'There's a wimple in here somewhere that should suit.'

Speechless with gratitude, Catrin donned the red gown. The sleeves and hem were slightly too long, but otherwise it was a good fit, and the colour was a perfect foil for her black hair and hazel-green eyes.

'Catrin, you look beautiful!' Edon FitzMar circled her, twitching the gown into place. 'You'll have all the knights falling over each other to share your trencher in the hall!'

Catrin pulled a face. 'Reason enough to take it off this instant,' she said, but really she was pleased, her confidence buoyed by the luxury of the new garment and the admiration she saw in the other young woman's eyes. Nor did the cold envy in Rohese de Bayvel's disturb her, for it only served to confirm that the red dress must suit her.

The Countess found a wimple of cream-coloured silk, edged with crimson embroidery, and secured it lightly over Catrin's braids with a brass circlet. Then she stood back to admire her handiwork. 'Much better,' she declared. 'Child, you are quite lovely.'

Catrin reddened at the compliment. Fine feathers, it seemed, did make a fine bird.

For the rest of the morning, she and Edon sat in a corner of the bower, cutting and sewing the linen and wool into new garments. Catrin did not want to parade about the keep in the red gown. It was too fine to wear except in the hall at night and on special occasions. Rohese did not offer to help with either the cutting or the sewing, and Catrin was glad, for it saved her the bother of refusing. She had a strong suspicion that given the opportunity, Rohese would have ruined the fabric in some way. Catrin resolved to keep her distance as much as she could.

Edon proved a competent seamstress in her own right and was brisk with a needle. As she stitched, she asked tentative questions about Catrin's past. She was obviously curious, and just as obviously trying to be tactful. Unfortunately the two did not marry.

'I'm so sorry about your husband,' she said, after Catrin had reluctantly yielded the information that he had been killed in a fight. 'It must have been horrible to lose him when you had been wed so short a time.'

Catrin fought the urge to snap at her companion. Edon could not know how deep the wound was, but she was doing an admirable job of grinding salt into it.

Edon looked at her sidelong, and her face fell. 'I shouldn't have said that, should I?' She touched Catrin's arm in an apologetic gesture. 'Geoffrey's always telling me that I never stop to think.'

'It doesn't matter.' Catrin's voice was ungracious.

'Yes, it does, I can see that I've hurt you.'

Catrin's needle flew. 'It is in the past, it cannot be changed, and there is no use in grieving.' She gave Edon a tight smile. 'There is no use talking about it either.'

'No, no of course not.' Edon bit her soft lower lip and returned to her sewing.

Catrin had said that she did not want to talk about the past, but now that it had been called to mind it was not so easy to banish. She could still see Lewis on the last day of his life with perfect clarity; his wind-ruffled dark curls and burnished mail, his hands on his mount's bridle, quick, clever and graceful.

'The last night we were together we quarrelled,' she said. The words emerged of their own volition, as if the edges of the wound could no longer be held together. 'He had come late to our bed after a night of gambling and drinking with the other men. There had been a woman too – one of those dancing girls you sometimes see – and his skin stank of her scent. We had never argued the way we argued that night. I refused to kiss him in the morning before he rode away. I turned my cheek and I turned my back. By the time I had regretted the deed and run after him, he was gone.' She took three swift stitches. 'I never saw him again.'

'Oh Catrin!' Once more Edon touched her.

Catrin laughed bitterly. 'Reason and good sense were never mine where Lewis was concerned. I gave him my body before we were wed and he took it with never a second thought – my heart too, and that he broke.'

Edon gave the suspicion of a sniff. 'I cannot bear anyone to be sad. I wish I'd never asked you.'

Catrin was irritated, but tried not to let it show. It was not Edon's fault that she appeared to have feathers for brains. She was the kind who would weep over a minstrel's song in the hall and wax sentimental at the smallest opportunity.

Although she knew that Edon wanted to be embraced, Catrin could not bring herself to such an intimacy so soon. 'Then let us talk about it no longer.'

Edon nodded and sniffed again, her small nose pink. 'You're not angry with me, are you?'

'No,' Catrin said. Irritated certainly, she thought. And yes, at her core, she was angry, but not with Edon. Biting off the thread, she selected a new strand. 'Tell me about yourself instead.'

For the next half hour, Edon took Catrin at her word and poured such a glue of mundane trivia into her ears that she became almost insensible. Edon's husband Geoffrey was, it seemed, a paragon among men. He was tall, exceedingly handsome, gentle, witty, brave and kind. Catrin doubted that such a male existed, except in Edon's imagination. A man without flaws was one without a soul. But she kept her counsel and smiled in the right places whilst her eyes glazed and her jaw ached with the effort of preventing a yawn.

She was rescued from purgatory when an elderly woman appeared in the chamber doorway.

Edon ceased her litany of 'Geoffrey says', and put her sewing down with brightening eyes. 'Here's the midwife,' she murmured to Catrin. 'She's going to attend my lying in. I asked her to find me an eagle stone; I wonder if she's got it now.' Raising her arm, she beckoned.

The woman had paused to catch her breath after the

arduous climb up the winding stairs from the hall. She returned Edon's salute and, after a moment, came over to them. Catrin noted that she moved slowly with a slight limp on the left side, and she was still panting as she sat on the bench beside the two young women.

'When you pass three score years and ten, you shouldn't go climbing twice that number of stairs in one attempt.' She placed her hand to her breast as if the motion would calm her heart.

'Did you bring it, did you bring my eagle stone?' Edon demanded like a greedy child.

Catrin could have kicked her for such lack of consideration. 'Would you like some wine?' she offered. It was perhaps not her place to do so, being the newest addition to the Countess's women, but Catrin had no time for such conventions.

'Bless you, child.' The woman smiled, exposing her worn teeth. The lines on her face deepened and crinkled, revealing humour and endurance.

Catrin went to a vast oak sideboard where stood a flagon of wine and several pottery cups. As she poured, she was aware that the other women were watching her action. Let them judge, Catrin thought, affecting not to notice their disapproving looks.

When she returned with the drink, Edon was enthusing over a smooth, egg-shaped stone the colour of dried blood. There was a gold mounting at the apex of the oval and a ribbon had been threaded through it.

'Look at my eagle stone!' Edon said, dangling it in front of Catrin. 'It's to protect me during my labour. I have to tie it round my thigh and pray to Saint Margaret.'

Catrin gave the cup of wine to the old woman and duly admired the object. 'Do they really work?'

'Of course they do.' The midwife had been about to take a sip of the wine, but she lowered the cup and gave Catrin a warning glance. 'I've been using them at childbeds for more years than you've lived, young woman. Give any wife an eagle stone to hold and she will have an easier labour. Lady Edon will have no difficulties, I promise.' She smiled again, including Edon in the gesture, and raised her cup in a toast before taking a long drink.

'I haven't seen you in my lady's solar before.' She smacked her lips in appreciation of the Countess's best wine. 'Although I hope you'll be here next time.'

'Catrin's home was raided by mercenaries,' Edon said before Catrin could speak for herself. 'She had nowhere to go, so Countess Mabile took her in. There's a little boy too, the Earl's half-brother. He kept us awake all last night with his bad dreams, but I feel sorry for him.' Edon jumped to her feet. 'I'm going to show Alais my eagle stone. She's getting married soon. Perhaps she'll want one for her trousseau.' Edon wrapped the ribbon round her fingers and took her treasure across the room to a plump young woman seated at a small weaving loom.

The midwife shook her head and her eyes twinkled. 'There is no malice in her,' she said. 'Young and giddy, that's all.'

'Did you truly mean what you said about the eagle stone?'

'Of course I did. Belief is the strongest power we have. Tell a wench that one of those things will ease her travail, and sure enough her pangs diminish.'

'And what if the birth goes wrong?'

The woman finished the wine in the cup and pinched her lips to wipe them. 'I sell hope, not miracles,' she said. 'Sometimes a skilled midwife can rescue a mother and babe in difficulty, but if not, then it is God's will, and all the belief in the world will not change matters.' She nodded sagely as she spoke, then gave Catrin a shrewd look. 'I thought you must be Lord Oliver's lass the moment I set eyes on you. "Forthright and sharp of wit," he says to me, "looks so dainty, you'd never believe she was as stubborn as an ox." '

Catrin's face flamed as she was assailed by several emotions at once, not least among them embarrassment and anger that Oliver had seen fit to discuss her with another. She was bewildered too. 'I'm not his "lass",' she said frostily, 'and he has no right to talk about me behind my back.'

'Oh, don't take on so.' Etheldreda gave her a reproving look. 'You turned him upside-down and he had to talk to someone.'

'But why you? I don't understand.'

'I've known him since I delivered him into my apron back in the time when life was safe. Helped to birth his older brother too, God rest his soul.' She crossed herself. 'Master Oliver's the last one now, and one of Stephen's godless mercenaries sits in the hall that should be his.'

Catrin frowned, feeling more bewildered than ever. The woman patted her hand. 'In the winter, I had to flee my old home, so I came here to Bristol. There's always call for a wise-woman and midwife among the troops. Oliver's good word and my skill have granted me work in the keep as well as the camp. He makes sure I don't starve.'

It was then that Catrin made the connection between the midwife and Oliver's mention of an 'Etheldreda'. She stared at the elderly woman sitting at her side, one age-spotted hand curled around a cup, the other lying in her lap and showing a slight tremor. The only features that might have belonged to the dark-haired temptress of Catrin's imagination were the snapping black eyes. Defensiveness and anger were replaced by chagrin and amusement.

'I thought you were his mistress,' she laughed.

Ethel laughed too, a loud, throaty chuckle that caused the other women to cast censorious glances in their direction. 'His mistress, God save us!' she whooped. 'Well, I admit to holding him naked in my arms, but he was new-born at the time, and I've never heard a yell so loud.' She wiped her eyes on her sleeve and coughed.

Her humour was infectious, and Catrin too found her eyes filling as she found release in laughter instead of tears. It was difficult to sober, but before she crossed the line between mirth and hysteria, she sought a scrap of spare linen from her sewing to wipe nose and eyes, and changed the subject.

'Oliver said that you would give me a sleeping potion for Richard.'

'Yes, I've got it here.' Etheldreda rummaged in her shoulder satchel and produced a small leather flask with a stopper. 'Four drops in a cup of wine is all you should need. Time and healing will do the rest.'

Catrin removed the stopper and sniffed the contents. 'What's in it?'

'Mainly white poppy. Master Oliver brought a store back from the Holy Land. In small amounts it induces sleep, calms and soothes, but too much can be dangerous.'

Catrin nodded. 'I wish I knew more about herb-lore,' she said wistfully. 'My mother taught me a little, but usually she sought out the castle's herb-wife or asked at the abbey if she had need of a cure.'

The old woman watched her replace the stopper and set the flask carefully to one side. 'Would you truly like to learn?' she asked, adding swiftly, 'It is not an idle question.'

Catrin did not hesitate. 'You would teach me?'

'As much as can be taught. Knowledge of the hands is inborn, and other things can only be learned by experience, but if you have the healing gift, then I could help you to make it grow and be of use to others.'

Somewhat bemused by the turn that events had taken, Catrin wondered why the old midwife was giving her such attention. Surely she did not make such offers to her other clients. 'Did Oliver ask you to take me under your wing?' she asked suspiciously.

'Hah!' Etheldreda snorted. 'If he knew I'd offered to train you, he'd burst his hauberk. If I take you under my wing, 'tis as much for my sake as yours.' She raised the recumbent left hand from her lap and laboriously waggled her fingers. 'Look at this. Hasn't been right since I suffered a seizure in last winter's cold. My body is weakening. I was born the year of the great battle on Hastings field, and by my reckoning, that makes me well beyond three score and ten. If I reach four score I predict 'twill be a miracle, and I've neither daughters nor kin to bequeath my knowledge. Unless I find someone soon, it will all die with me.'

Catrin absorbed this and felt a little daunted. She had always been fascinated by the twin skills of midwifery and herb-lore. Perhaps it was because of their mystery, or the power that possessing knowledge conferred on their owner. Or perhaps it was the need to feel less vulnerable. 'Why would Oliver object?'

Etheldreda snorted again. 'He's a man, and like all men he's wary of women's matters. Besides, he's afraid.'

'Afraid?' Catrin blinked.

'His wife died in childbed. Three days she was in labour, and nothing I nor anyone could do to save her. Mouth of her womb wouldn't open, so we couldn't even take the child out in pieces to save her life. Had to make Caesar's cut in the end when she was dead.' The midwife shook her head. 'He took it mortal bad.'

'I knew his wife died,' Catrin said unsteadily, 'but I did not know the details.'

'Well, now you do.' Etheldreda raised a warning forefinger. 'And best keep it to yourself. I ain't a gossip, and it's not my habit to carry tales. A midwife should be as close-mouthed as a priest in the confessional except on rare occasions, and this be one of them. Master Oliver tolerates me out of family obligation and old affection, but he don't like midwives or women's business. He's better than he was in the early days, but he still fights shy.'

'I won't say anything.' Catrin thought about him comforting the dying Amice at Penfoss. How difficult that must have been for him in the light of what had happened to his wife.

'So,' said Etheldreda briskly, 'do you still want to learn?'

Catrin looked at the elderly midwife in her plain homespun gown and thought of the fear, respect and hostility that her trade engendered. Lives depended on her skill. She surmised that there must be great satisfaction on one side of the coin, despair and danger on the other.

'It is not for those with a weak stomach or heart,' Etheldreda said as if reading her mind.

Catrin swallowed and seized the horns of fate. 'Yes,' she heard herself say. 'I do want to learn. I need a sense of direction.' She glanced around the Countess's bower. There was little sense of direction here. A morning's sewing with Edon for company had left her feeling cooped-up and frustrated. She had to have more. 'There is still my duty to the Countess,' she felt honour-bound to murmur.

Etheldreda wagged her forefinger. 'If there are stones in your path, then you either cast them aside or find your way around them. Otherwise, you might as well just stay where you are. I know the Countess Mabile. She'll see your learning as a boon. It'll suit her not to send all the way to the camp when she wants a calming tisane, or some rosewater cream to rub into her hands.'

Catrin gave a doubtful nod, still not quite convinced. The midwife returned the cup to her and eased to her feet. 'Well, I'd best be on my way. I'll come and talk with you tomorrow, and if you're still of the same mind, we'll begin your training.' Again she delved into her satchel, and brought forth a small, exquisitely fashioned piece of knotwork, the loops woven in red, black and white wool, and suspended from a red cord.

'Here,' she said. 'Take this and wear it around your neck. All wise-women have a healing cord to remind them of the grace of the Trinity.'

Catrin took the talisman. 'Father, Son and Holy Spirit,' she said.

The old woman studied her narrowly. 'Maiden, Mother and Crone,' she contradicted. 'Women's magic.'

Catrin returned Etheldreda's stare, and a thrill of apprehension ran up her spine. 'Is that not dangerous?'

'Only inasmuch as men choose it to be. Is not the Blessed Virgin Mary a maiden and mother? Was not John the Baptist's mother beyond child-bearing age when she bore him?'

Catrin began to have more of an inkling why Oliver would 'burst his hauberk' if he knew what Etheldreda was proposing. It was not just the midwifery, but the integral weaving of the old female religion, albeit disguised in the lore of various female saints.

'Of course,' Etheldreda said with a little shrug, 'you do not have to wear the token at all. It only means as much as each individual wants it to mean and, in my case, I intended it as a gift.'

Catrin looked at the cord lying across her palm, the knot woven with loving, beautiful intricacy. With sudden decision she slipped it over her head and tucked it down inside the neckline of her gown. 'Then I accept it as such.'

Etheldreda gave a firm nod, obviously pleased, and some of the sharpness left her eyes. 'I would not have you think that I am not a good Christian,' she said, 'but the old gods – and goddesses – have their place too.' Then she put her finger to her lips as Edon returned from her rounds with the eagle stone.

'I must take my leave, mistress,' she addressed Edon. 'Tomorrow I will return and see how you are faring, but you seem in fine, good health to me.'

Edon preened at the compliment. 'Geoffrey says I'll make the perfect mother.'

'Aye, well I'm sure he's the perfect husband and father,' Etheldreda said. Not by so much as a flicker of expression did she betray what she was actually thinking, but she did avoid Catrin's eyes and needed suddenly to turn aside to cough.

Catrin watched the midwife make her way slowly across the bower. Near the door the old woman paused and approached the corner where Rohese de Bayvel sat at her own needlework. There was a brief, muted conversation and another flask changed hands in return for a glint of silver. Etheldreda went on her way, and Rohese concealed her purchase in the folds of her gown, her colour high.

Power indeed, Catrin thought wryly, to bring a blush to the face of the haughty Rohese. She fingered the red cord at her throat, and listened with half an ear to Edon's chatter, but her thoughts were upon the sudden changes wrought in her life and the old woman descending the tower stairs.

CHAPTER 6

The black stink of smoke still hung on the air, but Oliver was almost glad, for it served to disguise the aroma of putrefying flesh. The high summer weather and the open wounds on the corpses had advanced the decomposition at a rate which would have been unbelievable had not Oliver seen its like many times during his years of pilgrimage.

The burial party worked with covered faces, and Father Kenric swung his incense burner in long, low arcs. It kept the flies away to a degree, but the sickly sweet smell of the burning spices only added to the stomach-rolling stench. Oliver had taken his turn to dig the soil. He had helped lift the bodies on to linen shrouds, and wrapped them up. Not one of them wore a single item of jewellery. Fingers had been hacked off to steal rings too tight to remove.

The sight, the smell, the silence were worse to Oliver than his first discovery of the scene. Two days ago, the fire had been a raging, living thing, and there had been survivors in its midst. Now there was nothing but distasteful, tragic duty among the ashes and the dead. At least there had been survivors, he told himself as he walked around Penfoss's perimeter stockade. If Catrin and Richard had been in the compound at the time of the attack, they too would be lying amongst the slain. He shied from that image, and thought instead of Catrin standing in Bristol's bailey, her head tilted to one side, her hazel eyes bright with suspicion as she spoke to him.

In the five years since Emma had died, there had been few women in his life; he could count the occasions on the fingers of one hand, and they had made the approaches. It was the first time since Emma's death that he had been moved to make an approach himself. He wanted to discover the Catrin behind the shield that held him at bay, but getting her to lower her defences was likely to be as difficult as lowering his own to let her in. He found himself envying men like Gawin, who had a wealth of experience with women and the brash confidence to pick and choose at will.

In the early days of his bereavement, he had entertained thoughts of becoming a monk. His brother had talked him out of the impulse, saying that he did not have the nature to dwell in the cloister. 'It takes more than a hair shirt and a scourge to make a monk,' he had said. 'Christ, if every husband who lost his wife in childbed entered a monastery, half the men in England would wear tonsures.'

Simon had been right, Oliver acknowledged, although at the time he had thought his brother unfeeling and obstructive. The pilgrimage had been the compromise. Oliver touched his belt, and felt beneath his fingers the pewter badges that were both proof and reminder of the time he had spent as a wanderer, changing from lost boy to man – or at least growing a hard shell over the lost boy, so that no one knew of his existence except himself.

He came to the broken gates and stared up the rutted track and into the deep green of the forest. The leaves swished and rustled softly in the breeze. Now Simon was dead in battle and his wife of the sweating sickness. A stranger sat in the great hall that had belonged to Oliver's family since before the coming of William the Conqueror. He was the last one to carry his name. Responsibilities to the dead were sometimes greater burdens than those to the living.

Impatient with himself, he was turning back to the burials when a movement caught the corner of his eye. 'Ware arms!' he bellowed over his shoulder to the digging soldiers.

The compound erupted, men throwing down their spades and drawing their weapons. Oliver freed his own sword and backed within the gateway, his breathing swift and hard.

A troop of riders and footsoldiers emerged from the forest on to the track, steel hissing from scabbards, shields surging to the fore. Oliver saw that their numbers matched those of his own men, but the strangers had the advantage of horseback.

'Halt in the name of Robert, Earl of Gloucester, on whose land you trespass!' Oliver cried.

'Land's for the taking these days,' their leader sneered, but he drew his fine bay stallion to a stand. A new shield with bright red chevrons on a blue background covered his left side and he carried a honed lance in his right hand.

Without removing his eyes from the soldier, Oliver gestured over his shoulder. 'Then come and take six feet of earth for your grave.'

'Six feet of earth, eh?' The man grinned and hefted the lance. 'That would be poor payment for saving your life on the road to Jerusalem, Oliver Pascal, or do you choose to forget old friendships and debts?'

Thrown off balance, Oliver stared at his adversary. 'Randal?' he said, dragging the name from the depths of the past. 'Randal de Mohun?'

'Ah, you do remember then?' Tossing the lance to one of his troop, the soldier swung down from his saddle with an athletic bounce. An expensive grey mantle lined with squirrel fur swirled around his shoulders and was pinned with a silver brooch of Welsh knotwork. 'Call off your dogs; put up your sword. You don't really want to fight.' His teeth flashed like a snare within the full bush of black moustache and beard.

'You shouldn't take the risk,' Oliver said, but gestured his men to return to their grisly work, and sheathed his sword. However, he did not relax. For all that Randal de Mohun had saved him from certain death at the hands of brigands and been his companion on the pilgrim road for almost six months, his liking for the man had never been more than tepid. 'What are you doing in these parts?'

Removing his helm, de Mohun waved his own men to dismount. Sweat glittered on his forehead and made tiny dewdrops in the thinning peak of hair on his brow. 'Riding through on the way to Bristol to seek employment.' He nodded towards the compound. 'What happened here?'

'A raid by a band of wandering mercenaries,' Oliver said with a hard glance at de Mohun's men. 'Riding through' had been spoken far too glibly. 'Prowling' or 'scavenging' were more appropriate descriptions. Randal de Mohun was a man with an eye to every opportunity that came his way. To judge by his manner of dress and the strength of his troop, he had been fortunate of late. 'They butchered all the occupants, plundered what they could, and torched the rest.'

Randal clicked his tongue and shook his head. 'Godless,' he muttered, 'the world is burning, Oliver.'

They were the right words, but spoken without any degree of sincerity. 'Yes, godless,' Oliver repeated. 'Where have you ridden from?'

Randal gave an irritable twitch of his shoulders. 'We were employed further up the march but we were not being paid regular wages so we left. Rumour has it that Earl Robert does well by his troops.'

'You look well enough paid to me.'

Randal snorted. 'We persuaded His Lordship at swordpoint to open his money chest before we left, and we've found casual employment along the way.' He stepped closer to Oliver and lightly punched his bicep. 'You told me to halt in the name of Robert of Gloucester. Do I take it that you are in his service already?'

Somewhat reluctantly, Oliver nodded.

'Hah, then you can recommend me to him. You know from experience the kind of fighter I am, and I've twelve trained men at my back, eager and ready to do his bidding.'

Oliver knew that Earl Robert would be only too pleased to employ the likes of Randal de Mohun. Seasoned warriors with good equipment were both invaluable and hard to find. In effect they could, and did, sell themselves to the highest bidder. While Oliver had no strong liking for de Mohun, he did owe the man his life.

'I will be glad to recommend you to Earl Robert,' he said, but without any warmth. 'Bring your men into the compound.' He stood aside so that the gateway was open and made a sweeping gesture with his hand. 'One thing though,' he said, as de Mohun turned with alacrity to his horse, 'as a token of goodwill and the quicker to be quit of this place, perhaps your men could assist mine to bury the dead.'

De Mohun's dark eyes narrowed and the white grin lost some of its width. But it did not disappear altogether. 'Why not,' he said, and faced his men. 'It is the least we can do, isn't it, lads?'

'So you stayed in the Holy Land for two more years?' De Mohun whistled. 'Penance enough for ten lifetimes I would say.'

Oliver smiled bleakly and watched the ferry approach from the opposite side of the river. Sunset glimmered on the Severn, turning the water to a sheet of beaten copper. Midges danced on its surface, and fish plopped in sudden ripples of white-gold. After the sight and stench of death, the fragrance and peace were incongruous but soothing. 'In the end, the penance was coming home,' he said, but more to himself than to de Mohun. 'In Rome and Compostella, in Antioch and Nazareth and Jerusalem, I did not have to tread the same ground that I had trodden with Emma.'

De Mohun gave a single grunt which eloquently said without words what he thought of such reasoning.

'I didn't spend all the time on my knees. I took service with King Fulke of Jerusalem for a time and joined his bodyguard.' Oliver heard the defensiveness in his own voice and tightened his lips. He owed de Mohun neither explanation nor excuses and was irritated to find himself giving both.

De Mohun punched him on the arm again, reminding Oliver that it had been one of the soldier's irritating habits from their earlier acquaintance. 'That's more like it,' he declared. 'Did you see much fighting?'

'Enough.' Oliver pointed to a small curved scar on his jawline. 'Someone tried to barber me with a scimitar in one skirmish.' He did not add that it had been a fellow soldier during the throes of an ugly tavern brawl.

De Mohun grinned. 'Aye, well, you were always one for a fight, Pascal.'

Oliver did not return the grin. What de Mohun said was true, and probably the reason that they had stayed together for six months. Picking fights had been a way of venting his anger at Emma's death, and he had half hoped that the sweep of an Arab blade would send him to join her. Looking back now, it was immature and foolish, but at the time it had seemed a simple solution.

'What about the women? Kept yourself cosy with a little dancing girl, eh?'

Oliver watched the approach of the ferry and willed its keeper to haul it in faster to their side of the bank. 'What do you think?'

'Don't be a miserly bastard. Go on, tell me.'

'There's nothing to tell that you don't already know for yourself.' Oliver rose to attend to his horse as the ferry pulled mercifully closer.

'All right then. What about the women at Bristol? Are there enough for my men? I don't want them falling out over whose turn it is.'

Oliver concealed a grimace of distaste within his mouth. He was indebted to this man for his life, and de Mohun had helped to dig the graves with a strong and willing arm. 'There are enough women,' he said, thinking of the outskirts of the camp where the whores plied their trade in exchange for their daily bread. 'You'll find what you want.'

Yet again, de Mohun thumped Oliver's shoulder. 'Fortune favours the bold, eh?'

Grasping the grey's bridle and leading him down to the water's edge, Oliver harboured his own thoughts about the favours of fortune and fate.

Richard stood quietly beside Catrin as his mother's shrouded body was lowered into the grave. He threw the obligatory handful of soil into the hole with everyone else, and at the end tossed in the chaplet of gillyflowers that Catrin gave to him. Then he wiped his fingers down his tunic and abruptly turned away.

Catrin watched him with folded lips and a frown in her eyes, for she did not know how to reach him. That part of his life had been shut away, but Catrin could almost see it hammering on the door to be let out. Until it was, she did not think that Richard would have any peace. Running after him, she set her arm around his shoulders.

'It's all right,' she murmured. 'I understand.'

Richard shook his head. 'No, you don't.' He kicked at the ground.

'Then tell me, so that I do.'

He looked up at her, his eyes dark with misery. 'I can't.'

'Well, when you can, I'm ready to listen,' Catrin said gently.

He fought with himself for a moment, his throat working, then he blurted out, 'I wished them both dead. I saw them go into the bedchamber together and set the dog across the door, and I wished them both dead. Then I went into the forest to practise with my bow, and when I returned the soldiers were there. It's all my fault.'

'Oh, Richard, sweeting, of course it isn't!' Catrin was appalled, but she understood his guilt all too well. If she had not turned her back on Lewis on that last morning and refused him her lips, perhaps he would still be alive now. Knowing that such thoughts were foolish did not prevent her from thinking them in moments of melancholy. She tightened her arm around the child's shoulders. 'If it was possible for wishes to harm people, then there wouldn't be anyone left in the world at all. How many times have you said "Devil take you" to me when you've been in a bad mood – oh, behind my back I know,' she added with a laugh that was tight in her throat, 'but I'm still here, aren't I?'

'Yes, but . . .'

'No buts. I know that you did not like some of your mama's "friends" but you have no more power to put a death wish on someone than . . . than that pile of dung over there has to grow legs and walk and talk!'

Richard grimaced and wriggled free of her embrace. 'But I still wished it.'

'Then confess it to a priest and put it behind you. If you want to explain it to your mother, perhaps you could go and pray at her graveside. I'm sure she will hear you.'

Richard's expression grew thoughtful. 'Do you think so?'

'I am sure of it,' Catrin said in a strong, positive tone.

'Can I go and tell her now?'

Catrin stopped and turned round so that they were facing the graveyard. 'The sooner the better,' she said. 'Do you want me to come with you?'

He shook his head. 'I'll be all right on my own.'

She watched him retrace his steps, and compressed her lips to steady the wobble of her chin. Distance made him seem smaller and more vulnerable. She wanted to run after him and wrap him in her arms, but held back, respecting his pride and privacy. Strange and sad to think that for the first time in his life, he had his mother to himself.

The time Richard spent at Amice's graveside was obviously a catharsis for the boy. That night, as the women prepared for bed, he seemed relaxed and sleepy rather than strung with exhaustion. Catrin still made him drink Etheldreda's potion after she had tucked him beneath the linen sheet and woven blanket on his pallet.

'No dreams,' she promised, crossing her fingers behind her back and trying not to imagine how the Countess's women would react to a second disturbed night in a row.

Richard handed the cup to her and lay back on the pillow. 'Can I sleep in the squires' dorter with Thomas tomorrow? He said that I could.'

Catrin smoothed the dark hair from his brow. 'You seem to have made a friend in him, don't you?' she murmured.

'He's going to teach me to throw a spear tomorrow.' There was relish in Richard's voice which did nothing to soothe the alarm his statement had roused in Catrin.

'On your own?'

'Oh no, with the other squires and one of the Earl's ser- jeants. I can go, can't I?' Alarm filled Richard's own voice. 'I don't have to stay here with all these women?'

Catrin did not know whether to be annoyed or amused. A typical male, she thought, wishing that she was one too and could abandon the bower for the freedom of a grassy field and a lesson in spear throwing. At least he would be occupied and benefiting from the experience. 'No,' she said with a smile, 'you don't have to stay.'

'And I can sleep in the dorter?'

'The Earl will have to be asked about that, and the Countess too, but I cannot see that they will object. On the morrow, I will ask them. Time for rest now.' She arranged the blanket over his shoulder and gave his hair a final smooth. Then she went to prepare herself for bed. By the time she had removed her wimple and gown, he was sound asleep.

'Bless him,' said Edon, glancing his way with a soft look. 'Let us hope he sleeps sound tonight.'

'Etheldreda said that her potion would ease his slumber.'

'Then it will. She might look like a hag, but she knows her nostrums. Do you want me to comb out your hair?'

It was on the tip of Catrin's tongue to say that she could manage. Since Lewis had died, no one had touched her hair. Lewis had loved to comb it and then spread it over his lean, brown hands. In those days she had scented it with rosemary and jasmine, and dressed her braids with bright ribbons and bindings. 'If you wish,' she said. At least it was clean. Before Amice's funeral that afternoon, she had begged a small container of the Countess's scented soap, purloined a pail of warm water from the kitchens, and scrubbed herself from crown to toe. A mark of respect to the dead, she had told the others when they looked at her askance, but it had been more than that, the cleansing almost a self-baptism as she began another life.

Unfastening the strip of leather at the tail of her plait, she pulled her fingers through her braid to loosen the twists, then sat still for Edon to do the rest.

'Your hair's quite pretty to say that it's black,' Edon remarked as she began to draw the comb down through Catrin's tresses. 'I wish mine was as shiny.' She fingered one of her own locks. 'Still, I should not complain. Mine is fair, and that's the sort that all the troubadours worship. Geoffrey says it reminds him of a cornfield rippling in the wind.' She gave her head a small toss.

Catrin remembered Lewis saying that her hair put him in mind of black silk, but she kept her silence. She had no intention of using her dead husband to compete with the paragon Geoffrey. Besides, it was true that to conform to the romantic ideal of beauty, a woman needed hair the colour of a parsnip, eyes of insipid pale blue, and a nature as sweet as a nectar-filled flower. Possessing none of these traits, Catrin had long since learned to live with what she had, and good luck to those more fortunate.

Still, it was pleasant to have someone dress her hair, and when Edon finished Catrin reciprocated gladly.

At the far end of the room, Rohese de Bayvel and another young woman were performing the same task for each other, whispering and giggling.

Edon cast a glance in their direction. 'Rumour has it that Rohese has a lover among the castle knights,' she murmured, leaning back at the tug of the comb, 'but no one knows who it is. I asked Geoffrey, but he said he had no truck with women's gossip.'

'No,' Catrin said drily.

'I wonder who it could be.' Edon caught her full lower lip in her teeth. 'She was betrothed until last year, but he changed allegiance and married someone from Stephen's party. For all her airs and graces, she has but a small dowry.'

Catrin was disgusted to find herself enjoying these details at Rohese's expense. The atmosphere of the bower, the pleasure in gossip was insidious and harmful. 'Finished,' she said with a last smoothing stroke of the comb, and handed it back to Edon in a manner that was almost brusque.

Edon seemed not to notice. She stowed the comb in her small personal coffer of carved beech wood. 'Did you see old Etheldreda give her that flask? Any guess that it's a love philtre. Ethel must have sold one to nearly every woman in the keep by now.'

Catrin shook her head. 'I would not want a man if I had to resort to love potions to make him desire me.'

Edon reddened slightly, making Catrin suspect that her companion had not been above slipping a little persuasion into Geoffrey the Wonderful's wine. Involuntarily she raised her hand to touch the cord at her throat. *Women's magic. Maiden, Mother and Crone.*

'I'm tired,' Edon said querulously, and then arched her

spine. 'Jesu, but my back aches tonight. It must have been all that sewing earlier. I should not have sat for so long.'

'Best retire to bed then,' Catrin said solicitously, managing to keep the irritation from her voice. 'I am grateful for the help you gave me today.' Which she was, but thought it unfair that Edon should blame it for her aching back. All women in the last month of pregnancy suffered thus. Catrin did not have to be a skilled midwife to know that; it was common female knowledge.

Edon gave her a smile, her mouth corners tight and, still rubbing her back, went to her pallet. Catrin raised the covers on her own mattress and lay down beneath them. The linen was scratchy against her bare shins, and the pillow had a musty smell, threaded through with the scent of dried lavender. This wasn't home, she thought dismally; she could never belong here, and yet, as she closed her eyes and courted sleep, she could not think of anywhere else that she had belonged, except perhaps Penfoss which, like the rest of her past life, no longer existed.

Once more, screams tore the night and roused everyone from sleep. This time the culprit was not Richard but Edon, her mouth open in a square wail of pain, and her chemise drenched in birthing fluid.

'God save us, she's started early with her pains,' said Dame Aldgith, the most senior of the women. The Countess was abed with her husband and therefore beyond summoning.

'I don't want to have a baby!' Edon screeched. 'It hurts, it hurts!' The final word ended on a hair-raising note of pure hysteria, and she threw herself back on her pallet, clutching at her taut belly and drumming her heels.

'Want or not, you're in travail, my girl,' said Aldgith, and swung round to the other women who were gathered round the bed, eyes huge with shock. 'Don't all stand there like sheep. Poke up the fire, set the cauldron over the hearth and find some old linen.'

Rohese gave the older woman a murderous look before sweeping away in a cloud of red-chestnut hair.

'I'll fetch Mistress Etheldreda,' Catrin murmured, and

quickly set about dressing again. Borrowing a cloak, she threw it around her shoulders and, draping a scarf over her hair, hurried from the room.

Running down to the great hall, she realised that she did not know where to find the elderly midwife. Somewhere in the camp was her vague notion. None of the other women would know either, so it was pointless turning back to ask. No respectable lady would step beyond the forebuilding door unescorted. The thought of venturing amongst the soldiers and camp followers made her baulk, but Etheldreda had to be summoned.

In the hall, she approached the guard on duty and told him of her difficulty.

Narrowing his eyes, he looked her up and down, then strode from his post to kick one of the knights who was rolled in his cloak near the fire. 'Hoi, Geoff, that little wife of yours has started with the babe. Take this lass and find the midwife.'

A young man sat up, yawning and knuckling his eyes. He had a mass of sleep-mussed curly blond hair and regular, but plain, features. When he stood up, he was a little below average height and stockily built, the hint of a bow to his short legs. Catrin warmed to him immediately. Edon's paragon was an ordinary man, his Adonis-like appearance a figment of his wife's over-fertile imagination.

'Edon, is she all right?' he demanded anxiously as he stumbled over the other sleepers and, latching his swordbelt, arrived at Catrin's side.

'Yes, of course she is,' Catrin said, with a silent apology to God for the lie. 'But she needs the midwife, and I have to find her.'

He dropped his scabbard with a clatter and, stifling an oath, picked it up again, fumbling with the lacings and causing Catrin to wonder anew at the human propensity for self-deception.

'It's too soon, isn't it?' Still fastening the leather strips, he followed her out into the summer darkness.

'Babies come when they will,' Catrin answered evasively. 'It is always hard to tell in the last month.'

'Is she in pain?'

'A little back-ache. Do you know where to find Dame Etheldreda?'

He nodded and led her across the bailey at a rapid walk, his anxiety tangible. Clearly Edon's worship was reciprocated and Geoffrey FitzMar saw his wife as a fair and flawless lady dwelling in her ivory tower. And how each viewed the other probably increased their confidence to face the world.

He led her to the second bailey. Fire embers glowed red, and here and there people were still awake. A fractious infant wailed. Dice clattered in a wooden cup and wine sloshed from flagon to drinking horn. Under a blanket, two forms moved together, one moaning softly on each upward stroke.

Geoffrey cleared his throat and steered her aside from the lovemaking couple.

They came to Etheldreda's fire. The old woman was still wide awake and busy grinding dried leaves with a pestle and mortar, but she set her work down the moment that she saw Catrin and her escort. Almost before Catrin had told her the news, she was reaching for her satchel and cloak.

'Always come in the dead of night, they do,' Ethel said, and then gave Geoffrey a nudge. 'Mind you, with a first babe, you'll be lucky to greet the sprog much before next dusk. Slow down, young man. My legs don't have the same spring as yours.'

Catrin and Ethel left a thoroughly unsettled Geoffrey in the great hall, and mounted the stairs to the bower. Ethel paused frequently to rest and breathlessly cursed her own failing body. 'Once I'd ha' run up these like a deer,' she panted. 'Time and past time I had someone to help me.' Fumbling in her satchel, she unstoppered a small flask and took several swallows. 'Lily of the valley,' she said. 'Sometimes it works, sometimes it don't. Come, wench, we've a babe to deliver.'

Harbouring misgivings at the 'we', Catrin led Etheldreda into the women's bower.

CHAPTER 7

Edon had decided that she did not want to bear a child. The romance of impending motherhood had been replaced by the reality, and she was made furious by the indignities visited on her body, and terrified by the increasingly powerful surges of pain.

She swore at Etheldreda and she swore at Catrin, setting the blame firmly on their shoulders. Then in the next moment, she was pleading with them to help her.

'You're spoiled, m'girl, that's your trouble. Never had to face the world before, have you?' Ethel said, but not unkindly. 'Here, swallow this brew to keep up your strength. You're going to be a while yet.'

'You cheated me, you hag. The eagle stone doesn't work!'

'Mistress, it works as much as you will it to do so,' Ethel said with a glance across the bed at Catrin. 'What do you expect if you keep thrashing and fighting like a fish out o' water? Now, do as I say, and drink this down.'

Throughout the rest of the night, Edon laboured and so did Ethel, alternately soothing and scolding, whilst keeping an eye on the progress of the birth and explaining details to Catrin.

'This un's coming out feet-first,' she said. 'Contrary as its mother.'

'Does it make a difference?'

Ethel glanced at the patient and lowered her voice. 'Makes me work for my living,' she said. 'I gets most of them out alive, but there's some as can't be saved. Head comes last, you see, and sometimes the babe suffocates. But if you bring the head out too fast, you damage the skull.'

Catrin winced, and Ethel gave her a tired smile. 'Do you still want to be my apprentice?'

'Not at the moment,' Catrin said with a small shake of her head. She looked at the elderly woman sitting on a stool by Edon's pallet side. It was not just the darkness of the room that was staining Etheldreda's eye sockets and dragging the flesh in dark shadows from her bones. While Edon's young body strove to bring forth new life, Ethel's was striving to hold life's end at bay.

Reaching out, Ethel patted one of Catrin's hands with her trembling left one. 'You have the gift, you have the hands and, despite what you say, you also have the calling.'

On the pallet, Edon whimpered and drew up her knees. Visibly gathering her strength, Ethel turned to her with words of encouragement and palpated her abdomen with a gentle, sure touch.

As the dawn brightened over the land and the shutters were thrown back to admit a flood of light into the women's chamber, Catrin witnessed an expert midwife at work. Any doubts she had harboured about entering the trade were banished by the birth of Edon's son.

Squinting, the better to focus, Ethel peered intently between Edon's quivering thighs. Taking a sharp knife from her belt, she made a single, swift cut in the young woman's flesh. 'Have to be stitched later,' she said without looking up, 'but this way the child has a better chance o' life. See both cheeks of its arse now.'

Edon had screamed at the sharp incision. Now she screamed again as another contraction forced her to push. Catrin held her hand and murmured soothingly, but her gaze was upon the tiny, bloody buttocks and legs that were emerging from Edon's birth passage.

'A fine little lad,' Ethel encouraged Edon. 'Five more minutes and we'll have him bawling in your arms. Just look at the ballocks on him!'

Edon half laughed, half sobbed and clenched her fists in the pillow.

Ethel waited until the body had been born as far as the mid-section. Then she freed the legs and gently pulled down a loop of the pulsating birth cord. 'Next the shoulders,' she said to the fascinated Catrin, and when Edon had pushed these out, Ethel watched closely again, not touching the baby, but waiting until the nape and hairline appeared. Then she grasped the infant's ankles and very carefully tugged him in a wide arc towards Edon's belly. His nose and mouth came free of the birth passage.

'Here, hold him like this,' Ethel commanded. 'Don't pull at all; we don't want him popping out all of a sudden.'

Catrin found herself grasping the baby's slippery little feet, their size so tiny that she could scarcely believe they belonged to a human creature. Ethel took a strip of linen and deftly cleaned the infant's nose and mouth of birth fluids. A huge wail filled the space around the bed and the new-born's colour improved from dark red to pink.

'My, my,' muttered Ethel. 'Ballocks and a bellow. He's going to be a regular little bull.'

Taking charge from Catrin again, she slowly delivered the rest of the head and lowered Edon's new-born son on to his mother's abdomen. 'Backside first,' she said, shaking her head as she cut the cord and wrapped the baby in a length of warmed linen. 'He's as awkward as his mother.' There was a note of deep satisfaction in her voice. Breech births were notoriously difficult and not all had a happy outcome.

'I'm not ready to be a mother,' Edon croaked, her voice filled with tears and joy.

'Too late now,' Ethel said, and placed the child in her arms. 'Never fret, you'll grow accustomed.'

The afterbirth was delivered and the other women crowded around mother and baby, offering their services now that the main one had been performed. Edon's son was bathed and oiled. His gums were rubbed with honey to soothe him, and the wet nurse was sent for. Rohese kept her distance, her nose in the air.

In the broad light of day, Ethel's features were positively grey. Once more Catrin broke protocol to bring the older woman a cup of Countess Mabile's best wine.

Ethel took it gratefully, together with another swig from

the small flask in her satchel. 'Hope you learn quick, girl,' she said ruefully. 'By the feel o' my bones, my time's almost run into the bottom of the hourglass.'

Catrin shook her head, not sure what to say. She was indeed a fast learner, but knew that Ethel had so much to teach, it would probably take years to absorb it all.

'Where's that cord I gave you?'

'I have it here.' Catrin fished the knotwork necklace from the throat of her dress. 'Did you fear I would take it off?'

'No, but I wondered.' Ethel looked pleased. A spark of colour had returned to her cheeks and her breathing had improved.

'I wondered too, but I don't any more.' Catrin glanced over her shoulder to the far end of the room where mother and child were being fêted by the other women.

'Aye, it's a miracle and a mystery,' Ethel said. 'One I never grow tired of seeing.' Recovered, she rose to her feet and turned towards the door, but before she had taken more than a step Richard appeared at Catrin's side.

He was wearing a clean, if slightly large, tunic that had been found for him yesterday, and from somewhere he had obtained a comb and smoothed the night-tangles from his hair. 'Can I go and find Thomas?' he demanded.

Catrin nodded. 'If you want,' she said, but caught his sleeve to hold him back. 'You slept well?'

Richard wrinkled his nose. 'I didn't dream if that's what you mean, but all the noise woke me up.' He shrugged. 'I'm glad the baby's alive.'

Catrin felt the tug of resistance against her hand and let him go. He bolted from the room like a young hare, and the midwife shook her head with envy. 'Wish my old legs were as springy as that,' she said, adding thoughtfully, 'He does well to shoulder the burdens he has.'

'I suppose Oliver told you about him.'

Etheldreda limped towards the door. 'He told me enough but I still have eyes to see. God's Mother, if I had to rely on information from Master Oliver, I'd still be sitting at my fire now! Sometimes it's like drawing a tooth!'

Stifling a smile, Catrin escorted Ethel down the draughty,

winding stair. As they reached the foot, the new father greeted them on his eager way to see his infant son.

'A boy!' he cried. 'It's a boy!'

'Aye, so it is, my lord,' said Etheldreda drily. Geoffrey grabbed her, plonked two smacking kisses on her cheeks, pressed a silver penny in her hand, and shot on up the stairs.

Ethel rubbed her cheek and chuckled. 'I warrant he'll not still be sober the other side of prime.'

Catrin glanced up the stairs to the sound of his receding footfalls and warmed to Edon's husband a little more.

She escorted Ethel as far as the bailey, whereupon the midwife insisted that she could see herself the rest of the way to her shelter. 'I'm for a cup of ale and a wink of shut-eye, but I'll return to look in on mother and babe before noon.'

'What about all those stairs?'

The whiskery mouth pursed stubbornly. 'I'll manage, young woman,' she said and then looked sidelong at Catrin. 'Leastways for today, while I show you what to do. After that you can check on mistress Edon and report to me.'

'But I don't . . . I'm not . . .' Catrin began.

'You will and you are,' Ethel interrupted firmly, her tone brooking no argument. 'Leave me now, I can manage from here.'

Chewing her underlip, Catrin watched the indomitable old woman make her way towards the main camp. Only four days ago, Catrin had known what to expect from daily life. Now she felt as if she were a stone, rolling down a hill and gathering speed with terrifying momentum. But it was exhilarating too.

Turning back to the keep, she was surprised to see Rohese de Bayvel hurrying across the bailey in the direction of the camp. The seamstress was wearing a hooded cloak, but Catrin recognised the skilful embroidery on the hem of Rohese's gown, and the shoes with their distinctive silk braid side-lacings. The image of the haughty embroideress entering the human stew of Earl Robert's camp of her own volition, and at a run, was enough to make Catrin stare with widening eyes. She remembered the furtive exchange of money for a pouch of herbs and wondered if Rohese had taken a lover among the Earl's common troops. She was curious and interested, but not shocked. After serving Amice for three years, there was very little that could surprise her about men and women.

'Have you lost him again?'

Stifling a scream, Catrin spun round and discovered Oliver grinning behind her. His hair was wet and bore the sleek sheen of silver gilt, and there was a barber's nick on the point of his chin, showing a pin-prick bead of red. It was the first time that she had seen him unencumbered by his mail. He seemed taller and thinner without the bulk of hauberk and gambeson, the dark blue tunic emphasising both traits. The colour was expensive, affordable only to the nobility, but the garment bore evidence of hard wear. There was a patch in one elbow of a slightly different shade of blue, and the cuffs bore much evidence of darning.

'Lost who?' Catrin asked, momentarily taken aback by his sudden and changed appearance.

'Richard of course.'

'What?' She rallied her wits. 'Oh, no. He's gone off with Thomas FitzRainald again.'

'Did he wake last night?'

She shook her head. 'Not for dreams, but he was woken.' She told him about Edon, but avoided the details about her part in the baby's delivery. 'I was escorting Ethel back to her shelter.'

His expression remained neutral as she mentioned the childbirth, but he seemed eager to change the subject. 'Have you broken your fast yet?'

She shook her head.

'Neither have I, and they'll be serving bread and cheese in the hall by now.' He held out his darned sleeve in a formal gesture. She hesitated for a moment, then laid her own along it. She was wearing her blue-green undergown, and in quality and wear it matched his own appearance. Suddenly she was glad that she was not dressed in the rich, dark red tunic.

'I did not think that you would return so soon,' she said, as they entered the hall and found a place at one of the rapidly filling trestles.

'It would have taken us longer,' he admitted, 'but we had help. A group of mercenaries happened by on their way to seek employment with Earl Robert, and they lent us their aid.' Drawing his knife, he expertly divided a flat loaf of bread between them.

'Mercenaries,' Catrin repeated, the word emerging with revulsion.

He laid the knife on the board. 'I know their leader. He saved my life a long time ago when I was a pilgrim. If not for Randal's intervention, I would have been slaughtered by brigands and my bones scattered by the vultures. We journeyed together for a six-month and I owe him a debt from that time – not only for my life, but for the lessons he taught me.' He tore a morsel off his portion of bread and put it in his mouth.

'Then how did they come to "happen by"?' Catrin asked. 'Penfoss was a small settlement serving a hunting lodge. Hardly the place for mercenaries to seek employment.'

'It has a water trough for thirsty horses,' he said, swallowing and pulling off another chunk of bread. There were tense lines at his eye corners. 'And it is simple enough to find – there's that wide cart-track leading through the trees.' He threw her a sideways glance, his grey eyes bright with hostility. 'Randal was riding a bay stallion and his shield was blue and red.'

Catrin took up her own portion of the loaf and picked crumbs from the broken crust. She knew that she owed him an apology, but the words stuck in her throat. When he spoke of mercenaries, all she could see in her mind's eye was the wanton destruction at Penfoss.

'And if he had found us as the others found us, what then?' she demanded. 'Would watering the horses have been enough?'

Oliver chewed the bread with powerful rotations of his jaw. A flush spread from his throat to the flaxen hair curling and drying on his browline. 'You go too far,' he said huskily. 'I owe Randal my life. Insult him and you insult me.'

'I . . . I didn't insult him, or you. I just asked a question.' Catrin flushed as well, anger brimming in her eyes. 'And you would ask it too if you had been a witness to . . .' She broke off, unable to continue. Crumbs showered the board as she dug her fingernail into the soft, brown core of the bread.

He looked away, swallowed, and after a moment sighed and looked back. 'Randal de Mohun has led a far from blameless life, but that does not make him an ogre. You accused me of judging Amice. Should I now accuse you of judging Randal?'

Catrin shook her head. 'I'm sorry,' she forced out, feeling wretched.

The hardness left his face, and the glint of anger died in his eyes. 'And I am sorry for being so swift to take offence. Let us call a truce before you've nothing to make a meal but crumbs.'

Catrin glanced down at her mangled bread which, in truth, she did not feel very much like eating. But to show that she was willing to agree to his truce, she raised a morsel to her mouth. Once she started to chew, she discovered that she was ravenous. The previous night's vigil had taken its toll on her energy, and she polished off the remains of her bread in short order, together with a large lump of cheese.

'So,' he said, adroitly changing the subject as he finished his own meal, 'is life in the bower any more appealing for the sake of another day and night?'

'It would stifle me if I had to remain there the day long.' She took a drink of the cider which had been served with the bread and cheese. 'The Countess has been very kind, but I cannot bear all the shrewish remarks and tittle-tattle. Trivial matters are exaggerated out of all proportion. What does it matter if the hem of a gown is not quite straight, or someone spills a drip of wine on the napery?'

He looked amused for a moment, but then he sobered. 'So, you are not content?'

'Oh, no, I would not have you think me ungrateful. I am happy enough and I do have other matters to occupy my time.' She used the moment of drinking her cider to look at him through her lashes. She did not relish the thought of another confrontation, and Etheldreda had said that he would 'burst his hauberk' when he discovered that she was embarking on a career of herb-lore and midwifery.

'Other matters?' He raised his brows.

For an instant Catrin was trapped by his scrutiny. His eyes were grey; not the light, sharp hue of glass which she would have associated with such fair hair, but a darker, storm-water colour that in dull light could be mistaken for brown. Less to be seen, more to be discovered and, like dark water, to draw her down. Catrin mentally shook herself. Lack of sleep was making her fanciful. 'Things that concern women,' she fenced.

His brows twitched together and she saw a question gathering behind them. Now it was her turn to change the subject. 'Richard wants to sleep with the other squires in the boys' dorter,' she said quickly. 'Could you approach Earl Robert on his behalf? Etheldreda's sleeping potion has worked its wonder on him, and he slept much better last night – or he would have done were it not for Edon's travail.' Her voice was swift and breathless, and his frown remained.

'Gladly I will speak to the Earl. I have to make my report to him anyway concerning Penfoss.' He drained his cup. 'But first, will you show me where Amice is buried?'

Catrin was ashamed at the alacrity with which she rose from the board to show him a dead woman's grave. But she could not have endured to sit much longer beneath the darkness of his gaze. Outside in the open air, it was diluted, less potent.

He looked at the freshly turned scar of soil and the chaplet of gillyflowers lying on top of it, the petals drooping a little now, but still brave of colour. He picked it up and turned it round in his hands. 'Rest in the garden,' he said softly, then laid it back upon the grave and made the sign of the cross.

Catrin's throat swelled and she shed a few tears, but they were of healing and lightened her heart.

For a moment, Oliver stood in silent contemplation, then turned to leave. 'Now to Earl Robert,' he said, but paused to brush his thumb across the tear-tracks on Catrin's face. 'I'll seek you later and tell you the outcome.'

She nodded and thanked him, but stepped away from his touch and replaced it with a quick swipe of her palm. His expression became rueful. 'If you were a plant, you would be a thistle,' he said, but there was a smile in his eyes, if not on his lips, as he inclined his head and went on his way.

Catrin watched his progress across the bailey; his lean, blue-clad form and the glint of his hair, dried now to flaxen brightness. Since Lewis had died, she had lowered her guard to no one except Richard and Amice, and only then in small measure. Now she was perplexed to find it dissolving, and herself powerless to prevent it. Perhaps it was time to forget the pain left by Lewis's death and salve the wound with the balm of another man's attention.

Catrin pondered the thought as she followed slowly in Oliver's wake. Lewis had been slender, handsome, quick as a fox, with all a fox's charm and cunning, and a voracious appetite too.

Oliver was tall, big-boned and fair, with a powerful sense of duty and a dry sense of humour that matched her own. But for the rest, what did she know? He had grieved long for his young wife, as she had grieved for Lewis. His lands were forfeit to the vagaries of war, and his friends were mercenaries whom he would not stand to be questioned. Ethel said he would be furious to know that Catrin intended learning midwifery skills. But it was no concern of his and he had no right . . . unless she gave it to him.

Frowning deeply, Catrin wandered back into the keep, her mind so occupied that she almost collided with Rohese on the stairs leading up to the bower.

'Mind where you're going!' the embroideress snapped.

Catrin looked at the flush on the high, perfect cheekbones, the slightly swollen red lips, and the wimple set askew, tendrils of hair snaking around Rohese's hectic face. 'At least I don't have to mind where I've been,' she retorted nimbly, and was pleased to see her barb hit home as Rohese recoiled, her blue eyes growing first wide, then narrow.

'There is no place for you among the Countess's women!' she hissed. 'Who are you to call me to account when your former mistress was nothing but a whore!'

'At least she did not need love philtres to make a man take notice.'

'What has that old hag been saying to you?'

'Nothing, I have eyes to see. Does the Countess know where you go?'

'If you so much as open your mouth to my lady, I will sew it shut! Stay out of my business!'

'Gladly, if you leave me in peace to go about mine.'

Rohese glared at her, then whirled and ran on up the stairs. Catrin followed more slowly. Her knees were weak, but nevertheless there was a smile on her lips, for she judged that she had got the better of the argument.

CHAPTER 8

Both of Oliver's petitions to Earl Robert were successful.

'I would have sent the lad to the boys' dorter myself, eventually,' Robert said. 'If he is ready to go now, then it shows his resilience. He can take up his own squire's duties too, instead of doing half that rascal Thomas's work.' His thin lips curved. 'I had noticed.'

Once more Oliver was in the Earl's solar. He kept his back to the mural painting, but felt its presence like a pressure between his shoulder blades. 'Yes, my lord.'

Robert tilted his head. 'You seem to have set yourself up as a guardian to him and the woman,' he observed. 'I saw you sitting with her during the breaking of fast.' His glance travelled from Oliver to the Countess who was sitting in the window embrasure, a piece of sewing in her lap and a small, silky dog sleeping at her side.

'She took me to see Amice de Cormel's grave, and I did promise that I would not abandon her and the lad once I had brought them to Bristol.'

The Earl grunted. 'Commendable,' he said.

The Countess spoke up from her corner. 'I suppose you had a hand in arranging for the midwife to take Catrin beneath her wing? Etheldreda used to be one of your family retainers, did she not?'

Oliver stared. 'My lady?'

Mabile's cow-brown eyes widened 'I assumed it was at your instigation. Was it not?'

'My lady, I know nothing of what you speak.' Completely baffled, Oliver spread his hands. 'All she said to me was that she had found "women's matters" to occupy her time, and I took it to mean of the sewing and weaving kind.'

Mabile clucked her tongue. 'Then she did not tell you that she is to train as a midwife under the guidance of Dame Etheldreda? I have given Catrin leave to remain in the bower or sleep in the hall, as she chooses. I have also promised her that Etheldreda can have one of the permanent shelters against the bailey wall, instead of living under a linen canvas as she does now.'

Oliver shook his head. 'She told me none of this,' he heard himself say in a reasonable voice, whilst within him all reason was gathered up and cast aside by disbelief. Small wonder that she had looked at him sidelong and said, '*Women's matters.*'

'Ah, well, it was before she had petitioned me for my permission. Perhaps she wanted to keep it to herself until then.'

'Yes, my lady,' Oliver said, managing to be civil by the skin of his teeth.

'You like it not?' The Countess looked at him askance. 'Dame Etheldreda saved the life of Edon FitzMar's son, and Catrin assisted her most competently. Catrin will make an excellent midwife – far better than she does a bower maid. And she is young and strong. With the best will in the world, Dame Etheldreda's health is failing.'

'Yes, my lady, you are right,' Oliver said courteously and made a conscious effort to unclench his fists. 'I am surprised, that is all.' And he turned to the Earl before the full extent of his discomfort was betrayed. 'There is also the matter of the soldier I mentioned, and his troop – Randal de Mohun.'

The Countess eyed Oliver from behind his back and then resumed her sewing, a thoughtful purse to her lips.

Earl Robert's own thoughtful look was in response to the subject that Oliver had now raised. 'You recommend him?'

'Yes, my lord. I first knew him many years ago when we were pilgrims in the Holy Land. He is no half-trained Fleming or green boy in search of glory, but a warrior full-fledged, the kind you have been seeking to recruit.'

'Trustworthy?'

Oliver hesitated. 'Yes, my lord, providing he receives his wages.'

'I see.' The Earl brushed his palm across the neat, dark beard on his jaw. 'Where did he come from?'

'He did not say, except that it was further up the border and that he and his men had not been paid although, in truth, I believe that he was probably working for a baron of Stephen's faction.'

'Hardly a reason for me to employ him.'

'Perhaps he has information that will be of use to you, my lord,' Oliver said, barely concealing his impatience. It was the final remark he was going to make in de Mohun's favour. While he owed the man a debt, he was not entirely at ease with the notion of sharing his proximity, and now he had concerns other than promoting an old and outgrown acquaintance.

Robert pondered for a moment, then snapped his fingers.

'Very well. Bring him to the battle-practice in the bailey at dusk and I will have a look at his skills. And if they are good, I will employ him.'

'Yes, my lord, thank you.' Dismissed, Oliver bowed and made his way down to the hall, his feet carrying him independent of his boiling thoughts. He could not believe that Catrin had apprenticed herself to Ethel, and that the Countess had sanctioned it. Ethel was always talking about finding a younger woman to replace her, but Oliver had largely ignored her hints and grumbles, knowing full well that what kept Etheldreda alive was her trade and her pride in her skills. While she was needed, her will had the dominance of her body. Never would he have guessed that she would choose Catrin when there were other midwives, already with a grounding of skill, to whom she could pass on her knowledge. And if he had guessed, he would have done his best to stop it, although it was easier to be angry than to examine why.

Burning with agitation, he went to find Ethel, but her fire was cold and no one had seen her since mid-morning. Nor had she taken up residence in any of the shelters clustered against the inner bailey wall. In a thoroughly bad temper, Oliver set about the first of his day's duties, which involved going down to the wharves to count and escort a cargo of wine back to the keep.

Gawin, in contrast to Oliver, was in high spirits, a whistle on his lips and a glint in his eyes. 'Women,' he said with a grin. 'They spurn you until you turn away, and then suddenly they're interested.'

'Women,' Oliver said tersely, 'are more trouble than they are worth.'

'Depends on the woman. The one I've got is trouble through and through.' He grinned. 'But I'd count her worth an empty stable and an hour of my time any day!'

Oliver snorted with disgust. 'That is how you count them all,' he said. 'An empty stable and a willingness to lift their skirts.'

Gawin shrugged. 'Better than not counting them at all and wearing a scowl like a thundercloud.' He cocked his head on one side. 'It's the wench we rescued, isn't it? She's itching under your hauberk like a hair shirt.'

When Oliver snarled at him, Gawin's grin deepened. 'There's only one cure when they've got you by the balls,' he said cheerfully. 'You give them your prick as well.'

Oliver closed his eyes and swallowed. To have struck his fellow knight in front of the citizenry of Bristol would be to cause unnecessary scandal and discomfort to the Earl, and Oliver's moral conscience was somewhat more polished than his companion's. Raising his lids, he fixed Gawin with an icy glare. 'A pity your brains dwell in your cods and you can't refrain from spilling them.'

'My brains work perfectly,' Gawin retorted, refusing to be set down and giving as good as he got. '*They* haven't withered from lack of use.'

Oliver withdrew from the exchange, aware that if he did not the tit-for-tat would continue, cutting closer to the bone each time. Whilst he did not mind about filleting Gawin, he had no intention of having the same treatment meted out to himself.

Catrin was indeed itching beneath his hauberk like a hair shirt, but that did not mean he wanted to throw her down on her back in the nearest stable. What he wanted was to talk to her, to see the changing agate glints in her eyes and watch her nose wrinkle as she smiled. He wanted to keep her from all harm, but at the same time for her to be free and unfettered, her chin jutting in defiance, and the crimson hose peeping from beneath the hem of her gown. He most certainly did not want her to become a midwife. A mass of contradictions churned within him, and he had to make an effort to ignore them and concentrate on the task in hand.

Having performed the escort duty and delivered the wine into Earl Robert's care, Oliver returned to the bailey and made his way to the wooden shelters built against its walls. The loud braying of a donkey drew him to the furthermost shack. Whereas this morning it had been occupied by a pile of straw and three sheep awaiting slaughter, it now housed Etheldreda and the motley contents of her canvas shelter. The old midwife was directing a young soldier to dig out a firepit, and Catrin was unloading a pallet and blankets from the donkey's back.

Oliver gnawed his lip. So it was true. He had been half hoping that he had misunderstood the morning's conversation, but the sight before his eyes saw it confirmed. Catrin staggered into the shelter with her unwieldy bundle, set it down and began smoothing it out. Ethel glanced up from supervising the digging of her firepit and her eyes met Oliver's. What might have been a smile twitched her lips but was concealed as she turned and murmured to Catrin. The younger woman straightened from her task and stared at Oliver. Then she laid her hand on Ethel's sleeve, said something, and left the shelter to meet him.

He planted his feet apart and squared his shoulders. The blue-green underdress clung to her body. There was still a slight mark on the breast where the eel liquor had soaked through her outer garment. Tendrils of black hair had escaped the kerchief she wore in place of the more decorous wimple and her cheekbones were flushed with exertion. The full lips, the glints of green in her eyes, the defiant jut of her chin; all were as he had imagined, and the effect was vastly unsettling.

'The Countess Mabile told me that you had embarked on a

scapegrace scheme to become a midwife,' he said without preamble. 'I did not want to believe her, but I see that I must.'

She tilted her head to one side in that maddening way she
had and considered him, her eyes narrowing slightly. 'I know
that you like it not,' she replied, 'but it is none of your concern,
and nor is it a "scapegrace scheme". I have the Countess's
sanction. I do not need yours.'

'That much is obvious, since you disguised your intent to
me this morning when we broke fast together.'

Catrin glanced back towards the shelter. 'If you are going
to shout and lose your temper, I ask you not to do it in front
of Ethel. Her health is not robust and she has enough on her
trencher already.'

'I do not need *you* to tell me about Ethel,' he said, throwing
his own glance at the old midwife. She was going astutely
about her business, but he knew that her ears were pinned.
Whatever inroads age had made into her health, Ethel's
hearing remained needle-sharp. Taking Catrin's arm, he led
her not only out of earshot but out of sight, tugging her
around the corner of a storeshed. The remark she had made
about him shouting and losing his temper was probably an
attempt to shame him into doing neither, but her suggestion
that he lacked control only made him angrier still.

The moment they were out of Ethel's range, Catrin freed
herself from his grip and rubbed her arm. 'And Ethel certainly
does not need to be told about you. She said that when you
heard, you would burst your hauberk, and to look at you she
was right.'

'Did she tell you why?' His tone was full of angry contempt
as he folded his arms, pressing his fingers against the cold
metal rivets of his hauberk. To have Ethel, who knew more
about him than any person living, discuss him with Catrin,
was both a betrayal and an intrusion.

Colour flooded her face. 'Yes, but in confidence. She said
that a midwife should be as close-mouthed as a priest in the
confessional.'

'A pity she seems not to practise what she preaches,' he
said angrily. 'What gems of wisdom did she impart, or is
that too much of a "confidence" to break?'

Catrin drew herself up. 'She had no intention to wound or harm you in telling me. It was to make me understand why you might prove difficult. She told me about your wife, and said that you had a dislike – a fear – of midwifery and women's business.'

Catrin's eyes, full of battle-light, were a luminous tawny-green. There was anxiety in them, but it did not detract from the determination he saw too. He loomed over her, glaring down. 'After the way Emma died, it would be strange if I did not avoid conversation about matters of childbirth.' His lip curled. 'Fear it is not. If I am at risk of bursting my hauberk, it is at the thought of the danger that you risk by taking up the trade.'

She held his gaze with stubborn courage. 'No more danger than any other. I could prick myself on a sewing-needle in the bower tomorrow and die of a poisoned finger. Look what happened at Penfoss! But for a quirk of fate, you would have buried me yesterday with all the others.'

'So I might, but there is no cause for you to go shortening the odds with this lunatic folly. Did Ethel also tell you how she came to Bristol?' he asked brutally. 'How she was burned out of her cot for witchcraft? Did she tell you about journeys through the worst parts of the camp and the town in the middle of the night? Of the thieves and pimps to whom a young woman alone would be easy prey? Christ on the Cross, I didn't bring you to Bristol to see you squander your life down some stinking alley and wind up just another corpse in the river!' Unfolding his arms, he took her by the shoulders to emphasise his point.

'Then for what purpose did you bring me?' she spat. 'To sit among the Countess's women until the pettiness and boredom drives me to cast myself out of the bower window to a "clean death"! If I had known you were going to make a chattel of me, I'd have stayed amongst the cinders!'

'If I had known you were going to be so foolish, I'd have left you there!'

She glared at him. 'You do not own me. The choice is mine and freely made. If you had my welfare at heart, you would wish me well, not seek to strew stones in my path.

Now let me go. Ethel needs help to unpack her belongings.' She shrugged him off, her frame bristling with anger. 'Face yourself, not me!' Turning on her heel she stalked off, the red hose flashing with each step.

'Hellcat!' Oliver choked in her wake, and kicked at the blameless storeshed wall. The action rebounded on him, for he stubbed his toe and thus felt all the more aggrieved. It was a long, long time since his control had been so precarious, but then it had been a long, long time since anyone had so thoroughly upset his equilibrium, and never before had it been a woman. Emma had been too gentle and obedient to criticise her adolescent husband, and his relationships since her death had been transitory and, for the most part, conducted between the sheets.

For a moment he almost strode after Catrin to continue the exchange, but when he did move it was in the opposite direction. As she said, the choice was hers and freely made. Well and good, let her stew in her own soup. His pace lengthened with determination as he set off to find Randal de Mohun and relay Earl Robert's message about the tiltyard.

'You were right, he did burst his hauberk,' Catrin said ruefully, as she swept the beaten-earth floor of the shelter with a birch besom and then covered it with a thick layer of straw. 'I even feared that he was going to strike me.'

'He didn't raise his hand against you?' Ethel ceased feeding twigs to the first fire in her new hearth and looked at Catrin sharply.

'No, only his voice. And to my credit, or shame, I shouted straight back at him, told him to face himself instead of railing at me.'

Ethel gave a small snort through her nose and, nodding to herself, continued to build up her fire. 'Aye, you're the one,' she said with a note of satisfaction.

'What do you mean?' Catrin demanded suspiciously. But Ethel only shook her head and chuckled softly to herself. When Catrin persisted, Ethel made her set up the iron tripod and cooking pot over the fire and put her off by showing her a recipe for building up a mother's strength in the days after the birth.

'Hah, double sixes, I win!' Randal de Mohun clenched his fists in triumph and scooped the silver pennies off the table and into his pouch. If the dice had not belonged to someone else, Oliver would have sworn that they were loaded, for Randal's luck that evening had been phenomenal. But then the mercenary had been enjoying good fortune all day, and this drinking session in The Mermaid, a dockside alehouse of unsavoury repute, was to celebrate the hiring of his sword by Robert of Gloucester. Oliver would not usually have stayed in such a place beyond the obligatory first cup to toast Randal's success, but tonight a second cup had followed the first, and the third was well on its way to joining them.

Sharp edges of colour and noise grew comfortably blurred. Weak jests suddenly became hilarious, and the serving wenches seemed far more attractive than when he first entered the place. So much so, that one of them was soon sitting in his lap and helping him to finish his wine. She had a loose plait of greasy brown hair, and pale blue eyes. Her giggle was irritating, but her figure was ample, and she seemed thoroughly willing to share its delights with him. He ordered a fresh flagon. The dice rattled across the trestle and Randal's laugh rang out, huge and confident. Oliver laughed, echoing the sound, but it rang hollowly in his own ears, and he muffled it within the girl's abundant breasts. The flagon arrived, brimming with cool red oblivion, and Oliver sought it greedily.

He woke to a blinding headache and a stomach that was boiling like a dyer's vat. The sound of someone pissing nearby set up a fierce aching in the pit of his belly.

'Jesu,' he groaned and, against his better judgement, opened his lids a crack. Daylight seared his eyeballs and for a moment he was insensible to anything but the pain. The noise of urination went on and on. Turning his head he saw Randal de Mohun taking a piss against the bailey wall. Oliver stared blankly. He had no recollection whatsoever of leaving The

Mermaid and returning here, but must have done so, although apparently he had not reached the hall, for his bed was a heap of stable straw pulled down from a wagon standing in the bailey. The last time he had been as drunk as this had been during his pilgrimage, when a chirurgeon had drawn an abscessed tooth. Back then he had not known which pain was worse; now he did.

Trying to ignore the clamour from his bladder, he dragged his cloak high around his shoulders, closed his eyes and rolled over. The straw rustled and there was a soft murmur of protest. Oliver's lids shot up again and he stared in dismay at the girl from *The Mermaid*. In the pitiless morning light, she was a sight less appetising than she had been the previous evening. Her hair straggled about her face and he could see the lice wandering amongst its strands. The stink of her breath almost made him gag, but he knew that his own must be no sweeter. Three quarts of Gascony's worst red and a pottage bowl full of leek and garlic stew were not ingredients for freshening the mouth.

The girl began to snore, a thin string of drool at the corner of her mouth. Oliver groaned and turned on his back. He could not remember lying with her. Surreptitiously he groped beneath his cloak. He was still wearing his braies and his hose were still attached, apart from one fastening. He was also sporting a magnificent, swollen erection. Of course that did not mean he had refrained from fornication last night, it was just a measure of how badly he needed to piss. The girl's gown was rucked and stained and her body stank of vigorous effort.

Struggling to his feet, he lurched over to the wall and joined de Mohun who was shaking the last drops from his organ.

'Rough night.' De Mohun's broad grin and gleaming eyes revealed that he was in considerably better case than Oliver. 'I hazard you've a head as thick as a thundercloud after the amount of wine you sank.'

Oliver gave an inarticulate murmur and Randal's grin became an outright guffaw. 'I had to carry you back, more or less. God's bones, you didn't even stir when I tupped the wench and she started screaming like a vixen on heat. Should have stayed sober, man, we could have shared. Not a beauty, I'll admit, but she's got a grip like a vice.' He thrust his right forefinger expressively into the cupped fist of his left.

Trapped by the slow emptying of his overfull bladder, Oliver could only stand and wait. Like the wine, de Mohun's company had been considerably more acceptable the night before. 'I've forsworn women and drink,' he said shortly. 'Have you paid the wench?'

'Three times and then some,' Randal said with a flash of his brows.

Oliver grimaced.

'Hah, knew you'd turn priest on me the moment you sobered up! Good Christ, man, there's nothing wrong with wenches and wine.'

'There is when you can't remember either, except to know that they were both bad bargains,' Oliver retorted. Relieved to have finished, he adjusted his clothing and walked away as fast as his pounding head would allow.

Randal watched him through narrowed lids, then walked back to the girl and seized her roughly by the elbow. 'Come on, slut, you've outlived your use,' he growled, jerking her to her feet, and slapping her face when she was slow to waken and take her own weight. When she protested, he slapped her harder and, dragging her to the gates, threw her out.

She screamed invective at him and shook her fist, but when he lunged after her she took to her heels.

Randal returned to her sleeping place and stooped to pick up her purse from the straw. He lost the few silver coins it contained in his broad, scarred palm, and tossed the purse away. She had not been worth the payment and he considered himself owed a refund.

Walking across the bailey, he saw Oliver's young adjutant, Gawin, making his own fond farewells to his leman. A braid of chestnut-red hair peeped from beneath her wimple and her features were thin and fine. There were rings on the fingers that curved around her lover's neck, and the edge of her gown beneath her green woollen cloak was embroidered with silks. Envy curdled in Randal's gut as he contrasted this thoroughbred creature with his partner of the night before.

He watched her break away from Gawin, and hurry in the direction of the main household, her head down and cloak folded high around her face. A highborn woman seeking a little coarse cloth to make her silks less boring, he thought. She ought to know how it felt to have a real man hard up inside her instead of playing with boys like Gawin.

'A remedy, eh?' Ethel peered at Oliver through a haze of woodsmoke. 'Would that be for a sot's head, or the more incurable disease of cracked wits?'

'I'm here for your help, not to be sliced into little pieces by your tongue.'

'Humph,' Ethel said, and pointed to a low stool. 'Sit.' Taking a cup, she set about mixing the same betony and feverfew tisane that Oliver had given to Catrin on the road.

Oliver watched her and nursed his thundering skull. It did not help matters that he had received orders from the Earl, and was expected to depart Bristol with letters for Gloucester as soon as he had saddled up. Even the thought of wearing a helm was beyond bearing. The only mercy was that he would not be riding with de Mohun who was being sent out in a different direction.

'Drink,' Ethel commanded, and handed him the steaming cup.

Grimacing, he took it from her. She had closed her lips on further sour remarks, but her expression spoke instead. Avoiding her gimlet stare, he glanced around the neatly arranged shelter and the bed-bench at the back covered with a cosy woven rug. 'I thought Catrin might be here,' he said.

'Well, you thought wrong. She's sleeping wi' the other women and keeping an eye on Edon FitzMar to save my old legs those stairs.' Ethel cocked her head on one side. 'But if you want to apologise to the lass, it'll be worth the climb to fetch her.'

'Apologise!' Oliver choked, then clutched his bursting skull with his free hand. 'Good Christ, her tongue's sharper than yours!'

'In self-defence,' Ethel retorted, folding her arms. 'Your

own ain't slow to clear the scabbard . . . my lord.' She sucked her teeth and considered him, the look in her eyes softening. 'Think carefully about what you will say when you see her next. The lass can match you, word for word, but she is wounded as much as she wounds. You went out in the city, had three skins too many in bad company and bedded a whore for your comfort.'

'What of it?' he said defensively.

'The lass came down at dawn to report to me on Edon. Then she went across the ward to the bake house and saw you snoring in a sodden heap beside that slut from The Mermaid. If you angered her yesterday, then she has nothing but contempt for you this morn, and I cannot say I blame her.'

Oliver cursed softly and sipped the hot brew. He could hardly say that it was Catrin's fault that he had drunk himself out of his senses. It might be true, but it was also a feeble excuse. It had been easier to set his back teeth awash with wine than 'face himself'.

'I just want her to be safe,' he said. 'And taking your place will put her in all manner of jeopardy.'

'Aye, so it will, but a gilded cage is your desire, not hers. She has the gift and she has the need. If you want to keep her respect, let alone her friendship, then you have to accept that.'

'I'm not sure I can.' Oliver finished the brew, screwing up his face at the particles of herb in the dregs, and rose to his feet.

Ethel gave him a hard look. 'Try,' she said, and turned her back on him to make herself busy with her pestle and mortar.

His head still pounding fit to burst, Oliver took his leave.

CHAPTER 9

Over the following weeks, Catrin threw herself into learning her new trade. She assisted at births and was told which prayers to recite and which saints to invoke. Ethel showed her how to perform external examinations to gauge the position of the child within the womb. The old woman took her around the market place and the dockside in search of herbs and remedies, and together they sought among the fields for fresh plants and herbs to make unguents and poultices.

When she was not busy with Ethel, Catrin served the Countess. There were always errands to run and tasks to perform, from simple pieces of sewing to strewing the rushes with toadflax after a sudden plague of fleas. Catrin's days were so full that she had small time to think beyond her physical duties. When she fell into bed at night, it was to deep and dreamless sleep. In the morning, she would awaken refreshed and hungry for the experiences of a new day.

Occasionally the thought of Oliver crossed her mind, but she had no time to dwell on him. The sight of him sprawled beside the whore in a heap of straw had filled her with contempt, but no great degree of surprise. She had told him to face himself and he had chosen a wine cup as his mirror and a slut to aid his forgetfulness. Still, she had been disappointed, for she had thought better of him. She had half expected him to seek her out before he left on the Earl's business, but he had not and she had put him aside for more worthwhile concerns.

The thought of Oliver made one of its brief, troublesome appearances now as she attended the Countess in Earl

Robert's solar. Thomas and Richard were present in their capacity as pages to pour the wine and run errands, should the need arise. Richard was self-consciously resplendent in a new tunic of holly-green wool with scarlet braid. Although he tried to keep a straight face, a grin kept threatening his mouth corners whenever he looked at Catrin. She had not seen a great deal of him since he had migrated to the squires' dorter, but enough to know that he was happy in his new position and making rapid progress.

He served her wine, and the grin split all the way across his face. Catrin yearned to give him a big hug, but made do with complimenting him on his fine new clothes and the polished manners he was acquiring.

'He's learned all that he knows from me,' Thomas interrupted cheekily as he returned his own flagon to the enormous carved sideboard.

'Well, that's a mixed blessing,' Catrin said dryly.

Richard was summoned away to put fresh logs on the fire. Catrin's gaze drifted to the garden mural of the two young women. Some of the paint had begun to flake. The dark girl's yellow dress was in need of refurbishment, and the blond one had lost part of her hand, but still their vibrancy dominated the room.

Richard went the rounds with the flagon, returning to her last. 'That's my mother,' he said, seeing the direction of her gaze.

Catrin was startled. 'How do you know?'

'Earl Robert told me. He said he had it painted when she lived here as his ward.'

'Truly?' Catrin stared at the mural with new eyes. Apart from the swirling blond hair, there was a slight resemblance to Amice, although it was more of essence than actual physical feature.

'Truly,' nodded the boy. 'The Earl says that I can come and look whenever I want.'

Behind Amice the second girl danced, a chaplet of flowers in her winding, dark tresses. Her features were thin and sharp, and she had the darting quality of a bird in flight. 'Who is her companion?' Catrin asked, and thought that she already knew.

'Her name's Emma and she used to be the Earl's ward too. She married Sir Oliver, but then she died.' The boy gave a small shrug and departed to another summons from the Earl.

Catrin stared at Emma Pascal and thought of Oliver, of what it must be like to see his dead wife's effigy every time he had to attend upon the Earl. Small wonder if his wounds were slow to heal.

She was still pondering the matter when the Countess dismissed her, so it was a shock to enter the courtyard and almost bump into Oliver himself, his garments travel-stained and his eyes red-rimmed by the irritation of dust.

Catrin greeted him in a flustered fashion, feeling embarrassed and guilty, emotions she would certainly not have experienced had Richard not told her about the painting. It was as if she had poked into a private corner of Oliver's life and been caught in the act.

He returned her greeting politely, but avoided her eyes and showed no inclination to stop and talk. 'I have to report to the Earl,' he said.

Catrin nodded. He would go to the Earl's solar, she thought, and be forced to gaze upon that mural. Perhaps she was misjudging him. Perhaps it gave him comfort. How would she feel if a wall in the keep bore the image of Lewis? She did not know. Before she could speak and break the awkwardness between them, Oliver excused himself and hastened on his way.

Catrin gnawed her lip and wondered if he had decided to wash his hands of her after their last volatile encounter. That would explain why he had avoided her before he left and his aloofness now. But she would rather he 'burst his hauberk' than keep her at arm's length.

Later that afternoon she was simmering honey and wine with powdered mustard seed to make a soothing syrup for sore throats when Oliver came to the shelter. Ethel had hobbled off to visit a newly delivered mother and had dissuaded Catrin from accompanying her. Catrin was amused at the midwife's insistence that she remain behind and mix potions. It was gratifying that Ethel trusted her to make the easy ones on her own, but she knew that it also gave the old woman a chance to sit and gossip with the new infant's grandmother who was a particular friend.

Catrin stirred the mixture and used a thick woollen mitt to set it on the hot hearth tiles to simmer. Then she stole a dribble of honeycomb and smeared it on an oatcake. It still lacked a couple of hours to the evening meal and she was already starving.

A shadow darkened the entrance of the shelter. Her mouth bulging, crumbs on her bosom and her fingers and cheeks sticky with honey, she gave a squeak of alarm and stared at Oliver with huge eyes.

'I didn't mean to startle you,' he said. 'I've come looking for Ethel.' He still wore his quilted gambeson and sword belt but had removed his mail.

Catrin shook her head and, putting the syrup to one side, pointed to her mouth.

He looked at her and his lips twitched. Glancing around the shelter, he located the bowl of oatcakes and helped himself to one. 'She's been busy with the baking stone, I see,' he remarked.

Unable to speak, Catrin chewed frantically and forced herself to swallow, almost choking in the process. Jesu, why couldn't he appear just once when she was neat and presentable? She poured herself a beaker of water and helped the last remnants down her throat. 'Ethel won't be back for a while. She's gone to check on a mother and stayed to gossip with the relatives.'

'And left you to mind the fire?'

She shrugged. 'It's no hardship.'

'With these for company, I can see why.' He bit into the oatcake.

'There's honey if you want.' She brought him the comb, her embarrassment fading. At least he was meeting her gaze and speaking to her. Perhaps looking at the mural of his wife had been of benefit after all.

Actually, Catrin was closer to the truth than she realised. When he had encountered her in the bailey, Oliver had been preoccupied with the report he had to make. He had also been caught off his guard, unsure of his reception after the way they had parted, and he had opted for distance. Standing in the Earl's solar, confronted once again by the mural's macabre charisma, he had cursed himself for a fool. If not buried, the past was dead. It was stupid to yearn after a two-dimensional portrait rendered by another hand when the full-blooded colours of life were all around him.

'Why did you want Ethel?'

'Lice,' he said. 'I've been bitten to death the past fortnight, and one of them has rubbed on my gambeson and turned septic. I need to take a staves-acre bath.'

'Lice?' Her eyebrows rose towards her kerchief, and then she pursed her lips. 'Serves you right,' she said. 'I'll warrant you caught them off that whore.'

He cleared his throat. 'Likely I did.' There was no point in making excuses. 'I suppose she had to give me something for my money.'

Catrin sniffed and turned away to seek amongst Ethel's earthenware pots and jars. 'Well, if lice are all that you got, you can count yourself fortunate. There is a disease going around the dockside whores that rots the private parts of any man who lies with them, and Ethel says that there's no cure.'

'I lay beside her, not inside her,' Oliver defended, his complexion darkening, for even to think of the incident filled him with chagrin. 'Christ knows, I was too deep in my cups to have either the will or the way when it came to the act.'

'Praise God for small mercies,' she muttered sarcastically. 'It's the first time I've heard drunkenness extolled as a salvation.'

'It was better than facing myself,' he said deliberately, his eyes on her spine as she swooped in triumph on two small blue jars.

Her back remained turned, but he saw her pause. 'Not better,' she said, 'but easier.'

'Jesu, you're hard. I come to make amends and all you do is assault me with your scold's tongue.'

Now she did turn round, hazel eyes flashing. 'Amends?'

she said scathingly. 'I thought you were here to rid yourself of lice. Am I supposed to heal your sore conscience as well?'

'You could try not grinding salt into it for a start.'

She glared at him, then made a small sound through her teeth and thrust one of the blue jars into his hand. 'Fill a tub with water as hot as you can bear, and mix this in,' she said. 'Then bathe in it until it grows cold. You will need to take daily baths until the lice are no more.'

He cupped the jar in his hands, and wondered if it was a dismissal. He did not want it to be.

She removed the stopper from the other jar and looked at him with pursed lips. 'Show me where the bites are septic.'

'They're under my shirt.'

'Well, take it off then,' she said with laboured patience. 'How can I treat the place without seeing it?'

Oliver set his jar on the floor and stood up. Unlatching his sword belt, he removed his gambeson, tunic and shirt. He was uncomfortably aware of people pausing to stare as they went about their business. There was a woven hanging that acted as a screen, but it was tied up out of the way.

'Don't scowl, it's bad for custom,' Catrin said tartly, and indicated that he should be seated again. 'I need the light to see what I'm doing,' she added, as if reading his mind.

The fresh air was cool on his naked skin and soothed the hot itchiness of the rash. He heard Catrin cluck her tongue as she looked at the patch which his gambeson had inflamed. 'If you're riding out again, you'll need to keep it bandaged, but otherwise you must leave it open to the air as much as you can.'

'You mean walk around shirtless?'

'Yes.'

He heard a glimmer of amusement in her voice. Her hand on the back of his neck was cool and sent a small shiver through him, but not of cold.

'This will hurt,' she murmured, 'but only for a moment.'

'I knew you were going to say that.' He braced himself, but still hissed in pain as she cleaned the affected area with a cloth soaked in astringent lotion.

'Salt water with scabious,' she told him. 'Then I'll put on a light smearing of comfrey ointment to soothe the itching. After you have bathed, you must anoint yourself again or, if you cannot reach, get someone to do it for you.'

The stinging pain of the first lotion was replaced by the soothing cool of the balm. He felt the gentle touch of her fingertips, and sensed her closeness behind him. 'You have learned a great deal in a very short space of time,' he said, probing gently at the subject which had caused their quarrel, seeking an opening.

'I am keen to learn and Ethel is a good teacher.' Her voice was suddenly wary.

Keeping his own voice quiet and reasonable, he said, 'I know that it is your chosen path and I have no doubt that in time you will make a worthy successor to Ethel, but I meant what I said before.'

'Which part?' Hostility had joined the wariness now.

He turned on the stool to face her so that she could see his expression was open and candid. 'The part about midwifery and herb-lore being dangerous trades. No, hear me out.' He raised his hand as she drew breath to argue. 'I admit, I would far rather that you stayed in the bower or took up ale-brewing or spinning to support your widowhood, but it's not worth the quarrel. Trying to change you would be like warping a loom out of true, and I doubt I would like the end result.' He glanced down at her feet, prepared to make a humorous comment concerning her scarlet hose, but she wasn't wearing any at all.

'But you don't like the one presented to you either,' Catrin said, eyeing him narrowly.

'Only part of it, and I would rather learn to live with it than without the whole.'

Colour flooded Catrin's face. She moved behind him again and continued smearing the salve. 'And if I say like it all or nothing?'

'Then you also would be warping a loom out of true.'

There was a long silence. Catrin attended to her task with a thoroughness that insulated her. He felt the touch of her fingers, but not of her mind.

'If it is not enough, then I am sorry. There is no more I can say to mend the rift between us.' He tensed, preparing to rise, but the pressure of her fingers increased, bidding him stay.

'Then say nothing more. If not all, then it is indeed enough.'

He turned again to look up at her. Her colour was still high and the wariness had not entirely left her expression, but there was a gleam in her eyes and the hint of a curve to her lips. 'And is it not said that enough is as good as a feast to a starving man?'

She snorted with reluctant amusement and gave him a gentle push. 'Go and take your bath. Even if we are to be friends again, I don't want to share your lice!'

'Scold,' he grinned.

'I give as good as I get,' she retorted, laughter dancing in her eyes.

Oliver was enchanted. He wanted to grab her waist and swing her round in his arms, but wisely forbore. Their relationship was on an even keel again and he was not about to rock the boat. 'Well, may all your "gettings" be fortunate ones,' he answered mischievously for the pleasure of seeing her blush. 'Just one question. What happened to your red hose? Have you suddenly become a staid and respectable matron?'

'I have always been a staid and respectable matron,' Catrin said flippantly, then shook her head with a regretful sigh. 'The Countess's lap dog took a fancy to chew them when I left them on my pallet, and they're beyond repair. The Countess gave me a pair of her own, but they're brown wool and they wrinkle and fall down unless I add yards of leg binding. I have never considered myself a vain woman – how could I and wear a dress like this? But until the cold weather bites, I would rather go without. You need not laugh,' she added, setting her hands on her hips.

'I wasn't.' Oliver swallowed so hard that he almost choked. 'I count it a great tragedy.'

'Your bath,' she said sternly, and made a shooing motion. Oliver leaned back into the shelter to grab another of Ethel's oatcakes, and made off with a spring in his stride that had not been present before.

Shaking her head, Catrin took an oatcake herself and stooped to revive the fire with the bellows, her own movements light and joyful.

CHAPTER 10

The summer months ripened into autumn, and autumn in its turn yielded to the fallow season of winter. Catrin spent less time with the Countess and her women, and more in Ethel's shelter, absorbing knowledge about herbs and simples, and attending births with the elderly midwife. Catrin did not care that Ethel made her work her hands and brain to the bone, for she was learning and she was happy. The world of the bower was a stultifying cage of petty jealousies. Ethel might be grouchy and irascible on occasion, but whatever she had to say was said and then forgotten, not whispered behind her hand or left to fester.

Measuring Catrin's progress, Ethel began to delegate responsibility. In late August, Catrin delivered her first infant under Ethel's supervision. A month later, she attended the birth of one of the soldier's women on her own.

From diagnosing and treating simple ailments, she moved on to those which required more complex remedies, blending the herbs and mixing the potions under Ethel's watchful but uninterfering eye.

Oliver supped at their fire when his duties did not take him away from Bristol. Catrin warmed to his companionship and found herself missing him on the nights when he did not come by. Sometimes Ethel would retire to her bed-bench, grumbling about her old bones and late hours, leaving Catrin and Oliver talking softly over the dying fire. Other nights, they would stay in the keep, listening to the minstrels and playing at dice and tafel.

One bitter evening in late November, they were sitting over

Oliver's wooden tafel board in the great hall. The wind could not pierce the thick stonework of the castle, but it whistled in at the window embrasures with a vengeance and thrust icy fingers beneath the door at the hall's far end. The huge fireplace gave off little heat except to those sitting almost on top of the flames and belched smoke at them for the privilege.

'Emma used to hate the winter,' Oliver said with a glance around the barn-like hugeness of the room. 'If she had had her way, we would all have hibernated like squirrels or hedge-pigs until April.'

He occasionally spoke of his dead wife these days. Catrin had noted that when he did, it was always with a slight narrowing of his eyes, as if he were seeing her from a distance. He ought to let Emma vanish over the horizon rather than try to draw her closer, Catrin thought, but did not say so. She felt the same way about Lewis and it was easier said than done to let go of the past.

'I mislike the chilblains and the way that the days are over before they can begin,' she said. 'But there is much to enjoy as well – the Christmas feast, the beauty of snow seen from within a room lit by a roaring fire, with the comfort of mulled wine. Lewis and I used to . . .' She bit off the rest of the sentence and gave a short laugh, realising how easy it was to fall into the trap of 'once upon a time'.

'Used to what?' He looked at her with a poignant half smile on his lips.

She shook her head self-consciously. 'Nothing, it doesn't matter.'

'Yes, it does. What used you to do?'

Catrin sighed. 'We used to lie beneath the covers, wrapped in each other's arms, while the wind howled like a wolf. There was nothing but us and the winter storm . . . nothing.' Her throat tightened and she swallowed.

'With us it was the summer, on a cloak beneath a night thick with stars,' he murmured.

They looked at each other. 'Lord, what fools,' he said with a down-turned smile and a shake of his head. Without any purpose, he picked up one of the tafel pieces and turned it round in his fingers.

'I know that it is Emma in the summer mural in the Earl's chamber,' she ventured cautiously. 'Richard told me. She must have been very pretty.'

'She was.' His expression was distant with remembering. 'I was offered the pick between Emma and Amice. Both had similar dowries and status. My family thought that I would choose Amice because she was as lovely as a ripe peach, but she held no appeal for me. I had grown up with a brother and parents all large and fair-haired. I craved difference, not more of the same.' He set the tafel piece gently down. 'She was dark and fey, gentle and shy as a doe, with a way of looking at me that made me feel like the king of the world. When she died, I became a beggar.'

'I know,' Catrin murmured.'It was the same for me when I lost Lewis.'

Once more their eyes met and held. He started to speak, but Catrin had heard no more than: 'I still have my begging bowl, but I no longer need—' when Ethel appeared at their side. Her cloak sparkled with water droplets and her ankle boots were splashed with greenish muck from the quagmire of the bailey. She was leaning heavily on a stick of carved hickory wood.

'I've to interrupt your gaming,' she said, the hint of a wheeze in her voice. 'Lora the soap-maker's wife is in travail and we're needed.' She touched Catrin's shoulder. 'Should be an easy birth. 'Tis her first, but she's broader in the beam than an abbot's barn. I've left everything ready by my hearth. We can pick it up as we leave.'

Catrin nodded and lifted her cloak off the bench. Another gift from the Countess, it was fashioned of grey wool with a fleece lining. It insulated her excellently against the cold, and it was so thick that it took a long time for rain to penetrate. There was no hood, but Catrin had bought one of those for herself from the market place. It was a perky, bright brown with a border of scarlet and yellow braid. She pulled it on now, over her wimple.

Ethel turned away, already limping towards the door. 'Make haste,' she said over her shoulder.

Oliver pushed the pieces aside. 'Do you want an escort?'

Ethel paused and shook her head. 'No, they've sent the journeyman and the apprentice to fetch us.' She turned fully and looked at him, the seams around her black eyes deepening. 'We'll be home 'afore cock-crow, whole, hearty and rich.'

'I hope so,' Oliver said woodenly.

'Folk know better than to interfere with a midwife about her lawful business. 'Tis as deep as an unspoken curse. At dawn, you come to my fire and I'll give you fresh oatcakes to break your fast.' She gave him a nod of supreme confidence and went on her way.

'She's right, you know,' Catrin said, and lightly touched his arm. 'Our trade endangers us, but equally it protects us.'

'Just have a care.' He gave her a dark look from beneath his brows.

'We always do.' She tightened her grip on his sleeve for an instant, then hastened after Ethel, her midwife's satchel bouncing at her side.

'They're gaining a reputation as the best midwives this side of the Avon, and not without cause,' said Geoffrey FitzMar, who had also watched the women leave the hall. He sat on the bench that Catrin had vacated, and rearranged the tafel pieces. 'I know for sure that they saved my son's life. Do you want another game?'

Oliver could hardly refuse. Besides, it was probably better than nursing his worries alone with a flagon. He gestured assent.

'You must be proud of them.'

'Hah, I have small say in the matter!' Oliver declared somewhat bitterly.

FitzMar looked puzzled. 'I thought they were beholden to you.'

Oliver opened his mouth to tell FitzMar about Ethel in precise detail, but thought the better of it before the words emerged. She frequently enraged and exasperated him, but beneath her tough exterior was an ailing and vulnerable old woman. And as to Catrin . . . He thought of her frowning in concentration over her next move on the tafel board because she was determined he would not defeat her. He remembered how she had squeezed his arm. 'Be that as it may,' he said, 'they go their own way, and yes, I am proud of them – your move.'

As Ethel had predicted, the birth of Lora's baby was simple and straightforward. The infant, a son, was large and yelled lustily the moment he emerged into the air. Lora neither tore as she pushed him out, nor bled more than a trickle, and the afterbirth emerged smooth and whole within moments of the infant's delivery.

The ecstatic father paid the midwives twice the agreed fee of a shilling each, presenting them with twenty-four silver pennies apiece. He also gave them both a jar of soap. It was not the usual grey, strong-smelling liquid used for washing linen, but was thicker, flecked with green and delicately scented with lavender and rosemary. This was a much rarer and more costly soap for washing of the person, and increased their wages twofold again.

Their thanks were waved away with a declaration that it was no more than their due, and after a warming drink of spiced mead they set out for the keep, escorted by the two manservants and in high good spirits.

They passed the church of Saint Mary and took the lane that ran through the butchers' Shambles, the crowded wattle and daub houses to their left and the Avon gleaming on their right. Fishing craft and rowing boats were moored up for the night. There were piles of nets and twists of rope, the plash of starlit water and the heavy smell of the river.

'What I would like to do,' Catrin announced, touching the outline of the soap jar in her satchel, 'is to immerse myself in a steaming hot tub, and perfume my skin all over.'

'Hah!' Ethel wheezed. 'If you did it in this weather, my girl, you'd freeze your nipples off!'

The men escorting them snorted with laughter. Catrin put her nose in the air. 'It was only a wish,' she said, feeling foolish.

'Aye, well, you'd do better to sell it and buy yourself an

extra chemise for when the snow comes. 'Tis what I'm going to do.' Ethel looked at her slyly. 'But then I don't have a man to impress, do I?'

Before Catrin could find a suitably withering retort, there was a shout behind them, and they turned to see a thin, middle-aged woman in threadbare garments crying at them to stop.

'Are you the two midwives from the castle?' she demanded as she ran up to them. Her breath crowed in her throat and her eyes were wild. A lantern guttered in her hand. 'Someone said they had seen you pass.'

'We are.' Ethel leaned on her stick and appraised the woman shrewdly.

'Then praise God. Come swiftly, I beg you, it's my daughter.' She gestured over her shoulder to the maze of lanes and alleys in the darkness of the Shambles. 'I can't stop the bleeding, I don't know what to do!'

'All right, calm yourself, mistress, we'll come,' Ethel said, and waved her hand at the two men. 'Best return to your master. I do not know how long we will be.'

The woman led them into the dark thoroughfares of the Shambles. Despite the straw that had been thrown down to make walking easier, mud still splashed their clothing and seeped through the stitches in their shoes. Behind the fairly prosperous houses that fronted the street were others which were not as well kept – mean dwellings with scarcely room for a meagre central hearth. Ethel could spare no breath to ask questions as they walked, and so it was left to Catrin to interrogate and discover that they were being called to attend not a birth, but a miscarriage.

'Four months she's been carrying,' the woman said. 'My first grandchild. I'm not saying as we wanted the babe, but once she caught, we never tried to get rid of it.'

'Husband?' Catrin queried.

'Hasn't got one. Father could be one of several.'

By which Catrin understood that they were being taken to see one of the town whores who had got herself into difficulties. It never occurred to her to baulk. Having served Amice and having seen the lot of women who were forced to sell their bodies to earn a crust, her censure was reserved for the men who used and misused them.

'If I ever catch the bastard who did this to her,' said the mother, 'I will geld him with my own two hands and make him eat his own ballocks. And then I will cut his throat.' She brought them to a wattle and daub dwelling, its low thatched roof rank and damp. They paddled through the muddy soup to reach the single door and entered a dark, fetid room. The smell of poverty was all-pervading and filled the air which was almost as cold within as without. A fire burned, but it fed on a single log, and there were only two pieces of split wood left in the wicker basket by the central hearth. The cooking pot that hung over the single lick of flame contained about two quarts of lukewarm water. Light, such as there was, came from the weak glow of the fire and a sputtering mutton-fat dip pinched in a rusty iron holder.

By the dim illumination, Catrin could only just make out the shape of a young woman lying on a bed-bench along the hut's side. Her knees were drawn up towards her belly, and she was stifling small, animal sounds of pain against the back of her hand.

The mother went straight to the bed and, kneeling, smoothed her daughter's wet hair. 'It's all right, sweetheart, look, I've found the midwives. They'll help you now.'

Catrin joined the woman and, with a soothing murmur, drew back the threadbare blanket the girl was clutching. There was blood but, with so little light, it was hard to tell how much. Very gently, she eased the stained chemise above the young woman's hips, and then caught her breath at the sight of the bruises and bite marks on her belly and thighs. 'Jesu!' she whispered, recoiling despite herself.

'Aye,' said the mother grimly. 'Gelding's not good enough for the likes o' him.'

Catrin swallowed, feeling nauseous. There were red lines on the girl's body too, as if someone had impressed her flesh with the mark of a sharp fingernail or the point of a knife. 'Who did this?'

'She won't say. He told her he'd rip her properly if she made a complaint, the hellspawn.'

Ethel pushed her way forward. She was still wheezing after her brisk walk, but able enough to take command of the situation. Bringing out the pouch of coins that the soap-maker had given her, she counted some into the mother's palm. 'For firewood and candles, if you can find someone to sell them to you this time of night,' she said curtly.

For a moment, the woman stared numbly at the silver in her hand, then shook herself. 'The Star might have them,' she said. 'Adela works there – or she did.' She looked at Ethel. 'I cannot repay you.'

'Never mind about that, just go,' Ethel said with an impatient wave of her hand. 'If we are to save your daughter, we need light and warmth. If you're off to an alehouse, a jug of wine wouldn't come amiss either.'

The woman vanished and Catrin and Ethel set to work, although there was not a great deal they could do except clean the young woman, apply a pad of folded, soft linen between her thighs, and ease her pain with a tisane made from the tepid water in the cooking pot. The child, visibly a little girl and perfect in every way except her ability to exist outside the womb, was born a little after dawn. The room by then was warmer and the morning light augmented the extra rush dips burning around the bed. Catrin could see now that their patient was very young. Sixteen the mother said, but a sixteen stunted by years of malnutrition. Whoever her partners had been, their desire had been for a child, not a fully fledged woman, and what the last one had done to her to slake his lust was sickening. The girl would not speak about him. Even a gentle question brought terror to her eyes. The most they could glean, and this from the ale-wife at The Star who brought a fresh flagon of wine and a loaf of bread to break their fast, was that it had been a soldier from the castle, one of the Earl's mercenaries, and she too was reluctant to speak out.

'Even if we make a complaint, the Earl will just put it down to high spirits going too far. Fighting men have to vent their hot blood when they're not in the field. He'll not listen to the likes of us. He'll say that she knew the risks when she became a whore.'

Which was probably true, Catrin thought unhappily. God might have time to see the fall of the meanest sparrow, but Earl Robert, despite his kindness to herself and Richard, was not so well disposed towards every waif and stray.

At least the girl was going to live, she thought, and then wondered how much of a blessing that was. Her mother was a widow who literally earned their bread by selling loaves on the street for a baker, in exchange for some of his produce. Adela had been selling her body for the past year to keep them warm and shod.

In a spurt of guilt and compassion, Catrin gave the girl's mother all but six pence from her twenty-four. Ethel watched and said nothing. She had parted with coins herself for light, warmth and wine.

A dull, grey November day had reached full light by the time the two women left the house and started back through the mud towards the castle.

'Good thing she lost the babe,' Ethel said, leaning heavily on her stick. As she walked, the base of it disappeared in three inches of mud. 'Her hips are too small to carry a nine-months child, kill her for sure.'

Catrin's eyes were so hot and gritty that it was difficult to keep them open, and one of her spectacular headaches was just waiting to pounce. She could feel it growing at the back of her skull, rather like the gathering of a thunderstorm. 'She might yet die if the fever sets in.'

'Oh aye, she might,' Ethel agreed, and paused for a moment to rest. The night had taken its toll on her too, and she was blue around the lips.

Catrin thought unhappily of the young whore she had seen snoring in the straw at Oliver's side in the summer. How easy it was for men to get hold of these undernourished girls to slake their lust. So easy that they did not stop to think. For the whores it was simple too; sell their bodies or starve.

Her thoughts were abruptly curtailed by the sight of two men slinking out from a noisome entry to block their path. They brandished nail-studded clubs and their garments were patched and tattered although, incongruously, one of them wore an expensive wool hat trimmed with ermine fur. Ethel tightened her grip on her stick and drew herself upright. Catrin backed up, shielding Ethel with her body.

The ruffian with the cap smiled, revealing a mouthful of worn-down teeth. 'Two plump pigeons ripe for the plucking. Give us your pouches.' He thrust out his free hand.

Catrin's breathing quickened. 'We have no money. We're honest midwives about our duties. Let us go our way in peace.'

'No such thing as an honest midwife,' the other sneered, and took a menacing step forward. 'Come on, your money now, or you'll make the acquaintance of my cudgel.'

'Touch either of us, and I will set a curse on you!' spat Ethel, shaping her hand like a claw. 'I can, you know, and by Hecate, I will.'

They hesitated, licking their lips, looking at each other. Catrin tried to feel for the small, sharp knife at her belt without being conspicuous. She also filled her lungs with a huge breath, ready to scream for aid at the top of her voice.

'Reckon as we're damned already,' the man with the hat said. 'Your curses mean nothing, old woman, except they'll send you to hell before us.' He made a grab for Ethel, whilst his companion leaped on Catrin. She released the scream, shattering the morning air with its power, and at the same time jerked her knee hard upward. Her assailant recoiled, clutching his genitals, and Catrin whipped the small dagger from its sheath, full knowing that it was an act of bravado. She could cut umbilical cords and prepare herbs with the blade, but never had she used it in aggression or even self-defence.

She dodged a blow from the cudgel, but was not fast enough, and it caught her arm, breaking no bones but severely bruising. As Ethel was thrown to the ground by the other thief, Catrin screamed again in desperation and prayed for doors to open and people to come.

Oliver spent a restless, uncomfortable night. Being one of the Earl's hearth knights meant just that, and he had to sleep beside the fire in the great hall, rolled in his cloak. The snores and coughs of the other men kept him awake, as did the knowledge that Ethel and Catrin were abroad in the city. The fact that they had an escort dampened his worry, but did not quench it entirely. They were still so vulnerable. And yet he dared not protest too hard lest he be accused of obstructing and stifling.

'Women,' he muttered to himself as he turned over for what seemed the hundredth time.

'Aye, bless them,' muttered Geoffrey FitzMar who was rolled up beside him.

Despite himself, Oliver gave a short laugh. 'Aye, bless them,' he repeated, and closed his eyes.

For a while he slept, and chased brightly coloured images through his dreams. He was in a garden looking for Emma, but he could not find her. Amice was there and she kept pointing towards a grove of apple trees. But when he entered the grove in search of his wife, all he discovered was a mound of green earth that looked like an overgrown grave. He turned away, but when he looked back Catrin was sitting on it, stark naked except for her masses of raven-black hair and her crimson hose which ended just above her knees, in bright contrast to the white flesh of her thighs.

With a gasp, he snapped awake to find himself tangled in his cloak. Dull heat pulsed at his crotch and his body was damp with sweat. It was not the first erotic nightmare he had ever had, but it was certainly the most disturbing. The man beside him still slept, oblivious, but all around him others were rising. The fire in the hearth was blazing strongly and tendrils of steam rose from the cooking pot set over the flames. A glance at the high windows showed him that dawn had broken.

Untangling himself from his cloak, he went outside to piss and then washed his hands and face at the trough by the well. It was a murky November morning with a hint of drizzle that swiftly cooled the sweat on his body and banished any carnal residue from his dream. Although it was not long past dawn, a steady exchange of traffic between castle and town was well under way. Supplies and traders entered. Soldiers left.

Oliver watched the activity while he pinned his cloak and accustomed himself to the idea of being awake. His stomach rumbled, and he thought with anticipation of Ethel's hot griddle cakes, smeared with honey and butter – far better fare than the bowl of gruel he could expect in the hall. But it was not the thought of breakfast alone that sent him in the direction of Ethel's shelter. As he walked, he smoothed his hair and plucked a stray stalk of straw from his cloak. He also cupped his chin and grimaced to feel the prick of stubble. He should have taken the time to shave, but it was too late now.

With a swift step and rapid heart, he approached Ethel's shelter. The woven hanging was drawn across, but when he parted it to glance inside and see if the women were sleeping, it was empty, the hearth cold, and the coverlet on the bed-bench neatly arranged.

'They're not here,' said one of the laundry women as she passed by with a basket of soiled linen. 'I called at first light for something to cure me toothache and there was no sign.'

'They've been out all night then,' Oliver said, with a sinking heart.

'Like as not. I ain't seen 'em for certes, but I wish they'd hurry back. Me gob's killing me.' She went on her way, leaving Oliver gazing around the shelter. Despite the cheerful bedcovering, the rows of jars, sealed pig bladders and bunches of herbs, the place looked forlorn without its occupants. Ethel had said that they would return by daybreak. He glanced at the sky which had been light for perhaps an hour. They were not unduly late, but he could feel the apprehension gathering within him.

He forced himself to return to the hall and act as if this was just another morning. He ate a bowl of hot gruel without any enthusiasm, barbered his stubble, and returned to check on the shelter, but it was still as empty as before. Thoroughly unsettled by now, Oliver hitched his belt and set off at a determined pace towards the castle gates.

Once in the city, he made his way to the home of Payne the soap-maker and was greeted first with surprise, and then some consternation when the household learned of his enquiry. The manservant and journeyman were fetched from their tasks and made to tell their tale about the poor woman who had come begging Ethel and Catrin's help in the Shambles.

With increasing apprehension, Oliver turned his feet in that direction, but he had little idea where to look among all the back entrances that twisted through the quarter like the animal guts from which the Shambles took its name. Enquiries led him nowhere. The butchers had all been abed in the early hours, and those who had not had good reason to avoid a man with a sword.

His right hand on its hilt, Oliver left the main thoroughfares and entered the narrower alleys, his shoes squelching in mud and dung. A dog growled as it dashed past him, a dead rat dangling from its jaws. Two grimy little boys contemplated throwing pats of mud at him, but changed their minds when he drew an inch of blade from his scabbard. A door opened a crack and then slammed shut. Oliver drew another inch of steel, both as a warning to any hidden watchers and as a reassurance to himself.

Then he heard the scream over to his left, piercing and shrill. Cursing, he began to run – something of a feat in the November sludge of Bristol's back alleys. A second scream brought him to a narrow thoroughfare and a scene that drew his blade clean out of the scabbard in a single rasp of steel. The two men turned, cudgels raised, but on seeing the calibre and rage of their opposition, took to their heels.

Already breathless from his run, Oliver didn't pursue. Sword still in his right hand, he used his left to raise Ethel gently to her feet. Her breath wheezed in her throat, and she was trembling from head to toe. She braced herself upon her stick for support, but her eyes were bright and black with the light of battle.

'They'll come to bad ends, the both of them,' she panted. 'And I need neither my wise-woman's sight nor a curse to predict that certainty.' She gave him a sharp look. 'How did you know?'

'You said you would be home before cock-crow. When you weren't, I came looking for you.' His tone bore no expression, for he knew that if he began to rant at the women he would never stop, and this time there would be no healing the breach.

He looked at Catrin. Her hood was down, her wimple

askew, baring her black braids. A spot of colour branded each cheekbone, and there was a small knife clenched so tightly in her hand that her knuckles were bone-white on the wooden haft. She was still gasping like a man on a battlefield.

The street had begun to fill with people, both the concerned and the morbidly curious. Ethel was offered a drink of ale, and someone brought out a three-legged stool so that she could sit down. Oliver returned his sword to his scabbard. 'Put up your knife,' he said quietly to Catrin, with a nod at her right hand.

'What?' She gazed at the small weapon blankly for a moment, then with trembling fingers did as he bade. A wooden beaker of ale was pressed into her hand. Everyone was talking at once, but their chatter meant nothing to her.

'A young woman had been raped by one of the castle soldiers and was miscarrying her child,' she said defensively. 'We couldn't just leave her to die.'

'No, of course you couldn't.'

Her jaw tightened. She looked at him with glittering eyes.

'I mean it,' Oliver deflected swiftly. 'It is no less than I expected you to say, although I suspect that this,' he gestured at Ethel, 'is more than you had in mind.'

'We were unfortunate,' Catrin said stiffly.

'To the contrary, you are more lucky than you know.' When she opened her mouth to argue, he laid a forefinger against her lips. 'No more, or we will both say things that we will regret. For now, my priority is to see you and Ethel safe back to the keep and alert the watch about those two ruffians.'

She swallowed and nodded. Then she swallowed again and compressed her lips, her complexion greenish-white.

His gaze sharpened and he swore softly beneath his breath. Turning to the woman who had brought the ale and the stool, he haggled the use of her donkey for a penny and deliberated which of the two women was going to sit on it.

'I can manage,' Catrin said grimly between clenched teeth. 'Let Ethel ride.'

Oliver studied her, then nodded. Pride, if nothing else, would keep her upright until they reached the castle.

While the woman held the ass, he helped Ethel on to its

bony, scooped back. He had always viewed the old woman as being physically solid and strong. In his youth, the back-swipe of her arm had floored a village brat on many an occasion, so he was disconcerted to discover that she weighed next to nothing. She was like a bird, her bones hollow for the flight of her soul. Her spirit, however, had no intention of departing just yet, and it was with relief that he heard her remark tartly that she was not a sack of cabbages.

Clicking his tongue to the donkey, he turned it round. 'A sack of cabbages would not cause me so much trouble,' he retorted, and held out his arm for Catrin to lean on. It was a measure of her own wretchedness that she took it without demur.

CHAPTER 11

'Go on, say it,' Catrin challenged.

'Say what?' Oliver spread his hands, his breath clouding the air. Around them frost glittered like loaf sugar. Ice, a fingernail thick, lay in clear, angular patterns on the waterbutts and troughs, and the mud in the bailey had become a pliable, white-crusted clay.

'That you were right and I was wrong.'

'About what?'

'About being open to attack.' She stamped her feet, with both impatience and cold. She could see that he was going to make her pay by drawing the incident out. He had been absent on the Earl's business yesterday. She and Ethel had stayed by the fire, nursing their bruises. 'You told me that I was vulnerable, and I ignored you.'

'No less than I expected.' He blew on his cupped hands. 'You were bound to learn the hard way.'

'I hate you,' she said calmly.

'That's no less than I expected either. How's your head today?'

'It aches, but it belongs to me again.' She touched her forehead and grimaced slightly at the niggle of pain still lingering behind her eyes.

'And Ethel?'

'Somewhat shaken despite all her brave words. I've left her by the fire with a hot tisane and one of her gossips for company – old Agatha from the laundry.'

'So your time is your own for a little while?'

'Unless the Countess sends for me.' Catrin cocked her head on one side and eyed him suspiciously. 'Why?'

'I have something for you.' He took her arm, and led her across the bailey towards the Countess's garden.

'Where are we going?' Utterly baffled, Catrin hung back a little. She hardly thought that he was going to present her with a flower in this bleak weather, or take her for a stroll around the dormant herb beds. If he wanted somewhere private to talk, there were warmer places than a pleasance at the end of November.

But his direction did not alter, and within moments they had entered through the gate and into a world on the edge of dormancy. The soil was turned and brown, each clod wearing a frill of hoar. The herb beds still held tinges of colour, the sage and lavender standing bravely against the cold. The mint was straggly and the tansy and rue had bowed their heads. Of the gardener, the only sign was the scent of frying bacon wafting from the tiny thatched hut on the far right near the rows of leeks and cabbages.

'Well?' Catrin repeated.

He led her down one of the marked-out paths to a grassy ring, surrounded by stone benches. The Countess's women often came here in summer to sew and weave. Occasionally Mabile would hold small feasts and entertainments for selected guests. They would sit out until the moon rose in the sky, cooking morsels of marinated food over an open fire. Today the place was frozen and deserted, the grass blades wearing a white scaling of frost, and the stone benches bleak grey, untouched by any kindness of sun.

'Oliver, why have you brought me here?' she persisted, and hugged herself with cold.

For answer he reached beneath his cloak, tugged at his belt, and presented her with a knife – not one for eating or midwifery work, but a man's weapon with a sharp blue edge and a haft of decorated bone. 'I want you to carry this with you for protection when you go out into the city at night,' he said.

Catrin took the weapon but could not prevent a shudder. 'I don't know how to use it.'

'That's why you're here now – to learn. I saw the way you were holding that blade of yours when you were attacked. If you are going to draw a knife on someone, you have to know how to fight – not only that, but how to survive.'

Catrin shook her head. 'Oliver, I cannot . . .'

'No such word,' he said in a tone that refuted argument, and handed her a piece of wood which had been carved to the same shape as the knife. From his belt, he drew a similar piece. 'It's a skill as indispensable as any that Ethel's taught you.'

For the next hour, Catrin was instructed in the art of self-defence. At first she was self-conscious and unsure, her lunges half-hearted, because she felt foolish. 'Christ, who's to see you?' Oliver demanded. 'Why do you think I chose the gardens? There's only the old man and he's too busy breaking his fast to pay any attention to us! If it does not bother me, then it shouldn't bother you.'

'You're a man,' she said. 'This is customary to you.'

He rolled his eyes in disbelief. 'And it was a man who attacked you in the street! You are doing this for your life, woman. Don't tell me it is not in your nature to fight back. I know full well the measure of your mulishness.' He looked at her broodingly for a moment. 'Imagine that I am a robber, out for your purse and perhaps other things in the dead of night. How would you fight me off?'

'Throw pepper in your face and run,' she said quickly.

'With Ethel at your side?' he snorted. 'Or supposing I emerged from a side alley too swiftly for you to reach in your satchel for the pepper? If it was your intent the other morning, you failed miserably.'

Catrin reddened, but could not deny the truth of what he said. There had indeed been a pouch of pepper in her satchel, but buried near the bottom.

'Come at me again,' he said, beckoning.

Catrin sighed, pursed her lips and thrust with the wooden knife. Grey eyes dark with anger, Oliver grabbed her wrist and twisted it round, making her drop the knife; then he hooked his leg around hers and brought her down hard on the frozen grass. Straddling her, pinning her wrists above her head, he snarled, 'This is what could happen to you, and in no more space than an eye-blink . . . and worse.'

Catrin swallowed and stared up at the harsh planes of

his face, mere angry inches from hers. The frozen grass struck through her clothes and chilled her flesh. His grip was bruising, his weight took her breath. 'Let me go,' she said shakily.

'You know what an attacker would say,' he answered grimly, and held her down a moment longer before relaxing his grip and drawing her to her feet. Her teeth chattering, she glared at him as he brushed the frost from her cloak with the flat of his hand.

'Jesu, Catrin, I don't want to lose you. If you must go abroad in the street, then at least let it not be like a lamb to the slaughter. For all your fire and spirit, you would not survive as you are now. I am not suggesting that you become an Amazon, only that you should learn to defend yourself long enough to live. If you cannot unbend enough to do that, then what chance do you have?' His voice took on a pleading note.

She continued to scowl at him, wanting to capitulate but hampered by her pride. With a sigh, he turned from her and retrieved her wooden knife from the grass. 'When you can hold me off for a turn of the cook's small hourglass, I will consider that you have evened the odds. If you're angry with me, Catrin, then use it.' He held out the weapon. 'Take it and show me.'

'Angry with you?' She shook her head and closed her hand around the wooden haft. 'I am angry with myself.' She tilted the blade at the angle he had shown her earlier. 'Tell me again. The sooner I master this, the sooner I'll be rid of your lecturing.'

Their eyes met, held in challenge for a moment, then sparked at the same time with reluctant humour.

'My "lecturing" might just save your life,' he pointed out, struggling not to grin. 'Now, let's begin again. Disable, disarm and run.'

By the end of an hour, Catrin was no longer cold. Flushed and panting, all self-consciousness forgotten, she strove to hold Oliver at bay, making up for her lack of skill in sheer determination. Indeed, her moments of success, brief though they were, filled her with exhilaration and a certain rashness.

'Disable, disarm and run!' he yelled at her, laughing despite himself as he parried a swipe aimed at his belly. 'God's bones, you don't have to stay for the kill!'

'But what if I want to?' she gleamed back at him.

'Resist it, you're not good enough yet!' He wove beneath her guard, grabbed her wrist, and sent the dagger flying over her shoulder into the grass where their feet had imprinted patterns of green amongst the silver hoar blades. First she struggled against his grasp, then she didn't. She was acutely aware of the touch of his fingers on her wrist, the swift beat of her pulse against his encircling palm, their rapid breath mingling in the frozen air.

His hold relaxed and he ran his thumb over the delicate skin he had just been gripping. 'Disable, disarm,' he murmured again, and his other hand circled her waist and drew her against him. He lowered his head and, with closed eyes, Catrin raised hers.

'You must be desperate to seek a tryst out here.'

Catrin shot out of Oliver's embrace with a gasp and saw the old gardener leaning on his spade, watching the two of them with relish.

'And kill,' Oliver muttered beneath his breath.

Catrin was not sure if she was relieved at his intervention or not. Her loins were heavy, her flesh sensitive. How far would lust have progressed in a winter garden? She was not sure about that either.

'I like a woman who can fight, myself,' the gardener continued. 'Makes the conquest more interesting, doesn't it?'

Cheeks blazing, Catrin retrieved her wooden knife from the grass. Her plait had become unpinned and swung down beneath her wimple.

'I won't tell if you won't.' The old man hefted the spade. 'Long time since I been to confession anyway.' He screwed up his eyes. 'You're old Ethel's assistant, aren't you?'

'Yes, I am,' Catrin said, mustering the shreds of her dignity.

'You got anything for the ague, a nice warming liniment rub?' He waggled his eyebrows suggestively.

'You'll have to ask Ethel.' Despite herself, Catrin felt the urge to laugh at the old rogue. 'I'm learning still.'

'Aye, I can see that. It's a pleasure to watch.' With a wink at Oliver, the gardener stumped off to prod at a heap of manure. 'You let me know when you've got some experience, girl.'

Catrin stared after him, her arms akimbo, not knowing whether to laugh or be angry.

'I think I might wring the old buzzard's neck,' Oliver said softly.

Catrin turned and saw her own irritation and amusement reflected in his eyes. 'But he is right,' she replied. 'It is a desperate place for a tryst – in winter at least.'

For a moment he did not answer, then he spread his hands. 'Then would you consider somewhere warmer?'

She tilted her head on one side. 'For fighting or trysting?'

'Both, but I cannot promise the order.'

Despite the cold, Catrin felt as if she was melting. The last man to look at her like that had been Lewis in the early months of their marriage, when a single glance was all that it had taken to tumble them breathless into the nearest bed. But she was no longer a green and innocent girl and had no intention of tumbling into any sort of bed with Oliver – yet. She held back, keeping the two feet of distance that separated them, and holding her wooden knife as he had shown her. 'I never hold much trust in men's promises anyway,' she said.

'I keep mine.'

She bit her underlip and nodded. 'Aye, I know you do. So when you say that you cannot make one, it behoves me to be cautious.'

Before he could defend himself, their banter was curtailed by Gawin's arrival, his stride swift and agitated. 'Found you at last,' he addressed Catrin, not Oliver. 'You had best come swiftly. Ethel's taken a fall.'

'Oh, sweet Jesu!' Catrin thrust the wooden knife into Oliver's hand and pushed past Gawin at a run. Oliver followed hard on her heels.

Ethel lay on her pallet, her face grey. The laundress who

had been visiting sat beside her, offering comfort. When she saw Catrin, a look of deep relief crossed her face.

'She was standing up to bid me farewell, and she just turned giddy and fell,' said the woman, as she gave her place to Catrin.

'Fuss over nothing,' Ethel mumbled. 'Everyone feels light-headed when they rise. I just stumbled, that's all.' An egg-shaped lump was ballooning at her temple and there was a deep cut on her hand where she had caught the cauldron tripod as she fell.

'Maybe so, but better a fuss over nothing than paying no heed,' Catrin admonished and ran her hands lightly over the old woman to make sure that there was no other damage.

'You think I would not know if it was more than a trip?'

'Yes, I think you would,' Catrin said shrewdly and, with gentle hands, drew the fleece cover up over Ethel's shoulder.

Ethel met Catrin's stare. Then she closed her eyes. 'Tell the others to be gone. They block my light.'

Catrin rose and turned.

'I heard,' Oliver said with a wry smile and deliberately raised his voice. 'It is common knowledge that healers always make the worst patients.'

'There's nothing wrong with my hearing either,' Ethel rallied from her pallet. 'If there was, I wouldn't have to listen to you.'

Oliver's smile became a grin. 'I'm going,' he capitulated. Facing Catrin, he tugged the end of her black braid where it showed beneath her disordered wimple. 'Fight or tryst,' he murmured, 'don't let me wait too long.'

Catrin reddened and responded with a brusque nod. 'I won't.' She glanced over her shoulder at Ethel who was watching them through supposedly lowered lids.

Oliver stooped to kiss Catrin's cheek. As his lips brushed her skin, he murmured, 'She does not befool me for one moment either. Let me know how she really fares.' Then he straightened, saluted, and went on his way, ushering the laundry woman with him. Gawin had already left for an assignation with one of the kitchen maids.

Catrin returned to Ethel. The old woman's eyes were fully shut and she was breathing slowly and evenly, but Catrin was wiser than to believe the outward evidence.

'Ethel.' She knelt at the side of the bed-bench. 'Ethel.' No response. Catrin raised the coverlet and reached for the midwife's gnarled left hand. It was cold in hers and when she squeezed it, there was the merest tremor of response. 'Ethel, I know you're not asleep.'

The seamed eyelids fluttered, and Catrin saw a sudden glisten of moisture in the bruised pouches beneath.

'My hand,' Ethel whispered. 'Catrin, I can scarcely feel my hand.'

'A slight seizure,' Catrin reported to Oliver later that day. 'A repeat of the first one I would say. It hasn't affected her speech, praise God, but she cannot hold a cup in her left hand and the leg on that side too is affected.'

'Will she recover?'

Catrin shrugged. 'I cannot tell at the moment. It is not as if I have had much experience of treating folk of her age.' This being because there were few folk of Ethel's age on which to practise. 'I have done what I can.'

Oliver sighed and nodded. 'I have known her since my birth and, despite what you see between us, there's respect and affection.'

'That *is* what I see between you,' Catrin responded. 'You are as concerned for her as she is not to concern you.'

He pulled a face at the truth of her statement, and after a pause asked, 'What of your midwifery? You cannot go out into the city alone – knife or no knife.'

Catrin's expression became wary. 'I will tackle that obstacle when I come to it. Besides, escorts are usually provided. Whoever fetches me will see me safe.'

'As they did two nights since?'

'That was different.' Catrin began to bristle.

'Indeed it was,' he agreed. 'But you don't need many different occasions like that to wind up another corpse in the Avon.'

'Then I'll hire someone to escort me,' Catrin snapped. 'Jesu, you're like a dog with a bone!'

'Be grateful,' he said. 'If I wasn't, you'd be dead.' And this time it was he who walked away, without giving her further opportunity to flay him with her tongue. This time too, she knew that he was in the right.

CHAPTER 12

As winter deepened its grip, Earl Robert gave Oliver command of a patrol in the Forest of Dean, its purpose to protect the Earl's interest in the iron ore diggings and forges which provided the steel to make tools and weapons for the Empress's cause. There had been raids, and the Earl judged Oliver a competent deterrent.

He had ridden out at dawn on the day following Ethel's seizure. Concerned for the women, he would rather have remained in Bristol, but orders were orders and Earl Robert's word law. It irked him that there had been no opportunity to talk to Catrin before he left – either for fighting or trysting. He missed her; he needed to know that she was safe, and was so chafed by his anxiety that he was unbearable to those around him.

'Still, we'll be back in Bristol for the Christmas feast,' Gawin said, trying to lighten Oliver's heavy mood. They were riding along a forest track not far from the forge at Darkhill. The wind was bitter, sown with sleet, and the trees gave small protection, their branches winter-black and fluttering with a ragged tracery of dead leaves.

'More than three weeks away,' Oliver growled, not in the least co-operative. 'And that's three more weeks of this and worse.' He cast a jaundiced glare at the sky and eased his position in the saddle. 'It hasn't even been light today.'

'At least we'll soon have a fire to warm our hands.' Gawin's tone was placatory.

Oliver grunted. Actually, the thought of warmth and food was welcoming, albeit that he would have to spend the night rolled in his cloak guarding a cartload of horseshoe bars before the morrow's journey to the ferry barge. 'I suppose so,' he yielded grudgingly, then raised his head at the sound of a furious yell from the track in front of them.

Wrestling his shield round to his left arm, Oliver drew his sword and urged Hero to a trot. Gawin fell into line at his left shoulder, and the other soldiers in the troop closed formation. Moments later, they rounded a sharp bend and came upon the sight of three ragged men with knives being held at bay by a single giant who was swinging an oak quarterstaff with accuracy and gusto. One of his attackers was on his knees, clutching his broken arm and screaming. As Oliver watched, the giant threw another one off his feet with a heave from the quarterstaff. The third man ran in low, attempting to slash the quarry's hamstring, but the quarterstaff arrived before the knife and dropped the attacker with a hefty blow to the temple.

Feeling somewhat superfluous, Oliver uttered a yell and spurred forward. The two robbers who were capable took to their heels among the trees. Oliver signalled to Gawin and two others, who detached from the troop and cantered after them.

The giant faced Oliver, his beard bristling and his quarter-staff at the ready. Sweat beaded his brow and he was visibly winded, but not to the point of being incapable of defending himself.

Oliver sheathed his sword and put his shield on its long strap to show that he posed no threat. 'What happened?'

'You can see,' the man said, with a brusque gesture. 'They were waiting at the roadside and they set upon me.'

One of Oliver's troops had dismounted to investigate the robber in the dust. 'Dead,' he announced. 'Skull's stove in.' He picked up the ragamuffin's knife and handed it up to his master.

Oliver examined the weapon thoughtfully. It was an evil tool, with a bone haft and a notched blade a full handspan long. 'Fortunate that you are more handy with that staff than he was with a knife,' he remarked, as he thrust it in his saddle pouch. 'Are you bound for Darkhill?'

The giant narrowed his eyes at Oliver, considering, then gave a curt nod. 'To visit with my sister,' he said. 'I've been absent a year and eight months.'

'On pilgrimage?' Oliver indicated the pewter badges stitched to the man's brown cloak.

'Rome, Jerusalem,' came the shrugged reply. 'I made a promise to our father.'

The stranger had given enough account of himself to gain Oliver's respect and curiosity; now feelings of empathy were roused too. The gathering murk of dusk with two miles still to cover was not, however, the place to explore their common ground. 'I too have been a pilgrim,' was all he said. 'You are welcome to journey with us the rest of the way. You can use one of the re-mounts.' He jerked his shoulder towards the spare horses at the rear of his line.

The man eyed him then gave a jut of his beard in assent. 'My name is Godard,' he said, and offering no more information than that shouldered his quarterstaff, stepped over the body of the predator who had become a victim and advanced on the waiting horse.

The two thieves who had survived their assault on Godard proved to be outlaws who had been plotting to sneak into the village and steal some of the horseshoe bars to sell for their own gain. Whilst lying up in the forest, they had caught sight of Godard, a lone traveller, and had chanced their luck once too often. They were the sheriff's meat now and, without a doubt, would swing from a gibbet when the time came. The dead man was consigned to the care of the priest, and a length of sacking was found to make his shroud.

Godard went off to visit his family, but later that night, when all but a few rush lights had been dimmed, he returned to speak with Oliver, who was keeping warm in Darkhill's small alehouse. There was a pitcher to hand, but Oliver had taken no more than a cup from its bounty. Wits were for keeping when there was a cartload of hammered steel to be protected. His own watch was due when the hourglass had turned three times. For the moment, Gawin commanded the men on guard.

'You say you've been a pilgrim too,' Godard stated without preamble, and sat down beside Oliver. For such a huge man, he moved lightly and although considered, there was nothing slow about his actions.

Oliver pushed the jug at him. 'Rome and Jerusalem like you, and a few other places.' He parted his cloak and showed Godard his pilgrim belt. 'For my wife's soul, and my own.'

Godard pursed his lips and nodded. Oliver could see him struggling not to look impressed at the weight of pewter punched through the leather.

'Not that I feel any more worthy for the effort,' he added, 'but I saw places and things that most men will not see in their lifetime.'

'Aye,' Godard agreed, and poured himself a cupful of ale. He took a long draught and then pinched moisture from his moustache. 'But you try describing a camel to a sister who's never been further than five miles in her life. A horse with a hump don't hardly fit.'

'No.' Oliver grinned at the thought, and his companion responded with the merest glimmer of a smile, although it was hard to tell, so thick was his beard.

For the next hour they talked of their experiences, both men reticent but with each exchange the ground thawing between them. Then, in a lull, Godard refilled his cup for the third time and pushed the pitcher aside, signifying that he would drink no more. 'Are you looking to recruit men?' he asked, with an abrupt change of tack.

Oliver stared at him for a moment, nonplussed, but quickly rallied. 'Earl Robert is always looking for men,' he said, and shook his head. 'This war eats them like a foul serpent and spits out their bones. Is there not a place for you at your sister's hearth? Do you have no trade?'

Godard nodded. 'I'm a shepherd, but my father's wealth did not stretch to providing for eight sons and four daughters. If I lived here with my sister and her husband, I would be a madman within a sennight. We'd kill each other so we would.' Reaching to his cup, he drained his ale. 'But you heard me a-wrong. I asked if you yourself were looking to recruit men.'

Oliver snorted with dark amusement. 'Not unless they want paying in beans! My own patrimony lies in a stranger's hands, and until I can regain it I'm beholden to Earl Robert for the money in my pouch and the clothes on my back – Jesu, even the oats and stabling for my horse.' The bitterness in his own voice surprised him. Nor was it the ale talking, for he had consumed no more than a quart.

'You're not beholden to him,' Godard said in his measured way. 'You give him your service, and he only repays what is owed.'

Oliver shrugged, acknowledging the point without any great conviction. His hand twitched towards the flagon and then withdrew. He looked at Godard, taking in the taciturn but honest features, and the sheer bulk of the man. All he knew of him was that he was a doughty fighter who would not cry over spilt milk, that he could look after himself, and had a healthy sense of duty, if not respect, towards members of his family. What was more important, Oliver felt that he could trust him.

'Why are you staring?' Godard asked suspiciously.

Oliver folded his elbows on the ale wife's old, splintered trestle. 'I am not looking to "recruit men" as such. If I did, it would be for the Earl because, as I have said, I do not have the coin to employ them. But if you are interested, I could afford to pay you to perform a certain task for me.'

The large man raised his brows. They were thick and dark, just beginning to salt with grey. 'That depends what it is.'

'It might be dangerous,' Oliver said, 'but it is very important to me.' And told him what he intended.

Throughout a bitterly cold snap, Catrin nursed Ethel devotedly, massaging her stricken hand, keeping up her spirits, and watching with relief as the old lady began to rally and recover some of her old sparkle. Fortunately, there was a lull in her summons to women in labour. She attended a couple in the camp, both during the day, and was escorted to and from one in the town, also during the hours of daylight.

Catrin knew that the lull would not last. There were several

women in the camp who were heavy with child, and she knew
of at least four more in the town.

'And go you must when they summon you,' Ethel admonished, wagging the forefinger of her good hand when Catrin
expressed her worry. 'Don't you mind about me. You just
make sure you've got someone to accompany you there and
back.'

But Catrin did mind. Although Ethel appeared to be on
the mend, she was still visibly frailer than she had been at
the onset of autumn. It was almost as if she was a tree, slowly
losing its leaves one by one. It was a fancy that Catrin tried
to ignore, but seeing Ethel every day made it impossible. She
did her best to hide her worry, and Ethel tried to conceal her
weakness from Catrin, but neither woman was deceived.

In the third week of December, Catrin returned from
buying fish and vegetables in the town to find an enormous
stranger sitting with Ethel and warming his hands at their
fire. An imposing quarterstaff was propped outside and tied
to one end was a travelling bundle.

Ethel was smiling crookedly, a tiny trickle of saliva at the
corner of her mouth. When she saw Catrin, her eyes lit up
and she beckoned vigorously. 'Just look what Oliver's sent
us!' she cackled. 'A fine, strong man!'

The stranger rose to his feet, but remained hunched over
since the roof of the shelter would not accommodate his massive height. 'My name is Godard, mistress,' he announced in
a gravelly voice. 'And I have been employed by Lord Pascal
to be your protection, should you have need. He said to tell
you that as far as he is concerned, my arrival here has buried
the bone.'

Catrin started, her mouth open. His very size was cause
for wonder, but what he had just said left her speechless. She
did not know whether to be pleased or indignant.

'You should bury the bone too,' Ethel said from her stool
and tucked her cloak more securely around her affected hand.
'No point in fighting when there ain't no need.'

'I can look after myself,' Catrin said, the words emerging
with the flatness of oft-repeated litany. Ethel's mention of
'fighting' made her think of 'trysting' too, and she knew

without recourse to a gazing glass that her cheeks were pink.

The huge man stooped a little further in acknowledgement. 'My lord told me that I was not to interfere with your independence, only that I should make sure you lived to enjoy it.'

Ethel gave a snort of amusement and Catrin scowled in her direction.

'Bend, girl, before you break,' Ethel warned, and again the forefinger wagged.

Catrin sighed heavily, but she knew in her heart that Ethel was right. And if the truth were known, the thought of having such a giant at her side, if she had need to go out into the city at night, was comforting. 'Then be welcome, and best be seated before you break your back.' She gestured at the stool, and wondered where on earth he was going to sleep. There was certainly no room in Ethel's shelter to house his great bulk.

As if reading her mind, he said, 'I've arranged to lodge with the kennel-keeper. His daughters have not long married and there's sleeping space on his floor. It's only across the bailey should you need to summon.'

Catrin nodded, feeling relieved. 'Oliv . . . Lord Pascal, is he well?' She ignored the sudden sharpness of Ethel's stare.

'Indeed he is, mistress.' Godard held out his hands to the fire. 'He said to tell you that he is sorry that he cannot be here himself to continue with your lessons . . .' He frowned, seeking the memorised words. 'He said that you make far better company than wagonloads of horseshoe bars and he hopes to be home before the Christmas feast.'

This time the pinkness in Catrin's cheeks was accompanied by a flush of warmth through her body. 'I'll be pleased to see him,' she murmured and looked down at her hands where Lewis's gold rings still shone on her finger.

Godard took his leave shortly after that, and Catrin made Ethel a hot posset of milk and honey, sprinkled with nutmeg. 'Only ten days to the Christmas feast.' Ethel looked thoughtfully at Catrin. 'Be a good excuse to use that scented soap you were given, eh?'

Catrin scowled at Ethel from beneath her brows. 'What is that supposed to mean?'

'Whatever you take it to mean, girl, but I think you know.' Ethel laboriously raised her left hand and held it against the hot side of her cup. Her eyes gleamed. 'He's sent you your first gift early.'

Catrin glanced over her shoulder. 'My bodyguard, you mean?'

'Aye.' Ethel took a one-sided sip of the hot posset. 'The question is . . . what are you going to offer him for the twelve days of giving, in return?'

Fortunately, at that juncture, a woman came asking for some cough syrup for her sick child, and Catrin was spared the problem of answering.

Christmas Eve arrived and there was no sign of Oliver. Despite, or perhaps because of, the continuing civil war, Bristol was in a fever of anticipation and celebration. Rumour abounded that Empress Mathilda herself was coming to Bristol for the Christmas feast. The cooks were run off their feet, their cauldrons and ovens so busy that they had no time to feel the bone-deep cold that settled in a white mantle of hoar over the land. Cartloads of firewood and charcoal made their way through the keep gates daily and were devoured by the numerous fires – great logs for the hall, smaller pieces of split branch for the fires in the private chambers, and charcoal for the braziers and the forge.

Catrin attended at several more childbirths, and was glad of Godard's company. He spoke little, but his very presence was comforting, and her initial indignation at Oliver's sending him vanished. Sometimes he would eat at their fire, but even then he was about as forthcoming as an ox. He split wood for them and drew water. When Richard came visiting he showed him how to wrestle with a quarterstaff, much to the boy's delight, and near dusk on Christmas Eve presented him with a cut-down version of the weapon.

When thanked, he just shrugged and looked a trifle sheep-ish. 'I've nephews of your age,' he said gruffly and turned away to pump the fire with the bellows, signifying that the matter was at an end.

Not long after that, Catrin was called away to a labouring woman. When she returned it was almost midnight, clear, bright and cold. Ethel was sound asleep beneath her covers and the fire had been banked by a neighbour to last until dawn. Godard took his leave and retired to his own bed.

Lantern in hand, Catrin gazed around the bailey. Apart from the guards on patrol and a pen of sheep awaiting slaughter, it was empty, everyone buried under their blankets for warmth. It was one of the strands of a midwife's existence, seeing a world that others slept through. Tonight, on the eve of the celebration of the Christ child's birth, she should have felt a sense of quiet satisfaction, but her pleasure was marred by a stronger sensation of emptiness. Oliver had not come, and anticipation was becoming anxiety and disappointment. She could not celebrate without him. The realisation hit her like a lungful of the crystalline air. It was too late to step back; she was trapped.

With a heavy sigh, she turned to push aside the screen, and had to stifle a scream as she realised she was not alone. A cowled figure was standing beside one of the shelter's wooden supports.

'Who is it . . . Rohese?' Catrin held up her lantern and peered, her other hand at her throat to steady the leaping of her heart. 'What do you want?'

'I have to speak with the old one,' said Rohese de Bayvel, and glanced anxiously round. Within the depths of her cowl, her face was narrow and pinched. Catrin had not been much in the bower this last month; most of her time had been taken up with nursing Ethel, and she was shocked at how ill Rohese looked.

'Ethel is sleeping,' she said. 'She is very frail and I do not want to wake her. Can you not wait until the morning?'

Rohese shook her head. 'I need her now. Wake her up.'

'Ethel can do nothing for you that I cannot,' said Catrin. 'If it's more of that love philtre you want, then I am sure I can mix it for you.'

Rohese stiffened. 'I want nothing from you,' she said with a curl of her lip.

'Then come back when it's light.' Catrin held her ground. Although not as tall as Rohese, she was more than her match in stubborn courage.

Rohese chewed her lip. 'It is a private matter.'

By which Catrin judged that it was more than a simple love philtre that Rohese required.

'How can a biddy sleep with all that noise?' The hanging was tugged aside and Ethel poked her nose into the biting cold. She was clutching a blanket to her bosom and her hair swung in a heavy grey braid.

Catrin glared at Rohese. 'I'm sorry we woke you.'

'Don't matter, I was wakeful anyway.' Ethel opened the hanging wider. 'Won't you come in, my lady.'

Picking her way daintily like a skittish horse, Rohese entered the shelter. 'I want to see you alone,' she murmured, with a meaningful glance at Catrin.

It was with some difficulty that Catrin kept her tongue behind her teeth. Ethel, however, had no such nicety of restraint. 'What's meant for my ears is meant for hers too. Like it or leave it, my lady. I promise we'll not spread tales.' Dragging herself over to the fire, she began to poke it to life with a long iron bar. Catrin knew better than to try and take it from her. Instead, she dusted off the stools, which were clean anyway, and kindled a rush light.

Rohese fidgeted and even cast her eyes across the bailey towards the gleam of the whitewashed keep as if she would return to the bower. But then, with a sigh, she stepped across the threshold and dropped the curtain. 'I need something to bring on my flux,' she announced. 'I'm more than two weeks late.'

Catrin compressed her lips. Small wonder that Rohese did not want her present after all that the woman had said about Amice. An unmarried woman whose flux did not come was wading in deep water.

'Well, what can you do for me?' Rohese snapped.

'Depends on the reason you haven't bled.' Ethel leaned the poker against the small spit at the side of the tripod and went to consult her jars and bundles of herbs. 'Is it likely that you're with child?'

'No, of course not!' Even in the dim light of the shelter, Catrin could see that Rohese's complexion was dusky. 'How can you say such a thing!'

'Easy. 'Tis the most likely cause. Only other ones I know are starvation or a deadly sickness of the vitals.'

'I tell you, I am not with child!'

'Suit yourself, my lady.'

Catrin watched Ethel reach to the bag containing the penny royal and gromwell. They were herbs used to promote menstruation in women whose fluxes had ceased for whatever reason. Sometimes they worked, but their efficacy was haphazard. Stronger herbs carried stronger penalties such as vomiting, purging and even death. Ethel only gave them when a woman was certain to die anyway if she carried a child to term.

'Take three pinches, my lady, in a cup of wine, and say a prayer to Saint Margaret,' Ethel instructed, handing Rohese a twist of linen. 'I'm not saying that it will work, but happen you might be fortunate.'

Rohese took the pouch, put a silver quarter penny into Ethel's cold, left palm and, without looking at Catrin, swept out.

'Well, well. Wonder who the father is?' Ethel fetched a blanket and seated herself at the hearth. She transferred the penny from her bad hand to her good, then tucked her fists in her sleeves.

Catrin thought of the occasion she had seen Rohese slipping away into the camp and shook her head. 'Will she bleed?'

'Might, but I doubt it.' Ethel clucked her tongue. 'No good playing with fire and not expecting to be singed.'

'No.' Catrin drew her cloak around her body and stared into the revived red embers.

'Still,' Ethel murmured, 'a little singeing on occasion is no bad thing.'

Catrin watched the flames licking the life from the wood and wondered if she was right.

* * *

Following mass on Christmas morning, there was feasting and merriment in the keep's great hall. Outside, the air sparkled with a clarity that hurt the eyes. Inside, it was a smoky fug, scented with apple-wood from the fire, with evergreen from the branches of holly and fir adorning the walls, and with the aroma of spices from the numerous dishes that crowded the trestles. The bailey was deserted, for almost every member of Bristol keep not on duty was in the hall feasting and merry-making.

Ethel had been found a relatively quiet corner by the fire with others who were elderly or infirm. There was a jug of hot wassail wine to keep them occupied, and several platters of small delicacies – cheese-wafers, slices of smoked sausage, small salted biscuits, fried nuts, and candied fruit. Tucked in a new blanket, that had been a gift from the Countess, Ethel was highly content with life.

Catrin, however, was less so. 'He's not coming,' she said, sitting on the bench at Ethel's side. Before going to mass, she had washed from crown to toe in the scented soap and donned a new undershift of soft embroidered linen, topped by the gown of crimson and gold that Oliver had yet to see. While still damp, she had bound her black hair in braids and secured the ends with fillets of enamelled bronze. She knew, with a certain degree of pride, that she could match any woman present in the hall today, but it was swiftly becoming an empty triumph.

'Time aplenty yet,' Ethel answered around a mouthful of cheese-wafer. 'Besides, there's plenty more fish in the sea for an attractive young woman. Do you a world of good to dangle one on your line.'

Catrin pulled a face. Several men had inveigled her to dance or tried to manoeuvre her beneath the mistletoe to steal a kiss, but she had kept her distance. One or two would be quite interesting to 'dangle on her line', but Catrin was wary of hooking a fish larger than she could handle. It was one of the reasons why she was sitting here amongst the old and the infirm, instead of joining in the games and dancing at the hall's centre. Indeed, if the truth were known, the merriment daunted her a little, for there was a wild undercurrent, a predatory edge to the playing that could so easily turn a crowd into a mob.

She watched Richard and Thomas FitzRainald. The boys were playing a boisterous game of hoodman-blind with some other youngsters, and thoroughly enjoying every moment. She smiled wistfully at their pleasure and helped herself to a cup of the wassail wine, welcoming the trickle of the hot liquid down her throat. She thought of the last Christmas when Lewis had been alive. Her feet had not touched the floor for dancing. She had been one of the crowd out there, brimming with laughter, giddy with drink . . . probably insensible in the end too, for the memories would not focus, remaining a colourful blur.

'Go on, wench.' Ethel gave Catrin a nudge and almost spilled the wassail wine. 'Get you gone. Spend your life waiting and it'll be over before you know it.'

With a small sigh, Catrin drank down the wine to the spicy dregs and stood up, pondering where to go next in search of a haven. Perhaps she ought to stand beneath a kissing bunch and let fate take its course.

A sudden fanfare at the hall door made her swing round in surprise. People began falling to their knees and bowing their heads, almost like wheat beneath a reaper's scythe. Catrin stared, wide-eyed.

'The Empress Mathilda,' someone hissed and, tugging on her sleeve, dragged her down. For a moment, she held the same pose as everyone else, but then could not resist a half glance upward.

The sole-surviving legitimate child of the old king was a little shy of forty years old. There were few lines on her face, but those that did exist were deeply graven, like sharp pen strokes. She was gorgeously dressed in royal purple and gold, with a lining of ermine tails to her cloak. Escorted by her half-brother, Earl Robert, she walked with a regal glide, her head carried as high as those of her subjects were bowed. The pride, the elegance, the very severity of feature led to an impression of beauty, but in the way that a killing winter day was beautiful. To touch was to freeze.

Reaching the dais and mounting it, Mathilda sat down upon the high-backed chair that had been appointed for her.

She surveyed the hall without expression and, having taken her due from those who bowed, she flicked her fingers in dismissal. Catrin continued to regard her, thinking it small wonder that many of the barons chose to support King Stephen instead. Hauteur of such a degree was unlikely to endear men to her cause, men who were already suspicious of taking orders from a woman. A smile, a word, would have cost nothing and repaid the effort tenfold.

'Take more than a cup of wassail wine to prize that one out of the ice,' Ethel muttered. 'Still, if I had the husband she's got and that pack of fools for followers, I'd be frozen too.'

'Her husband's supposed to be one of the most handsome men in Christendom,' Catrin said. 'Geoffrey le Bel, they call him.'

'Geoffrey the ten years younger and as tricky as they come,' Ethel snorted. 'They've fought ever since they've been wed.'

'Yes, I'd heard the rumours and the scandal.' She looked again at the Empress, who was leaning to listen to her brother, her white fingers curled around the stem of a fine silver goblet. How much pain, Catrin wondered, did that cold façade conceal? How deep was the ice? Her first husband had been an emperor. Recalled home at his death to become the heir to England and Normandy, she had been forced into marriage with Geoffrey of Anjou, the mere son of a count and still in adolescence. The marriage had foundered, but parental pressure had shored the broken edges and forced it to hold together in mangled shards. Three sons later it still did, but everyone could see the gaping holes beneath the shoring. If not for their children, if not for their political need of each other, Geoffrey le Bel and Mathilda Domina Anglorum would gladly have let their marriage sink.

'I would not change places with her for the world,' she murmured.

Ethel gave another little snort. 'Speak for yourself. I'd change places in return for a night with Geoffrey le Bel.'

'Ethel, you're drunk!'

The old woman chuckled and did not deny the accusation.

Catrin felt a tug on her sleeve and turned to find Richard and Thomas at her elbow. Both of them must have been outside, for their cheeks were red with cold, and there were sparkles of melting snow on their tunics.

'You've to play a game!' Richard cried, wafting the hood at her from the hoodman-blind.

'Ah, no,' Catrin laughed, starting to shake her head, but she did not really mean it. Having viewed Mathilda's coldness, she needed the relief of laughter.

The boys dropped the hood over her head, so that the face opening was at the back, and her vision cut off by a layer of itchy, dark wool. Then they spun her three times round, but instead of releasing her to feel her way and try to capture one of them, they took her arms and drew her where they wanted. For a horrified moment, Catrin thought they were leading her up to the dais to present her to the Empress. But then she felt cold air on her skin and the delicate sting of sleet.

'You know that you two will pay for this,' she said with a shiver, as her shoes slipped in the soft, dark mud of the bailey floor.

The response was a muffled giggle. One of them let her go, but the other tightened his grip on her arm.

'How much had you in mind?' a deep voice demanded with amusement.

Catrin seized the hood in her free hand and dragged it off her head, the movement taking her wimple and circlet too. 'Oliver!' Suddenly her breath was short and, despite the cold, her cheeks were burning. Giggling, his two accomplices ran off back to the hall.

He laughed and swept her up in his arms, crushing her face against the sodden wool of his cloak and the hard rivets of his mail hauberk. 'I suppose you'd given up on me.'

'The thought of you never crossed my mind,' she retorted with spirit, as he set her back on her feet. 'I've had no lack of offers to stand beneath a kissing bunch, you know.'

He sucked in his cheeks. There was a grizzle of beard encircling his mouth and pricking his jawline, its colour copper-blond in the light from the blazing pitch torches guttering in the wall sconces. 'Taken any of them up?' he enquired.

'What do you think?'

He looked at her a moment longer, the sleet glimmering silver and fire-gold between them. 'I think,' he said softly, 'that I have missed you beyond all reason, and that there is not a kissing bunch large enough in that hall to show you how much.'

Catrin swallowed. Jesu, she wanted him, and not just beneath a sprig of evergreen and mistletoe. 'Ethel has one in her dwelling that might suffice,' she offered, looking at him through her lashes, and was gratified to hear his hoarse intake of breath. She circled her toe on the muddy ground of the bailey floor. 'Unless of course you'd rather join the feast and try the others.'

He shook his head. 'All the sustenance I need is here with me now.' Taking her hand, he pulled her against him once more. Their lips met in a tingle of sleety cold, and heat spread like a sun. He crushed her close and Catrin lost her breath against the hard, steel hauberk rings. His beard scratched her and the feeling was bliss; his hands gripped and she gasped against his mouth in pleasure.

A nobleman staggered out from the hall and vomited against the keep wall. A companion followed him and stood by laughing. Oliver and Catrin broke their embrace and, by mutual consent, turned towards the haven of Ethel's dwelling.

Once within, the headlong rush towards fulfilment was curtailed by practical considerations. Whilst making love in a hauberk was merely difficult and uncomfortable, tearing one off in haste was nigh on impossible. After three attempts at unbuckling his sword belt alone, Oliver had to take several deep breaths and slow down.

'Shall I help you?'

The thought of her nimble fingers in the area of his crotch was both heaven and torture. He could see from the gleam in her eyes that her version of 'help' had wider connotations than just unfastening a buckle. She reached to the decorated strap end and tugged the excess length of leather until she had freed the latch from the hole and the belt, complete with scabbarded sword, snaked free.

She wrapped the leather around the scabbard, and propped it carefully in a corner of the room. Next came the hauberk itself. This, even for the two of them, was tricky, for the garment was full-sleeved, and clung to the gambeson beneath. Catrin was panting by the time she finally peeled it over his head and, as she took the weight, she staggered and almost fell. Gasping himself after being doubled over, Oliver grabbed it from her and laid it across the small trestle to one side of the fire. The rivets crunched and jingled on the wood.

The gambeson was simpler to remove, but it still took an effort. As Oliver laid the garment on top of his hauberk, Catrin said, 'It's like peeling an onion.'

Oliver grinned. 'Or unwrapping a gift.'

She wrinkled her nose at him, but her eyes were alight with humour. 'And do you think I'm going to like this gift, or will it wring tears from my eyes?'

'There's only one way to find out.' His fingers curled around her waist and again drew her close. This time, there was no padding of steel and quilted linen between them, no drunkards to break the moment. They kissed and clung, swayed and sat down on the bed-bench.

From the awkwardness of buckles and heavy chain-mail, Oliver found himself struggling with the pin of the round brooch at the throat of Catrin's crimson gown, and the tie on her braid belt. A part of him wanted to ignore all the complications of such intricacies, push up her skirts and take her to ease his swollen urgency, but he held off because it mattered to him that she should derive pleasure from the encounter. Besides, he sensed that any such move on his behalf would receive short shrift. Catrin was not like Emma, to murmur soothing words in his ear and shine with pride at a wifely duty successfully performed.

And so he made a game of the undressing, lightening the moment with teasing and laughter, holding back so that Catrin, in her turn, could unwind the leg bindings on his chausses and unfasten the laced drawstring on his shirt.

She nibbled his collarbone, bit his earlobe, and rubbed

playfully against him. He put his hands beneath her skirts and tugged at the threading on her garters. Then he ventured higher and drew her down on top of him, spreading her legs and deftly positioning the juncture of her thighs over his swollen flesh.

She made a soft sound and rubbed upon him, their bodies separated by the thin linen of his braies and the fine wool and linen of her dress and chemise. It was too much and not enough. He groaned and tried to think of other things, but the scent of her hair and skin drove all sanity from his mind and filled it instead with raw need.

He arched his spine, thrusting up towards her, but she pulled away from him in order to remove her dress and chemise. Her breasts were high and round, with small, pinkish-brown nipples that tightened in the air. Her belly was flat, and her legs smooth and well proportioned. The sight of her took what little breath remained to Oliver. Apart from his wedding night, he had never been granted so open a view of a woman's body. Emma had preferred to make love in the dark, or wearing her chemise, and it would not have occurred to him to make a whore remove her clothes during his brief encounters with such women.

Catrin, however, was different. He had known it from the moment that she swung pillion behind him as he took her away from Penfoss. The mannerisms of nun and hoyden were inextricably combined and utterly bewitching.

She returned to the bed, squeezing in beside him on its narrowness, and now there was no barrier. His shaft pressed against the rough triangle of hair, sliding, searching blindly. He cupped her breasts and buried his face against her soap-scented throat. She arched her thigh over his flank, allowing him the merest fraction of entry, and he groaned. Her fingers stroked, gliding over his skin with the tips of her nails, and she altered her position so that he entered a little further. He felt her muscles tighten around him, squeezing gently, and strove with every shred of will not to burst there and then.

As if sensing his dilemma, she ceased to move. Oliver stared at a bunch of herbs suspended from the rafters and contemplated the texture and pattern of the dried leaves. He recited a troubadour song inside his head to try and distract himself. *Blow, northerne wind, Send thou me my swetyng, Blow, northerne wind, Blow, blow, blow.* The sensation of imminent crisis diminished. He ran his fingertips very lightly over her skin, teased her nipples, sucked the pulse at her throat. He ventured lower, finding the furrow in her pubic hair with his index finger and the tiny, sensitive knurl of flesh that Gawin had told him was a woman's source of pleasure. His touch was light and tentative, for he had half wondered if Gawin was telling him tales, but Catrin shuddered and moaned and he felt the sudden leap of her blood against his lips. He stroked her again and felt her clamp around him. *Blow, northerne wind, Send thou me my swetyng* . . . He closed and tightened his eyes; continued to rub.

Making mewing sounds in her throat, Catrin shifted her position again so that she was fully over him and, pushing down, she sheathed him completely. Oliver abandoned all attempts to divert his mind. It was futile. Nothing existed but the pleasure and pressure in his loins. Catrin was gasping above him. He seized her hips and thrust into her. Her flesh flexed, then grasped him smoothly.

'Jesu,' Oliver groaned. Unable to hold back any longer, he lunged powerfully, once, twice, and was overcome by his climax. Catrin sobbed and ground down, and he felt her fierce contractions pulsate around him.

Panting, Catrin collapsed against him, her hair brushing his face, her body moulding to his. He could feel the resilient, tender flesh of her breasts, the satin curve of her thigh, the gentler ripples of after-shock swallowing along his shaft.

'Ah, God,' she said, her breath still heaving. 'I had forgotten.'

'Forgotten what?'

She raised her head. Her hazel eyes were glazed and heavy-lidded. A pink flush stained her face, throat and breasts. He could see a reddish mark flowering where he had sucked her throat. 'What a pleasure it could be.' She tilted her head on one side, a smile curving her lips. 'You were right. I do not think a kissing bunch in the hall would have encompassed this.' She ran her finger down his wiry chest hair, following a trail down his belly towards his pubic bush, at that moment meshed with hers.

'It's not only a red beard that you sport, is it?' she teased.

'It's a sign of vigour,' he answered, in the same vein.

She laughed, and squeezed him gently with her internal muscles before rising off him. 'I'm glad to hear it, but even a vigorous man needs sustaining.' Leaving the bed, she went to a jug set near the hearth and poured golden liquid into a cup. 'Mead,' she said, 'from the clover hives in the river meadow. Ethel insists it puts a spring in her step.' She looked at his crotch with a suggestive arch of her brows.

Oliver snorted with amusement. 'If Ethel swears by it, then it must be good.'

'It is.' Catrin sat down beside him. She was totally at ease with her nudity, and this too was new for Oliver. Emma had been shy of her body, always crossing her hands in front of her breasts and refusing to look at him. Catrin was completely spontaneous, her hazel stare candid with humour and lust.

He took a sip of the sweet, golden brew, passed the cup to her and stroked her silky hair where it had loosened from its braid. The faint perfume of lavender drifted to his nostrils and mingled with the scents of love-play and mead. 'It is long and long since I was so content,' he murmured. 'Years in fact.'

Catrin drank. A drip spilled down her chin and she scooped it up on her forefinger and licked it off. 'It is the same for me too,' she said, 'perhaps more so, because I had begun to think that I was going to spend the Christmas feast alone.'

He grimaced. 'I would have been here yester-eve, but I became saddled with providing part of the Empress's escort from Gloucester. We had to wait until my lady was ready to leave, and she took her own sweet time about it. Then we had to ride through the streets of Gloucester in full array for the benefit of the people, with Mathilda waving a haughty hand and casting handfuls of silver as if she despised the act.' He shook his head and drew the cup, still in her hand, to his lips.

'And yet you have sworn your oath to her.'

'Because Stephen has rewarded one of his mercenaries with

my lands; because Earl Robert commands more respect in my eyes than ever Stephen could – than ever Mathilda could come to that. But she has sons to continue her line, and they could never, even in a nightmare, be any worse than Stephen's son, Eustace. If he mounts the throne, then I will return to the Holy Land and offer my sword to the King of Jerusalem.' He took another long swallow of the mead, as if swilling a bad taste from his mouth. 'Ach, I don't want to talk of rulers and their petty ways, not when there are more interesting things to discuss.'

'Such as?' She finished her drink and set the cup to one side, her eyes luminous as she knelt above him.

'Such as what do you think of Godard?' Oliver banded his arms around her and rolled her over. There was a welcome surge of heat at his groin.

'First I was angry, then I was pleased,' she answered and spread her legs invitingly. 'He is very useful to have around, and Ethel dotes on him. So do half the laundry maids.' She dug her nails into his back. 'You took a risk sending him. I find his company quite pleasing myself.'

'But not as pleasing as this?'

Her thighs clasped him. 'Ask me again in a while,' she murmured, then arched and gasped as he thrust into her.

Leaning heavily on her stick, Ethel limped across the bailey. The sleet had turned to wet snow and was settling although, behind the clouds, a haze of moon still glimmered fitfully. On reaching her dwelling, she paused outside, her head cocked on one side like a listening bird. Very carefully, she unfastened one of the hooks holding the door screen and peered inside.

By the faint red glow from the embers of the fire, she saw Oliver and Catrin entwined upon her bed, both of them sound asleep. Oliver's arm was draped protectively across Catrin's shoulder, and her head was snuggled beneath his chin.

Quietly, Ethel secured the screen and turned back towards the hall. It was warm in there, and she had no complaint about dozing by the fire with hot, spiced wine for company.

As she paused against the forebuilding to gain her breath, she saw a couple arguing in the lee of the wall. In a moment, she recognised them both. The man was young Gawin, still wearing his hauberk from escort duty, and the woman was the Countess's sempstress Rohese. She stood shivering in a dress of thin, wheat-coloured silk, no cloak to protect her from the bite of the wind.

'You've had your pleasure!' she cried in a voice high with panic and petulance. 'You can't walk away from your duty to me now!'

Ethel saw a look of impatience cross Gawin's face. She could tell that he was the worse for drink – as were more than half the young men in the hall tonight. Swaying forward, he braced his arm against the wall. 'Oh, but I can, sweetheart. It wasn't just my pleasure, don't deny it. Besides, how do I know it's my duty? More than one dog will mount a bitch in heat.'

Her hand shot out towards his face, but he caught her wrist with a soldier's reflexes and twisted it round, forcing her to her knees in the settling snow. Then he pushed her away. 'Find someone less choosy,' he sneered, and lurched back into the hall.

Ethel watched the encounter with tightening lips. Gawin was a decent, if shallow, young man when the drink was not upon him, but there was no excuse for what she had just witnessed. Knowing his personality, she could see that seducing the Countess's haughtiest maid had been a challenge impossible to resist. Now that the consequences had come home to roost, he did not want to know.

Although Rohese was about as approachable as a stinging nettle, Ethel limped forward, intending to help her up and offer comfort. 'Child, come within before you freeze,' she said gently, and extended her hand to the weeping young woman on the ground.

Rohese flung her off and struggled to her feet, her beautiful gown marred by a damp patch of melting, muddy snow. 'Leave me alone, you hag!' she sobbed, her face raw with pain. 'Your nostrums don't work! He doesn't love me and I haven't bled!' Shoving Ethel out of her way so hard that the elderly midwife staggered, Rohese fled across the snowy bailey towards the gate.

Ethel cried for her to stop but her voice was snatched by

a swirling gust of wind and her chest cramped painfully. Knowing the warning sign too well and unable to pursue, the old lady turned and made her way laboriously towards the hall.

Rohese rounded a corner of the bailey, and the full force of the wintry night slashed through her garments like a knife. Shuddering, the tears icy on her cheeks, she pressed herself against a storeshed wall and hugged her frozen arms.

With a soft jink of chain-mail, a man materialised out of the whirling darkness, a spear in his right hand, a shield on his left arm. A thick cloak blew back from his shoulders, its lining one of glossy squirrel fur.

Rohese was about to scream when she realised that it was one of the guards on his rounds.

'Well, well,' said Randal de Mohun softly. 'If I'm not mistaken, it's one of the Countess's maids, and in need of a little warming.'

Against banks of mounding white, the river Avon flowed like black glass. The snow struck its polished surface and vanished with neither sound nor trace. It was the same for the body. A single swirl and eddy in the obsidian surface, then nothing to show that it had ever been cast upon the water.

Within an hour, even the footprints had vanished, covered in a powdering of white.

CHAPTER 13

The hose were woven of the softest red silk with ribbon garters of the same. Catrin gazed at them in pure delight. Fond though she had been of her old pair, these surpassed them a hundred fold.

'Another reason I was delayed.' Oliver smiled at her pleasure. 'I had to scour Gloucester for them. Fortunately, I found a hosier who fashions the Empress's undergarments.'

Winding her arms around his neck, she kissed him. 'So I'll be wearing hose fit for a queen!'

'I hazard they will look better on you than they would on Mathilda.'

'Shall I show you?'

His eyes lit up and, with a husky laugh, he gestured her to continue.

Catrin was wearing her chemise, ready to start the day. Outside, Saint Stephen's morn was dawning in pallid grey light. The fire had almost died, just the faintest glimmer of red among the ashes, and the room was cold, but she cared little for that just now. Last night had set a gloss on her world that nothing could diminish. Her only guilt was that they had denied Ethel her bed, but Catrin suspected that the old lady would be highly pleased at the turn of events.

Sitting on the edge of the bed, she raised her chemise to a tantalising level, took one of the hose and arched her toes into it. Then she drew it slowly up over her calf, watching Oliver all the time. When she reached her knee, she paused. 'How good a lady's maid are you?' she enquired, and dangled one of the binding ribbons at him.

'I have small experience, but large ambition and a great willingness to learn,' he answered with a grin and, taking the ribbon, accepted her invitation to slide the hose on to her thigh and bind it in place. Of course, as she had known, he could not resist exploring further. His fingertips were delicious, but she yelped at the prickle of his beard stubble.

'By the Virgin,' came Ethel's voice from without. 'I thought if I left you two alone last night, I'd at least have my house back by the morning!'

Oliver shot backwards and up, colliding with a bunch of drying herbs tied to the rafters. Aromatic scraps of leaf showered down on him. Catrin flailed for a moment like a cast-over crab, righted herself and dragged her undershift down over her knees.

Ethel unhooked the door and stumped into the room. 'God's bones, you've been so busy kindling your own fire, you've let mine go out too!' she snorted, and cast her gimlet eye over the couple. There was a gleam in her expression, but Catrin could sense the old woman's irritation.

So too, it seemed, could Oliver. He had already been wearing his shirt and braies. Now he quickly donned his tunic and chausses, and set about rescuing the fire from the brink of extinction. Catrin flashed him a rueful glance and pulled on her dress.

'If you're going to live here, best find a space for a pallet of your own,' Ethel muttered, sitting down on her stool and glowering at the embers. 'If, of course, you've thought that far.' Her tone was so crotchety that Catrin wondered if she had misread Ethel's earlier attempts at being matchmaker.

'To be honest, neither of us have thought much beyond the moment,' Oliver replied mildly enough, but his eyes were wary as he gently piled dry twigs upon the embers.

'Hah, then you should.'

'In our own good time,' Catrin said with a frown.

Ethel chewed her lips and scowled. 'Time and tide wait for no man – and no woman neither,' she retorted ominously.

Oliver blew gently on the fire and soon tiny flames were licking and crackling around the twigs. Leaving it to gain hold, he fetched a folded-up bundle from the corner of the room and presented it to Ethel.

'What's this?'

'Your Twelfth-night gift, but I thought you should have it now to sweeten your mood. I'm sorry if we kept you from your bed last night.'

She gave him a severe look. 'I'll not be bought,' she said, but began unfolding it all the same, waving him aside with a tetchy 'I can manage,' as he stooped to help her.

Casting a glance heavenwards, Catrin swung the cauldron over the new fire. Ethel was always grouchy in the mornings but she seemed to be uncommonly so today.

Oliver had bought the old lady a mantle of fine, soft, green wool. It was warmer than a cloak for it was donned over the head, the full drapes of fabric falling to the front and back. Nor did Ethel have to fumble with a cloak pin to secure it.

'You stand need to buy me fripperies like this when your own cloak is nigh on threadbare,' Ethel said gruffly, the suspicion of a glitter in her eyes.

'The Countess has promised me a new cloak as my own Twelfth-night gift,' Oliver shrugged. 'And for escorting the Empress, I'm to receive an extra day's pay. Don't go looking gift horses in the mouth.'

'Aye, then thank you, lad, but I still say you've more money than sense.'

'And you have more pride,' Oliver retorted, and this time made her sit still while he unpinned her cloak and gently drew the mantle over her head.

Ethel's good hand stroked the soft, green wool. 'Your father would be proud of you,' she murmured. 'He always set store by seeing those who depended on him clothed and fed, God rest his soul.'

'Amen,' Oliver said, thinking that his father's soul would have small rest whilst a Flemish mercenary sat in his hall. Every time the usurpers visited the church, they would trample on his grave.

The water in the cauldron started to steam and Catrin made them all an infusion of elderberry and rosehip, sweetened with honey. Ethel took the first, warming swallow and, closing her eyes, sighed.

'Shall I tell you why I'm being a cantankerous old woman?'

'I had scarce noticed any different,' Oliver said flippantly, then sobered as her gaze opened on him with a spark of warning. 'I thought it was because of Catrin and me – because we had stolen your bed and become lovers?'

Ethel shook her head. 'Don't be so foolish. I've been hoping for that since the day you told me about her. It's been all I could do sometimes to stop myself from knocking your two stubborn heads together. No, what's set me on edge is that foolish young adjutant of yours.'

'Gawin?'

'Aye, Gawin.' Her tone was eloquent. 'He's been bedding one o' the Countess's women and got her with child.'

Oliver's eyes widened and his jaw dropped. Catrin ceased patting out oatcakes for the griddle and stared. 'It's Rohese de Bayvel, isn't it?'

Ethel sucked her teeth. 'Saw them together last night and they was arguing like cat and dog. She was all for calling him to account and he was having none of it. Soused as a pickled herring he was, but that ain't no excuse for the way he treated the lass, forcing her to her knees in the snow and calling her a slut. She might be a haughty bitch but she deserves better than he gave last night.'

Oliver sighed. 'I'll speak with him as soon as I've broken my fast, for what good it will do. You know his morals where women are concerned.'

'Speaking's no good,' Ethel said sourly. 'Just take him by the scruff and dunk him in the nearest horse-trough. That's what he deserves.'

Gawin looked blearily at Oliver. 'It's none of your business,' he said belligerently. 'I'm only seconded to you, you're not my feudal lord.' His breath was heavy and sour and he was still drunk.

Around them, the hall was groaning to life, everyone sluggish and the worse for wine. It would be the same again on the morrow, and the morrow after that, all the way to the twelfth and last day of the Christmas feast.

'If I was, your back would be flayed raw,' Oliver replied coldly. They were sitting at the trestle near the door. A freezing draught fluttered the rushes on the floor and helped to dispel the vinegary stench of stale wine. 'Rohese de Bayvel is not some Shambles whore you can toss a coin and forget. She's one of the Countess's own maids.'

'I know that.' Gawin's voice was an irritated snarl. He pushed his fingers through his hair.

'From what Ethel overheard last night, I would doubt it.'

'Look, she pursued me.' Gawin gestured impatiently. 'Good God, she even put one of that hag's disgusting love philtres in my drink.' He glared at Oliver. 'If you push me, I will claim that I was bewitched, and then see what happens to yonder midwife and her assistant.'

Oliver saw red. Seizing Gawin by the tunic, he drew him face-to-face. 'If anything happens to Ethel or Catrin, you will pay the reckoning to me, in blood. If you cannot tell honour from shame, I do not want you riding at my side!' Throwing Gawin down, he strode from the hall into the clean air of the bailey where he leaned against the forebuilding wall, breathing hard, mastering his fury.

When Gawin was sober and had his nose to the grindstone, Oliver would have trusted him with his life. But given leisure and a cup, the young man's personality degenerated with alarming speed. Usually his follies were set right with a handful of silver and a visit to the confessional, but getting Rohese de Bayvel with child and then spurning her was a different matter entirely – as was the petty, vindictive threat against Ethel and Catrin. Oliver was not sure that he could forgive him for that.

The Earl's younger squires and pages were out in the bailey having a boisterous snowball fight. As his breathing slowed, Oliver became aware of them; the flung snow, the joyful shouts. Thomas FitzRainald and Richard were part of the throng and playing their part to the hilt. A half-grown tan mastiff lolloped between the boys chasing the missiles and tossing lumps of snow between its black jaws. Oliver was spied and became an immediate target for both dog and boys. Sweeping up his own ball, he answered vigorously, flinging the last of his anger from him, before he retreated behind raised hands, begging for mercy and spluttering on showered snow.

The dog jumped up at him, barking and scrabbling with blunt claws. Richard grasped its collar and dragged the animal down. 'His name's Finn,' he said. 'Earl Robert gave him to me for a Christmas gift. He's even allowed to sleep with me in the dorter.'

Oliver dutifully admired the brute, slapping its taut, golden hide, and wiping his hands on his cloak after it slobbered upon him. He accepted that dogs had their role to play in castle life, but he was not particularly fond of them, much preferring the independent aloofness of the cats that stalked the kitchens and stables and occasionally found houseroom as pets. Still, if Robert had given the pup to the boy, it was a mark of how seriously he was treating the blood bond between them.

Richard turned to run back to his snow game but paused and looked hesitantly at Oliver. 'Will you come with me later to visit my mother's grave and lay a wreath of evergreen?'

Oliver was touched. 'Of course I will, lad. I'm glad that you think of her.'

Richard shrugged. 'It's my duty,' he said, then redeemed himself by adding, 'I don't want her to be lonely.'

There was a hint of forlornness in the boy's voice that told Oliver more than words. 'We'll pray for her.' He squeezed Richard's shoulder. 'I know that if she were here, she would be very proud of you.'

Richard nodded and squirmed, embarrassed by the sudden moment of intimacy. Pulling away from Oliver, he ran to join the others, his dog gambolling at his side.

Oliver watched them for a moment, then made his way across the bailey to Ethel's dwelling. Richard's mention of his mother's grave made him think of Emma's. Was it still attended, or had the passage of time and the new Flemish lord caused it to be neglected and forgotten? A pang went through him, wistful and forlorn like the boy's. But in the same manner he was also aware of the life flowing in his veins. How could he not be after the previous night? Head up, a curve to his lips, he approached the small house.

'You know how to protect yourself, girl?' Ethel demanded, once Oliver had gone. 'I don't think for one moment that he's like yon young wastrel, but it's best not to bear a babe unless you're sure you want to.'

'Yes, I know.' Catrin managed not to sound impatient. 'Sheep's wool or moss soaked in vinegar. Besides, it's not as if I'm blessed with fertility. I was wed to Lewis for a year and a half and never once did I miss a flux.'

'Hmph, t'aint always the woman's fault.'

'I know that.' Catrin smoothed the crimson gown beneath her fingers and looked at the grain of the fabric. 'But I know that my former husband's seed was fertile because he confessed to me that he had got one of the kitchen maids at Chepstow with child – although she miscarried in the third month.' She raised her head and gave Ethel a look both candid and sad. 'He found it difficult to resist a pretty face, and they, most certainly, had few defences against him. He could have charmed the very birds down from the trees had he so chosen.' Suddenly there was heat behind her eyes. How foolish to be mourning Lewis when she should be rejoicing that she had Oliver. 'Let the past lie,' she said with a toss of her head, 'I take your advice to heart and I will be careful.' Surreptitiously she rubbed her eyes, but Ethel was sharp and saw.

'I doubt such a man is worth weeping for,' she said.

'I'm not weeping. It's the smoke from the fire.'

'Oh, aye, it is that,' Ethel said with double meaning that caused Catrin to flounce on her stool.

Unrepentant, Ethel sucked her teeth. 'So tell me, will Oliver move his pallet in here or will you go to him?'

'It is too early to make a decision like that.' Ethel was making her feel ever more defensive. Catrin would neither be led nor pushed. Her own free will or nothing. Between her and Oliver there was respect, liking and sheer, honest lust, but it was too new, too soon.

Her face must have shown her thoughts, for Ethel ceased to

badger her, saying only, 'You are the daughter I never bore. I want to see you settled and happy.'

'Of which I am both – Mother.'

Ethel gave a tired smile and patted Catrin's cheek. 'I think I'll rest for a while.' She went to lie down on her pallet.

Catrin watched her with a mingling of affection, exasperation and concern.

She knew that Ethel was failing. The unspoken knowledge lay between them, but not for one moment would the old lady admit that each day was becoming more of a struggle. Ethel too was stubborn and in that, indeed, they were as mother and daughter.

Catrin leaned forward to mend the fire and add two more pieces of split log. A shadow darkened the entrance. Glancing up, a welcome on her lips for either Oliver or Godard, she was surprised and alarmed to see a different man blocking her light. He was not one that she had noticed before, but then she paid small heed to the Earl's mercenaries except to be cautious of them and keep her distance.

He was taller than Oliver with thick, black hair and beard, the latter salted with grey. Attractive creases defined his eye-corners and his lips were thin, cruel and sensual. He wore a rust-streaked gambeson and beneath it a tunic of very fine blue wool with a hem of red and gold braid. The design on the latter looked familiar, but there were several braid weavers in Bristol who had their own personal colours and patterns.

Catrin stood up and dusted chips of bark from her hands. 'Can I help you, sir?' Usually it was women who came to her and Ethel. Soldiers were a rarity, for which she was glad. His height and the way he looked at her as if she was a morsel to be devoured, were intimidating.

He showed his bandaged right hand. 'A dog bit me and the wound is festering,' he said. 'I have heard that your healing skills are without compare in Bristol.'

'A dog?' With some misgiving, she gestured him over her threshold.

'One of the bitches in the hall.' He entered the dwelling, glanced round, and sat down before the fire, the brass tip

of his scabbard scraping on the rushes. On the bed-bench,
Ethel did not stir.

'How long ago?'

'Yesterday eve.' He glanced up at her. The look in his eyes
clung to her like oil.

Catrin wanted to say that she could not help him and bid
him leave, but since she had not even looked at the wound, it
would have been a patent lie, and ousting him, she suspected,
would not be as easy as inviting him in. Swallowing her misgivings, she asked for his hand and unwrapped the grubby
linen bandage. Beneath his gambeson, the cuff of his tunic
bore the same braid pattern as the hem, and again she was
struck by an elusive sense of familiarity.

His hand was that of a seasoned soldier; its texture halfway
to leather and marked with the stigmata of a swordsman's
blisters. It was also marked at the moment by a nasty bite
wound. The teeth had gouged deep and the whole area was
red and inflamed. It looked unlike any dog bite that Catrin
had seen before, but she held her tongue on that score.

'It needs to be cleaned,' she said, 'and then anointed with
woundwort.'

He gestured brusquely for her to do so. As she turned away
to inspect the stores of herbs, she knew that he was watching
her, sizing her up like a wolf planning its next meal.

'I thought that wise-women were all old hags,' he said,
when she came back to him and held open the jagged lips
of the wound to receive a swabbing of strong, salt water.
His tendons grew tight at the pain, but his face revealed
none of it.

'Well, now you know differently.' Catrin's tone was as
brusque as her motions.

'Oh, indeed I do.'

Tight-lipped, Catrin rubbed woundwort ointment into the
injury, positive now that no animal had bitten him. The shape
of the teeth, the angles were all wrong. She bound a fresh linen
strip around his hand and tied it off neatly. 'You must try and
keep it clean or it will fester.'

He flexed his palm. 'It's the slack season; I won't be
wielding a sword for a while . . . well, not one of steel

anyway.' Rising to his feet, he stood over Catrin. 'Well, Mistress Wise-woman, how much do I owe you?'

'A halfpenny is the usual fee.' She swallowed, hating the closeness.

'A halfpenny,' he repeated, and paid her a coin from his pouch. 'But I hazard that I am not a usual customer, sweetheart. Perhaps, since it is Christmas, I should give you a gift to honour the season.'

Catrin could see what was coming. Even as he took a step towards her, she took one back and grabbed the iron poker resting against the spit bar.

He stared at her, then he laughed with genuine amusement. 'Surely a small kiss is not cause for such fuss. I'll pay you the other half of the penny for it.'

'I sell healing, sir,' Catrin said icily, 'not myself.'

He snorted. 'Every woman has her price.'

'You could not afford mine.' Catrin tightened her grip on the poker.

He laughed again but this time the sound was unpleasant. 'What do you think you could do against me with that little stick? I could break your wrist with a single snap if I so chose.'

It was with the utter weakness of relief that Catrin saw Oliver walking up, and behind him, chopping-axe on shoulder, the massive form of Godard.

Sensing someone behind him, the mercenary turned, but to Catrin's dismay, instead of making himself scarce, he threw open his arms and embraced Oliver heartily, slapping his back. 'Pascal, you whoreson! Where have you been lying low!'

Catrin watched Oliver return the embrace with considerably less enthusiasm, his entire body stiff and the smile on his face strained. But nevertheless, it was a smile. 'Nowhere. I've been on the Earl's business. And you, Randal?' His eyes went to Catrin and she gave an infinitesimal shake of her head.

The mercenary shrugged. 'Got bitten by a dog, so I had the wench here take a look at it.' He grinned. 'Her charity's as cold as an arse on a winter latrine though. Threatened me with that poker when I offered her the compliments of the season.'

'It was no compliment, but an insult,' Catrin said with revulsion.

'How can that be? Every pretty woman expects to be kissed more than once beneath the mistletoe.' He flashed his eyes at her and grinned.

Oliver pushed past Randal de Mohun and joined Catrin. Godard began to split some fresh logs for the fire, one eye cocked for trouble. 'Not this one,' Oliver said tersely. 'I will warn you now that she is under my protection and her life is mine.'

The mercenary stared at him with narrowing eyes. Oliver stared coldly back, and the tension bristled between the two men like a wall of spines. Then de Mohun shrugged. 'And your life is mine, Pascal, or have you forgotten the road to Jerusalem?'

'I forget nothing, but I'll not have you calling in the debt for every petty whim and fancy. There are women aplenty in Bristol if that be your need.'

'But this one is too good for me, is that what you're saying?'

'I am saying that she does not appear to want you.'

'Women never know what they want,' said the mercenary with scorn. Then he shrugged and a forced, white grin appeared beneath his moustache. 'It is the feast of Saint Stephen, our beloved King – a lost cause if ever there was one. I won't quarrel with you on this day and, besides, my sword hand is out of commission.'

Oliver regarded him stonily.

'But I warn you,' de Mohun wagged a finger, 'taking waifs and strays under your wing is a dangerous occupation, especially when you prefer them over old comrades to whom you owe your very life.'

'I'd rather live with the danger.'

Still grinning, with contempt now, de Mohun shook his head and turned away. 'You're a self-righteous fool, Pascal. No woman's worth it, even on her back. Seek me out when you come to your senses and we'll share a flagon at The Mermaid.' He touched his temple in farewell. 'Since I'm generous at heart, I'll leave you to enjoy your waif in peace.'

He took off across the ward, his stride jaunty and arrogant. Catrin shuddered. 'Who is he, Oliver?'

He grimaced. 'You remember I spoke in the summer about a band of mercenaries who happened upon us digging graves at Penfoss and stopped to help? Well, that is their leader, Randal de Mohun.'

'The one who saved your life when you were a pilgrim?' She recalled the conversation very well, since it had almost ended in a quarrel, with Oliver defending de Mohun's reputation. At the time, he had told her not to judge. Now that she had had opportunity she found little to commend.

'Unfortunately, yes.' His expression hardened. 'The years have not improved him. When I knew him in the Holy Land, he was not so brutish.

'There is something familiar about him,' she murmured with a frown, 'but I don't know what, and it disturbs me.'

'He's been employed by the Earl since midsummer and, like me, in and out of Bristol all the time. You have probably seen him in passing. He will not trouble you again, that I promise.'

Catrin smiled without humour. 'Another of your "promises"?'

'Do I not always keep them?' He slipped his arm around her waist and drew her hip-to-hip against him. Then he smoothed the frown from her brow with the tip of his finger and kissed her. Beneath his lips, hers curved into a smile and, for a moment, the world blurred at the edges.

Catrin pressed against Oliver, taking refuge from her anxiety in physical sensation until both of them were hot and gasping. Unfortunately, there was no bed to hand, unless they went looking for an unoccupied hay loft, and it was too cold a day to make love against a wall or spread a cloak in the fields. By mutual consent they broke apart. Holding her hand, Oliver sat on Ethel's stool before the fire and drew her on to his lap. She wriggled playfully and he squeezed her buttocks, but it was an ending, rather than a prelude, to their sport, for they were both aware of the sleeping old woman. Not that Ethel would have been much shocked, but she needed her rest, and they were loath to disturb her.

'Did you speak to Gawin?' Catrin left his knee to pour them each a cup of mead.

Oliver sighed. 'Yes, for what good it did. He was still in his cups and not inclined to pay any heed. Indeed, he went so far as to say that if I pushed him, he would claim that he had been bewitched by Ethel's potions.'

'But that's not true!' Catrin flashed a look over her shoulder, but Ethel slept on oblivious, the coverlet drawn up to her withered cheek. 'There's nothing in her love philtres that could cause anyone to be bewitched. It's only rose petals and cinnamon steeped in water. What nonsense!'

'That depends on your belief,' Oliver said. 'I told her that it was dangerous to meddle in such things.'

'Do you think Gawin believes?' Catrin asked shortly.

'Of course not, it is just a convenient excuse to abstain from responsibility for his actions.' He took the drink that she handed him and made a dismissive gesture. 'It was the wine talking. I threatened him with death in return and told him what I thought of his character. Whether it will be of any benefit once he sobers, or have no more effect than water off a duck's back, remains to be seen.'

Avoiding the temptation of Oliver's lap, Catrin sat in the straw at his feet and, cupping her hands around the hot mead, gazed into the red heart of the fire. 'I feel sorry for Rohese,' she murmured.

'I thought you disliked her.'

Catrin looked at him. 'That does not mean I cannot have compassion for her situation. I admit we have not been friends, but I don't hate her. Countess Mabile will likely send her to a convent for the birth and then to live as a penitent for the rest of her life. Unless Rohese has a vocation, her life will be a living hell.' She shook her head and her lips were twisted, as if the sweet mead had suddenly turned to vinegar in her mouth. 'Men such as Gawin act on their lust and think later, if they think at all. My husband was a little like Gawin, I know the kind.'

Oliver's complexion darkened. Catrin gazed at him blankly

for a moment, then realised that he had taken her words to heart. 'I do not number you among them, you fool!' she cried. 'Yes, we acted upon our lust, but it was mutual and I know that you still honour me.'

He lifted his shoulders. 'With my life,' he said, 'but I want others to know of that honour too. How can I chastise Gawin when I am not in a state of grace myself?' He cleared his throat, then said tentatively, 'Catrin, would you become my wife?'

Catrin felt a hot chill of delight and fear run down her spine. Both acceptance and refusal hovered on her tongue and left her speechless. The silence stretched and began to strain.

She gnawed on her underlip, seeking with difficulty the words that would make him understand. 'I was married to Lewis on a winter morning just like this,' she said at last. 'I do not want a second joining to hold memories of the first.'

He frowned. 'I should not have asked you.'

She felt him tense to rise and swiftly clamped her hand around his leg to make him stay. 'Perhaps not quite so soon,' she said, her throat dry. 'Although I can see why you did.'

'Then the answer is no?'

His voice was far too expressionless for her comfort. She had hurt him and that had not been her intention. The only grounds she had for refusal were caused by old wounds that were not of Oliver's making.

Drawing a deep breath, she said, 'I swear that before the next Christmas feast, in a different season, I will become your wife. Is that grace enough?' Finishing her drink, she returned to his lap and curved her arms around his neck, sensing that he needed more than words as reassurance.

After a moment, his own arms tightened around her, the mead sloshing over the rim of his cup. 'More than enough,' he muttered against her throat. 'I thought you were going to refuse me.'

Catrin laughed shakily and curled her fingers into the thick hair at his nape. 'I may have panicked, but not to the point of losing my reason.' She toasted him with a sip from his mead. 'To our future.'

'To our future,' Oliver repeated, and drank from the place where she had set her lips.

Later that day, they visited Amice's grave to lay a wreath of evergreen and pay their respects. It was Richard who put the wreath on the grave and crossed himself. He had grown since the summer, his face elongating and his nose developing a sharpness that was more than reminiscent of his father, the old king. He bore himself with assurance, no longer a bewildered and bitter child but a boy on the verge of adolescence.

In the frozen, cold twilight the snow sparkled, and Catrin shivered within the warmth of her cloak as she looked at her former mistress's grave. For no reason she could fathom, the memory of Randal de Mohun intruded on her prayers and disturbed the melancholy beauty and silence of the cemetery. Oliver reached for her hand and squeezed it. Gratefully she squeezed his in return and stepped a little closer to his reassuring presence.

CHAPTER 14

The remainder of the twelve days of Christmas passed in a blur of feasting and celebration. Earl Robert's court played boisterously, releasing tensions pent up by the winter confinement. Each table was set for twelve people and twelve courses were eaten, beginning with thin broth and dumplings and progressing through various elaborate fish and meat dishes, including the obligatory roast boar. The feast culminated in the presentation of a magnificent marchpane subtlety in the shape of Bristol Keep, the rivers Avon and Frome winding in blue almond paste around the edge of the serving-board.

Each night Oliver and Catrin ate until they could eat no more, then joined the rough and tumble of the games in the hall. Hoodman-blind, hunt-the-slipper, hot-cockles. They danced caroles around the apple wassail tree in the centre of the great room and laughed at the antics of the mummers and jugglers.

Sometimes they would slip away from the carousing – to be alone, to make love. Ethel's home gave them a haven, if she was absent. If not, there were hay lofts and byres to shelter them. They also took to riding out on the snowy roads beyond the city, and once they joined the court in a hunt but did not stay long with the jostle and noise of the dogs and horns. After the exhilaration of the first gallop had worn off, they turned aside for the untrammelled silence of other woodland paths, abandoning the loud belling of the dogs and the tantivy of the hunting horn.

Their breath rose in white puffs on the wintry air as they rode amongst the stark, black trunks. Oliver's cloak was a splash of blue brightness, Catrin's crimson gown and hose as rich as blood against the backdrop of crunching snow. The only signs that others had passed the same way were the tracks of wild animals: the narrow elegance of a fox, the dainty spoor of a lone roe deer.

Catrin and Oliver drew rein on a ridge overlooking the winding grey of the river. Fields stretched away on the other side, punctuated with coppices of hazel and hornbeam. It was a common enough view, but its very tranquillity in the winter cold made it beautiful. Catrin inhaled the crystalline air and sighed with pleasure.

Oliver tugged off his sheepskin mittens, and from the pouch beneath his cloak drew out a smaller drawstring bag. 'Hold out your right hand,' he said.

Her eye on the bag, Catrin pulled off one of her own mittens and did as he bade.

'I spoke to a goldsmith a few days ago,' he continued. 'A man well-versed in Irish knotwork. Although he was busy and it was the holiday season, I told him of my urgency and he fashioned me this.' Into his palm, he tipped a gold ring worked in cunningly twisted gold wire to form the shape of a triple knot. 'I had it blessed by the Earl's chaplain.' His tone was diffident. 'It's a betrothal ring, if you please, or a Twelfth-Night gift, if you don't.' Taking it in his hand, he slipped it on her middle finger.

Catrin blinked, her eyes suddenly full. The only other rings she possessed were the ones that Lewis had given her on their wedding day, but they were hidden beneath the mitten on her left hand as well Oliver knew. 'It's beautiful,' she whispered, touched to her core. 'And it fits perfectly.'

Oliver grinned. 'Well, I confess to measuring your finger with a piece of string while you slept.'

Catrin sniffed and turned her head to wipe her tears. The new gold shone in the winter sunlight. 'I can give you nothing so perfect in return,' she said, her throat tight with emotion.

'You've already given me more than perfection,' Oliver said. 'My pleasure is in your promise to be my wife.' He leaned across his horse to kiss her. Their lips met, tingling with cold, and their breath mingled in a single cloud.

Her step so light that they scarcely heard her, a doe pattered through the trees and leaped past them on to the crown of the ridge. Her thick, winter coat was shot with glorious hues of red and gold. Beneath the thick pelt, her flanks heaved with effort. The noise of hounds in full cry belled the air and there was terror in the doe's huge brown eyes.

Catrin gasped and broke from Oliver to gaze at the deer. She loved the rich flavour of venison but, watching the animal flee for its life, she found herself willing it to escape.

The doe poised on the ridge, cloven hooves dancing, ears flickering, then she gathered her haunches and took off in a series of enormous bounds, her legs showering spangles of snow with each leap. At the foot she did not stop but sprang straight into the grey water and began swimming strongly.

Catrin clenched her fist upon her new ring and silently urged the doe on. Ripples arrowing her breast, head carried high, the deer reached the opposite bank, scrambled from the river, and shook the water from her coat. Then she was away, fleeting across the fields towards the bank of woodland in the distance.

'She's free.' Oliver's taut expression relaxed and there was a sudden cloud of vapour as he let out the breath he had been holding. 'The hunters will never chance the hounds, or themselves, in that freezing water.' He too was fond of venison, but today his soul was with the deer, not her flesh.

As the huntsmen and dogs swirled around them, then ranged the top of the ridge in frustration, Oliver and Catrin turned for home in the pleasure of their own company.

The only item that marred the joy of the season was the continuing absence of Rohese de Bayvel, who had not been seen since the early hours of Christmas morning. A search had proved fruitless. She had left her gowns and all her personal effects, even the double-thickness cloak that had been a Christmas gift from the Countess. The guards on duty had seen nothing. It was as if she had been swallowed off the face of the earth in a single gulp.

Gawin spent three days hiding in a drunken stupor, but when finally he sobered he was filled with guilt, if not remorse.

He confessed his sins to a priest, who gave him a penance of twenty days on bread and water and absolved him. But he remained ill-at-ease. He searched the town, the wharves, the leper hospital and convents, all to no avail.

'She cannot just vanish, someone must have seen her,' he said, with a frustrated shake of his head. He was sitting in the hall with Oliver, a January wind whistling at the shutters and sending occasional gusts of chimney smoke belching into the room.

Oliver considered the younger man. There were dark circles of late nights and heavy drinking pouched beneath his eyes, and a slight tremor to his hands. 'No one in the keep or the city has seen her. Catrin has asked on all her rounds. I think you must accept that you are not going to find her.'

'Say what you mean. You believe she's dead, don't you?' Gawin picked up the flagon they had been sharing and tipped the dregs into his empty cup. It would be his fourth to Oliver's two.

Oliver rested his chin on his hand. 'I think it likely. All you can do now is pray.'

'Pray!' Gawin snorted. 'Do you think if I kneel down here and now that she'll walk back into the hall as if she had never left?' He tipped the wine down his throat.

Oliver shook his head in disgust and started to rise from the table. 'You are drinking yourself into a state of idiocy,' he said tightly.

'It gives me pleasure.' Gawin filtered the sludgy dregs through his teeth. 'And it helps me forget how much more trouble the bitch has been than she is worth.'

Oliver was saved another session of grabbing his adjutant by the scruff, as Richard appeared before the two knights, his dark blue eyes agleam. 'Lord Oliver, you're summoned to Earl Robert's presence immediately,' he announced, hopping from foot to foot with excitement.

'Am I now?' That was interesting news. A half-hour since, as he and Gawin were sitting down, Oliver had seen a messenger out of the corner of his eye. The man had looked hard-travelled with mud spattering his garments and eyes red with fatigue. After a lull, the game, it seemed, was afoot once more.

Gawin took his cup, and lurched off in pursuit of another flagon and the company of a group of knights around a dice game. He would not spend time alone if he could help it.

Oliver followed Richard above-stairs, taking the familiar route to the Earl's solar. He was keen to know what news the messenger had brought but he refrained from asking the lad. Part of the responsibility of being a squire was learning to keep a closed mouth, and he did not want to tempt or compromise Richard when the boy was so obviously trying not to burst.

The solar door was open and the guard gestured them to enter. The Earl was already surrounded by other adjutants and knights, and two scribes were frantically writing at a trestle set off to one side. Even as Oliver stepped over the threshold, an older squire left at a trot, a sealed parchment in his hand.

Oliver approached the group surrounding the Earl and heard the tail end of a conversation involving the words 'move fast' and 'catch him while he thinks he's safe'.

'My lord, you sent for me?'

Earl Robert glanced up. His eyes were bright and his complexion flushed. 'Ah, Oliver.' He beckoned vigorously. 'I need you to ride out and recruit men for me. Go into Wales and along the border. Offer whatever it takes to obtain them – within reason,' he added, with a jerk of his brows. 'I want them sooner than now, whatever you can get. If they have mounts and weapons, all the better, but it is not necessary. You will leave immediately. Take de Mohun with you. He's got a good eye for a likely man.'

'De Mohun?' Oliver recoiled and then, seeing the look in the Earl's eye, said, 'Yes, sir. May I ask the purpose?'

'My son-in-law has snatched Lincoln Castle out of Stephen's hands and garrisoned it with his own men. Malde is holding it for him while he recruits troops to strengthen his position. He has asked me for aid. Without it, he cannot hold Lincoln Keep, and by law it is rightfully his. I have said I will come to him with all haste. For all that Stephen is a chivalrous man, I will not make him the gift of my daughter as a pawn.'

'No, my lord.' Oliver knew that the Earl doted on his eldest daughter, Malde. She was married to Rannulf, Earl of Chester, whose power on the northern marches of Wales made him almost a prince. Thus far, Rannulf had been loyal to Stephen, but it was not a cloak that had ever fitted the power-hungry Lord of Chester particularly well. Robert and Rannulf had a healthy respect for each other but were not the fondest of in-laws. Malde, and the desire to extend their mutual influence along the Welsh borders, were the ties that bound them together. But Rannulf's defection to the Empress's cause would bind them closer still. 'How long do I have?'

'Ten – twelve days at the most. Stephen has the town, Rannulf the keep. Or rather, Malde has the keep,' he added, with a swift hiss of anxiety. 'Rannulf is in North Wales summoning levies to march on Lincoln. I have to muster troops with all possible haste. My exchequer will equip you with funds.'

'My lord.' Oliver bowed out of the room and hurried down the stairs into the hall, his mind working to the swift pace of his feet. Grabbing Gawin, he commanded him to run and pack a saddle roll.

'What for?' Gawin looked at him slack-mouthed over the rim of his cup.

'We're going into Wales. Stop staring, we've to ride out now!'

Gawin lurched to his feet and almost over-balanced. 'Wales?' he repeated.

'Yes, to recruit troops. You can sober up in the saddle. Go!'

Shaking his head in bemusement, Gawin steadied himself and reached for his cloak.

Oliver collected his spare tunic and cloak from his pallet, then went to tell Ethel that he had to ride out on the Earl's business. He could not make his farewells to Catrin for she was away in the city at a childbirth.

'Will you be gone long?' Ethel asked. She was huddled

by the fire in her new green mantle. The hands that poked out from beneath the garment to absorb the heat shook with palsy.

'No more than ten days, but then we'll all be marching north.' He stooped to help himself to a flask of mead and several of Ethel's oatcakes. 'Give Catrin my love and tell her that I wish she was here, but I'll speak to her when I return.'

'From your ten days or from the North?'

'The first I hope,' he answered with a grimace and, saluting Ethel, strode off in the direction of the stables.

Somewhat to Oliver's surprise, the recruiting went smoothly and well. Randal de Mohun might have been obnoxious in camp, but on campaign, with responsibility, he was efficient and professional. He was also a good judge of the quality of fighting men and, by a mixture of emotive words and material promises, attracted an excellent number of recruits to join Earl Robert's banner. His ebullience and boldness, the expansiveness of gesture and dress, were well-contrasted with Oliver's more reserved approach. Men saw that there was room for more than one sort of soldier in Earl Robert's ranks. Those who did not take to Randal de Mohun could talk quietly to Oliver and make their decision at a more measured pace.

'We've done well,' grinned de Mohun, as they sat over a camp-fire on the last evening before their return to Bristol. 'The Earl will pay us a bonus for this lot.'

Oliver nodded agreement, his jaws busy with a chunk of gristly mutton from their supper stew.

'Lincoln, eh?' De Mohun rubbed the side of his beard with his thumb. 'It's a rich city, so I've heard. Plenty of pickings, and its citizens deserve no more than what they get for supporting Stephen.' His eyes gleamed with relish.

Oliver gave up and spat the meat into the fire where it sizzled and hissed. 'I know it is the nature of war,' he said, 'but I do not enjoy burning people out of their homes and taking away their livelihoods.'

The mercenary gave him a sharp, sidelong look. 'To the victor, the rewards,' he said. 'I could not afford a sword or tunic like this out of my own pay. I risk my life. It is only right that I be recompensed.'

Oliver shook his head. 'In the end there will be nothing left. If you bleed the river dry, the landscape turns to desert.'

'Oh yes, I agree.' De Mohun smiled. 'But a little running-off now and again does no harm. You are too tender, Pascal.'

Oliver shrugged. 'The more I see, the more tender I become,' he said grimly, and thought that it was perhaps the opposite for some men. He suspected that his companion actually enjoyed the acts of looting and rapine. They were probably the urges that had driven him to be a mercenary in the first place.

De Mohun snorted and shook his head. 'You're a strange one,' he said. 'If you came to me as one of these raw recruits, I'd leave you behind and tell you to tend your sheep.'

Oliver smiled without humour. 'And I'd be glad of it,' he said, and used the excuse of checking on his horse to quit the fireside and company that chafed him.

Catrin was returning to the keep from the market place, her basket full of Ethel's favourite eels to tempt the old lady's waning appetite, when she heard the riders bearing down on her from behind. Spinning round, she clutched her basket to her bosom and stepped aside.

The leading horse was a powerful bay, its rider clad in chain mail, his bright cloak blowing in the brisk wind. For the briefest instant, Catrin had the terrifying sense of standing in the woods at Penfoss watching just such a troop gallop through their gates, except the leading horse had been a chestnut, the shield had borne a different blazon and weapons had been bared. The sensation was gone in a flash, but it still seemed like a true memory rather than a trick of the imagination and it made her shiver.

A grey destrier swung out of the line and headed straight towards her. Again Catrin's heart swooped and plummeted, but in response to a different blend of emotions. 'Oliver!' she cried.

His grin dazzled beneath the nasal bar of his helm. During ten days in the field, his jaw had sprouted an embryo beard of startling Viking-red. Riding up to her, he leaned from the saddle and extended his palm. She took it, set her foot over his and, in a flash of scarlet silk hose, straddled the stallion's rump. Lodging one hand in his belt, she clutched the basket of eels with the other.

'Have we not met somewhere before?' Oliver jested, his eyes flickering from her face to the basket, to her red hose, as if he could not decide where to look first.

'I am sure I would remember if we had,' Catrin retorted, her eyes dancing.

'And do you?'

'I could be persuaded.'

He laughed and twisted in the saddle to embrace her, then made a hasty grab for the reins as the horse jinked sideways. Catrin uttered a small scream and, laughing, gripped his belt more tightly.

Randal de Mohun watched the play with a half-smile on his lips and contempt in his eyes. 'I did not realise your "protection" extended that far, Pascal.' There was an edge to the jesting tone of his voice.

Returning to the ranks, Oliver gave de Mohun a cool look. 'As of Twelfth-Night, we have been betrothed,' he said. 'Catrin is my wife in all but the final blessing.'

After one glance at de Mohun, Catrin lowered her eyes. There was something about the mercenary that caused her flesh to crawl. It was more than just the incident when he had tried to kiss her as she tended his hand.

'Then I congratulate both of you.' De Mohun inclined his head in a mocking salute. 'I'll drink to your happiness the moment I'm free of my duty.'

If he hoped for an invitation to do that drinking with Oliver's coin, he was disappointed. Oliver fixed a polite expression on his face and held it there, refusing to be drawn.

Just to be irritating, de Mohun needled them with his presence for a while longer, but finally he gave up and rode off down the line to snarl at the recruits.

Catrin's scalp prickled. She did not know whether she preferred him in her sight or out of it.

'Yes,' Oliver murmured as if reading her mind. 'He is a

wolf. A very fine wolf who will sit at your fire and save your life from other wolves, and then, because it is his nature, he will snap your hand off in his jaws.'

'I thought he was your friend.'

'Only in the days when I thought it was daring to have a wolf at my fire and I had nothing to care about.'

'Well, you do now,' she replied, 'so have a care to yourself too.' She was not just speaking of de Mohun, although he was cause enough for concern. Now that the first joy of greeting was over, she had time to remember that Oliver's return was fleeting; that very soon he would be on the road again, this time to full war.

Oliver laughed. 'You need have no fear on that score,' he said vehemently.

While they were dismounting in the castle bailey, Gawin approached them. 'Has there been any news, Mistress?'

She dusted down her skirts and glanced at him. 'News?'

'About Rohese?' He bit his lip.

Catrin shook her head and could not help but feel pity for him. 'No, I'm sorry,' she said. 'There has been no word in the town.'

He nodded his thanks and, downcast, turned away. Oliver watched him and sighed. 'I would not usually say this, but setting out on campaign will be the best thing for him – clear his mind, help him find his balance. It's the first time that he's had to face the reaping of what he has sown.'

Catrin nodded sombrely. 'It was probably the first time for Rohese too.'

Oliver sighed heavily. 'God have mercy on them both.' Which was the nearest he would come to saying that he thought Rohese was dead. Gathering Catrin into his arms, he kissed her. 'I have to go and make my report to the Earl and I don't know when I'll be free, but save some eel stew and a seat by the fire.'

'I can think of warmer places,' Catrin said mischievously, 'but only if you shave that stubble.'

He cupped his jaw. 'I promise, if you promise.'

Laughing, she pushed herself out of his arms and went to tend to the dinner.

Ethel was waiting for her. 'He's back then,' the old woman said, and eased her stool away from the fire so that Catrin had room to cook the eels she had just put down.

'How do you know?'

Ethel chuckled. 'Your face gives you away. Besides, I saw the horses in the bailey.'

'There are always horses in the bailey these days,' Catrin said with a small shrug. Sitting on her heels, she looked at Ethel. 'But he won't be staying for long. I don't want . . .' Her voice betrayed her. In silence she donned a linen apron and picked up a sharp knife.

'You will not lose him, lass.' The old midwife touched her breast. 'I know it in here.'

'Lightning does not strike in the same place twice, you mean?' She stripped the skin from an eel with a sharp, downward tug.

'I just know it. Time was when I could command the sight by scrying in a cauldron of simmering water. I ain't got the art any more, lost it when I had my first seizure, but I still have inklings at times. He'll come back to you, never you doubt.'

Catrin finished preparing the eels in silence. Then she wiped her hands on the apron and looked intently at Ethel. 'Truly? You have truly seen?' Her breathing was suddenly short.

Ethel made the sign of the cross. 'I swear it on the Heavenly Virgin. He was riding that grey of his in the midst of a victory procession. I could see a crown shining and there was great rejoicing.' Her voice tailed off and her eyes grew dark and distant.

'What else did you see?' When Ethel did not respond, Catrin gave her a little shake. 'Ethel?'

The midwife came to with a start and shook her head. 'What else did I see?' she repeated vaguely. 'I don't remember. It was confusing and I was tired. All I know is that you need not fear for Oliver's well-being on this march.' She rummaged beneath her mantle. 'You could give him this though, as a talisman.' She handed Catrin one of her famous knots, threaded on to a strip of leather. It was woven with three colours of hair – raven-black, flaxen-gold and dark, rich copper.

Catrin gave Ethel a questioning look. 'Mine and Oliver's I can see,' she said, 'although I will not ask how you came by them, but whose is the red hair?'

Ethel shuffled self-consciously on her stool. 'It is mine. Do you think I was always this dirty sheep colour?'

'No . . . I . . .'

'Time was when I could put autumn herself to shame.' She leaned for her satchel and, with shaky fingers, unfastened the latch. Delving to the bottom, she drew forth a pouch of light green silk and from it produced a plait of hair, thick as a wrist and the colour of a copper beech leaf. 'I had it cut off when the first grey threads started to show. It was a hot summer and I didn't miss my hair – I had to wear a wimple anyway. Sometimes I use strands in weaving my knots, but not often. You can see how full and thick it still is.' There was pride in her voice.

The sight of the plait filled Catrin with poignancy. She narrowed and blurred her eyes and tried to imagine Ethel as a young woman with glossy, auburn tresses and a spring in her step. 'You must have been beautiful.'

Ethel made a preening gesture. 'I had my admirers,' she said. 'I tell you something else too, something that I have never told anyone before.' She lowered her voice. 'Oliver is my great-nephew.'

Catrin raised her brows in startled question.

Ethel nodded. 'I am the bastard daughter of his great-grandsire. My mother conceived me at the midsummer festival in the fields beyond the bonfire.' She gave me a one-sided smile. 'Old lord Osmund had the red hair but, fortunately, so did my mother. She was able to pass me off as her husband's, but I always knew that I was different to my brothers and sisters.'

'So there is a family tie between you?' Catrin looked down at the knot in her lap. 'Did Oliver's great-grandsire ever know?'

Ethel shrugged. 'He never made a point of enquiring after me, but we never went short. Sometimes there would be gifts from the keep – a new goat when ours died, the end from a bolt of linen with enough on it to make me a chemise. He paid for my brother, Alberic, to be educated for the priesthood at Malmesbury. The bond was known but never acknowledged, and after he died it was forgotten.' She stroked the plait and returned it to its pouch.

'Why tell me now?' Catrin asked.

Ethel shrugged. 'Perhaps it is a secret that I don't want to take with me to the grave.'

Catrin looked at her with dismay widening her eyes, and Ethel looked back serenely.

'I would be a fool not to realise how frail I have become,' she said. 'I am a herb-wife. I know what can be healed and what has to be.' Then she smiled and gently shook her head. 'That stew is not going to be ready before midnight.'

Taking the hint, Catrin tucked the hair knot away and resumed chopping the eels. She did not want to think of Ethel dying, but she saw the truth as clearly as the old woman, and knowledge was a two-edged sword. She could not decide whether it was better to live in ignorance or know what the future held in store. Oliver was going to be all right. Ethel was going to die.

Gazing into the fire, Ethel watched the flames dance, but they did not speak to her again and she was glad. She did not have the energy to discern their meanings. They could be so ambiguous, and that troubled her. Behind the shining crown and Oliver's return, there were dark currents that threatened to ruin the future of those that Ethel loved best, and she knew that there was nothing she could do.

CHAPTER 15

In years to come, Oliver would always remember Lincolnshire as a flat, waterlogged land, devoid of colour in the bleak January weather. He would see again the boggy roads over which Earl Robert's army floundered and trudged, smell the mud, taste the all-pervading frozen damp that numbed the flesh and rusted mail overnight. He would also remember the anticipation and the sense of power as Robert's army united with Chester's and marched with dogged, inexorable purpose upon Stephen and Lincoln. The cold, the discomfort, were not lessened, but they were made bearable by the knowledge that the tide was no longer running in Stephen's favour but in theirs.

To reach Lincoln, the combined armies had to find places to cross the river Witham and an ancient Roman ditch called the Fossedyke, which protected the city. Their guide, a local villager, swore that there was a shallow ford on the latter, but when he led them to it, squelching and cursing across the boggy floodplain, it proved to be a swift-running channel of brown spate-water. On the other side Stephen had set a small company of guards. As Robert of Gloucester and Rannulf of Chester approached the water's edge to try and gauge its depth, they were assaulted by a barrage of stones, clods of mud and yelled insults.

Oliver drew rein and, with frozen hands, fumbled in his saddle pouch for his wine flask. Hero was caked belly-deep in stinking marsh mud and bore scarcely any resemblance to the groomed, silver-dapple stallion that had set out from Bristol less than two weeks since.

Oliver drank from his flask and as he washed the pungent red wine around his teeth, thought that he seemed to have been on the road for ever. Although it was only Candlemas now, the peace of Christmas was a distant star on a fast vanishing horizon. His glance strayed to the woven knot of hair laced to his scabbard attachments. Catrin had given it to him on their last night together as they lay in the loft above the stables, wrapped in their cloaks and each other's arms.

The thought of her added warmth to the wine as it flowed through him, and he touched the knot. It made the physical distance between them seem less. The threads of bright copper-auburn trapped his eye, causing him to shake his head in bemusement. Strange to think that Ethel was his kin in truth. He had not known her when her hair was this colour, for she had been well past her fortieth winter when he was born, her red colouring faded to a sandy-grey. He wondered if he would have treated her differently had he known she was family and was glad that he had been unaware until now. The obligation of blood was weighted with guilt, whereas the obligation to an old woman who had once lived on his family's lands was considerably more simple. He took another drink of wine and then hastily looped his flask back on his saddle as Miles of Gloucester and a companion drove their horses into the icy, swift-flowing water of the Fossedyke.

On the other side, King Stephen's men watched with growing apprehension. Their horses backed and circled. They hurled further flurries of mud and stones as Earl Robert's men plunged into the dyke. A spear flashed in the air and fell harmlessly between the horses. Before it could sink, someone leaned down from his saddle, caught it up and cast it back at Stephen's men. It landed in front of them, its tip quivering in the mud of the far bank as both a threat and a promise. A horse panicked and flailed into one of its companions, creating mayhem. Bravado evaporating, Stephen's small band of sentries turned tail and fled to raise the alarm, leaving their post unguarded and the way free.

Oliver set his teeth and spurred Hero into the churning spate of the dyke. He had been prepared to be frozen but still the shock took his breath away as the water immersed the stallion to the saddle girth and spray flew up drenching Oliver through mail and padding. He heard Gawin cursing the icy tug of the current as his dun splashed and floundered. Any man who fell off his horse or failed to keep his feet would drown, dragged under in seconds by the weight of his mail and sodden gambeson.

The first troops to gain the opposite side set about securing a rope across the dyke for the infantry to grasp as their turn came to dare the chest-deep water. There were many Welshmen among them, accustomed to fording deep streams and plodding through inhospitable terrain as part of their daily existence. They took the crossing with such a flourish that they encouraged their less experienced English counterparts to do the same.

'Hell's mouth, I want double wages for this!' declared Randal de Mohun as he rode past Oliver on his bay stallion, water spraying from the high-stepping hooves. 'No one said anything about being a fish!'

'If we win, you'll doubtless get them.'

De Mohun snorted and set about mustering his men. 'It will be us that will have to do the winning first.'

Oliver shook his head and went to seek Earl Robert for orders.

It was Candlemas: the feast of the purification of the Virgin, the ceremony based on the Roman worship of the Goddess Juno Februata, and Catrin was attending another childbirth amongst the soap-makers of the city, where she and Ethel had made a reputation for themselves. It was Aline Saponier's seventh confinement, and the baby came swiftly and smoothly into the world and immediately began bawling with lungs like a set of smithy bellows.

'A fine boy,' smiled Catrin, receiving him into the waiting sheet. 'You scarce needed a midwife at all, Mistress.'

'I'm told your skills make for an easy delivery,' Aline panted from the birthing stool. 'Has he got all his fingers and toes?'

'Whole in every sense of the word.' Catrin gently rubbed

the infant in the towel then folded over the ends and gave him to his mother.

Aline's sweaty face creased with a surfeit of emotion as she peered into the baby's new-born, unprepossessing features. 'He's beautiful!' she sniffed, and started to weep.

'He is that, Mistress,' Catrin said diplomatically, as she knelt to cut the cord and competently delivered the after-birth.

The other women of the household crowded round, cooing, touching and commenting. There were three aunts, a cousin, and a toothless grandmother, all present to help and bear witness, thus making the event a tremendous social occasion. Catrin was accustomed by now to such gatherings, but there had still been a couple of times when she could cheerfully have gagged the grandmother with a swaddling band.

One of the aunts trotted from the room to announce to the waiting household that a new son had been safely delivered. Catrin saw the mother cleaned up, made comfortable with linen pads and helped back into the freshly made family bed.

The grandmother mumbled into her gums and patted Catrin on the shoulder. 'You've not done so badly for one so young, who's never borne a babe herself,' she allowed.

'Thank you,' Catrin said sweetly.

'Heard about you from Mistress Hubert at the house on the end. She said as you and the old woman were competent.'

Catrin gave a preoccupied smile and set about returning her midwife's tools to her satchel, of which only the oil and the sharp knife had been required.

'But you came alone,' her assailant persisted.

'My companion is not well enough to make the journey into the city,' Catrin replied. 'The winter and her years weigh heavily on her.' She compressed her lips. Ethel had been sneezing all morning and, despite being crouched over the fire wrapped in both her green mantle and a cloak, had been shivering fit to slough the flesh from her bones.

'Aye, well, I'm nigh on three-score-and-ten winters myself and I've had a cough worse than a dog's bark,' said the old woman, not to be outdone. 'I tell you, sometimes it is as much as I can do to ease myself from my bed in a morning.'

Which Catrin took with a substantial pinch of salt. She glanced round. Two of the aunts were bathing the baby in a silver basin while the cousin aired its swaddling before the charcoal brazier. A serving maid went round the room lighting the candles from a long taper. Catrin noted that the light was provided not by spindly, tallow dips but proper, heavy wax candles, the kind that burned in the Countess's bower.

Seeing the direction of her gaze, the old woman went to an aumbry in the wall and returned with three more of the candles, their surfaces smooth and creamily glossed. 'Here, take these,' she said, 'in honour of the blessed Virgin whose feast it is.'

Catrin accepted them with pleasure. She knew how fond Ethel was of beeswax candles. The gifts and tokens that grateful householders presented were one of the more pleasant aspects of being a midwife.

Outside, the February daylight was dull grey, and the wind was sharp on Catrin's face. She tugged her hood up over her wimple and secured the clasp on her cloak, her teeth chattering with cold. The church of Saint Mary le Port rang out the hour of Nones and was joined by the bells of Saint Peter. She thought of Oliver and wondered what he was doing. Was he riding blue-fingered in the cold or had they reached their destination? Was there peace or bloodshed? Two weeks of silence on the matter had shredded her equilibrium. She had taken to biting her nails and, despite Ethel's assurances that he would return, she worried constantly.

Godard's dark shape loomed out of the shadows at the side of the Saponiers' dwelling and he fell into step beside her, as huge and solid as a walking wall. She was grateful for his presence and his taciturnity. Talk for talk's sake only set her teeth on edge, when all she longed for, and dreaded, was news of Earl Robert's army.

They walked along the path between the riverbank and the boundaries of Saint Peter's church. Fishing craft and galleys bobbed on the tide and seagulls wheeled like detached portions of cloud, their cries poignant and harsh.

A sea-going cog had docked at the castle's wharf to be unburdened of its cargo of casks and barrels. It was a scene re-enacted every day, and at first Catrin took small notice. But as she and Godard drew nearer, she saw that no one was working, that all the men were gathered around something on the ground. One of the younger labourers had staggered away and was vomiting into the water. Others had drawn cloaks and capes around their mouths.

Natural curiosity drew Catrin to go and look at what the men had found. She suspected that it was probably a porpoise or a whale. Such creatures were occasionally washed up along the river in the tidal flow and they were always a cause for wonder – and disgust if they were dead and their corpses had begun to rot. She craned her neck at the white thing she could see lying on the dock between the legs of the men. It seemed too small to be a porpoise, or even a baby whale – too insubstantial.

'Mistress, come away,' Godard said suddenly and grasped her arm, but it was too late for she had already seen the gleam of bone through shredded flesh and realised that the form they were all looking at was – or had been – human. A length of hemp rope was snagged around what had been one of its legs, and twisted around the rope was a rag of pink cloth, embroidered with a darker pink flower motif. Strands of hair still adhered to its skull, which had broken away from the body as the men had lifted it free from where it had lain, caught in the mesh of a lost fishing net. The colour, streaming with water, was the same hue as the red hair woven into the knot that Catrin had given to Oliver, but when dry it would be a lighter, more chestnut shade. Catrin felt bile rise in her own throat. Now she knew what had happened to Rohese de Bayvel.

'It is the Countess's sempstress,' she said jerkily to the gathered men. 'She vanished on Christmas Eve and no one knew what had become of her.' Her throat was so tight that it was hard to speak. 'For decency's sake, cover her and fetch a priest.'

Oliver positioned his shield on his left arm and drew his sword. All around him men were fretting their mounts and preparing for the charge. The bitter wind cut through his garments, still sodden from the crossing of the Fossedyke, but he was too focused on the coming battle to feel the cold. He had fought in skirmishes before but this was his first taste of a major engagement. It was the same for many of the men sizing each other up across the flat stretch of land to the west of the city. Despite the state of constant warfare in England, battles on a large scale were rare. All or nothing casts of the dice were impractical . . . unless, of course, the dice were loaded in your favour, or you were cornered and there was no other way out. Today, Earl Robert had the luck of the throw and Stephen was cornered, but both armies were evenly matched in number and fighting skill. It was not yet a foregone conclusion.

On the hill above, Oliver could see the banners on the keep walls, bravely fluttering the colours of Chester and Gloucester in defiance of Stephen's siege engines. Stephen himself had come roaring out of Lincoln with his entire army when he heard the news that the ford at the Fossedyke had been breached.

'He wasn't expecting our arrival on his threshold so soon and in such great numbers,' Gawin said scornfully, as Stephen's troops fell into hasty formation opposite their own.

Oliver nodded agreement. 'No, and because we've caught him unprepared, he's reacted with his gut.' He blew on his frozen fingers. 'If I was Stephen, I would stay behind the town defences and force us to bring the battle to him – make us charge up the hill. He's thrown away his advantage by facing us on the level.' He looked round at the solid position of his section of Robert's force on the left flank. The Earl had assembled most of the disinherited knights and barons in that sector. Opposing them were the forces of Stephen's earls and magnates – Richmond, Norfolk, Northampton, Surrey and Worcester. Rannulf of Chester held the centre, facing Stephen and his infantry, and Earl Robert had taken the right flank with the Welsh levies to face Stephen's Flemish mercenary troops.

Rhetoric was spouted and commanders rode up and down their lines, inciting the men, raising them to battle fever. Earl

Robert's voice was a strong, carrying baritone. In contrast, Stephen's voice was so thin and husky that one of his barons, Baldwin FitzGilbert, had to deputise.

Opposite Oliver, a challenge to joust went out from Stephen's magnates, who appeared to favour a formal opening to the fight.

'Hah, as if they think it's a feast day,' growled Randal de Mohun in Oliver's ear. Although not one of the dispossessed, he had elected to fight with them – in the hopes of being given a fief of his own, Oliver suspected.

'To them, it is,' Oliver replied, without taking his eyes off the opposing line. He wondered if the man who had usurped Ashbury was numbered among the troops that Waleran of Worcester had brought on campaign. 'To them we are nothing but landless mercenaries, and that invitation is a mockery.' He watched the opposing knights prancing and prinking in their bright colours, and did not need the rhetoric of the battle captains to fuel the smoulder of his anger. It was to feed the ambition of the men he was facing that his brother had died and he had been made a rebel, dependent on his sword for his income. Well, by God, today he was going to earn his wages.

He pushed his way forward, offering to reply to the challenge to joust. Randal de Mohun lined up beside him, his lance couched.

'I'm going to rend holes in that fancy mail of theirs that no armourer will ever mend.' De Mohun licked his lips hungrily. His eyes were bright and his breathing swift.

Oliver looked at de Mohun. The mercenary had slackened the reins on all that vicious aggression lying beneath the surface. And why not? Oliver reached down to the fire in his own belly and allowed it to spread through his veins. A little behind him, he could hear Gawin breathing swiftly through his mouth. A glance showed him that the young man was trembling, but more with anger and excitement than fear.

'Ready?' Oliver asked.

'More than,' Gawin replied, and fretted his horse with rein and spur.

In front of them, their commander, Miles FitzWalter,

Sheriff of Gloucester, rose in his stirrups and bellowed aloud. *'Laissez Corree! Vanquez le Stor!'*

Oliver clapped spurs to Hero's flanks and together with Gawin, de Mohun and thirty knights, thundered over the soft ground towards the posturing opposition. Instead of courteously drawing their blows and making a chivalrous play of the encounter, they attacked in earnest, their charge never slackening and their weapons driving for their enemies' vitals and punching through.

King Stephen's languid cavalry found themselves at the mercy of men carried forward on an impetus of rage and outrage. Each blow aimed was intended to disable or kill, rather than politely take for ransom – of which the latter had been custom throughout the war. No quarter was given. Steel bit, then bit deeper still. Earl Robert's left flank surged in the wake of the first, vicious charge and hammered home a second assault.

It did not matter that the numbers were about even; Stephen's men could not compete with the ferocity of their opponents. Oliver found himself fighting thin air, for no one would make a stand and meet him blow for blow. To a man, the five earls who should have held Earl Robert's cavalry at bay fled the field with their troops, leaving the men of Gloucester in control and Stephen hopelessly outflanked.

Catrin replaced the ordinary rush tapers of daily use with the fat wax candles that old Mistress Saponier had given to her. Light blossomed in Ethel's dwelling, clear, bright and perfumed with the honey smell of summer. Catrin inhaled deeply, trying to banish the stench of the wharfside discovery from her nostrils.

Propped up on two bolsters to ease her congested breathing, Ethel watched her from the bed. 'So she threw herself into the river,' she wheezed, as Catrin told her about Rohese. 'Well, 'tis no surprise. Too much pride to live with the shame.'

Catrin shuddered. 'But she was vain as well, and she liked the fine things of life. I cannot imagine that she would do that to herself. Besides, it was too soon. There was still a chance that she might have bled.'

Ethel gave her a shrewd look. 'There but for the grace of God,' she said, her cracked voice soft. 'Was that how it was for you?'

Catrin drew a sharp breath at Ethel's uncanny intuition. For a moment she was cast back to the days immediately following Lewis's death. She saw an image of herself standing on Chepstow's battlements at dusk, staring down into the sleek, dark waters of the river Wye. 'I didn't drown myself,' she said tautly. 'I thought about it, I admit, but only for an instant.'

'An instant is all that it takes, one slip of the foot on a wet stone.' Ethel closed her eyes.

Catrin gave a little shiver. 'How did you know?'

'Your fear, the way you spoke. I sensed a link with water . . . dark water, flowing fast.' Her voice sank to a mumble. 'And I saw a man too, dark of hair and eye.'

Catrin felt cold to her marrow. 'Lewis,' she whispered.

Ethel spoke again, a single word, clear and bright as the candle flame. 'Beware.'

Catrin went forward to the bed, intent on asking her what she meant, but Ethel did not answer except by way of a chesty snore.

Lincoln Castle was ablaze with light as the leaders of the Empress's army celebrated their victory. Lincoln town was ablaze too – with fire – as the common troops plundered the wealth of the citizens who had made an error of judgement in choosing Stephen as their protector.

Oliver had declined to follow Randal de Mohun into the streets of Lincoln in search of gain. To fight men on a battlefield was one thing. To harry women and children out of their houses, steal their goods and burn their dwellings, was another matter entirely. In every woman's face, he would have seen Catrin's, in every child's, Richard's. All war was dark, but this part stank as well, and Oliver remained within the castle precincts, his single act of plunder the appropriation of a flagon of the finest Gascon wine intended for the high table.

Despite his distaste, he was in high spirits. The ease of

their victory and the capture of Stephen himself meant that the tide had well and truly turned in the Empress's favour. If the impetus continued, then he would be lord of his own lands before many more months were out. It was a hope worth toasting in the rich, dark wine. He would celebrate the next Christmas feast at Ashbury's high table as his father and his brother had done: with a gilded wassail tree, great rejoicing and Catrin crowned in evergreen at his side.

For the moment, he was content with a simple trestle at the side of the hall and the company of Geoffrey FitzMar and a handful of other knights who had declined to venture into the town. They relived the battle blow by blow, as they had each seen it, exalting in the moment when Stephen, abandoned by his earls, abandoned by his mercenaries, had stood alone, swinging his Dane axe at all comers, until finally downed by a lucky blow to the helm which had stunned him for long enough to be taken and bound. He was now locked in one of the upper rooms. His wounds had been tended, he was treated with courtesy, but guarded so heavily that not even a spider could crawl under his door without being noticed.

'I'm to stand my turn of duty later,' Geoffrey said, declining Oliver's offer of wine. 'I'll need a clear head.'

'Hah, he's unlikely to break free, is he?' scoffed one of the others.

'Mayhap not, but Earl Robert's just as unlikely to tolerate a drunkard on duty.'

Oliver's own turn of duty was set for the following dawn. He could afford to drink but not to the point of inebriation. Filling his cup for the third and final time, he handed the flask to the others to finish. Despite his desire to see Stephen overthrown, he had to admire the man's bravery and his dignified conduct in defeat. Perhaps for the first time in his reign, Stephen was displaying the qualities of a king – although that still did not give him the right to be one.

'To victory.' He raised his cup. 'May it sweeten daily.'

'Victory,' Geoffrey repeated, and swallowed the last of his own wine. Wiping his mouth he looked around. 'Where's Gawin tonight?'

Oliver shook his head. 'In the town with de Mohun.'

Geoffrey picked his helm off the table and rose to his feet. 'I'm glad my duty to the Earl keeps me here tonight,' he said grimly. 'We are told that the townsfolk need teaching a lesson but I have no stomach for being a tutor.' He rumpled his free hand through his tawny curls and frowned. 'In truth, I would not have thought Gawin of that ilk either.'

'He isn't,' Oliver defended, without meeting his friend's gaze. 'He is just unsettled at the moment. I tried to make him stay but he would have none of it, not with de Mohun dangling the promise of treasure before his eyes.'

'Yes, well, one day de Mohun is going to trim his sails that bit too close to the wind.' Disgust curled Geoffrey's lip. 'Why you tolerate his company, God alone knows.'

'God alone does,' Oliver answered heavily, thinking of a bare mountain road near Jerusalem and the man to whom misfortune had made him indebted.

Reversing his sword, Gawin hacked open the lock with the hilt, shoved back the heavy oak lid and gazed into a coffer crammed with pieces of scrap silver ready for melting down. The house belonged to a goldsmith and the pickings were rich. He lifted the coffer, which was about the size and weight of a young pig, and staggered outside to the waiting pack horse.

Houses were burning, filling the sky with a lurid red light, the heat and gush of sparks making it seem to Gawin that he was standing in the mouth of hell. He felt that way too, but as if he was the sinner, not the people on whom this punishment was being visited. With a grim will, he shook off his doubts. Even if he was a sinner, he was going to be a rich one. That coffer of silver was worth a year's wages, and it was only the tip of the plunder. In the dwelling next door, he could hear de Mohun's men at work, prising up the hearth bricks in search of hidden wealth. No one had challenged them. The citizens had more sense than to resist mercenaries and had fled to take shelter in the churches or remote outbuildings of no interest to the looters.

Gawin led his horse back inside the house so that no one would steal his find and set about hacking open a second coffer – a clothing chest by its size. The lock quickly gave but the lid refused to open, as if held down from the inside. Gawin wedged his sword beneath the lid and heard a muffled cry of terror. Withdrawing the sword, he grasped the wooden edge in both hands and wrenched it back.

A young woman screamed and cowered down, her hands over her head. She had long fair hair tied back with a strip of braid. Her features were delicate, just beginning to emerge from the roundness of adolescence. Tear streaks had left clean white tracks through the grime on her face and she wore the ragged, threadbare dress of a servant.

'Stand up!' Gawin commanded. He flickered a glance around, but there was no evidence of anyone else in the house. For whatever reason, she had been left behind to take her chance with the routiers. Protectiveness and rage warred within him. 'I said stand up!' he snarled, when she did not move and, lunging forward, he seized her arm.

Sobbing, screaming, she lurched to her feet, and Gawin saw the reason why she had been unable to flee. She had a deformity of the hip that made it nigh on impossible to walk, let alone run, all her weight taken upon one side.

'Christ, are you witless, girl, as well as a cripple?' he demanded, his anger making him cruel.

She shook her head and wailed all the louder, her dirty blond hair tumbling around her face. He could feel the swift rise and fall of her shoulder against his arm as she breathed, the starved slightness of her bones. All the guilt and rage from Christmas flooded over him. He wanted to strike her to the ground and yet he held his hand. Perhaps if he saved her life it would somehow redress the balance that had been lost when Rohese disappeared. 'Can you sit a horse?'

She looked at him with frightened eyes and whimpered.

'Christ Jesu, I don't have the time,' Gawin said and, swinging her up in his arms, turned towards his mount. Then he stopped dead. She screamed, then buried her face against the mesh of his hauberk.

'Now then, what have we here?' Randal de Mohun shouldered through the doorway and, with feigned nonchalance, eyed Gawin and the girl. 'A wench, eh? Aren't you the lucky one?'

Gawin tightened his grip on her gown. 'She's mine,' he said quietly.

De Mohun entered the room and walked around the horse's rump. His gaze flickered to the ornately carved coffer strapped to the saddle and, behind it, a fine piece of blue Flemish wool. 'It's share and share alike amongst us, my lad,' he answered, in a tone equally quiet. 'The lass and the other loot both.'

The girl wept and huddled into Gawin's neck. He could feel her hair against his jaw, feel the terror in the bone-hard grip of her fingers. 'I'm not one of you,' he said. 'Your code is not mine.'

De Mohun narrowed his eyes. 'Then you should not be here, lad. Sheep that run with wolves end up being devoured.' Almost casually, he drew his sword.

Gawin uncurled the girl's clinging fingers from around his neck. She slumped to the ground, sobbing and screaming, as he drew his own blade. 'You promised Oliver that you would watch out for me!' he said, mouth open, breath coming hard.

'So I did, and I have kept my word, have I not? Every step of the way.'

Gawin licked his lips. 'Take the silver then. Do what you want with it, but leave the girl. You wouldn't want her, she's a useless cripple.'

De Mohun raised his sword and scratched his chin gently with the side of the hilt. 'You have a point there, and I can't say as I'm not tempted, but if I break the rule for you, then I'll have to break it for anyone who takes the whim to keep something for himself and that's not good for discipline. I tell you what.' He lowered the hilt and pointed it at Gawin. 'You can have first turn at her, and we'll let her live when we've all done.'

Gawin almost retched. What would remain of the girl after a dozen men had taken their turn would be worse than death. 'Just take the silver and be content. You can buy all the women you want without resorting to rape!' He braced his sword, protecting himself and the young woman.

De Mohun grimaced. 'You don't understand, do you? Buying *anything* is a blasphemy to me.' The flames from the burning houses around them gleamed on his sword as the blade came up.

Since there was no proof as to how Rohese de Bayvel had died, her death was recorded as a tragic accident and she was buried with all haste and ceremony in the grounds of Saint Peter's, her funeral attended by the Countess and all the ladies of the bower.

Edon FitzMar saturated her linen kerchief with tears and was so distressed that it fell to Catrin to make her a soothing tisane.

'I cannot believe it,' Edon wept, cuddling her small son on her knee. 'I thought that she had just run off.'

Not thought but wished, Catrin guessed, and in that endeavour, Edon was the same as everyone else. 'At least she has been found and granted Christian burial,' she said, mouthing the platitude with a grimace at her own hypocrisy. Perhaps the not knowing had been kinder than the reality.

'I wish Geoffrey was here.' Edon nuzzled the top of her baby's head.

Catrin nodded and thought of Oliver. They heard occasional reports from the Countess's messengers, but the information that filtered through was scant and did not mention the individual names that each woman wanted to hear. Geoffrey FitzMar and Oliver Pascal were minor cogs in the great mill wheels of Earl Robert's army. 'At least you have a keepsake,' she said, looking at the infant.

'Who might never see his father again,' Edon sniffed, and fresh tears sprang to her eyes. Cursing Edon's sensitivity and her own thoughtless tongue, Catrin urged more of the tisane on the young woman, soothed her with more platitudes and, as soon as it was possible, made her escape. She had a good excuse; Ethel's winter ague had thickened on her chest and she had a fever. Catrin did not like to leave her for too long.

Agatha, the laundress, was sitting with Ethel. Now and then she moistened the old woman's lips with a spoonful of watered wine, but there was little more she could do for her. Ethel hovered on the periphery of consciousness and each breath she drew made deep hollows of effort beneath her rib cage.

'I've sent for the priest,' Agatha sniffed, her double chins wobbling. She blotted her eyes on her gown. 'I'm not a healer but I know the signs, poor soul.'

Catrin gave the laundress a mute look and, sitting down at Ethel's side, took the old woman's good hand between hers, dismayed at how swiftly her condition had deteriorated. 'Ethel?'

The eyelids fluttered and the fingers found a squeeze of life. 'Catrin . . .' Ethel swallowed, the sound a dry rattle.

'I'm here. Save your strength, Agatha has sent for the priest.'

Ethel's face contorted. 'Don't need a priest, you know that.'

'Yes, but the rest of the world would rather see you shriven.'

Ethel made a wheezing sound that might have been a laugh or just a struggle for breath. Then she grasped Catrin's sleeve and strained towards her. 'He will ruin you if you are not careful.' She licked her lips. 'I dreamed of a man on a bay horse. He is a danger to you and to Oliver. Take great care.' The effort left her panting for breath, her lips blue.

'Lie still, Ethel, don't . . .'

But Ethel struggled against Catrin's restraining words and hands. 'There was water and darkness. You must not go near him!'

'I won't, I swear I won't,' Catrin said in a frantic attempt to calm Ethel's agitation. The old woman fought to breathe, her chest rattling, her grip like a bird's claw.

The priest arrived at a run and, taking one look at Ethel, set about the task of shriving with unprecedented speed, his Latin gabbled so swiftly that even another priest would have been hard pressed to understand him.

Even as he pronounced 'amen' Ethel slumped against Catrin, the holy oil trickling down her brow and sliding across one withered cheek like a tear.

Catrin held the old woman close, her head bowed against the wasted body, her nostrils filled with odours of incense, horehound and death. Agatha sobbed through her praying hands and the priest murmured softly, the Latin words offering the comfort of ritual.

Catrin heard the sounds but they had no meaning. Relinquishing her hold, she crossed Ethel's arms upon her breast and drew up the coverlet. The body was so hot with fever that it still bore the illusion of life. Ethel might only have been asleep was it not for the stillness of her chest. 'I will do what has to be done,' Catrin told the priest, her voice calm and practical.

'I'll help you too, Mistress,' Agatha snuffled. 'She were a good friend to me, God bless her soul.'

With a wordless nod, Catrin turned away and stepped outside to inhale the respite of the sharp February dusk. Light glimmered on the puddles in the dips of the bailey floor, and breath rose in curlicues of steam from a pen of sheep against one of the walls. Unseen, someone was whistling as they hammered at a task. It was all so ordinary, so unchanged from the morning, but now everything was different, distorted as if seen through thick green window glass.

The evening tranquillity was shattered as a courier rode in at the gallop, his tired horse splashing through the puddles, breaking the light on their surface, before staggering to a halt not far from Ethel's shelter. A groom came running to take the bridle, and Catrin found herself squinting at the animal in the poor light to see if it was the bay from Ethel's vision. Later she was to take herself to task, but at the time grief made sense of her action.

'Victory!' the messenger announced to the groom as he flung down from the saddle. 'Lincoln is ours and King Stephen taken prisoner. There was a pitched battle and we broke his army like straws in the wind!' Slapping the groom on the shoulder, the messenger ran on towards the keep.

Catrin gazed after him, his words ringing in her head without being absorbed. It was too much, too great a swing of emotion to encompass. All that she could salvage was that, as Ethel had predicted, Oliver would be returning, but the joy was marred.

'Why couldn't you have waited?' she said over her shoulder in the direction of Ethel's dwelling, and was so appalled at the anger she felt that she was immediately contrite. 'I didn't mean it, I'm sorry,' she whispered, and knew that even in opening her mouth she had told a lie. She did mean it, deny it as she might. 'Tell me how I am to be guided now,' she demanded, raising her face to the drizzly evening sky. Tears stung her eyes, brimmed and spilled, and she began to weep.

It was late in the morning when Oliver was fetched from guard duty and brought to the castle's chapel to identify Gawin's body.

'I told him to stay close, but he strayed off into a house on his own and was murdered by a citizen who had stayed to guard his hoard.' Randal de Mohun spread his hands in a gesture that absolved himself of all blame.

Oliver chewed the inside of his mouth. In the smallest corner at the back of his mind he had been expecting something like this to happen. He looked at Gawin's lifeless body with sorrow and anger but without disbelief. 'Where did this happen?'

'On the hill down from the Minster. The house is a ruin now. A spark from another roof caught the thatch and it went up so fast I only just got out alive.' De Mohun showed Oliver a patch of burned, blistered skin on the back of his right hand, and the charred cuff of his tunic. 'Don't look at me like that, I'm not a nursemaid. You should be grateful that I brought his corpse out of the accursed place instead of leaving him to burn!'

Oliver stared at Gawin's grey flesh, at the ugly slash in his throat that had bled his life away. 'I am damning your hide for ever taking him with you,' he said icily. 'And damning mine for ever allowing him to go.'

'Go swive a sheep, Pascal!' de Mohun retorted, curling his fists around his belt. 'He was seasoned enough to know the risks!'

Oliver looked from Gawin's torn throat to de Mohun's wolf-narrow eyes. 'I wonder if he was.'

'Hah, he's dead. There's no point in wondering, unless you want to bleed too. He took a chance, he died, God rest his purblind soul!' Turning on his heel, de Mohun stalked out of the chapel without even pausing to light a candle.

Staring in his wake, Oliver silently absolved himself of the debt he owed to Randal de Mohun. He did not think that Gawin's 'purblind' soul was going to rest easy with the end that his mortal body had received.

CHAPTER 16

The fire was low, just the faintest glimmer of red to lend warmth to the midnight hour. In the dwelling that had been Ethel's, Catrin and Oliver lay entwined, savouring each other's body heat, the presence of living flesh joyfully confirmed in the act of love.

'I feared for you,' Catrin admitted, and ran her fingers through the dusting of ruddy-gold hair on his chest. 'Ethel had some very strange visions in her last days. She swore that you were safe but I was afraid to believe her because she told me other things that made no sense.'

She felt him shrug. 'You say that she had a fever. Belike she was wandering through her dreams.'

'Yes,' Catrin said dubiously, but more to agree with him than out of any conviction of her own. 'Yet she did tell me that you would return, and with a crown shining above you, and she was right. When I saw you ride into the bailey, you were part of the guard escorting King Stephen, and because he is a captive, Mathilda will be Queen.'

He gave a non-committal grunt. 'I can remember that when I was a child, some of the women would ask her to scry for them, but I always thought that it was nonsense – like her weaving of the knots. I'm sure that she gave good advice, but I think it was wisdom rather than premonition.' He angled his head to look at her. 'What else did she see?'

'That is the quandary: I do not know.' Frowning, Catrin told him about Ethel's warning concerning a bay horse, darkness and water. 'But what she saw, she did not say . . . could not, for she was dying.'

He stroked her arm and was silent for a time. 'More than half the soldiers in Earl Robert's pay ride bay horses – Geoffrey FitzMar for a start. I cannot imagine him being a threat to you.'

Catrin pressed close to him, absorbing the comfort of his smell, the warmth of his body. 'No,' she murmured against his skin. 'My mind tells me that I am being foolish, but there has been so much death and wanton destruction of late that I cannot help but jump at shadows.' She tightened her fingers in his chest hair until he flinched and hissed.

'The only wanton destruction here is what you are doing to me,' he said. His tone was tender rather than playful, and he lifted her hand from his breast and kissed the fingertips. 'Sometimes good can come out of the worst happenings. If not for the raid that destroyed Penfoss, we would not be lying together now, would we?'

'No,' Catrin admitted, and nuzzled him. 'But I cannot see the good in losing Ethel, or in what happened to Rohese and Gawin.'

Oliver was silent for a moment, pondering. Then he sighed. 'As to Ethel, it was her time, I think,' he said. 'I can count upon the fingers of one hand the people I know who have reached three score and ten, and she was older than that. Rohese and Gawin . . . well, perhaps you are right. Only time will tell and, if it doesn't, at least it will heal.'

Catrin tasted the salt on his skin with the tip of her tongue and thought how much she had missed him. 'Yes, perhaps,' she conceded, and thrust from her mind the image of the white, rotting body on the wharfside.

'It doesn't matter what Ethel saw, or at least it doesn't matter now, immediately . . . does it?' He circled her palm with the forefinger of his other hand and stroked a slow trail up the soft flesh of her inner arm.

'No,' Catrin replied with a sensuous shiver, adding with forced determination, 'You are right, it doesn't matter now.'

'Will your family lands soon be restored?' Catrin asked. They were still in bed, sharing a cup of mead while the dawn brightened in the East.

Oliver raised himself up on his elbows to take the cup from her. 'I hope so, but I do not believe that it will be much before the summer. Despite Stephen's capture, the Fleming who holds Ashbury has not submitted to the Empress. It may be that I will have to fight for them yet.'

'But with Stephen a prisoner, surely the war is almost at an end?' Catrin protested.

He sighed. 'I would hope so, but it is not as simple as it first appears. Stephen might be a prisoner, but that does not mean that his supporters will kneel to the Empress. If they yield, they stand to lose the lands and the powers that they have enjoyed under his rule. Mathilda does not know the meaning of forgiveness or compromise. She will not let men submit with their pride intact; she will expect nothing less than abject surrender.'

Hearing the censure and distaste in his voice, Catrin was moved to ask, 'Then why do you support her at all?'

'Not her, but her cause. My family swore allegiance to the Empress as King Henry's heir, and I gave my oath of my own free will to Robert of Gloucester. I am bound by my honour to serve them.'

'Bound in knots by the sound of matters,' Catrin said a trifle acidly, having no bias either way. She wished both sides to perdition.

'When my brother rebelled against Stephen, his lands were taken by force of arms. I own nothing, except by Earl Robert's grace. If that be a knot, then I unravel it to my own impoverishment.'

'But still I . . .'

Their conversation was curtailed by a knock on the doorpost of the shelter, and Richard poked his head around the screen to peer in at them. 'Catrin, the Earl wants you. He says that you're to come to his solar and bring your satchel.'

'Is he ill?' Oliver demanded sharply, and reached for his shirt.

The boy shook his head. His hair was in need of barbering and fell forward over his eyes, giving him the aspect of a shaggy dog. 'No, but Stephen is. It's the manacles. One of them has a sharp edge and it has made his wrist all raw.'

Turning her back on the boy for modesty's sake, Catrin tugged on her undershift and donned her ordinary brown hose. Oliver eyed Richard in consternation.

'Manacles?' he queried. 'I thought Stephen was to be kept under honourable house arrest?'

'Empress Mathilda says that it is not enough – that he might escape. His word's not to be trusted. She says that he deserves the weight of chains for stealing her birthright.'

Oliver groaned, and rubbed his hands over his face. Catrin thought he muttered 'stupid bitch' but could not be sure.

Hastily she donned her remaining garments and grabbed her satchel from the corner. Into it, she put a pot of Ethel's goose-grease unguent and several strips of linen bandage. Kissing Oliver in farewell, she followed Richard across the bailey and into the keep.

Stephen was being held in a small, but pleasantly appointed, wall-chamber with painted murals and a sturdy charcoal brazier to keep the damp at bay. The iron ring bolted into the wall detracted incongruously from such comforts. Looped through it was a length of stout iron bear-chain which was attached at either end to the wrist manacles cuffing the prisoner. There were chains on his feet too, although only fashioned ankle to ankle rather than to the wall.

King Stephen was in early middle age, with a fleece of hair only a little darker than Oliver's. His beard was fair too, with a single badger-stripe of grey mid-chin. Stephen's eyes were weathered blue, framed in attractive creases which revealed that despite all the troubles visited upon him since his accession to the throne, he was a man accustomed to laughter. Catrin could not help thinking that Empress Mathilda was a termagant and a very foolish woman to issue the command to bind him thus. For all that he had snatched her throne, he was yet an anointed king and her cousin into the bargain.

'Ah, Catrin.' Earl Robert beckoned her into the room. His colour was high and he appeared ill at ease. She swept him a curtsey and gave one to Stephen too. King or not, he was still a man of rank. The gesture earned her a thin smile from the captive.

'I have sent for you to look at a wound on Lord Stephen's

wrist,' Robert announced, and gestured to one of the guards.

The soldier produced a key and unlocked the right manacle.

'Not afraid that I'll make a bid for freedom, are you?' Stephen mocked, a twist to his mouth.

Robert looked uncomfortable, and his eyes flickered away from his captive. 'No, I am not, but it is my sister's wish, and I abide by her ruling.'

'Ah, Robert, would you jump over a cliff if she so desired?' Stephen opened and closed his fist in relief at being free of the iron, no matter how briefly. 'But perhaps you already have,' he added.

Robert wriggled his shoulders as if at an actual, physical discomfort. 'I will not bandy words with you,' he said. 'I am sorry for your chains, but you will not otherwise have reason for complaint at my hands.' He nodded to Catrin, who had been observing the interplay between the two men, noting all that went unsaid between their words. 'Tend to Lord Stephen, Catrin, and see that you are thorough.'

Catrin inclined her head in deference but was stung to retort, 'I know of no other way, my lord.'

Stephen snorted with amusement. Robert turned abruptly to the window embrasure, his hands tapping behind his back in nervous impatience. Catrin took Stephen's wrist to examine the abrasion. It was raw and cruel where the sharp iron edge had gouged, and she shook her head over the wound. Now she was closer to him, she could see other marks on his body – those of the battle of Lincoln, she surmised. Even his most vehement detractors respected him for his bravery and prowess on the field. There was a fading bruise on his cheekbone in hues of purple, blue and yellow, and an almost healed cut on his lip. She could not feel sorry for him, but she could feel compassion. She also found that she liked him far more than the haughty Empress Mathilda. But then, as Oliver said, that was half the problem. Where Mathilda instilled loyalty, it was fierce, as in Earl Robert's case, but there were too few disciples and she would not set herself out to win others.

'This will hurt,' she warned. 'I have to clean the wound and make sure that there is no rust in it.'

'You cannot hurt me any more than I have been hurt

already,' Stephen replied and gave her a smile that deepened her liking for him all the more. She had heard that he was devoted to his wife, Maude of Boulogne, and Catrin thought it a good thing: otherwise he would likely have as many bastard offspring as the old king.

Catrin cleansed the abrasion and, although he stiffened, he did not flinch or cry out. She anointed his wrist with Ethel's salve and then bound the area with soft linen bandages. 'If you are to wear a manacle again, then it should be of a lighter weight and filed smooth,' she said, addressing Stephen but pitching her voice towards Earl Robert.

He swung round from the embrasure and looked at her with frowning eyes. 'Do not presume to meddle,' he said.

Catrin lowered her glance. 'I would never do that, my lord, but you did ask me to tend Lord Stephen, and when I spoke it was as a healer. If the wound continues to chafe and rub, it will become a weeping sore and wound-fever might set in.'

The Earl bit his thumbnail, and then gestured brusquely. 'See to it,' he growled at the guard with the manacle key.

'My lord.' The soldier bowed and left the chamber.

Again Stephen smiled at Catrin. 'My thanks,' he said. 'You are an angel to offer me comfort in purgatory. If I could reward you, I would.'

He was quite the courtier too, Catrin thought. She could not imagine Empress Mathilda finding kind words for what she would consider her due in the same circumstances.

'I will need to return on the morrow, my lord,' she addressed Earl Robert. 'The wound must be tended and dressed with fresh ointment.'

'As you will.' Robert gave her a coin from his pouch. 'Since I did not see Oliver in the hall last night, I assume he was with you.'

'Yes, my lord.' Catrin reddened, aware that Stephen was watching her with amused interest.

'Then send him to me. I've tasks for him.' He waved his hand in dismissal.

Catrin dipped another curtsey and made her grateful escape into the cold, clean air of the stairwell.

*   *   *

Oliver's tasks involved delivering messages to Gloucester and several of Earl Robert's holdings in Monmouthshire. Then he was commanded to scour the countryside for as many re-mounts as possible to replace those lost during the march to Lincoln and the subsequent battle. It was the day after the feast of Saint Valentine when he received the orders. The Empress was preparing to leave her Gloucester base for Cirencester and then Winchester.

'So you're not bringing the horses back to Bristol?' Catrin asked, as he marched around the shelter stuffing a clean shirt and tunic in his saddle roll and leaving behind his old shirt for Agatha to wash. Her voice was careful and she managed to keep the worst of the disappointment to herself.

'No. I've to find the horses and bring them on to our camp, wherever it might be.' He curled his lip. 'It will be like seeking for snow in July. People who have animals will hide them the moment they hear of my approach, or else they'll try and sell them for an outrageous price. The war has already taken the best beasts. Naught but nags remain.'

'Can you not tell the Earl?'

'Oh, he knows it already. It is his sister who refuses to listen.'

Catrin narrowed her eyes. The more she heard and saw of the Empress Mathilda, the more she disliked her. Even her sympathy for a woman's struggle in a man's world was wearing thin. 'Then no one will have time for her in the end,' she said, and handed him his hood which had been lying under the basket of linen laundry awaiting Agatha's collection.

Oliver shook his head. 'We do our best with what we have,' he said grimly. 'Look, I have to go. Geoffrey FitzMar's coming with me and I don't know where he is.' Pulling her close, he kissed her hard and she kissed him back, her fingers tangling for a moment in his wheatsheaf hair.

'Have a care to yourself.'

'And you,' he added, with wry meaning and a glance at her satchel where lay the knife he had given her last winter.

'Of course.' Her lips still tingling from the force of the kiss, she watched him stride off across the bailey and then, with a small sigh, turned to her own tasks.

Five minutes later, Richard dropped by, his young alaunt gambolling at his side, and begged one of the honey sweetmeats that Ethel had always kept in an earthenware jar for his visits.

The last batch, made by Ethel the week before her death, was almost all gone, and Catrin realised that she would have to continue the tradition and make some more. The sight of the few sticky golden lumps in the bottom of the jar made her blink and bite her lip. The boy sat for a moment on the stool by the fire. Cheek bulging, he fondled the hound's muzzle.

'If I go back to the hall, the Earl will only find me something else to do,' he said, looking aggrieved. 'I've been a pack mule all morning. I hate it on the day before an army moves.'

'But if you shirk your duties, someone else will have to do double,' Catrin pointed out.

'Only for a short while, and probably Thomas. I helped him with a load of shields earlier.' He swapped cheeks and sucked loudly. 'I'll go back when I've finished this.'

She offered him the jar. 'Best take the last two then, one for you and one for Thomas.'

He started to delve in, then raised his head and stared. Catrin turned round.

'Seen Oliver anywhere?' asked Randal de Mohun. He was leaning against the doorpost, one hand on his hip, the other braced on the wood.

Fear flashed through Catrin, but she stiffened her spine. 'He went to the hall,' she said, without expression.

De Mohun looked her up and down, and Catrin tightened her grip on the sweetmeat jar and thought about striking him with it – although it would be a pity to damage the attractive yellow glaze. Godard had gone to his lodging so there was no rescue from his reassuring bulk. The young mastiff growled, showing his teeth at the mercenary.

'That's what I like about this particular hearth,' de Mohun said, 'always a warm welcome.' Grinning, he uncoiled from the doorpost and walked away across the bailey. An involuntary shiver rippled down Catrin's spine.

'Who was that?' Richard demanded.

His tone was peculiar – thin and frightened. Catrin looked at him and saw that his face was ashen and his eyes so wide that the pupils were entirely ringed with white.

'His name's Randal de Mohun and he's a mercenary. What's the matter?'

'I remember him from Penfoss,' Richard said faintly. 'He was their leader.'

Catrin stared at him and felt as if she had been drinking ice. 'What makes you so sure?'

'His tunic. I recognised his tunic. It belonged to Lord Aimery, and they stripped it from his body before they cut his throat. I remember the red braid. My mother sewed it on for him not two weeks before and there was enough left over to trim my hat.' He rummaged in the pouch on his belt and produced a somewhat squashed and worse-for-wear phrygian cap. Sure enough, grubby but discernible, the opening was trimmed with the same braid. But he need not have shown her; Catrin could quite clearly recall Amice stitching both tunic and cap. She knew now why de Mohun's clothing had seemed so familiar.

'They might have sold the tunic,' she said, trying to be fair even through her revulsion. 'De Mohun's horse is a bay and his shield is blue. The man we saw rode a chestnut and his shield was green.' As she spoke, Ethel's warning rang in her ears: *Beware a man on a bay horse.* Nausea churned her stomach, not least at the thought that he was, or had been, Oliver's friend.

'Perhaps he sold them instead, or perhaps the horse was injured and the shield damaged and he had to get rid of them. It's always happening to the Earl. He's resting up his Lincoln destrier because of a foreleg strain and he'll have to ride out on the morrow with his second-string dun.'

'But de Mohun would not sell his bridle and saddle,' Catrin said. 'Do you remember his saddle-cloth? It was made of black and white cowhide. Two proofs are more damning than one.'

They gazed at each other. 'We could always go and look at his equipment,' Richard said. 'It would not take long, and then we'd know for sure. He won't be at his camp, he's gone to find Oliver in the hall.'

Against her better judgement, but driven by a need to know, Catrin donned her cloak, grabbed her satchel and went to the door. 'No,' she said, as Richard began to follow her. 'Go and fetch Godard and tell him to come to me.'

'But . . .'

'Quickly now.' She shooed him out in front of her, and as he ran off, the dog bounding at his heels, she took her own more pensive route towards the mercenary horse-lines.

Many of the soldiers knew her by now. She and Ethel had tended their women, and being a midwife, with women's secrets at her fingertips, guaranteed her a certain amount of protection. That she was known to have dealings with the Earl's wife and was betrothed to a disinherited knight counted in her favour too. Some of the comments made as she passed were ribald, but cheerfully so, and Catrin forced herself to retort in kind with a mock tilting of her nose and an admonishing finger.

De Mohun's serjeant was in camp and he watched her approach with narrowed eyes. She told him that she had been sent by de Mohun himself to look at a saddle sore on his mount's withers.

'First I know of it,' said the grizzle-haired mercenary suspiciously.

'He came especially to see me on his way to the hall,' Catrin answered steadily enough, although her heart was in her mouth. 'How else would I know where he was going?'

'Aye, well, the beast is there.' The man gestured brusquely to the tall, bay stallion.

Trying to appear calm and authoritative, Catrin approached the horse. It rolled its eyes and sidled. 'How long has Sir Randal had him?'

The soldier shrugged. 'Since last midsummer.'

'And before that?' She walked around the bay, pretending to look. A flicker of her eyes revealed a bridle and saddle to one side, protected from the ground by a folded-up blanket.

'Why do you want to know?'

'It's important for the charm to work.'

The man snorted, displaying what he thought of that notion. 'A chestnut with white markings,' he said.

'And did they wear the same saddle?'

The soldier rolled his eyes and gestured to the one in the corner. Catrin went over to it and bent down. The saddle-cloth peeped out from beneath the polished wood and leather – it was green with a border of red tassels.

Catrin stared, feeling disappointed. She had been so sure. She touched one of the tassels and then, to make it seem that she was conducting a necessary examination, she looked at the underside of the saddle-cloth.

'Something the matter?' enquired the soldier.

The cowhide was coarse against her thumb, black and white as she remembered it, but a little more bald with wear. 'No, nothing,' she said, and stood up, wiping her hand on her gown. 'Sir Randal used to have a green shield with a red cross, did he not?'

'What of it?'

'He did though, didn't he?'

The soldier gave a grudging nod. 'It got split in a fight,' he said. 'What is it to you?'

'I'll tell you what it is,' Randal de Mohun said, advancing to his horse-line, his movements casual and dangerous. 'It is meddling in affairs that are best left alone. Is that not so, Mistress midwife?'

Catrin's legs were suddenly weak. Her heart began to pound. She hoped against hope that Richard had found Godard. 'I do not know what you mean,' she said, and did not have to look at his face to know how feeble her defence was. 'I came looking for Oliver, that's all.'

'She said your horse was sick and that you'd asked her to tend it,' the soldier spoke out and stepped sideways, blocking her escape. Left and right, she was now hemmed in.

'Her and the boy are the only survivors from Penfoss,' de Mohun said over his shoulder, then looked broodingly at Catrin. 'Oliver told me. Full of pride he was, the fool.'

'It *was* you.' Catrin's voice quavered.

De Mohun lifted his brows. 'So you claim, but whose word will be considered law?' He stroked his beard in a parody of reasonable thought. 'There is room to negotiate. Tide's in, the river's high. A walk along the wharf should resolve matters.'

An image of Rohese de Bayvel's remains filled Catrin's mind; the ragged white flesh dragged up from the depths of the river. Her hand lay on top of her satchel and the latch was unfastened. She tensed her wrist and took a step back. 'Other people know where I am. They will raise the hue and cry against you,' she warned.

De Mohun snorted. 'You were never here. None of us ever saw you.' He took a step towards her, arms outstretched. 'You went out into the city, to a birth, and never returned.'

As he lunged, so too did Catrin, striking with the knife as Oliver had shown her. De Mohun recoiled with an involuntary cry of surprise and pain, blood dripping from a deep gash in the back of his hand. With a snarl, he drew his sword.

Catrin screamed at the top of her lungs. The other soldier made a grab at her arm and fetched up the same as his master with a bone-deep wound. But then the sword connected. Catrin swung desperately to avoid it. Her satchel caught the bulk of the blow and split open, spilling entrails of herb sachets, linen bandages, jars of ointment and oil, and a small plaster image of Saint Margaret which shattered on the straw-covered ground. The last of the blow bit through flesh to bone and although there was no pain, Catrin felt the heat of blood flooding her side. She screamed again, and her voice was answered by a huge, masculine bellow.

The sword glittered in the air again, but this time it was turned on the blade of another weapon. She saw a quarterstaff flail the air and heard the deep grunt of someone struck in the midriff. Oliver and Godard, she thought hazily, and swayed and fell. The smell of dung and straw filled her nostrils. It was very tempting to close her eyes and let the world disappear. Get up, she scolded herself, get away before it's too late.

There was pain now as she scrabbled to her hands and knees; hot, scalding, trickling pain, but it told her that she was still alive. She heard cries, the sound of running feet. A hand touched her shoulder and a woman's face, wide-eyed with shock, peered round into hers. ''Tis the young midwife,

she's wounded!' she cried over her shoulder to her companion.
'Help me with her.'

Between them, the two women lifted Catrin to her feet and
bore her over to their tent, where they laid her down on a
straw pallet.

Randal de Mohun parried Oliver's blow. A vicious upswing
sent chips of steel sparking from Oliver's blade. As he flinched
from the flying fragments, de Mohun grabbed a saddled
horse belonging to one of his troop, clawed himself across
its back, and rammed spurs into its flanks. Oliver lunged
for the bridle, but just as swiftly snatched his hand back
as Randal's sword chopped down and the horse lashed out.
Then the mercenary was free, thundering across the bailey
and through the open castle gates, leaving the guards staring
in blank astonishment.

Most of Randal's men made their escape in the mayhem and
confusion, the majority of them sneaking out as word spread.
Randal's hefty serjeant was constrained to stay, as Godard
finally got an arm lock on him, bore him to the ground and
sat on him.

'Don't kill him,' Oliver panted. 'He has a song to sing to
the Earl.'

'Do my best,' Godard growled, 'but I make no promises.'

Oliver nodded and, sheathing his sword, ran to the tent
where the women were beckoning.

Catrin was ashen, her eyes dilated with pain. Her gown
was soaked in blood from armpit to hip.

'Christ, only you could be so foolish and stubborn as to
walk into the den of a hardened mercenary like Randal de
Mohun!' He knelt at her side, his voice ragged and his hand
trembling as he drew his dagger to slash the green wool, north
and south.

'I'll need a new gown now,' Catrin jested weakly.

'In my estimation, you need new wits. Catrin, I swear you
will be the death of me, if you do not kill yourself first!'
Working rapidly, he tore open the dress and chemise and
was flooded with both relief and anxiety when he saw the
gash that de Mohun's sword had opened. It was long and
moderately deep but, as far as he could tell, it had struck no

vital organ and the blood was only seeping now. But still it required stitching, and quickly. After that came the dangers of wound-fever and the stiffening sickness, either of which could kill in short order.

Thanking the women for their care, he wrapped Catrin in his cloak and bore her back to the house against the bailey wall. In a faint voice she told him the nostrums to mix to ease her pain and clean the wound. Earl Robert's chirurgeon was sent for to do the stitching.

'I only wanted to look at his saddle-cloth, to find out if it was fashioned of black and white cowhide,' she said. 'I thought he was safely away in the hall.'

'He came to the hall, but did not stop for long.' Oliver chafed her hands, wishing her flesh was not so cold. 'He wanted to ask me about some new spear heads I'd promised to get him when I ordered mine. Just after he'd gone, Godard found me and gave me Richard's message. Fortunate for you that we did not delay in following de Mohun to his camp.'

'Will the Earl raise the hue and cry against him?'

'Of a certainty,' Oliver said, but the words were bitter in his mouth for he knew that there was small likelihood of Randal de Mohun being captured. Earl Robert's army was almost ready to leave Bristol and begin campaigning towards Winchester and London. There was little time and even fewer men available to hunt down a rebel mercenary. Good riddance would be Earl Robert's philosophy on the matter. Besides, they had de Mohun's second-in-command to make a confession and become a scapegoat for the rest.

The look in Catrin's eyes told him that she had about as much faith as himself in Randal de Mohun being brought to justice.

Oliver turned his head aside. 'I regret ever bringing him to the Earl's attention,' he said, his voice filled with loathing.

'You were not to know.'

'I knew his kind, which is almost as bad.' He rubbed his thumb over her knuckles. 'I could have lost you, and for no more than a sense of foolish obligation long outgrown.'

'But you haven't and you won't,' Catrin said fiercely, and drew herself up on the bolster, her eyes dark and bright in her otherwise bloodless face. 'Randal de Mohun's days are numbered. Ours are not.' She drew his face down to hers and kissed him with a vigour that revealed how strongly the life still flowed in her. And it was in that embrace that Earl Robert's chirurgeon found them as he arrived with his needle and thread.

'I don't want to go,' Oliver said.

He was sitting on the side of their bed, stamping his foot into an ankle shoe as he spoke. The warmth of the spring sun filtered through the door curtain and laid a sparkle of gold on the hair springing from the back of his wrists.

Catrin eased herself up on the bolster and felt the uncomfortable tug of skin where her wound had been stitched. Six weeks had passed since the incident with de Mohun but she still felt pain from the cut and, although it was healing well, the scar was a deep red welt against her pale skin. For a few days after the attack, she had been very ill indeed; not at death's door, but running a high fever filled with delirious, senseless dreams in which she was pursued by a faceless man on a bay horse. When the fever broke, it left her as weak as a new-born lamb, and it was only now that she was beginning to rediscover her original, robust self.

Persuaded to talk, de Mohun's serjeant had spun a horrific tale of murder and atrocity. Not only Penfoss, but several smaller hamlets had been destroyed, the mercenaries circling and raiding like a pack of wolves. Rohese de Bayvel had been their victim, and so had Gawin.

'I don't want you to go.' She laid a hand on his back and felt the warmth of his flesh through his linen shirt.

'Then I won't.' Turning round, he rolled over on top of her, careful to avoid her injured side, and for a moment they kissed and nuzzled. He pressed his hips down and she raised hers and then clasped her legs around him, only half in play. For a moment he groaned and almost yielded to temptation then, with a sigh, he sat up and pushed his fingers through his hair.

'Now look what you've done. Is that any way to send a man off on the road?'

Catrin giggled. 'The only way,' she said. 'You'll come home the quicker for the rest.'

'I had not suspected you of such cruelty.'

'Love is always cruel,' Catrin said, not quite in jest.

'And not always to be kind,' he retorted, and leaned over to fasten the toggles on his shoes.

'I will send you off with something else too,' Catrin said, her eyes upon the curve of his spine. 'The promise that when you return, we will be wed.'

He straightened and turned so swiftly that she actually heard the sinew crack in his neck the moment before he winced in pain. 'Jesu, that is grinding salt into a wound,' he said.

'Why?'

'Because I want to return even before I have gone, and I do not know how long I will be away this time.' He rubbed his neck. 'This damned, gory war creeps on and on like a leper dragging his useless limbs. The Londoners hate Mathilda. I do not blame them after the manner in which she dealt with them; she does not know the meaning of diplomacy. Every foothold gained is slippery and only made with the most arduous toil. I begin to think that Earl Robert is not losing his hair from age and wisdom, but from tearing it out in clumps at his sister's folly!' He shook his head and gave her a hopeless look. 'But I am locked to her cause. What else can I do?'

To which Catrin did not have an answer. Instead, she wrapped her arms around his neck and laid her cheek against his. 'Whatever you think now, it cannot last for ever. My talk of marriage was intended to cheer you and instead I have set you to brooding.'

'Nay. Without you, and the thought of you, I would have gone mad long before now.' They kissed and clung for a moment, but the dawn was brightening outside, and it was with reluctance that they broke apart. 'You will be Lady Pascal – a titled woman without lands,' he tried to jest.

Catrin smiled and gave a little shrug. 'I can live without them.' More easily than Oliver she thought, with a shrewd look at her betrothed through her lashes. 'But I know how much it irks you that a stranger sits in your hall and milks your estates.'

Rising from their bed, he donned his quilted gambeson and reached for his hauberk. 'Ashbury would not have been mine if my brother had lived, I freely admit it, but now he is dead the inheritance has fallen to me.'

'But surely Ashbury is only yours by right of Conquest in the first place?' Catrin ventured. 'Did not your grandfather or great-grandfather come to England with the Conqueror?'

'No.' He shook his head. 'My great-grandfather's name was Osmund, son of Leofric, and my family has held Ashbury time out of mind. He swore allegiance to the Conqueror and married a Norman noblewoman, Nichola de Pascal. Then, because all things French were in fashion, and he wanted to live, he changed his name to his wife's and christened his sons with Norman names. My colouring is true Saxon.' He tugged at a lock of his pale blond hair. 'Ashbury is mine by right of generations.'

'Why haven't you told me before?' Catrin eyed him curiously.

He shrugged. 'No reason why I should. It is not something that my family has ever bandied abroad. We are proud, but within ourselves.' His upper lip curled wryly. 'Or should I say within myself, since I am the only Pascal – the only Osmundsson – remaining.'

Catrin nodded thoughtfully. The pride was kept hidden because it went hand-in-glove with shame. Three generations after the Conquest, the nobility was dominated by men of French-speaking Norman extraction. It was true that their offspring were suckled by English wet nurses, and that their sons and daughters grew up speaking both tongues, but French was the language of the court and it was considered vulgar to admit to any great knowledge of English. Saxons were peasants and traders, occasionally merchants. Any who displayed overt signs of wealth were treated with suspicion and frequently harassed. For a man of rank to admit to Saxon heritage in public would be like throwing down a challenge to his peers. Older blood. A stronger claim, based on heredity not robbery.

She kept her perceptions to herself. To have spoken them aloud would have been cruel. Oliver must have them too. There was no need for words.

'Then our children will be true mongrels,' she said instead with a smile. 'Welsh and Breton from me, English and Norman from you.'

CHAPTER 17

SEPTEMBER, 1141

In the hazy light of a late summer morning, a young man groomed his horse, vigorously working the curry comb until the stallion's dark bay hide gleamed like peat water. He was stripped to the waist and well aware of the admiring glances cast in his direction by two young washerwomen, who had lingered on their way from the stream to watch him. Being accustomed to such feminine scrutiny, he played them on his line, pretending that he had not noticed them and working his arm to show his taut musculature to its best advantage.

His black, shoulder-length hair framed classical features that were preserved from effeminacy by an angular jaw and a scar high on one cheekbone. He had the dark, narrow eyes and sinuous grace of a marten, and his ready smile had opened more doors and charmed him beneath more skirts than he could remember.

He heard the women giggle and exchange loud whispers as they sought to draw his attention. Turning from the horse, he stooped to pick up his shirt and, still pretending ignorance, faced them. He knew full well that their eyes would go straight to the thin line of black pubic hair fuzzing above the drawstring of his braies, and the bulge on one side that spoke of a man well-endowed.

More gasps and giggles. He drew his shirt slowly over his head and knew that they were holding their breath, waiting for his braies to fall down or his penis to pop out of the top. The game was his; he was in control, and the women, although they fed his conceit, were of no importance. Indeed, women were only of importance when they were unavailable, and such a situation was rare.

He pulled the shirt down and tucked it inside his braies, making sure that he handled himself in front of the women, giving them a hint of what they were missing. Then, tired of the game, he donned his tunic and gambeson and led the horse down to the stream.

To his lord, William d'Ypres, Master of Kent, he was Louis de Grosmont, the grandson of a Norman border nobleman. To his men, he was Louis le Loup – the wolf – a name they liked because it rolled easily off the tongue and well-described their leader's hungry nature. They sometimes called him Louis le Colp too, in honour of the size of his manhood and his propensity for thrusting it into every sheath that came his way. Only Ewan, who had been with him in the early days, remembered him as Lewis, son of Ogier, common soldier in the Chepstow garrison and grandson of a groom; but since Ewan's identity and reputation had risen and changed as much, those days were seldom recalled. Louis had the instinct of being in the right place at the right time, a trait that had served him well during the past four years. William d'Ypres, captain of Stephen's mercenaries, had employed him among his household knights and bestowed upon him many a favour, including the costly dark bay stallion ruffling the stream with his muzzle.

Louis cupped the cold running water in his palm and splashed his face. He let the bay drink, but not too much, and returned to his horse-line to finish arming up. The laundry women had moved on, and Ewan was supervising the striking of camp. He was a small, dour Welshman; sallow of complexion, dark of eye, and horribly, and incongruously, bright red of hair.

'Ready, my lord,' he said, as Louis jumped up and down to help his mail tunic slink over his body and then donned his helm. 'We'll be dining in Winchester tonight, eh?'

'We might,' Louis said, and adjusted his swordbelt of decorated buckskin with its pattern on interlaced gilding. Everything about him spoke of wealth and exquisite taste. The best or nothing was Louis's philosophy on life. Why eat bread and be virtuous when there were delicacies and decadence to be had for the grabbing?

Those delicacies had been few since the battle of Lincoln, but his instinct had advised him to stay where he was. The tide which had turned in the Empress's favour had not swept everything before it and perhaps even now was changing. Which was why they were here in Winchester with the army of Stephen's queen. Robert of Gloucester and the Empress were hemmed within the city where they in turn were besieging Stephen's brother, Bishop Henry, in his palace. The cat stalked the mouse and the dog stalked the cat.

'Ever think about changing allegiance now that King Stephen's in prison?'

Lips pursed, Louis swung into his saddle. The Welshman's suggestion ran parallel with his thoughts, for he had been assessing the odds and trying to decide whether to stay or make himself scarce. How hard was the battle for Winchester going to be? And who would be the victor? The question begged consideration. 'What man in his senses would not think?' he said with a shrug. 'But there is small point in being too hasty. Wait and see how fortunes fare.'

Ewan nodded and a sly grin broke across his face. 'Last time you had to die before you could begin afresh.'

Louis grunted and said nothing, but his mind flickered briefly to the time four years ago on the banks of the Monnow where Padarn ap Madoc had accused him of lying with his young wife and challenged him to combat. Louis had no desire to fight, but a very strong desire to survive. Padarn had died from a single knife wound in the chest and Louis had found it prudent to disappear, leaving evidence to suggest that he had drowned – the Welsh being notorious for their vigour in pursuing blood feuds. It was not a conscious decision, more an effort to put distance between himself and Chepstow, which had brought him to Kent – from west to east. Along the way, he had been adopted by Ewan, himself a fugitive from Welsh law and a Chepstow man into the bargain. They knew each other; they had things in common and things to hide.

Neither of them ever thought of returning to their native

haunts. It was too dangerous. Ewan was of a nomad nature and Louis had a desire to be cock of a larger dunghill than the one awaiting him at home. His wings had been clipped by the monotony of garrison duty and the boredom of domestic routine with a wife who, although delightful, had no special tether to hold him, and who on occasion could be a nuisance with her demands on his affection and fidelity.

He thought of Catrin now, the wide hazel eyes, not quite brown, not quite green. The satin-black hair, the soft lips and the way they could tighten with displeasure or twitch with amusement. He had been fond of her . . . but not fond enough. Women were like food. They might taste different, but they all served the same purpose. He could get what he wanted from any he chose, without being bound to a single one. He wondered how hard she had grieved for him. It was an interesting thought, but one that intruded on his current need to decide how best to avoid becoming involved in a pitched battle.

'You always were a contrary wench, Catty,' he said aloud, making Ewan gaze at him askance. 'Nothing.' He shook his head and smiled ruefully. 'A memory from the time before I was dead.'

Louis was slender and not particularly tall, but it put him at no disadvantage when matched with other men for he was also wiry, fast and cunning. Such traits in mind, William d'Ypres bade him take his men out of line and ride reconnaissance along the Stockbridge road to the west of the city, to keep watch for valuable escapees, chief amongst them the Empress herself. To reach Andover, she would have to ride that way and negotiate the wooden bridge lying across the river Teste.

'There will be rich rewards for such a capture,' said d'Ypres, a cynical smile curving beneath his moustache, for while he valued Louis de Grosmont and recognised his talents, he also recognised the young man's acquisitiveness and knew his limitations. Louis was a hellion with a sword – but only to save his life or amass greater wealth.

Louis returned the smile in the same vein, showing that he

understood perfectly, and saluted. 'Not so much as a mouse
will cross our path unnoticed, my lord.' He swung the bay
out of line, his arm sweeping in a gesture that summoned
his men from the main body of troops. D'Ypres spared time
to briefly raise his eyebrows before directing soldiers to cover
the other main roads out of the city.

Smiling to himself, Louis set spurs to his mount's flanks.
The task suited him well. He would nail his gaze to the road
and stop anyone of substance riding along it, even if it involved
a fight. But, if the assault on Winchester was unsuccessful and
their own army was forced to flee, Louis had no intention of
remaining at his post. At the first sign of disaster he would
run and, if necessary, find an excuse for it later.

'Christ on the Cross!' Oliver wasted breath to swear, and
parried a blow with the blade of his sword. He had lost
his shield, but so too had his opponent, a frightened, but
determined, young Fleming. The chaos of battle clashed
around them. Earl Robert's knights were fighting a desperate
rearguard action, bearing the brunt of the assault so that the
Empress could flee to safety with her guard.

Oliver knew that they were buying time dearly; that they
too should be running while they still had a chance. They were
the only ones left. David of Scotland had fled, and Miles of
Gloucester had seen his soldiers melt like butter beneath the
hot stab of a Flemish knife.

Oliver aimed another cut at the youngster, a backhand
blow at the right collarbone. Break that and the sword arm
was disabled. The Fleming had expected the blow to come
forehand to the left side, and the full power of Oliver's arm
caught him square. He screamed. His guard fell and the
sword dropped from his fingers. Oliver whirled Hero and
spurred him back several yards to join Geoffrey FitzMar
in the circle of knights protecting Earl Robert. There was
no question of holding their position for long. They were
too greatly outnumbered by men thirsting to avenge the battle
of Lincoln and hot with indignation that King Stephen should
be held in chains like a common felon.

Fighting, running, fighting, the Flemish mercenaries of

William d'Ypres nipping at their heels, Earl Robert and
the remnants of his household knights retreated up the road
towards the ford of the river Teste at Stockbridge. They were
hoping against hope that it was either unguarded or so lightly
manned that they could force their way across.

'I begin to wonder why I never took up life as a hermit!' Geoffrey gasped, as a crossbow quarrel whined past
his helm.

'You wanted a life of lust and adventure!' Oliver replied,
and spurred his flagging grey. Behind him, footsoldiers were
discarding their armour the faster to run, and all thoughts of
saving the baggage wains had long since been abandoned.

'I renounce it gladly. Go on, you nag!' Geoffrey struck his
horse on the rump with the flat of his sword and the animal
grunted and strained, foam flying from the bit. 'He's not going
to last another mile. I . . . Sweet Christ!' He swept the bay to
a standstill and stared in dismay at the road before them.

Oliver slewed to a halt. Their way was blocked by a troop
of soldiers, their horses fresh, their armour and weapons fired
by the golden September light. They had formed up for a
charge, stirrup-to-stirrup, lances couched. 'It will take more
than "Sweet Christ" to save us now,' Oliver panted, and
braced his aching forearm. 'We are caught like grain between
two millstones.' With pinpoint clarity, he fixed his gaze on the
apparent leader of the new threat. He rode a magnificent dark
bay destrier and his equipment was of the best. Here was no
rag-tag Fleming but a hand-picked man in charge of other
men similarly chosen. Suddenly the option was no longer to
escape but to survive.

The young lord on the bay kicked his horse into a trot
and approached them alone. He turned his mount side-on
as he reached them, controlling the beast with hands that
were slender, fine-boned and filled with lean strength. He
had a thin, handsome face and eyes so dark that they were
almost black. Beneath his gambeson, a tunic of dark crimson
flashed, edged with gold embroidery. Not just hand-picked,
Oliver thought, but of high nobility too.

'My name is Louis de Grosmont,' he shouted in a rich,
carrying voice. 'I serve King Stephen and William d'Ypres,

Lord of Kent. My trade is bloodshed, but it is also diplomacy. If you will surrender, I will see that you are honourably treated. If not . . .' He gave a shrug and a half-smile that showed a hint of fine white teeth. 'If not, then I will see you honourably buried.' He gestured to the men behind him fretting their mounts.

Oliver heard the clamour of close pursuit and knew that they could not fight their way out, they were trapped like rats in a catcher's wheel. Perhaps they would take a few of the opposition with them when they died, but it would be a gesture as worthless as any in the war.

Earl Robert glanced over his shoulder and, as the chasing soldiers came into view, bowed to the inevitable, if not to the knight confronting him. Reversing the sword in his hand, he gave it hilt-first into the slender grasp of Louis de Grosmont. 'I am Robert de Caen, Earl of Gloucester,' he said. 'And I yield to you, but not because of your threat. If you killed me, I doubt you would live to see me "honourably buried".'

The young man took the sword and held it to the light, admiring its quality. 'I doubt it too,' he said, but there was a gleam in his eyes, and if he had been a cat he would have been licking cream from his whiskers.

Seventy miles away in Bristol, Catrin was in the women's chambers, sewing her wedding gown with Edon to help her. Countess Mabile had given her a bolt of finely woven, mulberry-coloured wool, and a bag full of seed pearls with which to trim the sleeves, throat and hem. Not that her wedding was any closer than it had been four months ago. The Empress's gathering of support was a protracted affair. London remained loyal to Stephen's queen, and now the Bishop of Winchester, whose backing was vital to Mathilda, had grown lukewarm. He was King Stephen's brother and his loyalties blew with the direction of the wind.

Messengers rode in and out of Bristol every day, bringing news to the Countess and to the men whose task it was to keep the Earl's administration running smoothly. Sometimes Oliver would appear with demands for supplies, but it was never for more than a day. There was scarcely even time to speak to each other, let alone consider the matter of a wedding.

'But surely they will all be home soon,' Edon said with a sigh in her voice. 'They have been at war all summer long. Geoffrey says that Stephen's supporters will have to accept Mathilda in the end.'

Catrin pulled a face, and not just because the seam she was sewing refused to lie straight. 'The bitter end,' she said to Edon. 'And they look as if they'll fight until they reach it.' She bit off the thread and examined her work with a depressed eye, knowing that she would have to unpick it and start again.

'I don't care, as long as it's soon.' There was petulance in Edon's voice. 'At least you see Oliver now and again. I haven't set eyes on Geoffrey the summer long.'

Knowing Edon well enough by now to recognise the signs, Catrin put her sewing aside. Making the excuse that she had promised to visit a groom's wife who was heavily pregnant, she left the bower. A storm of tears was the last thing that she needed, for she was liable to join Edon and weep her heart out.

At her dwelling in the bailey she paused to collect the things she needed. Godard had left kindling at the hearth, and the room was heavily scented with the cumulative aroma of smoke and drying herbs. As Catrin drew her satchel on to her shoulder, she was aware of another scent too, elusive, dry; one that had been absent from the house for seven months. The hair rose delicately on the nape of her neck.

'Ethel?' she whispered, and stared round. Undisturbed, the jars and bunches of herbs met her eye, but the scent remained in her nostrils and the air around her was suddenly as cold as ice. Her mind formed a picture of Ethel sitting by the hearth in the green mantle that Oliver had given to her at the winter feast. For a moment it was so vivid that she almost believed in its physical reality. Her heart began to thump and her armpits were moist with cold sweat.

'Mistress Catrin?' Godard's shadow darkened the doorway and almost made her jump out of her skin.

'Jesu, God!' she swore roundly, her hand at her throat, and glared at him. 'How can someone so large be so silent?'

He blinked at her vehement response. 'Didn't mean to frighten you.'

'Well, you did,' Catrin snapped, then, feeling slightly ashamed, she curbed her anger. 'Can you smell anything in here, Godard?'

Looking puzzled, he inhaled deeply. 'Smell anything, mistress?' He shook his great head slowly from side to side. 'Only the herbs and the hearth. Is there something amiss?'

Catrin drew a deep breath. The scent had gone and the atmosphere was equable. 'No, nothing,' she answered with a tight smile. 'Were you seeking me?'

'I've just seen two soldiers ride in at the gate, one of them wounded. There is news, mistress. I heard one of them say that Winchester is lost and the Empress put to flight. The Earl's been taken prisoner by the Flemings.'

The iciness returned, but it came from within. Catrin stared at Godard and felt herself freeze. 'Oliver,' she whispered. 'What of Oliver?'

Godard scratched his shaggy head. 'I am sorry, mistress, I could glean no more. The grooms took their horses, and they were escorted to the hall near-dead on their feet.'

'I have to find out.' She shook off the cold before it could engulf her and dashed to the keep as fast as her hampering skirts would allow.

CHAPTER 18

Having been raised at Chepstow, Louis was accustomed to imposing castles, but Rochester still managed to impress him with its combination of comfort and impregnable solidity. It was a young keep, less than twenty years old, and all the private chambers had a decorated fireplace and adequate window light when the shutters were not latched against the weather. There was a well on every level, which was far more convenient than drawing water from the undercroft or the bailey. There were numerous garderobes too, negating the need to go outside for a piss in the freezing dark.

It was the sort of keep that Louis would have chosen for himself. He knew that it was an ambition he would never realise, but there was no reason why he should not be given the custody of a smaller keep. He was in high favour with Stephen and d'Ypres for taking Robert of Gloucester's surrender.

His personal wealth was guaranteed too, since the ransom fees of Robert's knights belonged to him. On the strength of such fortune he had ordered himself a new tunic of the best Flemish wool in an expensive shade of lapis lazuli blue, a colour not usually seen on anyone less than a baron. The tunic was bordered with blue and white braid, the pattern a continuous chain of letter 'L's. Men said that fine feathers did not make fine birds, but Louis knew differently. To dress like a groom or a common soldier was to be treated as one. To dress like a noble was to be afforded respect and granted opportunities.

But Louis did not make the mistake of over-indulgence. He did not want men to see him as a fop. There were no rings on his fingers, and he made a point of telling folk that he did not wear them because they marred his grip on his sword. He frequently wore his quilted gambeson into the hall with only his tunic hem showing beneath to emphasise the fact that he was a soldier first. It was done with subtlety and it won him approval, even from his captives, who were kept under house arrest with their lord in one of the upper chambers.

When it came his turn to guard them, he often sat in their company exchanging soldiers' tales, winning them over with his wry, self-deprecating humour.

'You are not a Fleming,' said a flaxen-haired knight, as Louis drank wine with them one evening. His name was Oliver Pascal, and Louis sensed a certain reserve in the man. He was not as ready to be drawn in as the others. He was thus a challenge and Louis set out to woo him, entertaining a private wager that he would have Pascal eating out of his hand by the time the ransom was agreed.

'There are many in Lord William's contingent who are not,' Louis replied with a smile and a shrug, and poured wine into Pascal's cup.

The grey-dark eyes watched him shrewdly, their thoughts veiled. Thrusting his back against the wall, stretching his legs on the bench, Pascal said, 'Perhaps that is true; I do not have a great acquaintance with your lord's other men, but I wonder who you are and how you came to serve him.'

'Why should I arouse such interest?' Louis asked lightly.

It was Pascal's turn to smile and shrug. 'Why not? What else is there to do to while away the time except gamble and drink and gossip? Would you not want to know about the man who held your future in his hands?'

Louis laughed and combed back his hair with his fingers, exposing the taut, handsome lines of his face. 'I am not sure that I would.'

'Then we are different.'

A brief silence fell in which Louis deliberated between telling the truth, a pack of lies, or saying nothing at all. Pascal circled his finger around the slightly uneven rim of his clay goblet and waited the moment out with apparent aplomb. Louis narrowed his eyes, but it did not help him see through his captive any the better. Still, that was part of the challenge.

'Yes, I suppose we are.' He took a drink from his cup then set it to one side, for he had no desire to give his tongue a wine-loose rein. 'But since you ask, I will permit you the bones, if not the meat, of it.'

The lids widened, the grey eyes assessed then flickered down.

Louis spread his hands in a disarming gesture. 'There was some difficulty on my home territory. I killed a man I should not have done. Even though it was in fair fight, I knew that if I stayed my days were numbered. So I falsified my death – took my enemy's sword and left my own by the riverside where we had fought, together with one of my shoes.' He forced a grin. 'It was early spring and the weather as cold as witch's tit. But rather chilblains than death by a knife in the back. I travelled across England, heard that William d'Ypres was hiring, and I have been in his service ever since.' He spread his hands in an open gesture to show that was all there was. 'I have knelt in confession and paid my penance. Now you see a washed lamb.'

Geoffrey FitzMar had been listening to one side and now he leaned forward, his open gaze huge with surprise. 'But I thought you were high born with lands of your own!'

Louis gave a wry chuckle. 'High born certainly,' he said, 'but there are never many scraps for a younger son to glean. Lands of my own? I shall have them in the fullness of time.' The smile hardened at the edges. He looked at Oliver. 'Was it worth the asking?' The challenge in his tone surprised him with its defensiveness.

'Oh, I think so,' Oliver answered, and for the first time the eyes gleamed with humour. But Louis did not congratulate himself, for Oliver's expression was hard at the edges too, and he was still giving nothing away, while Louis had revealed rather more than was comfortable.

'Washed lamb, my backside,' Oliver said, when Louis had gone. 'A wolf in sheep's clothing, I think.'

'Do you not like him?'

Geoffrey looked so much like an anxious child that Oliver was moved to thaw. With a shake of his head, he laughed at himself. 'It is not so much that,' he admitted. 'I do not like being cooped up here in Rochester, knowing nothing – or only what they feed us. I have never been one to kick my heels with grace.' He grimaced. 'Yes, Louis de Grosmont is good company. It's all I can do not to laugh my belly out at some of his tales. That one about the woman and the parrot!' He snorted with reluctant amusement at the memory.

'Then why don't you?'

'Because it is what he expects. You can see him watching us, playing us like fish on his line. Well, this particular fish does not want to be hooked.'

'But why should he do that?' Geoffrey wrinkled his brow. 'What is there to be gained?'

'Esteem. Power. Do you not notice the way he feeds on us?'

'No.' Geoffrey looked more baffled than ever.

Oliver sighed and, rising to his feet, took his drink to the window embrasure. The sheds and workshops in the bailey were splashed with gold from the late October sunshine. Five pigs were being driven towards the pen near the kitchens. It was almost November, the month of slaughter and salting in preparation for winter. He should have been a married man by now. If fortune had smiled, he and Catrin would have been preparing to keep the Christmas feast in Ashbury's great hall. Instead, he was mured up in Rochester, with no more prospects than he had possessed on the day he returned from pilgrimage. He thrust his shoulder against the stone embrasure wall, watched Louis de Grosmont stride on his free and purposeful way, and knew jealousy.

'Well, I like him,' Geoffrey said, almost defiantly.

Oliver finished his wine and turned round. 'That's not difficult,' he said. 'You like anyone as long as they've a smile on their face.'

'Than that denies you,' Geoffrey retorted. 'You're so sour you'd curdle fresh milk in a dairy!'

Oliver arched his brow at this sharpness from Geoffrey, who was normally as mild as fresh milk.

Geoffrey swore and propped his feet on a bench. 'We are turning into a bowerful of women,' he said in disgust.

'Nothing to do but pick petty quarrels with each other to pass on the time. I want to go home. I want to see Edon and my son.'

Oliver's exasperation with Geoffrey was replaced by pangs of affection and empathy as he watched the young knight rub his hands together and then place his clasped palms against his lips.

'You've to dance at a wedding when we do,' he said by way of reconciliation, and somehow managed the all-important smile. 'I want you to be my groomsman.'

'Gladly,' Geoffrey said against his hands. Then he unclasped them and held them out before him. 'At least we're not in chains.'

Oliver said nothing, and thought that chains might be more bearable than this polite house arrest which was neither captivity nor freedom. He wandered back to the window. Louis de Grosmont was still in view, talking to a woman wearing a red dress and dark cloak. Then he swept her up in his arms and bore her behind a storage shed and out of Oliver's sight. His sweetheart, no doubt.

Oliver thought of Catrin and ached.

It had been a long road for Catrin, and the great keep at Rochester was both a welcome and a daunting sight. Now that she was close to her goal she was nervous, all the doubts and anxieties that she had suppressed on her journey threatening to overwhelm her. Faced by the fear that Oliver might not be there at all, she was almost tempted to turn back, on the principle that not knowing was better than knowing the worst.

'Mistress?' Leaning on his quarterstaff, Godard looked at her quizzically.

He had been her escort and protection on her journey from Bristol to Rochester, and she had been glad of his enormous bulk. People thought twice about tangling with him, even if it was only to pass the time of day, and it was he who carried the pouch of ransom money.

The Countess had tried to dissuade her from her quest, but Catrin was adamant. She had to know what had happened to

Oliver, had to find out at first hand whether he was safe or dead. Not for hell or high water, for the perils of war or personal danger, was she prepared to sit and wait.

Hearing that Earl Robert and those captured with him were being housed at Winchester, they had travelled there, only to find the city in smoking ruins, destroyed by the running battle between the supporters of the Empress and the King. The castle was intact, but it housed no prisoners. Robert of Gloucester had been taken to the greater safety of Rochester in Kent.

So now, deep in enemy territory, they were about to enter one of the most formidable keeps in the kingdom. Strangely enough, although Catrin was sick with nerves at the prospect of discovering news of Oliver, she felt no fear at entering Rochester itself. Soldiers abounded, but she and Godard had been left in peace thus far. William d'Ypres was a strict commander who demanded high standards of his men. She hoped that he would be amenable to her plea for Oliver's release. Surely an ordinary, landless knight could be of small political importance.

'Mistress,' said Godard again, 'why have we stopped?'

'To summon courage.' Catrin gave him a wan smile. Dismounting, she unfastened the bundle strapped to the mule's saddle. 'Besides, I'm travel-stained and in no fit state to plead my cause.'

Godard took the mule's bridle as Catrin disappeared behind a group of young hazel trees growing at the roadside. Behind their trunks, Catrin unpinned her cloak and stripped off her plain, homespun gown, replacing it with the crimson one that the Countess had given her last year. It was creased from the journey, but that could not be helped. At least the fabric and cut were of the best quality and would ensure her access beyond the gate. She replaced her plain wimple with the one of cream silk and secured it with a filigree circlet. Finally, she repinned her cloak with a fine silver brooch given to her by a grateful client and stepped back on to the road.

Godard gazed with approval, but not too much astonishment, upon the transformation from industrious peasant to lady of substance. 'Only pitfall is that when they see you dressed like that, they'll think you can afford to buy him back at double the price,' he commented.

Catrin wrinkled her nose. 'I had thought about that myself, but it cannot be helped. If I gown myself as a poor woman, then they will not let me past the outer bailey or listen to what I have to say. Looking as I do now, at least I have a certain authority.' She gnawed her lower lip. 'He might not even be here. For all that I know, we could have ridden past his grave in Winchester.' Her voice shook.

'No, mistress, I do not believe that,' Godard said stoutly. 'He is here.'

Catrin looked at him and swallowed her panic. 'Yes,' she said. 'He has to be.'

Cupping his hands for her foot, Godard boosted her back into the mule's saddle, and they set out upon the final half mile to the castle.

The gate guards were watchful, but their focus was upon the comings and goings of men of military rank bearing weapons. They gave Godard a cursory look because of his height and bulk, then dismissed him as a lady's prudent insurance against assault. To Catrin they yielded deference, and when she told them she had business with Lord William or his senior representatives, they directed her towards the hall without question.

Leaving Godard and the mule in the bailey, Catrin took the ransom money and made her way further into Rochester's defences. There was cold sweat on her palms and a sick churning in her stomach. The noise and bustle in the ward buffeted her like a sea around a rock and carried her forward in sharp surges towards the main building which rose above all the little islands of workshops, houses and storage sheds. Patterns of braided stone decorated the arched window spaces as they did at Bristol. She strained her neck, gazing towards the wall walk, and wondered if Oliver was locked up in one of the rooms, or whether they had imprisoned him in the gloom of the cellars as they had now done with Stephen at Bristol.

She sucked in a deep breath, summoned her courage and prepared to enter the lion's den and find out. But as she took her first, determined step, her way was blocked by a soldier striding in the opposite direction. When she side-stepped, so did he, then apologised with a laugh.

'We should become partners in the dance,' he said gallantly.

Catrin had been keeping her eyes down as befitted a modest woman, but now she raised them to his face and her reply died on her lips. Black curls; hot, dark eyes; white, even smile. 'Lewis?' she strangled out, and her hand went to her throat for suddenly it was difficult to breathe.

The laughter left his expression. He looked her up and down. 'Sweet Jesu in heaven,' he whispered and, reaching out, he took her arm. 'Catty?'

She felt the pressure of his fingers, the solidity of bone that challenged her disbelief. 'You're dead,' she gasped. 'I grieved over you so hard that I thought I would die myself. You cannot be real!' Drowning, sinking, she clutched for air, but there was only Lewis within her desperate grasp, and it seemed as if he was pulling her down. 'I don't feel well,' she said as her knees began to give way. She heard his oath of alarm as he moved to catch her and felt the darkness of his embrace close around her.

He swept her up in his arms and, ignoring the curious glances cast his way, bore her to a bench situated outside the kitchen entrance. Her head lolled against his shoulder; one of her braids tickled his hand. The smell of dried rose petals drifted from her garments and filled his nose with the scent of her. Tenderly, he set her down and took a moment to examine her properly without being examined himself.

Her face had lost the plumpness of adolescence, and the flesh clung smoothly to her bones. The curve of eyebrow was the same; she still did not pluck them even though it was the fashion. The tilt of her nose and set of her jaw reminded him with a pang of times past. It had not all been bad. His eyes strayed beyond her ice-white face to her garments. Despite being crumpled, her crimson gown was that of a wealthy woman, as was her wimple, and the fillets securing the ends of her braids were of polished silver. Whatever she had done with herself after he left, she had made her way well in the world. He looked at her hands and saw with a slight frown that she no longer wore the Celt gold wedding rings he had given her. Instead, on her heart finger, there was a different ring: gold in the shape of a triple knot.

'So, Catty, you've got yourself a man of wealth,' he murmured, with more than a pang of jealousy. His frown deepened as he looked at her hands. Wealthy or not, she still worked for her living. Her nails were clipped short and her skin had a slightly rough texture that suggested she spent her days doing more than spinning in a bower. Why, he wondered, was she here at Rochester? And what was he going to do about it?

Opening her eyes, the first thing Catrin saw was a tuft of grass growing through a dried-out crack in the soil and, either side of it, the toes of her shoes peeping out from the hem of her red gown. She realised that she was sitting on a bench, bending over, her head between her knees, but the wherefore and why escaped her.

'Drink this,' said a solicitous male voice. She was drawn gently into a sitting position and a cup placed in her hand. Lean brown fingers touched hers and, with a nauseous jolt, she remembered. A look into the face bending round into hers dispelled all notions that her imagination had been playing tricks.

'Lewis.' Her voice trembled. Once again the flutters of panic began in her stomach and tightened her throat. She tried to leap to her feet, but he held her fast.

'Drink first,' he said. 'I know it's a shock.'

Catrin tilted the cup to her lips with shaking hands. It was raw, red wine, sweetened with honey and spiked with Galwegian usquebaugh. She swallowed, coughed, retched and swallowed again, tears filling her eyes. The drink hit her stomach like a hot coal and flashed through her body. She sat back on the bench and breathed deeply, and each breath was filled with the scent of him; of orris root and horses, of a healthy, vigorous man in the full flow of life. 'Tell me,' she said shakily. 'I need to know.'

He drank from a cup of his own. She saw the familiar way he pouched it in his cheeks before he swallowed, and the unfamiliar line of a scar moving as he washed the wine around his mouth. What she had thought of as shattered bones and corrupted flesh was living, breathing, warm and vital.

'I killed Padarn ap Rhys,' he said. 'It was in fair fight, but do you think his followers would have accepted the outcome? It would be a matter of their clan's honour to see me dead. So I decided to "kill" myself before they did it for me.'

'And left me a grieving widow with never a word, so that you could save your own hide.' Catrin's lips drew back from her teeth as a spark of anger lit from within and carried her forward from that awful day on the banks of the Wye.

'I was intending to return for you.'

Catrin gave a cracked laugh. She felt as if all of her was breaking into little pieces; shattering like a fine and brittle mirror. 'When? Just how long were you intending me to wait? You must have an overbearing sense of your own attraction to think that I would still be dutifully pining four years later!' She took another vicious drink of the wine. Had she not, she would have thrown it in his face.

'I do not blame you for being angry, just as I don't blame you for not waiting.' He steepled his hands together in a prayerful gesture and gave her an engaging look from beneath his dark-winged brows. 'But I am telling you the truth. I—'

'Then it will be for the first time in your life!' Catrin interrupted furiously. 'How dare you say that you do not blame me when it was *you* who abandoned *me*, and in a fight over your seduction of someone else's wife!' Her hand trembled on the cup. 'I thought you were dead. You can stay dead!' She sought refuge in the burn of her rage, but her defences had been breached. Just the sight and scent of him brought everything back. Despite her rage, or perhaps part of it, there was a hot sensitivity between her thighs.

Lewis shook his head sorrowfully. 'First you say tell me; then, when I try, you bite my head off. I know I deserve it, but at least do me the grace of listening.'

She glared and drank, saying nothing, feeling the ground slip from under her feet.

He took her hand and rubbed her fingers gently with the ball of his thumb. 'I do not deny that I have been untrustworthy in the past, Catty. I took my responsibilities lightly. I misbehaved. I know that I was not a good husband . . .'

Catrin blinked as treacherous tears filled her eyes. She pressed her lips together and looked down at her lap.

'I admit that I flirted with the wife of Padarn ap Rhys. I admit that I visited whore houses with the other soldiers, but such women meant nothing to me. I thought I was proving myself, when all I was doing was being a fool and playing with dross when I should have been at home with my gold.'

Catrin sniffed. 'Spare me your honeyed tongue, I knew what you were like.'

'Well, that is the meat of the matter,' he said, still stroking her hand. 'I *was* like it then, Catty, but I'm not any more. On the day I fought with Padarn, I swore an oath to change. In a sense I truly am dead. I left the old Lewis on the banks of the Wye that day. I'm now Louis de Grosmont, and I serve William d'Ypres, Lord of Kent.' Very gently, he tilted up her chin on his forefinger, betraying the glitter in her eyes. 'I was going to come back for you, Cat, I promise I was. But not until I had proved myself worthy.'

'And you expected me to wait, thinking that you were dead?' She jerked her head away, but the wobble of her voice betrayed her.

'I thought you might stay a widow longer than this,' he said, and touched the gold knot ring on her heart finger. 'But then I made many misjudgements back then.' There was sorrow in his tone, and perhaps the faintest note of reproach.

'Yes, you did.'

'Are you then remarried?'

Catrin swallowed and shook her head. 'But for Winchester, I would be.'

'Ah. You lost him there then?' Although he spoke with gentleness and compassion, his eyes were sharp.

It was impossible to bear. A great wave of grief began to gather. 'I do not know. I came here to find out if he is a prisoner and, if he is, to pay his ransom!'

'And found me, instead.'

Tears spilled. 'I should never have come.' The final word
ended in a howl of self-reproach and she began to cry.

'Yes, you should, it was meant to be.' Louis took her in
his arms and held her firmly. When she tried to push out of
his embrace, he tightened his grip and murmured soothing
words at the same time. He wanted to know more about her
and until he did, he had no intention of yielding her up to
another man, if at all. What had once been stale was now
fresh and new and intriguing. Besides, it was several days
since he had last had a woman and he was hungry. And she
was, after all, his wife.

'Catty, Catty,' he crooned, kissing her temple and her wet
cheek. 'Catty, it's all right, I promise.' He let her weep, and
at the same time rubbed her back and her shoulders. He made
her finish the wine, and then gave her the rest of his. Only then
did he taste her lips, moist with wine and the salt of tears. His
hands soothed, stroked, and then manipulated. From her side
they moved to her waist and then to her breasts. His kisses
went from comforting, to questing, to passionate, and beneath
his touch her nipples budded and her body arched.

'Stop,' Catrin gasped as they broke for air. She tried to push
him away, but Louis ignored her protest and placed her hand
on the swollen bulge beneath his tunic.

'Catty, for God's love don't refuse me or I will go mad,' he
groaned. 'I have to have you.' He ended any attempt at protest
with another deep, probing kiss, and moved his own hand to
her lap. His fingers searched and then delicately rubbed. His
tongue thrust and stroked, and his hips rocked.

She made a small sound in her throat, and her hand closed
around him and began to squeeze and relax. It was good,
exquisitely so, and Louis had to struggle to keep his wits
about him. It was obvious that they could go no further
than this without seeking somewhere more private, but it
could not be too far or the impetus would be lost.

There was a storeshed a few yards away, in which was
stacked kindling for the great stone ovens in the kitchen. It
was not the best place for a tryst, but it would afford them
more privacy than this. Disengaging, he took her hand and
pulled her to her feet.

His voice was light with excitement and daring. 'Do you remember that time in Chepstow, Catty? In the keep undercroft before we were wed?' It was a rhetorical question. He knew she did because it was the first time that she had experienced the delight of climax, and he had brought her to that point time and again, panting, sweating, crying out and clawing him.

Now he pulled her into the small shed and wedged the door shut with a hefty chunk of split log. Anyone who wanted fuel would have to wait. Snatching off her cloak, he spread it on the bare floor in front of the kindling and removed his gambeson to use as a pillow.

'Lewis, I can't.' She tried to retreat, but he was blocking the entrance and there was a wall of wood at her back.

'That's what you said then too,' he answered with a grin. For all that she was shaking her head, her rapid breathing betrayed her. She wanted him as much as he wanted her.

He grasped her hand and brought it to his lips. The tip of his tongue flickered out and touched her palm, then trailed lightly to the pulse point on her wrist. 'Pleasure,' he said softly, 'nothing but pleasure.' Returning to her palm, he kissed her fingertips one by one, then bit down gently. His tongue circled. He was the hunter and she was the prey. He stalked her now, his other hand encircling her waist and pulling her against him. 'Remember Chepstow, Catty.' He angled his head, pushing her wimple to one side, and sucked her throat.

'Jesu God,' she whispered, and he felt her swallow. In the streaks of light showing through the cracks in the wood, he saw that her eyes were closed and that her breathing was short and shallow as she sought not to gasp.

'It's more than a memory now,' Louis murmured. 'It's here, it's real.' He claimed her mouth again and pressed his hand into the small of her back, at the same time pushing his hips forward and up so that she could feel his arousal. 'Please,' he said. 'Shall I get down on my knees to you?' And promptly did so, but only to lift the hem of her gown and caress her ankles, and then work his way up her calves and thighs. She shuddered but did not try to stop him, and her gasps grew more audible. He rose to his feet again, but now the folds of her gown were bunched upon his forearms and she was naked to the waist. He cupped her buttocks and rubbed against her, enjoying the cool smoothness of her flesh. The anticipation was often almost as exciting as the act itself, although what he liked best of all was to watch the effect he had on his partner.

Holding her against him, he unlaced the drawstring of his braies and rubbed his swollen penis against her belly and between her thighs. 'Feel how hot I am for you, Catty,' he muttered against her throat. 'I want to fill you until I burst. It's been too long.'

He drew her down on to the improvised bed of cloak and hauberk, and spread her thighs. His thumbs rested on the soft skin there, then stroked lightly upwards, opening her to the thrust of his body. She arched her throat, a soft cry escaping between her clenched teeth. Louis watched her response and avidly fed upon it. He pushed deeper, cupping her buttocks and pressing down upon the small pea of flesh that was her centre of pleasure. She whimpered and clutched him.

Despite saying that he was desperate, Louis had no intention of racing to climax too soon and he held back, his movements rhythmic and measured, keeping up a constant pressure on her, without driving himself beyond control. She began to thresh and toss her head, and the whimpers became louder cries. Louis studied her face: the tightly squeezed lids, the open mouth drawing air in rapid breaths and letting it out in shallow gasps of frustration and pleasure. His loins twitched at the sight. Near, so near. He held her there a moment longer, relishing the sight of her struggle the way a fisherman relished the sight of a newly caught fish flapping its silver body on the river bank. Then he went for the kill, plunging deep and surging hard.

'Jesu God!' Catrin uttered again, but this time it was not a whisper but a full-blown howl.

For a moment she went rigid beneath him, and then she shattered, the ripples of her climax engulfing him and bringing him triumphantly to his own.

He surfaced somewhat breathlessly from a well of pleasure

whose depth had taken him by surprise. But then lying with Catrin in the old days had often been rewarding. He liked her wild response. It was always better with a woman who cried and screamed. And now that he had taken her, he felt more in control.

Withdrawing, he rolled away and sat up. She was still breathing hard, but the straining hunger no longer filled her expression. Very slowly, as if reluctant to do so, she opened her eyes and looked up at him with heavy lids. Then she flung violently away and burst into tears.

It was not what he had expected and for an instant he was nonplussed. 'Catty?' He leaned over her. 'What's wrong?'

She shook her head and wept all the more. Louis sighed and pulled her dress down over her buttocks and bare thighs. She was wearing red silk hose like the ones he had given her all those years ago, and the sight sent a small aftershock of lust through him.

'I'll bring some more wine,' he murmured, and slipped out of the shed.

When he returned, she had pulled herself over to the wall and sat with her spine against the planks, her knees drawn up to her chin in a defensive posture. She had ceased to weep, but her eyes were swollen and she kept sniffing into a linen kerchief.

'I brought some bread too, else you'll be as drunk as a Bristol sailor,' he said, as he set the wooden platter down in front of her.

'Perhaps I want to be as drunk as a Bristol sailor,' she answered in a choked voice. 'Perhaps I want to consign what just happened to a drunken haze.'

'Not you, Catty, it's not in your nature. You always run to meet difficulties head on.'

'What would you know about my nature these days?'

'Not enough, although I've made a beginning.'

He started to grin, but she wiped it off his face when she said, 'Then I hope you're proud.'

'I never gave pride a thought, did you?' he retorted with some asperity, and poured wine into one of the cups. 'I wanted you, I still do and, as I far as I'm aware, the feeling is mutual.'

He took a drink from the cup and then handed it across to her. 'Is it not?'

She rested the cup on her knees and stared into the wine. 'I don't know. If you asked me my name just now, my tongue would stumble. I came to Rochester in search of the man to whom I am betrothed, and instead I find that betrothal null and void because I am no longer a widow but a wife.'

Louis tilted his head. 'Tell me about him,' he said. 'Tell me about your life since I left it and, in the name of Christ, eat some of this bread before you faint on me.' He thrust the platter beneath her nose.

She took one of the flat, golden loaves and bit into it without any enthusiasm. 'I thought about throwing myself into the river and joining you,' she said with a twisted smile. 'What a waste that would have been. But I was saved from myself and my grief by a lady named Amice de Cormel, who was in need of a maid for herself and a nurse for her seven-year-old son.'

He listened attentively and with developing interest as she told him her tale. Catrin the girl-wife, whose sole concern had been tending the hearth and pleasing his needs, had become Catrin the woman of independent strength and means. But that was only a small part of her appeal. Piquancy was added by the fact that her betrothed was his prisoner. Louis could see the attraction that the tall blond knight might have for Catrin. Oliver Pascal's laconic ways only hinted at the quiescent strength of the man, and the way he bore himself would be equally as appealing to women as a more bold approach. Still, Louis might yet have released Catrin from old vows had she not mentioned that King Stephen was in her debt for tending his wounds at Bristol.

'King Stephen?' he repeated, unable to believe his good fortune. 'You know King Stephen?'

She made a small movement of her shoulders as if it did not matter. 'They keep him in irons and the irons chafe. I tend his flesh with salve and I have spoken to him often. He knows me by sight and by name.'

Louis gazed at her while his imagination took flight. His young wife, whom he had once thought insignificant enough to desert, had the ear and the gratitude of Stephen himself. 'I have heard a rumour that Stephen will soon be exchanged for Robert of Gloucester,' he said.

'Then his men will be freed too?' She looked at him eagerly.

'That will depend on who holds their ransoms, but I should think so.' He rubbed his palm across his upper lip.

'I don't even know if Oliver's alive.' She gave a sniff and wiped her sleeve across her face. 'That's what I was coming to find out . . . and then this happened.' She looked at him, searching his face. 'What am I going to do?'

Louis considered her. He knew that he had to play this very carefully now; hold the balance, manipulate it in his favour. 'He is alive, you need not fear on that score,' he said. 'I saw him and spoke to him earlier this morning.'

Several emotions flashed across her face. Relief and joy, swiftly followed by the bitten lip and tear-filled eyes of guilt and grief. 'He is well?'

'Chafing at the confinement, but otherwise whole. I was one of the party who captured him and the Earl of Gloucester on the Winchester road, and part of my duty has been to guard them. I am promised a portion of the ransom price but, in the light of what he is to you, I dare say I could be generous enough to waive it.'

'You dare say?' Catrin looked at him through swollen, narrowed eyes. 'You could be generous?' She flung the words and then, with a rapid fumbling at her waist, she hurled a leather pouch in his face, making him duck. 'Take it,' she spat. 'Take it all. Go and count it in a corner and rub your hands!'

He looked down at the pouch where it had fallen into his lap. Silver coins spilled from its open throat. He scooped them back, laced the drawstring and placed it gently at her side. It was not as generous a gesture as it appeared. By the laws of matrimony, whatever was Catrin's was his. He would have the silver from her at a time of his own choosing.

'I confess that I am jealous,' he said, with the travesty of a smile. 'I would like to run him through with my sword, but how can I when, to all intents and purposes, you were a widow and, as far as both of you were aware, the road was clear? I am sorry if I cannot be as gracious about it as you wish, or as I indeed would wish it myself.' He paused and shrugged. 'But then, I realise that I have you and he has nothing. I will free him this very day.'

She made a choking sound and, turning to one side, retched up the wine she had drunk. He watched her and said nothing, his eyes brightly observing her response as he had observed it in the act of love. He was surprised to find that he really did feel jealous – although he had no intention of running Pascal through on his sword. There were other, subtler means of torture.

'Is that a condition of his release, you having me?' she demanded as she sat up. Her voice hovered on the verge of loathing.

Louis kept his own voice level, a little apologetic. 'I suppose you could take it that way, Catty my love, but I was hoping that you would cleave to me without such threats. You cannot marry him while I still live. You cannot give him legitimate heirs of his body or stand in church with him.' Taking her hands in his, he leaned towards her. 'I promise on my honour to be a better husband than I was before. I still love you and desire you. I always have.'

'But you don't love me enough to set me free,' she said flatly.

'Is that what you want?'

She jutted her jaw at him, and the old, stubborn look was back on her face. The one presented to him when he strolled home from the alehouse three hours later than promised with blond hairs on his tunic. 'I want to see Oliver.'

Louis eyed her thoughtfully, considering his options. He could run the risk of 'setting her free' and hope that she chose him, or he could hold her to ransom with Oliver's release as the price. The first was the more dangerous but ultimately the more satisfying if things went his way. The second would ensure him her body, her obedience and access to King Stephen, but not the devotion he craved from her.

He inclined his head. 'If that is your desire.' There was

a doubtful note in his voice. 'But I am not sure it is for the best.'

'I want to see him,' she repeated, her voice trembling.

Rising, Louis beat crumbs of soil and bark from his elegant tunic. Then he helped her to her feet, his expression one of tender anxiety. 'It is your decision.' He brushed gently at the creases and rumples in her gown.

'I know.' Trembling, she stiffened her spine.

Louis cupped her face with his palm and brushed away her tears with a gentle thumb. 'Then, Holy Christ, I pray you make the right one,' he said softly, and anticipation quivered through him at the size of the gamble he had just taken.

CHAPTER 19

Oliver was seated over a merels board with Geoffrey, half-heartedly considering his move, when their prison door opened and Louis de Grosmont returned.

Oliver eyed him with surprise. He had not thought to see de Grosmont again until his next turn of duty, especially after viewing him with the woman in the bailey. The satisfied glow on the man's face and the sated droop of his eyelids suggested that the encounter had been profitable. 'Now what does he want?' Oliver muttered out of the side of his mouth.

Geoffrey glanced over his shoulder. 'You by the looks of things. Perhaps he's still hoping to woo you.'

Oliver curled his lip. 'If he is, then he's in for a sad disappointment.' He straightened his expression as Louis sauntered over to their trestle.

'I need to speak with you alone,' Louis said to Oliver, and gestured to another trestle in the corner.

Close up, Oliver could smell the sweat of the man's exertion and the faint, but disturbingly familiar, perfume of rose attar. He raised one eyebrow, first at Geoffrey, then at Louis. In his own time he pushed to his feet. 'About what?'

'About your ransom.' Again Louis indicated the corner.

Oliver was tempted to dig in his heels and stay where he was but decided that it would serve no purpose. If Louis wanted to discuss his ransom, it was best to co-operate. Warily, he rose and went to the empty trestle. There was a wine stain on the wood and some drips of hardened candle wax from the night before.

'What about my ransom?' he demanded as Louis joined him. 'Have you suddenly decided to raise the stakes?'

'Let us just say that the stakes have changed.' Louis rested his hip on the table and leaned into Oliver's space.

Oliver immediately slouched back on the bench and folded his arms to show that he was neither impressed nor intimidated. 'In what way?' His expression was sardonic. 'Have I suddenly become so wealthy or important that my value has vastly increased?'

Louis smiled with his mouth but not with his eyes which remained as wary as Oliver's. 'Important, yes,' he said. 'In fact, so important that you are free to collect your weapons and go.'

All attempt at nonchalance fell away. Unfolding his arms, Oliver gazed at Louis with widening eyes. 'I am free to go?' he repeated on a rising note of disbelief.

Louis spread his hands. 'As soon as you will. Rise up and walk out of here and no one will stop you.'

'Hah, I do not believe that!'

'It is the truth, I swear on my soul.' Louis crossed himself as he spoke.

Oliver spread his hands too, in a gesture of utter bewilderment. 'But why?'

Louis dropped the hand with which he had been signing himself and hesitated. Then he looked at Oliver with avid, bright eyes. 'Catrin,' he said.

Colour filled Oliver's face and he felt a warm surge at his core. A vision, not so far from the truth, flashed through his mind, of Catrin riding into Rochester with a determined jut to her chin, letting naught stand in her way. 'She is here?' he said eagerly.

Louis nodded. 'Yes, she is here.'

Oliver's mind was so filled with the image of Catrin that it took a moment for other considerations to pierce the upsurge of joy. But when they did the cut was deep and sharp – the intimacy with which Louis said 'Catrin', affording no other title as if he knew her well; the woman in the red dress and dark cloak; the heaviness of recent pleasure weighting Louis's eyelids. Like a hammer blow the thought struck

Oliver that Catrin had paid his ransom to this snake with her body.

'If you have touched her, I will kill you!' he snarled and shot to his feet, his fists already clenched to strike.

In one nimble move, Louis sprang off the table and put it between them.

'And if you lay a finger on me, you will hang from these battlements until the crows have picked you clean!' His glance flashed to the other guards who had started forward, swords hissing from their sheaths. He waved them back to their posts with a terse gesture.

'Sit down,' he commanded Oliver. 'This avails us nothing, and there is much you do not know.'

With great reluctance and hostility, Oliver subsided on to the bench, but the battle light remained in his eyes and his heartbeat was a heavy drum in his throat.

Louis remained on his feet. He rubbed his palm across his chin and drew out the moment as he gathered his thoughts. At last, when he was ready, he struck without mercy. 'I have every right to "lay a finger" or whatever else I desire upon Catrin, because she is my wife,' he said.

'Your what?' Oliver almost gagged.

'Wedded, bedded and sanctioned by the church full six years ago. I have known my Catrin since we were children building mud castles together in the bailey at Chepstow.'

'Her husband is dead.' The words emerged from Oliver's mouth but he was scarcely aware of speaking them. 'My Catrin'? Christ Jesu, it was not to be borne.

'So she assumed until today, but she knows the truth now.' He gave a secretive smile as if at some pleasant memory. 'Of course, I do not blame her for abandoning her "widowhood", but she should have been more patient. I would have returned for her.'

'You were the one who "abandoned" her.' Oliver's voice was clotted with loathing. If there had been a sword at his hip, he would have used it.

'Every man makes mistakes in his life,' Louis answered with a shrug, as if the matter was trivial. He examined a fingernail and then clicked it on his thumb. 'I admit that

I am no saint, but she accepts that, just as she accepts the reason I had to flee Chepstow and play dead. Of course,' he added, giving Oliver a direct look in which there was complete self-assurance, 'if she wants to go with you, I will not prevent her, but I believe that you will find she prefers to keep her marriage vows.'

'You think so?' Oliver's voice was thick with revulsion. 'She didn't come here to find you but to ransom me. The past is dead.'

Louis shrugged. 'Believe what you will, but you are deluding yourself. I did not have to force her to lie with me just now. She was more than willing, and not because she was playing the martyr to pay your ransom. She still cleaves to me. You do not even have to take my word for it. You can ask her yourself before you leave.' Pushing to his feet, Louis sauntered to the door.

For a nauseous moment, Oliver thought that he was going to usher Catrin into the room and parade the situation before all the other hostages. But Louis spoke to the guard, there was a clinking sound and he returned with Oliver's pilgrim swordbelt and weapons.

'Your shield and hauberk are in the guard room and your horse is in the stables,' Louis said as he pushed the other items across the trestle. 'Take them and be far from here before dusk closes the gates.'

Oliver fingered his swordbelt and looked at the familiar pewter badges. It seemed to be the only recognisable item in a world gone awry. Very slowly, because all the power seemed to have drained from his body, he stood up and buckled on the belt. He had a powerful desire to draw his sword and slice off de Grosmont's handsome, smug head, but it remained sheathed. He could see that Louis was prepared and, perhaps even hoping, for just such a move so that he could lay claim to a justified kill of his own.

'Two more things,' Louis said, his voice pleasant, his expression marred by a twist of smug malice. 'There is a manservant of yours waiting in the bailey, a hulking oaf. Take him with you when you leave. My wife has no further need of his services. You will find her in the chapel. I do not expect your farewells to take longer than a few minutes.' He opened his hand. 'You are free to go.'

It was a lie, Oliver thought, staring into the obsidian-dark eyes with their challenge and mockery. Louis de Grosmont had just taken all hope of freedom from him and cast him into a deep, dark well of despair.

'God help you if we ever meet again on the field of battle,' he said through clenched teeth.

Louis smiled. 'Oh, he will,' he said smugly. 'God always helps those who help themselves.'

Catrin had tried prayer, but either she was not listening or the saints were not answering, for she had gained little comfort from the hour spent on her knees. Staring at the candles had made her vision blur, and now she viewed everything through a fuzzy, golden haze.

She was being torn in two. Lewis, Louis as he called himself now, or Oliver. She loved them both; Louis with the heartsick burning of her youth, Oliver with the quieter steadiness of maturity.

Whatever his excuses, Louis had once betrayed her badly, but when he said he had changed his expression had been so sincere and chagrined that she doubted her own judgement. His lovemaking still sent her soaring and he was, after all, her husband. She could not be wed to Oliver while her commitment to another man still stood; could not love him with a whole heart knowing that Louis was alive. Oliver deserved better than that. Besides, if he did regain his lands, any children that she bore to him would not be legitimate issue and their inheritance would be open to question.

How she was going to face him and say all this, she did not know. The prospect was so harrowing that she was tempted to hide until he was gone, but he deserved better than that too.

'Mary mother, Holy mother, help me to say the right words,' she entreated the statue of the Virgin before the altar. 'Help me to bear this.'

The mother of Christ gazed down on her with a face set in serene repose, the infant Jesus cradled in her arms. Catrin's mind remained blank.

A draught fluttered the candles on the altar and swayed the flame in the sanctuary lamp. Behind her, she heard the soft scrape of a leather sole on stone and the clink of a sword chap against mail. Slowly she turned, her belly a vast cavern, and watched Oliver come towards her.

He was wearing his hauberk, flecks of rust dulling the rivets. His shield hung on his back and his sword was girded at his hip. In the darkness of the chapel, his hair gleamed like ripe barley and his grey eyes were almost black. The look in them rooted her to the spot. He looked her up and down and she was conscious of the soil stains on her skirt from the storeshed floor.

'Did he force you,' he asked flatly, 'or was it of your own free will?'

Catrin gazed at him helplessly, with no inkling of how to reply. 'I . . . what did he say?'

'It doesn't matter what he said.' Oliver gestured impatiently. 'All I want to know is, did he force you?'

Heat stained Catrin's cheeks and she lowered her eyes. She felt smirched and ashamed. 'He did not rape me.' She twisted her hands together in the folds of her gown. 'It was he who made the first approach, but I . . . I was not unwilling.'

The look he gave her was like a blow and she crossed her hands on her breasts as if to shield herself. 'He is my husband,' she said raggedly.

'Who abandoned you in order to save his own hide. Christ, Catrin, can't you see him for what he is?' He took a step towards her, his armour jinking. 'He's about as faithful as a whore's oath.'

'He has changed, I know he has.' She hated herself for how weak the defence sounded.

'Although your view was from flat on your back,' he said with contempt.

Catrin gasped and recoiled as if he had struck her. 'I do not blame you your pain,' she said shakily. 'But I am suffering too. Before you condemn, think how it would be if your Emma were suddenly to walk back into the room and tell you that her death was all a mistake; that you could have her back in your arms. What would you do? Whom would you choose,

Solomon, in your wisdom? Your wife, or your promised wife?'
Her voice rose and cracked.

He stared at her, and then his shoulders slumped and he
shook his head mutely.

It almost broke her to see the defeat engulf him. 'While
Louis lives, I am his wife. It doesn't mean I love you less.' She
took a step towards him, her hand outstretched in entreaty.
For a moment she thought that he was going to strike her
aside or just turn and walk out. Both intentions flickered
across his face, but then vanished to leave a look of pure
anguish. He crossed the final three yards of space between
them and dragged her into his arms.

Crushed in his mailed grip, Catrin wept, and felt through
her hands the shuddering of his own body in grief. He took
her face in his hands and kissed her mouth, and she tasted
their mingled tear-salt.

The priest, returning from his errand to fetch fresh candles
for the chapel, made a shocked sound in his throat.

Oliver and Catrin slowly parted. 'If you have need of me,
seek me out.' He used his gambeson sleeve to wipe his eyes. 'If
not . . .' He swallowed hard. 'If not, then let me be. However
many sons you bear him, however great your fortune, I wish
you well, but I do not want to know.'

She watched him walk out of the chapel, and stayed where
she was until the sound of his footsteps faded away. Then she
genuflected to the altar and went in search of a small, dark
corner in which to curl up and weep.

CHAPTER 20

The Christmas feast of 1141 was celebrated on a grand scale by King Stephen's court at Canterbury. If no outright victory had been gained, at least the status quo had been re-established. Stephen and Robert of Gloucester had been exchanged for each other and both sides had drawn back from conflict to lick their wounds and regroup.

Louis and Catrin were given a place of honour at one of the high tables, below the salt of the magnates but on an equal ranking with the lesser barons. As the man who had captured Robert of Gloucester, Louis was in high favour, and he pushed that advantage for all it was worth. With style, with subtlety, with cunning. The wolf was running down the deer.

Catrin watched him set his snares with trepidation and pride. She was uncomfortable at the way he had reinvented her past with a mingling of half-truths and omissions. He told the curious that she had believed him dead and, as a skilled herb-wife, she had sought refuge and employment in Bristol, where her services had been invaluable in tending the King. Hearing a rumour that her husband might still be alive, she had braved the open road to find him. She was courageous, loyal, beautiful and wise. What man would not be blessed with such a wife by his side?

Catrin had not denied the tale, there was no point, but it worried her that the story flowed so plausibly off his tongue. Despite his promise that he had changed, he still used lies and manipulation to gain his ends.

She shied away from the thought that he had lied to her too, for it carried all manner of implications, not least about her own judgement. During the day, she could ignore the small, nagging voice that told her she should have stayed with Oliver and made her life with him, his wife in all but name. But in the darkest hours of the night she was vulnerable, and the voice would wake her from sleep, accusing her of skipping on quicksand instead of choosing firm ground.

She was full of guilt and grief over Oliver. She could not just act as if the year and a half during which she had come to know and love him had never been. But there was no one to whom she could talk about him. The women of the court already had their own friendships. Knowing the gossip of the bower, she would not have trusted them anyway, for all that they crowded around her and asked her advice for this ailment and that. She had never thought she would miss Edon's feather-brained companionship, but she did, terribly.

'Brooding again, Catty?' Louis leaned round to look at her. There was an evergreen chaplet set slightly askew on his thick black hair, making him look even more like a faun from the wild wood. He clutched a mead cup in his right hand but, although his breath smelt of the drink, he was only a little merry. He had been mingling with the guests seated at other tables, telling jests, laughing at jests told, making himself popular. She had even watched him juggle five leather balls before the King with expert sleight of hand. It had earned him applause from the royal table and the gift of a fine, silver brooch.

She shook her head and forced a smile. 'Reflecting,' she said.

'About what?' He leaned closer. His hand crept up beneath her wimple and his cool fingertips lightly stroked the back of her neck.

'About what I'm doing here.' A small, sensuous shiver ran down her spine.

He frowned. 'You made the right choice, you know that.'

'Yes . . . yes, I know that.' She gnawed her lower lip. 'It is just that I feel as if I don't belong.'

'Well, you don't . . .' He jerked his head at the high table. 'At least not to them.' He leaned closer, and her bones melted at the darkness in his voice. 'But you do to me, you've always been mine.'

She laughed shakily. 'Are you so sure of that?'

His dark eyes flashed a look that said he was supremely confident and she was foolish for even token resistance. 'Come,' he said. Dragging her to her feet, he led her to the large apple wassail tree in the centre of the hall around which guests were dancing to honour the season.

Catrin hung back, but Louis's grip was lean and strong and, with a laugh, he pulled her forward. From the tree's branches he grabbed a chaplet of evergreen like his own and pushed it down upon her wimple, the holly berries glistening like drops of fresh blood.

'Dance,' he commanded, and kissed her lips, his tongue flickering lightly round their outline before he withdrew.

And Catrin danced, because Louis was the piper and his dark glamour called the tune.

As the evening progressed, and the wine flowed freely, Catrin's sombre mood lightened beneath Louis's determined onslaught. First she smiled and then she laughed. Enjoyment crept up on her, and suddenly she could almost forget.

Louis led her to join in boisterous games of bee-in-the-middle, hoodman-blind, and hunt-the-slipper. Catrin discovered that she had a knack for the latter which involved passing an item of footwear among a circle of other players and trying to keep the owner, who stood in the middle of the ring, from guessing who was in possession. Once the owner did guess, the loser had to forfeit their own shoe and become the hunter in the middle.

By sleight of hand, an innocent expression, and great good luck, Catrin succeeded in never being caught out. Louis, by far the best dissembler of them all, was finally trapped by the pure guesswork of the flushed wife of a baron whose turn it was in the centre.

With much good-natured rolling of his eyes, Louis got to his feet and stepped to the middle of the ring to take her place. He presented the shoe to its owner with a courtly flourish and a kiss on the hand. The gesture met with jovial banter and cat-calls and the red-faced woman laughed and gave him a hefty push. Grinning, Louis gave an exaggerated stagger, stooped to remove one of his ankle boots and gave it to her. She swept him a mock curtsey, returned to her place amongst the hiders, and the game began again.

Catrin, the merrier now for three cups of wine, could not quite smother her giggle as the man on her right sneaked the boot beneath a fold of her skirt. Louis caught the movement from the corner of his eye and, whirling round, pointed straight at her.

Flushed, laughing, Catrin spread her hands to show that there was nothing in them. Louis, however, was not fooled, and continued to advance. 'Being your husband, I command you to lift your skirts, wife!' he declared, hilarity brimming in his eyes. There were loud guffaws at the sally.

Catrin sat a moment longer, hoping that her look of wide innocence would fool him, but he continued to advance. Grabbing the shoe from its hiding place, she sprang to her feet. 'Then you must catch me first, my lord!' she cried, and fled from the circle.

To loud laughter and cheers of encouragement, Louis set off in pursuit.

It was impossible to run through Canterbury's packed great hall, but Catrin wove her way determinedly through the crowds and between the trestles. To mark the Christmas season Louis had given her a new gown of strong grass-green that suited her colouring. It also made it easy for him to follow the path she threaded through the other guests.

Catrin glanced behind her and saw Louis shouldering after her, drawing closer. In the pit of her stomach there was a tiny spark of panic, a response to the primitive instinct of being hunted, but that only added to the thrill. Obviously, even hampered by the lack of a shoe, he was going to capture her in the end, but she would make him work hard for his victory.

Round the wassail tree she skipped, then beneath the batons of two jugglers entertaining one of the trestles. Briefly she joined a group of women admiring someone's new lap-dog – a fluffy creature resembling a burst pillow – that had been purchased for an exorbitant sum from an Italian merchant.

Louis lost her for a moment. She saw him over by the jugglers, his eyes travelling rapidly from face to face. She hid amongst the women for a little longer, then rose on tiptoe and, clutching the shoe, waved her arm on high. Louis's gaze met hers through the crowd like a hunter's in the forest. Hot, dark, dangerous. Her loins contracted. She stuck out her tongue, then gave a little gasp of excitement as he started towards her.

She took off again, squeezed past a group of knights who were discussing the merits of Lombard war horses, and scurried behind an embroidered curtain that screened off a twisting stairway. It was difficult climbing the wedge-shaped steps in her full skirts. She had been breathless when she reached the stairs. By the time she gained the next floor, she was gasping, her calves too tight to carry her any further than the arched, stone walkway leading off to the rooms beyond.

She looked at Louis's shoe. He had small feet, not much larger than her own, and she could have worn his footwear without any difficulty – especially these, with their embroidery and green braid lacing. Putting her hand inside the shoe, she inhaled the tang of new leather.

The sound of her own breathing and the rapid thud of her heart concealed the scrape of Louis's footsteps on the stairs. The first she knew of his presence was the moment when he lunged at her from the last step and caught her against the wall.

She barely had time to scream, and that was muffled by the cupped palm he pressed over her lips. 'I've caught you now,' he panted against her ear. 'I claim my forfeit.'

Catrin was unable to speak, but she poked out her tongue and licked the salty skin of his palm. The wine sang in her blood, and the wiry strength of him was delicious. Her arms went around his neck and she rubbed against him.

'My forfeit,' he repeated, his voice a little slurred, but more with lust than drink. 'I command you to lift your skirts.' He took his hand from her mouth and raised his tunic to reach down inside his braies.

Catrin's eyes widened. She glanced around. 'What, here, on the stairs?'

'Lost your daring, Catty?' he taunted with a devilish grin. 'Forgotten that time against the salted herring barrels in Chepstow?'

'I had bruises for weeks after,' she protested, but the spark in his eyes was kindling enough, and she began to gather up her skirts. 'Someone might come,' she added on a last thread of reason, as he seized her hips and angled her body towards his.

'I certainly hope so,' Louis said incorrigibly, and thrust into her.

It was not the most comfortable coupling, but the excitement and novelty more than compensated for the rough stone at Catrin's back and the jolt of pain in her spine each time that he lunged. Sheer, raw lust was what had fired their marriage before, and it was as incandescent as ever. Catrin cried aloud at the pleasure, then, remembering where they were, clenched her teeth and held the sound in her throat.

'No, Catty, let it go!' Louis panted in extremis. 'I need to hear you!'

She shook her head from side to side.

'Please!' Louis groaned.

Her climax struck, enhanced by his pleading, and her scream echoed along the walkway as her knees buckled. Louis took her weight and plunged into his own crisis with a long moan. Then he too lost his strength and staggered, pulling her down with him so that they ended in a tangle of limbs on the cold stone floor.

After a moment, Louis rolled on to his back, a blissful grin on his face. 'The best yet,' he said breathlessly.

Catrin struggled to sit up. Her spine was sore, her loins tingled and burned. The pleasure had been intense, but she was not sure that it was 'the best yet' for her. It was fun to couple in unexpected places, but she also liked the slower, sensual comfort of a feather bed, and the small, niggling voice that she preferred to ignore informed her that Louis seemed to derive his greatest pleasure from coupling with her where the danger of being discovered lent an added spice.

'You don't answer me, wife.' He glanced at her sidelong.

'You leave me no breath to do so,' she retorted, then turned her head sharply towards the stairwell. The sound of voices and the scrape of shoe on stone were far too close.

She scrambled to her feet and frantically shook out and smoothed the skirts of her gown. Louis, in no such rush, slipped his genitals back inside his braies and stood up almost lazily. He was bending over to pick up his shoe when King Stephen and William d'Ypres stepped on to the walkway that led to the private solar.

Catrin performed a flustered curtsey, her face flaming. Louis flourished a bow and, at the same time, grasped the shoe.

Stephen raised his brows. 'Is a place of honour in the hall not good enough for you that you should choose the royal apartments instead?' he asked with a smile. There were dark circles beneath his eyes, and weariness dragged at his mouth corners. The months of imprisonment had taken their toll.

'No, sire,' Louis responded smoothly. 'We are grateful indeed. It is just that I needed a quiet retreat to give my wife her Christmas gift.'

'I see.' Stephen eyed the shoe that Louis held in his hand, then looked at Catrin where she stood flushed and dishevelled. 'Was it well received?'

Louis smiled. 'Yes, sire.'

William d'Ypres snorted in amusement and shook his head. 'I do not know how you do it.'

'I could explain, sir.' Louis waggled his brows suggestively.

D'Ypres laughed and gave Louis a push. 'That wit of yours is sharp enough to carve you a path to success or cut you to the bone. Have a care which way you use it.'

'As ever, sir.' Louis bowed.

'As never,' d'Ypres retorted, but his tone was indulgent. 'Perhaps in the New Year, I'll see what you can accomplish.'

'You will not find me lacking, my lord.'

'As to that, a gambler takes his chances,' d'Ypres responded drily.

The two men made to go on their way, but Stephen stopped and turned round. 'Mistress healer, do you have a cure for a sore throat?' He rubbed his larynx to indicate the pain.

'Surely, sire,' Catrin answered, her colour remaining high. Louis had taken the brunt of the banter, and the King and his chief mercenary had been indulgently amused, hinting that they were well accustomed to discovering Louis in such situations. He had done no more than live up to expectations – theirs and his own. Catrin felt, rather ashamedly, that she had lived down to hers, and would gladly have remained overlooked. 'You must drink a tisane of blackcurrant, liquorice and horehound, sweetened with honey. It will ease, but not cure,' she added as a safeguard to her reputation.

'Then mix it for me, and bring it to my chamber.' His winning smile flashed across his face. It should have lifted his features, but instead it made him look all the more exhausted.

'Sire.' Catrin bowed her head, and the men continued on to the royal chambers.

Louis hopped into his shoe. 'If I didn't know that Stephen was so attached to his wife, I'd think he had a fancy to you,' he remarked with a grin.

Catrin gave her husband a withering look. 'Some men at least, carry their brains above their belts.'

Louis knelt to fasten the horn toggle on the side of the shoe. 'Now why should I think that your blade is aimed at me?'

'If the cap fits, then wear it.'

Louis stood up and looked at her, his expression suddenly serious. 'It doesn't fit me, Catty, whatever you think. I've made mistakes, but I've learned from them.'

'So you keep telling me,' she said. 'But I believe that actions speak the louder.'

'What do you want me to do? Have myself tonsured and profess a vow of chastity?'

Catrin smiled at the notion, but then she sobered. 'No,' she said. 'I would not put such a strain on our marriage. Keeping your faith to me will do. I am your wife, and you know how much I sacrificed to stay with you.' Her voice took on depth and vehemence. 'I won't remind you of it again; I am not a martyr, but hear this, Louis. I will not have our lovemaking used as cheap coin to feed your self-importance and your standing in the eyes of other men!'

'But you enjoyed it as much as I did!' he blustered, spreading his hands in a gesture of disbelief. 'Your cries weren't for me to stop!'

Catrin tightened her lips. 'It was the way you jested with the King and Lord William.'

'That was nothing, harmless banter. All men do it.'

'That is what I mean about the brains below the belt,' Catrin retorted smartly. 'Condemned out of your own mouth.' She gathered her skirts. 'I have a tisane to brew.'

He watched her go to the stairs, chewed his lip and tugged at his hair in perplexity. 'Catty,' he said as she set her foot on the first step.

'What?' She gave him a glance over her shoulder.

He made a contrite, prayerful gesture. 'You're beautiful and I love you.'

She gave him the ghost of a smile and put her nose in the air. 'That begins to make amends.'

'And I humbly promise to keep the faith.'

Still smiling, despite herself, Catrin went down the stairs.

'King Stephen is not well,' she said later, as she and Louis lay together in a daub and wattle shelter in the bailey. Usually it held sheep, but it had been swept out to provide accommodation for the overspill of troops. All around them, others were settling down to sleep, huddling in their cloaks for warmth against the sharp winter cold.

'Serious?'

'No,' Catrin said doubtfully, 'but he is so thin and he looks so tired. If he cannot throw it off, then it might grow worse. I told him that he should rest, but he just laughed, and asked what I thought he had been doing all those months in Bristol. I said fretting.'

Louis drew her close and nuzzled his lips against her throat. 'You are indeed a wise woman, Catty.' His voice was teasing, but his thoughts were troubled. She was the one who had changed, and she was proving more of a challenge than he had first complacently thought. Instead of leading a saddle-broken, if somewhat contrary, mare to a mounting block, he was discovering that he had his fist around the rope of an untamed wild horse. And yet he would not let go for the world. She was too valuable. He had seen her worth written in the eyes of a disinherited knight and of the King of England.

'Am I?' Her tone was almost forlorn. 'Sometimes I think I am very foolish.'

'That's just the lateness of the hour talking,' Louis dismissed easily, and pressed closer still within the cloak, letting her feel the swell of his erection, but making no greater move. After her earlier speech, he wanted to show that despite his needs, he was capable of consideration and restraint. 'Everyone thinks that sometimes.'

'Even you?'

He permitted himself a smile against the heartbeat in her soft, white throat. 'Even me.' His lips touched a fabric cord. Setting his finger beneath it, he drew it up out of her gown and chemise. It was warm from her body. In the light from the horn lantern burning on a shelf above their bed of straw, he examined the plaited knot of red, black and white wool. 'Why do you wear this thing?' he asked, unable to keep the distaste from his voice. It looked tawdry and cheap, the sort of trinket a peasant would own. 'Most women have crosses, or little religious badges.'

She grabbed it from him. 'I'm not most women.'

'True, but that does not answer my question.'

She sighed, as if he were being awkward. 'It was given to me by the wise-woman who taught me all I know. As a sort of badge of apprenticeship, if you like, but it means more to me than that. It's a reminder of her and the bond between us. She was like a grandmother to me.'

Louis concealed a grimace, imagining a toothless, smelly, old crone.

'In a way, it's a sort of talisman too,' she murmured. 'It represents the three strands of womanhood. Maiden, mother and crone.'

'Oh,' he said without interest or enthusiasm.

She tucked it firmly back inside her dress and chemise. 'But, if you want, I will wear a cross on top of my garments.'

'I will buy you a cross,' he said. 'A fine silver one inlaid with garnets from Midlothian.' He stroked her spine. 'If I had the coin, I would invest you with jewels like a queen.'

'I don't need jewels.'

'Mayhap not, but I would still dress you until you glittered to show the world how much I value you.'

She gave a little sigh – of contentment, he thought. Their lips met. The kiss could have been a preliminary to more lovemaking, but Louis kept it tender and gentle, proving what a good husband he was.

When their lips parted, he rolled half on to his back and stared at the rafters, the sparrow droppings illuminated by the glow of the lantern. Nearby, someone was softly snoring. He fixed the sights, sounds and textures in his mind. He wanted to remember this night so that in the future he could look back from a position of wealth and influence and see it as the threshold of his rise to fame. Once I slept in an animal shed. Look at me now.

He fell asleep with a smile on his face.

At Ethel's former hearth in Bristol, Oliver celebrated the Christmas season with wine and ginevra, with Welsh mead and Galwegian usquebaugh to deaden the pain. But although Oliver's body grew numb, his mind seemed to focus with all the more clarity. If anything, the grief of losing Catrin cut keener than his grief over Emma. Emma was dead and forever beyond his reach, but Catrin still lived, and breathed and loved. So near, and yet so impossibly far.

'You do yourself harm brooding out here,' said Geoffrey FitzMar, finding him there. The young knight had been released with Earl Robert a couple of weeks after Oliver. 'At least come into the hall and get drunk with everyone else.'

'I prefer my own company,' Oliver said with frozen dignity.

Geoffrey scrubbed a forefinger beneath his nose in perplexity and sat on the spare stool by the hearth. 'Richard wanted to come and fetch you, but I put him off, said that I would do it.'

'Is that supposed to bribe me with guilt?'

Geoffrey shrugged. 'I just thought that you wouldn't want

the lad to find you like this. I know you are deeply wounded, but it is the Christmas season. It might heal you a little to stand under a kissing bunch.'

Oliver gave Geoffrey a vicious look. 'I don't want to be "healed a little",' he snapped and took a gulp from the almost empty flask of usquebaugh. 'What is the point of having your heart ripped from your body time upon time? I will sleep with my sword from now on.' He touched his belt to emphasise the point and, in so doing, felt the decorative love knot that Ethel had woven. Now he tore this free and, with a look of loathing at the mingled red, raven and flaxen hair, cast it on the fire.

Geoffrey began to exclaim, but bit the sound between his teeth. Lunging to his feet, Oliver wove his way unsteadily to the hall. He did not suppose it mattered where oblivion came from, just as long as it did.

Godard lumbered out of the shadows, snatched the poker from the spit bar and, with a deft movement, flicked the knot from the fire and stamped on it. The outer edge was charred and singed, but the inside was whole and the pattern still visible. Oliver's aim had not been good.

'He might regret it later,' he said to a startled Geoffrey.

The young knight tugged at his curls and looked dubious.

'The old woman knew, but she never said nowt.'

'Knew what?'

'That the husband was still alive. Read it in the smoke she did – a dark-haired man from the enemy side who would bring misery and strife.'

The hair rose on Geoffrey's nape and his gaze flickered anxiously. 'She had the sight?'

Godard shrugged. 'Who's to say? All I know is that she knew.' He gestured to the blackened token half-hidden under his boot. 'I'll keep it for the nonce. It'll not be mended else.' With a nod, he set about banking the fire against any dangerous stray sparks.

Geoffrey turned to the keep. The sounds of merriment drifted like smoke on the wind. 'I'd best go and join his lordship before he injures himself or picks a fight,' he said with a sigh.

*   *   *

Catrin was binding the sprained ankle of one of William d'Ypres' knights when Louis came running through the camp to find her. The King's army was heading for York, but had broken the march to rest overnight at Northampton.

The weather had held fine, and a soft, late April sun was warming the thatch on the roofs and gilding the wooden tent supports.

'Catty, leave that,' Louis panted. 'The Queen wants you immediately.'

Catrin stared at her husband. 'The Queen?'

'Yes. The King's been taken with a high fever in the night, and he's refused all his doctors. Quickly, there's no time to lose.' He snapped his fingers at her.

Catrin resented the gesture. She was not a dog to come to heel, but in the next moment she forgave him as she saw the agitation in his eyes.

'A moment will make no difference,' she soothed, and wrapped the last layer of bandage around her patient's ankle, securing the support with a bone pin. Beside her, Louis fumed and bit his thumbnail. Finished, she picked up her satchel.

'More haste, less speed,' she could not prevent herself from saying.

Louis scowled but said nothing, obviously too preoccupied to either rise to the bait or make a retort. Instead, he set off at a striding walk that ought to have belonged to a much taller man.

Catrin ran along beside him. 'I am surprised he has not been taken ill before now,' she remarked. 'I said at Christmas that he looked exhausted. He has driven himself too hard, and Lenten fare is not the food to put flesh back on a man's wasted bones.'

'Just see that he recovers now,' Louis said grimly as they entered the great hall.

Catrin glanced at him. She had never seen Louis so out of countenance before. Life was lived with a gambler's jauntiness. That much had not changed since the Chepstow days. 'I will do what I can.'

He stopped abruptly and swung her round by her arm.

His face was so close that she could see the faint sprinkling of freckles across his nose, and the tiniest barber's nick on his cheekbone. 'You'll save him, and you'll let him know that it is your skill that has kept him out of a shroud.' His upper lip curled into what was almost a snarl.

'Louis, you're hurting me.' She tugged herself free and rubbed her bruised elbow.

He stepped back and, with a little shake of his head, breathed out. His tone softened and he stroked her cheek. 'Catty, if he dies, then so do my hopes of becoming a baron. Save his life, and you will have not only his eternal gratitude, but that of the entire royal party, and we can make what we want of it.'

Now she understood. He was in the midst of the largest gamble of his life and her skill was the luck that loaded his dice. 'Everything has its price in your eyes, doesn't it?' she said with contempt. 'I wonder about my own worth to you. If I had not been known to the King and desired by another man, would you have valued me enough to bind me with old wedding vows?'

His eyes narrowed. 'You know I would. Don't be such a shrew.'

Without a word she turned from him and approached the stairs to the royal chamber.

CHAPTER 21

On the second Sunday in May, the castellan of Wickham Keep drank too much, fell off his horse, landed on his skull and killed himself. The news was delivered to Stephen in Northampton, where he lay weak as a kitten but recuperating, under the watchful eye of the Queen, his senior retainers and Catrin.

During the first week of his illness, his brother, the Bishop of Winchester, had administered the last rites to a man delirious with fever and on the brink of death. The Queen had knelt in prayer by her husband's side the night through, while Catrin laboured over him with steam inhalants, aromatic chest plasters and honey and blackcurrant tisanes.

Another twelve hours passed before the fever broke. Sweat poured out of Stephen as if he were a leaky bucket, and as swiftly as the sheets were stripped and replaced he soaked them again. By the time it was over, he was lying on a table-cloth purloined from the dais trestle in the hall, and covered with blankets borrowed from his retainers. Catrin was as exhausted as a limp sheet herself, and scarcely had the strength to feel triumph as the King opened lucid eyes for the first time in three days.

Since then he had continued to improve and a fortnight later, although still possessed of a wheezy cough and confined to bed, was conducting daily business from his chamber.

'Fell off his horse,' he repeated, tossing the vellum message on the bed and scowling at the man who had brought it. 'I don't believe it. Good God, the man was almost born in the saddle!' He drew his furred bedrobe around his painfully thin body.

The messenger looked at the floor and shuffled his feet. 'Sire,' he mumbled.

'Oh, it's not your fault. Begone.' Stephen waved his hand in terse dismissal. As the man bowed and scurried gratefully to the door, the frown deepened between Stephen's brows. Picking up the letter he studied it again, narrowing his eyes at the scribe's untidy scrawl.

'He was a good man, de Chesham, but overly fond of his wine – to his cost and ours, God rest his soul.' He made the sign of the cross with the same irritation with which he had dismissed the messenger.

Catrin came to him from the hearth where she had been preparing a savoury milk broth.

'I cannot even rise from my bed but must lie here like a puling infant, supping food fit only for old men,' Stephen added with disgust as she placed the steaming cup in his hand.

Catrin reddened. 'It will help to replenish your strength, sire.'

Stephen glowered, but set the cup to his lips. 'It had better.' He took a swallow, grimaced for form's sake, and looked across at his brother and William d'Ypres. 'He'll have to be replaced immediately,' he said. 'But who can we send?'

'There's Thomas FitzWarren,' said the bishop. 'He's served me right well as a castellan in the past.'

'In the past, there you have it, Henry.' Stephen shook his head and took another swallow of the milk broth. 'He's nigh on three score years. You've already had the best out of him, brother.'

Catrin had become such a fixture of the royal bedchamber in recent weeks that she was treated as such. If she had possessed a loose tongue, she could have earned herself a fortune in silver from the things she heard. Prudently, she had spoken to no one, not even her husband. Oh, she fed him harmless details about the King's health, what he wore and what he ate. She told him about visits from the Queen and the royal offspring and seasoned the bland trivia with occasional items of gossip that were destined for the common melting pot anyway. Catrin preferred not to examine her reasons too closely. It was easier to dwell in the shallows than probe the murky depths.

Now, listening to the King and his senior advisors discussing the castellanship of Wickham, she remained nearby and, instead of being unobtrusive, deliberately clattered at her work.

Henry of Winchester threw her an irritated look. His eyes were like Stephen's in colour but were smaller and without the King's candour or good-natured twinkle. William d'Ypres followed the direction of the bishop's glower. His own gaze rested thoughtfully on Catrin, and the faintest suggestion of a smile curved beneath his moustache. 'I know of a younger man who has been chafing at the bit for some while, and to whom you owe a favour,' he said.

Stephen raised his brows. He too looked at Catrin. 'There are many men of that ilk,' he said, but his expression was considering. 'What experience?'

William d'Ypres shrugged. 'His father was commander of the garrison at Chepstow and gave him a grounding. Other than that, he's quick-witted with good soldiering abilities. Give him a chance, I say. If he proves unsuitable, then replace him.'

Stephen rubbed his beard. 'You're right,' he murmured. 'A man cannot be tried unless he's tested.' He drank down the rest of the milk broth and wiped his lips. 'Does that suit you, Mistress Grosmont?'

'Sire?' Catrin widened her eyes. She had almost choked when she heard William d'Ypres tell the King that Louis's father had been commander of a garrison, when he had been no more than a common serjeant at arms.

Stephen smiled. 'Come now, you have ears beneath your wimple and they hear very well, the times you have been at my side in the night with a cup before I have scarcely stirred. I am going to offer that husband of yours the custody of my keep at Wickham.'

Catrin knelt to him, her head lowered, her face flaming. 'Sire, I do not know what to say.' Which was true enough. She was breathless with surprise that it had been so easy; but her stomach was churning too. 'Thank you seems not enough.'

'In truth I am only repaying what I owe for my life,' Stephen said, a smug grin on his face as if the suggestion had been his in the first place. 'Go and find your man and bring him to me for confirmation. My scribes will make out the necessary letters for the constable.'

Catrin could not wait to leave the room. She knew that the King and d'Ypres were amused by her flustered response, and that Henry of Winchester was contemptuous. Whatever the angle they all thought her a foolish woman, never realising their own folly. As she descended the tower stairs, her joy for Louis warred with the tarnish of the lie he had told d'Ypres. How many other falsehoods was his reputation built upon? She tried to ignore the thought. Louis would make a good commander. What did his father's occupation matter?

A niggling voice replied that it was not his father's occupation that mattered at all. His lies were the real concern but, despite the acuteness of her hearing, or perhaps because of it, Catrin chose not to listen.

While Wickham was not a castle of significance in the mould of Windsor or London, it was nevertheless useful to Stephen. Together with Warwick, Winchcomb and Northampton, it served as a counter to the Empress's castles at Worcester and Hereford. It was of no great size, but solidly built, and reminded Catrin of a stout man standing with feet planted apart and arms akimbo. In a way, it was almost endearing.

The June sun turned the stone blocks to a deep, ruddy gold and flashed upon the roof tiles as their entourage approached the huge wooden gates. A hundred paces from the keep, Louis drew rein and leaned back in the saddle to study his new acquisition.

'It is smaller than I thought it would be,' he murmured.

'That is because you are accustomed to the likes of Rochester,' Catrin said. 'The King would not entrust you with one of his largest keeps for your first command. Only a week ago you were a hearth soldier.'

Louis grunted, and chewed his thumbnail. 'I suppose you are going to rub that in at every opportunity.'

Catrin rolled her eyes. He was like a spoiled child sometimes. The more he got, the more he wanted. 'I am just saying
that you cannot plant a seed one day and expect a full harvest
the next. There has to be ripening.'

'Sensible as ever.' He gave her a mocking smile, acknowledging her concern and at the same time telling her without
words that she was foolish. 'I bow to your greater wisdom.
Wickham will do to start.'

Their first night in the great hall, Louis sat in the lord's
chair at the high table and wore his crimson gown with
the gold embroidery, insisting that Catrin wear her finery
too. The best napery was fetched from the chests where it
had lain yellowing for the past ten years, Humphrey de
Chesham not being one for ostentation. As long as a trestle was scrubbed, it had been good enough for him, the
maid told Catrin as she handed over the keys to the linen
coffers.

The keep was militarily spruce, but almost completely
devoid of a woman's touch. Humphrey de Chesham had
been a widower who availed himself of the alehouse girls
when he felt the need, and relied on the maids to see to the
domestic running of Wickham.

Catrin could see that there was much to be done, but the
sumptuousness of the court had been stifling and she much
preferred de Chesham's style of austerity. Louis, however,
had plans which involved more than just strewing fresh,
scented rushes on the floor and adding a few cushions to
the benches.

'A lord should be seen to live like a lord, not a peasant,' he
said, when she questioned the advisability of extending the
stable block, rebuilding the kitchens, and totally renovating
the private quarters. 'I'll have craftsmen put glass in the upper
windows and . . .'

'Glass!' Catrin cried in horror. 'Do you know how much
that would cost? Where would you find the coin?'

'There are ways and means,' he said with a vague wave of
his hand and looked at her narrowly. 'You always were the
one to measure out each half and quarter penny.'

'And you always spent what you never had,' Catrin said waspishly.

He frowned, then, with an obvious effort, shrugged off his irritation and laid his hand over hers. 'I don't want to quarrel with you, not on our first night together here. Don't spoil it, Catty.' His look became pleading, with just a hint of long-suffering to make her feel as if she was a killjoy and a shrew.

If not the first night, then when? Catrin wondered with a glimmer of foreboding. As long as she held her tongue and gambled along with him, arguments were unlikely. But if she chose the wider, safer path, instead of dancing on the precipice, they were bound to quarrel – as they had quarrelled before.

'Catty?' he cajoled and peered round into her face. His expression was suddenly mischievous and he squeezed her thigh beneath the table. 'Wouldn't you like glass in the bedchamber?'

Despite her better instincts, she was forced to smile. He had a way with him that was impossible to resist. She had heard a tale about stoats charming birds from the trees into their jaws, and she thought that Louis was a little like that.

'Whether I like it or not, we couldn't afford it,' she said, but her tone was lighter now.

'We couldn't not afford it,' he grinned, and toasted her in the keep's wine with his free hand. 'Who wants to be cold at night?'

Henry FitzEmpress, heir to his mother's disputed kingdom, adjusted to the rolling deck of the ship like a sailor born, his legs planted wide for balance as he watched the haze of England's coastline sharpening on the horizon. He was nine years old, small for his age, but stocky, with a shock of bright red hair and light, glass-grey eyes. Those old enough to remember his great-grandfather, the Conqueror, said there was a family resemblance. All Oliver knew was that the child never sat still. In fact, he never sat at all. Questions poured out of him, one after the other like water out of a leaky spigot, and most of them were unanswerable. For a child of nine, his intellect was so sharp that those around him almost bled trying to keep it fed.

Oliver viewed the approaching land with impatience. They were heading for the port of Wareham. It belonged to Earl Robert, but had been seized by Stephen's troops, the reason why they came in a convoy of fifty-two warships with three hundred knights on board. He was ready to fight. Every one of Stephen's soldiers would wear the face of Louis de Grosmont and Oliver would yield no quarter.

He had travelled to Normandy as part of Earl Robert's deputation, to plead with Mathilda's husband, Geoffrey of Anjou, to come to England and lend his aid to their cause. Geoffrey had replied that he was too busy fighting his war in Normandy, but that his 'beloved wife', the words spoken with a sarcastic eyebrow, could have the custody of their eldest son and heir designate to prop up her ailing cause.

During Robert's absence in Normandy, Stephen had recovered from his illness. Taking the initiative, he had seized Wareham and marched upon the Empress at Oxford where he was now besieging her. After a lull of almost a year, the horns were locked again.

'I can speak English,' Henry announced proudly. '*Henry ist mon noma.*' He beamed at Oliver who was unfastening the heavy roll made by his gambeson and mail shirt. 'Do you know what that means?'

'*Gea, Ic cnawen, min lytel aethling. Oliver ist mon,*' Oliver replied, and was gratified to see the grey eyes widen and echo the open mouth. Prince Henry lost for words was a sight worth seeing.

'Do all my Uncle Robert's knights speak English?' There was suitable respect in Henry's voice.

Oliver kept the smile inside his mouth and answered gravely. 'Most speak a little, like you. Not many of us are fluent.'

'Then how did you learn?'

'My great-grandfather was English and kept his lands after Hastings.' Gazing past the child, Oliver judged the distance to landfall. He had no particular fear of ships or water, but it was a fool who put on mail armour in mid-crossing. They were closing on the land now though. He could see the thatch of the houses through the haze, and the spume breaking on the shoreline. All around him, other men were quietly donning their mail and checking their weapons.

Henry watched him. 'But you've got a Norman name,' he said stubbornly.

Oliver smiled through gritted teeth as he donned his gambeson and sought out the opening in the steel shirt. 'I'm a mongrel, like you, sire.'

Once more, Henry was taken aback. 'I'm not . . .' he started to say, then fell silent and looked thoughtful.

'Part English, part Angevin, part Norman.' Oliver began struggling into the hauberk. Absently, Henry moved to help him, tugging the mail shirt down over Oliver's gambeson with squat, competent fingers.

'Then I'm fit to rule all Saxons, all Normans and all Angevins,' he said, his childish treble quite at odds with the intensity of his expression.

And instead of the freckled face of a troublesome nine-year-old boy, Oliver saw the countenance of a future king.

Earl Robert had been both worrying and hoping that Stephen would abandon the siege at Oxford and come tearing south to relieve his garrison at Wareham. It would mean a tougher fight for Robert, but it would save Mathilda from danger. Stephen, however, resisted temptation and clung like a leech to Oxford, abandoning Wareham to its fate.

Oliver's vessel took no part in the storming of the harbour, for its cargo was too precious. Leaning against the shields that lined the wash-strake, Oliver and the young prince watched the other vessels ram-in amongst Wareham's outnumbered fleet. Grapnels and spears hissed through the air, striking wood, ripping through sails and tearing flesh. The shouts of men and the clash of weapons floated clearly across the water to the prince's vessel and the four others protecting it.

The boy drank in the sight and sound of battle, his nostrils quivering and his eyes as huge as moons but as much with curiosity as fear. 'Uncle Robert will win,' he said confidently.

'He's not as good a commander as my father, but he's much better than theirs.'

Oliver clenched his fists on the rawhide rim of a shield and longed to be involved in the battle. He wanted to become part of its welling dark core, to strike and strike, until he found oblivion.

Henry leaned over the side of the ship. 'What's "death to our enemy" in English, Oliver?'

Oliver looked at the livid marks the shield rim had imprinted on his palm. '*Deoth til urum feondum,*' he said, with intensity but no enthusiasm.

Henry cupped his hands and bellowed the words across the water. Very few members of the attacking force spoke English, but Henry yelled the command just the same.

Oliver watched him and wished for just a spark of that innocent vivacity. He supposed that to possess it, you had to be nine years old and supremely confident of your position in the world, items which had been missing from his own baggage for longer than he could remember.

Once Earl Robert's forces had claimed the harbour, Oliver's waiting was over. Shield on his left arm, sword in his right, he was one of the first ashore and into the town. The inhabitants cowered behind their bolted doors as the battle for control of Wareham raged through the streets towards the castle.

Oliver was a man possessed, all the pent-up rage and bitterness of the past few months flooding out upon the blade of his sword. Geoffrey FitzMar tried to stay with him but fell back, defeated by Oliver's sheer ferocity.

'Christ, man, do you want to die?' he roared, avoiding the swing of a mace and ducking behind his shield.

'Why not?' Oliver spared breath to respond and, slashing his own opponent out of the way, surged forward.

He might have received his wish and been sent to eternity on the thrust of an enemy spear had not an almost spent arrow struck him in the leg below his hauberk and downed him with a yell of surprise at the startled spearman's feet.

Cursing, Geoffrey sprinted and leaped to stand over Oliver, dicing with death himself as the spear thrust and jabbed. On the ground, Oliver seized one of their assailant's legs and toppled him over. More of Earl Robert's vanguard arrived and the unfortunate spear man was spitted on his own point by a Welsh knight.

'God's eyes!' Geoffrey sobbed, beside himself as Oliver lurched to his feet, the arrow clean through the fleshy part of his calf. 'Kill yourself if you want, you selfish bastard, but don't expect others to die with you!'

'Then go away!' Oliver snarled back. 'I didn't ask you to stay and save my life!'

'You didn't have to ask,' Geoffrey said tersely. 'I'm your friend, for what that counts with you.'

'Hah, if you were my friend, you'd have let him finish me.'

Geoffrey's jaw made chewing motions while he gained control of himself. 'Not to fulfil your own self-pity, I wouldn't. Your life's worth more than a wanton squandering in this miserable, muddy little port.' Geoffrey levered his shoulder beneath Oliver's. 'You can't fight on,' he added with grim satisfaction. 'At least that's a blessing in disguise.'

'It's a curse,' Oliver said bitterly.

By eventide they had taken Wareham castle and their victory was complete. Prince Henry dined in the keep's great hall, two cushions on the lord's chair to boost him above the table, and the gold circlet of royalty on his brow – a fact about which he complained in great detail. It hurt, it made his skin itch, it gave him a headache.

'When I'm King, no one will make me wear my crown unless I want to,' he said mutinously to his uncle.

Robert of Gloucester gave him a stern look. 'You may not yet wear one at all,' he said. 'And it is graceless to complain when so many good people have sacrificed themselves for your cause.'

Henry looked down at the table-cloth. His complexion reddened and his lips pursed mutinously. But as swiftly as the rebellion surged, it was gone. He touched the circlet on his brow. 'I am sorry,' he said simply, then looked beyond Earl Robert.

'Oliver, what's crown in English?'

'*Cynehelm*, sire,' Oliver inclined his head. He felt awkward. Henry had insisted that he be given a place at the high table instead of at one of the side trestles with Geoffrey and the other hearth knights. His leg was throbbing where the leech had removed the arrow-head and cleaned and bound the wound. All he wanted to do was lie down and sleep but, for the nonce, he was Prince Henry's pet, and the child was still as bright and fresh as a new-minted coin.

'Good.' Henry nodded. '*Ic wille awerian min cynehelm.*' He looked at his uncle. 'That means "I will wear my crown."'

Robert gave a pained smile. 'What's "time for bed"?' he asked Oliver.

For the next few days, Oliver was confined to the hall by his leg. It was healing well and showed very little sign of festering, although that might have had something to do with the fact that Oliver was treating it himself. The time to die had been during the battle, from a swift spear thrust. Not even a man desperate for death would choose to die from the lingering agony of a poisoned wound.

After the arrow-head had been pulled out, he had raided the pouch of supplies in his saddle bag. There was a perverse sort of comfort in anointing the injury with Catrin's goose-grease balm, one of the first recipes of her own. He had fond memories of watching her mash a paste of healing herbs into the pale fat, and then carefully pile the resultant mixture into small pots, one of which she had given to him.

'Kill or cure,' he had teased, as he took it from her hand.

Now he said the words to himself and his throat tightened even while there was a smile on his lips.

Prince Henry was fascinated by the little wooden pot of salve. 'What's that?'

'Ointment to heal my wound.'

'Where did you get it?' Henry sniffed at the green, pleasant-scented concoction and took a dab to rub between his fingers.

'From a friend – a wise-woman.'

'I've never met a wise-woman.' Hopeful curiosity entered the boy's eyes. 'Does she live close by?'

Oliver shook his head. 'Only in my heart,' he said.

'Oh, she bewitched you?'

Oliver laughed bitterly and was about to agree with the boy when common sense stopped him. There was already enough prejudice surrounding midwives and wise-women without him adding more, particularly where the future king of England was concerned. 'No, no.' He shook his head. 'She was a widow and we were betrothed, but then the husband she thought lost returned from the dead.' Jesu, that sounded just as bad. He could almost see the word 'necromancy' written in the child's eyes.

'Sit down,' he said, 'and I'll try to explain.'

Henry sat and, to his credit, scarcely fidgeted as Oliver told him about himself and Catrin. There was painful comfort in that too, Oliver discovered, as if the pressure of an abscessed wound had been relieved.

Henry looked at him thoughtfully, but with little comprehension. His own parents had lived apart for much of his young life, and when they were together they fought like cat and dog. His father had mistresses who came and went. Henry had a half-brother, Hamelin, from one such liaison. 'There are other women.' He gestured in the direction of three knight's wives who were gossiping over their embroidery. A tinkling laugh rang out and a hand preened at a wimple.

Oliver shook his head. 'In truth too many, sire.'

Henry narrowed his eyes, then nodded decisively. 'When I am King, I will restore your lands in full measure and give you a wealthy heiress in marriage.'

Oliver gave a pained smile.

Henry bristled. 'You do not believe me?'

'No, sire, I believe you entirely. It is just that I would be content with the lands alone.'

Henry shrugged. 'But you'd need a wife to provide sons to continue the line,' he said practically, and wiped his fingers on his chausses.

Oliver was spared from answering as Henry's tutor, Master Matthew, came looking for his charge, and the child was removed to the world of Aristotle, Vegetius and Thomas Aquinas.

Oliver gazed after the prince, watching his energetic bounce down the hall. He supposed that Henry was right. Would a wealthy heiress be so bad? Coin and companionship, the common yoke of duty. Gently he pressed the stopper into the neck of the wooden jar.

He knew all about duty.

Catrin's face was as green as the window glass through which the spring sunshine stained the floor rushes. She leaned over the wooden latrine board and retched agonisingly down the fetid hole. It was the third morning in a row that she had been sick and her flux was almost a month late.

Amfrid, her maid, presented her with a damp, lavender-scented cloth, and Catrin wiped her face. Her stomach quivered and gingerly settled. Although she knew that women suffered from sickness in the early months of pregnancy, although she knew the herbs and simples that helped to ease the discomfort, she had not been prepared for the overwhelming attacks of nausea and the permanent exhaustion.

Pressing her face into the cloth, she walked back into the bedchamber. The walls were hung with Flemish tapestries in shades so deep and opulent that they put her in mind of Earl Robert's solar at Bristol. There was a silk coverlet on the bed. Apparently it had come from the plundering of Winchester following Earl Robert's capture. There was a singe-mark along one edge where a piece of burning thatch had dropped on it as it was snatched to safety by Louis's acquisitive hands. The flagon had come from Winchester too. It was fashioned of silver, with amethysts encircling its base. Catrin hated it, and the coverlet too. They were gains made from someone else's disaster, or even death.

'Spoils of war,' Louis called them with a shrug and a smile, unable to comprehend her distaste.

His plunder had included some silver too, and he had spent it profligately. Not only was there glass in the windows but, for the first time in her life, Catrin was able to see her own reflection in a Saracen mirror of polished steel. Louis had not told her the cost, but Catrin knew that it must have been expensive beyond all dreaming. Not even Countess Mabile possessed such in her private chamber.

She was learning to be blind again; she was learning not to ask for fear of discovery. Staring at herself, she saw a trapped creature, hollow-cheeked and gaunt-eyed.

'I was much happier when I had nothing,' she murmured.

'My lady?'

Catrin shook her head at Amfrid, threw back the slippery silk coverlet and sat down on the linen bed sheet. She glanced at the bolster which still bore the imprint of Louis's head. Oh yes, there were still moments when he set her world alight, but so often it was here, in the bed. He would cajole, he would make her laugh, he would melt her, but it was all a part of the learning and the forgetting. All her worries were answered with kisses, with playful dismissal, with silence. If she persisted, she was punished with petulance and slammed doors.

Amfrid brought her a gown of blue wool, embroidered with golden lozenges. Catrin looked at it, sighed, and tugged it over her head. Donning her wimple and ignoring the hated mirror, she crossed the room and freed the window catch. Cold spring air blew into her face and filled her lungs. The sky was a tumultuous chase of streaky grey-and-white cloud.

As she gazed out, Louis returned from patrol, his dark bay horse lathered and fretting the bit. She watched the graceful way he dismounted, light even in chain-mail; his rumpled black hair as he removed his helm, the ready smile on his lips. Despite her misgivings, the flame swept through her. He was so lithe, so glowing and handsome. Other women would give their eye-teeth for a husband like hers.

She was about to turn away from the window when Wulfhild, one of the kitchen girls, came walking across the ward. Her hips swung seductively, and on her arm there was a basket of honeycakes. Her hair, blond as new butter, was tied back from her face by a kerchief, but hung loose below it, supposedly in token of her virginity, but everyone knew she had left that behind in a ditch some time ago.

Beneath Catrin's narrowing gaze, Wulfhild approached Louis. She said something to him, and he laughed and snatched one of the honeycakes from her basket. Then he stooped and murmured in her ear. Wulfhild giggled, covering her mouth with the palm of her hand. Then she sauntered on her way, pausing once to look over her shoulder, her expression full of suggestion and promise. Louis grinned from ear to ear and saluted her with his half-eaten honeycake.

Catrin tightened her lips and slammed the window shut. It meant nothing, she told herself. It had always been his way to flirt. But he had promised he had changed, and there had been more than flirtation in Wulfhild's eyes.

Louis was still chewing the last of the honeycake as he entered their chamber. Although panting a little from his run up the stairs, his stride was brisk and there was a gleam in his eye.

'Stirring at last, I see,' he said as he unfastened his belt and began to shrug out of his hauberk like a snake shedding its skin. 'I thought when I did not see you in the hall that you had chosen to become a slug-abed for the rest of the day.'

She came to help him with the heavy garment. 'I am sure you could find things to keep yourself amused.'

He eyed her quizzically and ran his tongue around his mouth to dislodge a fragment of honeycake. 'Such as?'

'Such as Wulfhild.'

He rolled his eyes. 'Jesu, she's a simple kitchen wench. I cozened a sweetmeat from her in passing.'

'Is that all you cozened?'

He made an impatient sound. 'Am I to have my every movement watched and judged from that window? I spoke to her, I took a cake from her basket. God's bones, what is the matter with you? Are you going to help me or not?'

Catrin compressed her lips and laid hold of the hauberk skirt. 'Your patrol went well?' she enquired tightly.

'Well enough,' he said, his voice muffled as he stooped over. 'The people never have anything to report. Too busy cowering behind their doors or hiding their best animals from my view, but I saw no signs of trouble.' He stood straight, his complexion slightly flushed. 'Besides, Mathilda's party are finished after what happened in Oxford at Christmas – Madam High-and-Mighty forced to flee through the snow in her night-gown . . .' He licked his lips and grinned. 'That would have been a sight worth seeing.'

'Apparently no one did,' Catrin answered shortly. She did not like Mathilda, but it did not prevent her from giving the woman her due against the mockery she heard in Louis's tone. 'From what I understood, she fled not in her night-gown but in a white robe so that she would seem a part of the landscape – and she succeeded.'

'Yes, but Oxford is Stephen's now. She has lost any initiative that she once possessed. It can only be a matter of time.' The gold braid on his robe sparkled as he crossed to the window embrasure and poured wine into a goblet. 'Oh, she is to be admired for her fight, but it's futile. She might as well take ship for Anjou and return to that husband of hers. At least he had the good sense not to leave his own shores.'

Catrin watched her husband drink the wine and was irritated by his confident posture and the glib contempt in his voice. 'I do not think she will do that,' she contradicted with a toss of her head. 'Earl Robert is as good a commander as Stephen, if not better, and each year that she holds her position, her son grows older.'

'I doubt she can cling on for another nine years.' Louis took a gulp of wine. 'Want some?' He held out the cup.

Catrin shook her head and fought a renewed surge of nausea.

'Of course, it will be a pity for her supporters,' he remarked, watching her narrowly. 'They will lose their lands, and those already dispossessed will have to find other employment. She won't need an army when she goes back to Anjou.'

'You mean Oliver, don't you?' Her voice was hard with anger.

He spread his hands. 'I mean them all. In truth, I feel for their misfortune.' He cast a complacent look around his magnificent bedchamber. 'I gambled, Catty, I won.'

Her belly churned at the note of self-satisfaction in his voice. He said that he felt for their misfortune, but it was probably pleasure, not compassion. 'Yes, you won,' she said, her lip curling with disgust, 'but how long before you have to gamble again, Louis?' She swept her hand around the bedchamber, encompassing everything that his look had done. 'How long will you keep this? You bleed the villages dry to support your pleasures. You spent the wool clip before the sheep were even sheared.'

He stiffened and his nostrils flared. 'I am the lord of a castle. I have to make a display of my wealth. Anyone would think that you prefer to live in a hovel.'

'I did once, and I still do!' she flung at him. 'You display wealth that is not yours. You're living a lie, Lewis of Chepstow, a paltry, pathetic lie!' The last word ended on a cut-off scream as he strode across the room and struck her across the face.

'Shut your mouth, you shrew!' he roared. 'It is a wife's duty to honour and respect her husband, and I see very little of either from you!'

'I'll give it where it's due!' Catrin spat back, her cheek numb where he had struck her. With growing fear and anger, she watched him reach for his sword belt.

'No, my lord.' Amfrid stepped forward, a look of horror on her round, homely face.

'Get out!' Louis snarled, repeating the command on a full-throated bellow when she hesitated. With a frightened glance at her mistress, Amfrid ran from the room.

Catrin faced her husband, her breathing harsh and swift, her stomach so curdled that her throat made small retching motions as she struggled not to heave.

'Give me a single reason why I should not beat the venom out of you,' he said, curling the leather through his slender fingers.

She tightened her lips. While she would not yield to save her own hide, there was more at stake now. She could give him all the reason in the world, if she could but manage the words. Cold sweat stood out on her brow, and the room tilted and swayed like the deck of a ship.

'Well,' he queried with an arched brow, 'has the leather got your tongue?'

She shook her head and swallowed. 'No, Louis. But before you mark me, you had best know that I am with child.'

He coiled the tongue around his fist. 'You're what?' His look changed from one of dominant, masculine challenge to delighted astonishment.

'With child,' she repeated, and fell to her knees, dry-heaving into the rushes.

Louis threw the belt away from him as if it were a poisonous snake and knelt beside her, his expression suddenly full of concern and tenderness. 'Why didn't you tell me?'

She shuddered and retched against the supporting strength of his arm, a strength that had almost struck her down for telling the truth. 'I have only just discovered it myself,' she said. 'I wanted to be sure.'

'I wondered what had made you so crotchety of late. Now I know, I can forgive you.'

Catrin was too wretched to treat his reply as it deserved. Besides, she did not have the strength to continue the fight.

'A son,' Louis said, his voice deep with exultation. 'I am going to have a son.' His hand possessively on her arm, he looked into her green, wan face. 'When, Catty, when will he be born?'

'It might be a girl,' she said, with a last flicker of perversity.

'No, it will be a boy.' Louis shook his head vigorously. 'My line always breeds sons. When?'

'November, I think, around the feast of Saint Martin.'

Gently, he raised her from the floor and bore her back to their bed. He took the damp, lavender-scented cloth from the bowl on the coffer and bathed her temples. 'I was hoping for such news,' he said, 'what man would not? You did not quicken in the first year of our marriage and I thought that you might be barren.'

'So now I am worth more to you than ever?'

He did not hear the sarcasm in her tone. 'Beyond value,' he said. 'You are carrying our son. I will hold a great celebration in your honour and I will send word to the King and William d'Ypres. They are bound to send christening gifts.'

Catrin closed her eyes. She was suddenly so weary that even breathing was a burden. Instead of being cause to plan steadily for the future, the tiny seed growing within her was just another reason for Louis to scatter the largesse he did not have.

CHAPTER 22

'I wish I could give you the troops and leave to besiege Ashbury, but I do not have the resources,' said Robert of Gloucester. 'And you are too valuable to me here.'

Oliver looked at his lord with dismay, but he was not surprised. Ashbury was not a great or strategic keep. It was true that it guarded a minor crossing of the Thames to the far west of Oxford and that it had a thriving market, but its capture was not essential to the Empress's cause.

'It is mine,' he said, 'and it has been my family's since the time of King Alfred. The waiting is hard.'

Earl Robert sighed and fondled the brindle head of his mastiff bitch. 'I know that, I am not blind to your need. But it cannot be. Perhaps later in the year I will be able to spare you, but not now. The great keeps need to fall before we can take the small ones.'

Oliver had been fed the 'perhaps later' speech so many times that it raised not a flicker of hope. Perhaps never was the more likely outcome. He would die a hearth knight, rolled in his cloak by the fire if he was fortunate, dead of his wounds on a battlefield if he was not.

'Yes, my lord,' he said, and turned from the trestle to give the next petitioner his chance at being denied. They had lost Oxford in the winter, but since then had reclaimed Wilton, defeating Stephen in a pitched battle that had almost been a repeat of Lincoln. They had captured his steward, William Martel, and Stephen had paid with Sherborne Castle for his release. The King was being held in check, and Oliver had dared to hope that his chance to regain Ashbury had arrived.

There was an ocean of restlessness in him that could not wait for time to turn Henry Plantagenet into a man.

Geoffrey FitzMar was waiting for Oliver in the hall. His two-year-old son perched on his knee chewing a hard crust of bread. The infant had a fluff of blond hair as pale as Oliver's own, and eyes the violet-blue of gentians. Edon was expecting a second child in the spring. Geoffrey had his family to keep him sane. Being a hearth knight by trade, a younger son without hope of land from the start, he had no roots dying for want of soil to plant them. Looking at his friend, the small child in his lap, Oliver knew bitter envy.

Geoffrey glanced up at him and the smile left his open features. 'He refused you,' he said.

'Ashbury's not strategic enough and I'm too experienced a soldier to be given leave. If I won, I wouldn't be a hearth knight any more, would I?' He pushed the toe of his boot moodily through the floor rushes. 'I can understand his reasoning, but it riles me nevertheless.'

Geoffrey shook his head and looked sympathetic. 'I wish I could help.'

Oliver watched the infant offer his father the sucked, soggy crust of bread. If Emma and their child had lived, his daughter would be almost eight years old by now. No wife, no child, no land. He imagined himself in years to come. A grizzled, embittered old man with a frozen heart and charity for neither man nor woman. It was a frightening prospect.

'Da,' said the little boy, and jumped up and down in his father's lap. 'Da, da, da.'

Oliver went outside. The late September sun was setting over the bailey in tones of rich, burnished red, and the sky was a hollow, perfect blue. Prince Henry was receiving a jousting lesson from two of the Earl's knights. Richard and Thomas were with him, and their boyish trebles rang out over the greensward as each in turn took a shortened lance and attacked the quintain post on their ponies. Oliver watched their juvenile attempts to hit the swinging shield on the end of the rotating crossbar and found a smile, remembering his own first lessons in the art. Having no desire to be drawn into the circle of good-natured advice being shouted at the youngsters, he sidled quietly along the wall of a storage shed. It was to no avail for, almost immediately, he heard his name being called.

Reluctantly he turned, and found himself being ridden down by Richard. The boy clung to his grey pony like a centaur, his face flushed with the speed and pleasure of the sport.

'There's a messenger looking for you,' he said.

'For me?' Oliver raised his brows. 'I do not know anyone who would send me messages.'

Richard shrugged. 'They were mostly for Lord Robert, but the man asked us in passing where he could find you.' The boy tilted his head. 'Do you think it could be from Catrin?'

Oliver's belly churned. 'I think not,' he said. 'I told her that it was best if she severed all ties.'

'Yes, but what if she's in trouble?'

Oliver flicked his fingers. 'Go back to your sport before your imagination runs away with you,' he said brusquely, while his own imagination gathered speed.

Looking doubtful, Richard wheeled his pony. 'Tell me, won't you?' he said over his shoulder.

Without answer, Oliver strode off in search of the messenger.

He found him breaking his fast in the kitchens with a beaker of milk and a heaped platter of new bread and curd cheese. The man was flirting with one of the kitchen maids, but broke off his teasing to present Oliver with a rolled-up strip of vellum secured with a length of braid. The seal bore the ubiquitous design of a warrior astride a horse, his sword raised on high. The letters around the outside of the seal were smudged and illegible.

'Who gave you this?'

'A merchant from over Winchcomb way.' He took a gulp of milk and sleeved his mouth. 'Brought it to Gloucester last night. Said he'd been paid to carry it by one of Stephen's lords.'

Oliver gave the messenger a penny, broke the seal and went outside. The letter was slightly travel-stained at the edges and bore a late August date. It was a scribe's writing, fluid and precise, and it wasn't from Catrin. It was from her husband, informing him in triumphant detail about Catrin's new status as lady of a fine keep. He was maintaining her in the manner of a queen; they were both ecstatically happy and anticipating the birth of their first son.

Oliver stared until the words danced on the page and lost their meaning. He knew that this letter was not Catrin's doing. Probably she was unaware that her husband had even sent it. Louis de Grosmont possessed a nature that took pleasure in torment. A tweak here, a pull there, a subtle manipulation of the truth. Catrin would not care whether she was kept as a queen or not. Indeed, her spirit needed freedom to be whole. The thought of her bearing a child was sheer torment. Had it been his own child he would have been frightened enough, but the thought of her carrying and bearing Louis's offspring so distant from him numbed Oliver completely.

Returning to the kitchen, he approached the fire and the two huge cauldrons bubbling over the flames. Crumpling the letter, he tossed it into the blaze and watched the vellum blacken and curl, the red seal melt and sizzle, until his eyes were hot and dry and nothing was left.

Louis de Grosmont was going to have a son. Never had such a child been born before, if the expectant father was to be believed. All and sundry were made aware of the fact; from the poorest serf struggling on the demesne land to feed his family, to William d'Ypres and King Stephen.

"Twill be an easy labour,' one of the midwives assured Catrin cheerfully. 'You're young and strong with good wide hips.'

Two had been installed for her lying in, the best that Louis could not afford. They were skilled, sensible women, and Catrin liked them both, but she would have preferred just one and less of Louis's bragging. After the first months of utter sickness, her body had adjusted and her pregnancy had passed without incident. She was untroubled by swelling ankles or giddiness. Her appetite was excellent, and she slept moderately well. Now the first twinges of threatened labour had started, but as yet there was no real pain.

'The labour does not bother me.' She stroked the taut mound of her belly. 'I know what to expect; I have delivered enough babies myself. But I don't want Louis to know until it is necessary.'

'He is very keen, my lady,' said the other midwife with an indulgent smile.

Catrin said nothing. She knew that her husband's fervour depended upon her producing a healthy son – to be named Stephen in honour of the King. He had refused to countenance the prospect of a daughter. It would be a boy because that was what he wanted. Fortune, he said, was running in his favour. But Catrin had her suspicions that it was not fortune which was running, but Louis, and as hard as he could to keep up.

Another pain, deeper than the last, tightened around her belly and squeezed.

Rising from the cushioned window seat, she paced the chamber restlessly. Walking helped. She counted her paces and breathed deeply, easing herself over the contraction.

Louis appeared an hour later, the news having leaked down to the hall where he was presiding over the quarter-day rents and exacting heavy fines from those who were not prompt to pay. He burst into the bedchamber where Catrin was still pacing and counting and pulled her into his arms, her swollen belly mounding between them.

'How long?' he demanded, his eyes bright with impatience.

'How long have I been in travail, or how long will it continue to be?' Catrin asked, and tried not to tense as her womb tightened.

'How long until I see my son, of course.'

Stripped of its gilding by his eagerness, Louis's selfish nature was laid bare to the bone.

'It will be a while yet, my lord,' the older midwife spoke out. 'First babes can take two or more days to show themselves to the world.'

'Two days!' Louis looked aghast.

'If waiting is all you have to do, then you are fortunate,' Catrin said waspishly. 'Go and make yourself busy. The time will pass.'

'No, it won't, it'll stand still.' He looked at the women as though they were involved in a conspiracy.

'Of course,' the midwife added quickly, 'it is frequently much sooner than that. Examining my lady, I would say that come eventide you will have cause to celebrate.'

'Eventide,' Louis said, grasping the word like a lifeline across a river in spate. He squeezed Catrin's hands in an echo of the muscular squeezing of her womb. 'Make haste, Catty. I'm eager to see my son.'

'I will do my best,' she replied, but her sarcastic tone was wasted on him as he bounced out of the door with the eagerness of a puppy.

The day progressed. Almost every hour, Louis sent to discover how the labour was advancing, and as dusk approached Louis himself took to haunting the landing outside the bedchamber door.

Panting upon the birthing stool, her body drenched with effort, her thighs streaked with blood and birthing fluid, Catrin gave the midwives a mirthless grin. 'Let him in,' she panted. 'Let him see me. All men should witness this.'

The women looked shocked and took her words as a jest. 'My lady, no man may enter a birthing chamber. It is not proper!'

'No, of course not,' she laughed savagely. 'But what kind of farmer sows the seed and then absconds the harvest?'

'My lady, you are distraught, you do not know what you are saying.'

'Yes, I do,' Catrin retorted. The pain returned and seared so hard that it destroyed all coherent thought. The midwives had given her various nostrums to drink, but none that had had much effect. She knew that she must be in the final stage of labour, for with each pain there was an overbearing urge to push down. It was now that the truth would be known. If the child was lying the wrong way in her womb or her pelvis was too small, then both of them would die. She grasped the smooth wooden sides of the birthing stool and bore down with all her strength. It was like trying to move a mountain, but the women encouraged her.

'Almost there, my lady, I can see the head. He's got dark hair, so he has.'

Catrin sobbed and, with the next contraction, pushed again. 'Oliver!' she screamed, the name surfacing from nowhere and bouncing off the walls.

'Is that to be his name?' one of the midwives enquired. 'I thought your husband had chosen Stephen.'

Catrin shook her head, beyond speech, beyond anything but the final struggle to push the child from her body and have relief. She was not even aware of the name she had screamed, only that it had been a cry for help.

Another surge, and the baby slithered from her body into the waiting, warmed towel, and immediately began a lusty bawling.

The midwives cut the cord and gently rubbed mucus and fluid from the infant's tiny body. Its furious wails filled the room, but there was no other sound. The women looked at each other in silence.

'What is it, what's wrong?' Catrin demanded with a sudden lurch of fear. 'Give me my baby, let me see.'

'No, my lady,' one of the women said quickly, 'nothing is wrong. See, you have a perfect little daughter.' She handed the screeching bundle into Catrin's arms.

The baby waved irate little fists and roared as if she had been insulted. She had masses of thick black hair and tiny, snub features. For Catrin it was love at first sight and, mingled with that love, a great flood of protectiveness. 'I wanted a daughter,' she whispered with a tearful smile.

Louis had been listening at the door and, as the raucous screams of the baby continued, his control snapped. Unable to wait any longer, he burst into the room. 'Let me see my son!' he cried, and advanced on Catrin, his arms outstretched to take the baby. She still sat on the birthing stool, the afterbirth as yet undelivered, her hair loose to her hips and sweat-soaked at the brow.

She tightened her grip on the bundle she held and immediately the new-born ceased to screech as loudly. 'Your daughter, you mean,' she said. 'Louis, we have a girl child.'

He stopped as if he had run into a castle wall and his

arms dropped to his sides. 'A girl child?' he repeated, the joy freezing, then falling from his face to leave an expression of deep affront. 'That is impossible. My line always breeds boys.'

'Well, God has seen fit to bless you with a daughter.'

Louis glared narrow-eyed at the baby in Catrin's arms. 'This is your doing, you bitch. Any other woman would have borne me a son. You have thwarted me deliberately with your wise-woman's tricks.'

Catrin opened her mouth to deny that she had done any such thing, but found that she was too weary to stand against his petulance and rage. She just wanted him to go away. 'You have thwarted yourself,' she said, 'at every turn.'

Louis clenched his fists. For an appalling moment, Catrin thought that he was going to strike her while she sat on the birthing stool, still in the last stage of labour. Raising her eyes to his, she saw the intent, but some tiny spark of control held him in check. Abruptly he turned from her, let out his breath with harsh contempt and strode from the room, slamming the door in a shudder of cold air.

Catrin hung her head over her tiny daughter. 'I chose the wrong man,' she whispered. 'God forgive me, I chose the wrong man.'

'Now then, mistress, don't you worry. He'll come around in time,' said the older midwife. Her face was pale with shock, but she had rallied bravely. 'Men need daughters to make good marriage alliances. He'll be right proud of her once she comes into her looks, you mark me.'

'His pride is the problem,' Catrin said, as her womb began to cramp and expel the afterbirth. 'He has boasted far and wide that he will soon have a son to follow him. He will blame me for failing him, not God for ordering.' She squeezed her eyes tightly shut and pushed down. The pains were not as bad, but they were still deeply uncomfortable.

'Things will seem better in the morning,' the woman soothed. 'Now, we need a name for this little lass.'

Catrin parted the linen towel and looked down into the baby's tiny, crumpled features. While she owed her a great debt, she could not saddle the infant with a name like

Etheldreda. 'Rosamund,' she said, 'after my mother, her grandmother.' She gave the slightest of bitter smiles. 'Our line always runs to girls.'

Louis stared down at his small daughter in her cherry-wood cradle. She was sound asleep, her eyelids no larger than telin shells and seeming too delicate for their edging of dense black lashes. Her name suited her; she was as pink and soft as a rose. Over the past six weeks some of his initial disappointment had waned. As several people had pointed out in the process of commiseration, daughters were useful providing you did not have too many, and at least Catrin had proved that she could bear children with relative ease. Only a few days after the birth she had been chafing at her enforced confinement in the bower. The next one would be a boy for certain. Catrin had been churched that morning and thus was free to take up her wifely duties again, amongst them those of the bedchamber. Not that Louis had been on short rations during her confinement. Wulfhild, the kitchen maid, had been most accommodating in the stables, and there were a couple of women in the village too. If Catrin suspected, she had said nothing. Since the baby had been born, there appeared to be no room in her life for anything else, including him.

Usurped by a puling infant, and a girl at that. Louis's lip curled. She had even insisted on feeding the baby herself, like a peasant woman, instead of doing what was proper to her rank and obtaining a wet nurse. When he protested, she stood her ground so firmly that he had been forced to retreat and sulk in the stables for an hour with Wulfhild.

'I am a midwife; I know what is best for my daughter,' she had said with quiet assertion, no blaze of temper on which he could feed his own. She was a bitch, a contrary, irritating bitch, but she was also comely and, despite his other amours, he still desired her, not least because of the way she ignored him.

She entered the room now, clothed in her undergown and chemise, her black hair curtaining her shoulders. It was not as long as it had been during her pregnancy. The child had apparently taken the strength from her hair, and she had shorn off a good six inches. Still, it did not detract from her looks. At least if Rosamund inherited them she would make an appetising marriage prospect.

Louis sat on their bed and began disrobing. Catrin went to the cradle and looked down at the swaddled baby. An expression of melting tenderness filled her face. It was a look that Louis recognised because once, back in the days at Chepstow, it had been bestowed on him.

'She's asleep,' he said brusquely. 'Come to bed.'

Catrin raised her head and looked at him, the softness fading. 'May I not check upon my own daughter?'

'I've checked already. That cradle is like a shackle around your ankles. You're never more than a pace from it.'

'That is not true.' She left the baby and approached the bed. He could sense the reluctance in her step, and it was made all the more galling for the alacrity with which she had approached the cradle.

'If you had done as I said and employed a wet nurse, we could still have the bedchamber to ourselves,' he complained.

'You need not sleep here if it troubles you so much.' She gave him a cool stare and pulled off her undergown, then, more reluctantly, her chemise.

He snorted. 'I'll not be thrown out of my own chamber by a couple of women!' Her body glimmered in the candlelight. Her breasts were full from suckling the baby. She had recovered her trim waist, if anything she was more slender than before. There were a few small, silvery stretch marks on her belly, and an area of raised pinkish-white flesh on her side from the sword wound she had sustained at Bristol. The scar itself never ceased to fascinate him, because it was the sort of wound seen frequently on men but never on a woman.

Taking her hand, he pulled her down beside him on the cold silk coverlet. She shivered and gazed past him at the rafters. Louis ran his thumb delicately along the scar and kissed her cold, goose-pimpled skin. 'Two months, Catty,' he murmured against her throat. 'It's been a long, dry wait.'

She shifted slightly beneath him and her hands clasped around his neck. 'Don't tell lies,' she murmured. 'I know you've been drinking at different fountains.'

He thought about making a vehement denial, but decided that it would begin another quarrel and he had patience for neither argument nor placation. 'Only because I could not have the one I wanted,' he muttered against her breasts. 'Open for me, Catty, let me in.'

Obligingly she raised and spread her thighs. He felt their satin touch against his flanks and then the clinging, liquid heat of her inner body.

'This time it will be a boy,' he panted as he worked himself deep inside her. Her body swayed with his movements, but she made no response of her own, except to wriggle a little and interrupt his rhythm now and again as if she was uncomfortable. When he looked into her face it was blank, apart from a slight frown between her eyes and the catching of her underlip in her teeth.

He ceased to move and rose on braced elbows. 'What is wrong with you tonight? You're as welcoming as a lump of venison on a slab.'

'Does it matter, as long as you obtain the son you desire?' She looked at him, her hazel eyes weary.

'Of course it matters,' he said furiously. 'I'm your husband. In the past I've made you scream like a banshee at the gates of hell. You know how much it pleasures me.'

She sighed. 'You want me to scream?'

'God damn you, woman, I want you to want me!' He felt himself begin to wilt inside her; something that had never, ever happened to him before with any woman. He lunged desperately, but the heat and strength had gone and he slipped from her body with a wet plop.

'Jesu, you witch, what have you done?' He looked down at his softened organ in growing horror.

'Nothing,' she said scornfully. 'It is your own mind that unmans you. You cannot always have what you want for the smiling, Louis. It is your right as my husband to command my body, but do not look for desire when all *you* desire is to slake your lust and beget yourself a son.'

'Christ, that would be the desire of any man. You put something in my wine, didn't you?' He seized a handful of her glossy, black hair. 'Didn't you!'

'Don't be so stupid!' she flared back. 'If I had put anything in your wine, it would have been wolfsbane and you wouldn't be worrying about a limp cock, you'd be dead!'

He wound her hair around his fist and seriously thought about strangling her. Heat pulsed in his groin as he imagined the act; her struggle. He pushed her flat, his wrist across her throat, sought, fumbled, and plunged.

This time she did scream, after a fashion, and her body arched against him. Louis fixed his eyes on her face, watching the war between her fury and fear. He had never taken a woman in rape before and the experience was so novel, his pleasure so great that it was almost a pain.

Catrin continued to spit and struggle, but Louis was in no hurry to complete the act and took his time, holding back, toying with the delightful sensations. Begetting his son was going to be a pleasure after all.

In her cradle, Rosamund started to cry. Catrin's struggles became desperate.

'Lie still!' Louis snarled, tightening his grip until she choked.

Above the sound of Catrin's fight for air, his grunts of pleasure and the baby's wails, came a vigorous pounding on the bedchamber door.

'Go away!' Louis yelled.

'My lord, come quickly, we are under siege!' an agitated voice responded. 'There is an army outside our walls!'

'What?'

'An army, my lord, with siege machinery!' the voice repeated, and pounded the door again.

For the second time, Louis lost his erection. 'All right, all right,' he bellowed. 'Keep the skin on your knuckles!' Releasing Catrin, he levered himself off her and flung on his clothes. 'We'll finish this later,' he snapped over his shoulder and, pushing his feet into his shoes, strode to the door and banged out of the room.

Coughing and choking, Catrin sat up, her black hair spilling wild. There was a raw throb between her thighs and her scalp was sore. She lurched to her feet and staggered to the cradle where Rosamund was now bawling for all she was worth. Stars fluctuated before her eyes and she had to steady herself for a moment before she was able to stoop and lift the screaming infant from the cradle.

'Hush,' she soothed, 'hush,' not knowing if she was talking to the child or herself. Holding Rosamund to her breast, she rocked the baby back and forth, her hand cupping the tiny, fragile skull. Rosamund rooted against her flesh. Catrin cradled her and put her to suck.

Until recently she would not have thought Louis capable of the kind of violence he had shown just now. Too late, she was coming to understand that the changes he had promised her were not for the better. The child in him was too strong for the man to defeat, and a wilful child in a man's body was so dangerous it was terrifying.

She brushed her forefinger over Rosamund's downy, dark hair, and wondered with quiet desperation what she was going to do. She could live the lie and play his soul-destroying game, or she could fight him every step of the way as she had fought tonight and lose not her soul but her life. Or she could, as she had taunted, put wolfsbane in his cup.

Afraid of her own emotions, she wrapped her cloak around herself and the suckling baby and, going to the bower window overlooking the gate house, freed the catch.

A bitter, rain-laden wind beat into her face. The fields were brown, the winter trees dark and skeletal. Where smoke should have been rising in gentle twirls from the village houses, there were thick black gouts instead, interspersed with the red lick of fire. Closer to the keep, she could make out the forms of the soldiers, both mounted and on foot. They were spreading out to encircle the castle and they had brought siege machinery with them.

Frozen to the marrow as much by what she saw as by the weather, Catrin jerked the window shut and, nursing her daughter, turned to the small charcoal brazier burning in the middle of the room. Part of her fear was for herself, but most of her terror was for the baby lying in her arms. The sight of the smoke and the soldiers flooded her mind with the images of what had happened at Penfoss. Only it was not Aimery de Sens who sprawled across the gateway with a cut throat but Louis, and she was lying where Amice had lain. She had heard the tales of what Welsh and Flemish mercenaries did to the small babies whose mothers they had raped and butchered. It did not help her state of mind that while Louis was a good reconnaissance soldier, he had never been faced with this kind of challenge before.

'Jesu, be silent!' she snapped at herself. Gently prising a sleepy Rosamund from her nipple, she returned the baby to the cradle and donned a chemise and warm gown. Worrying would only make the situation worse. If the maids saw her panic then they would panic too.

She bound her hair in a wimple, took Rosamund and carried her from the room and down the stairs. If the village was in flames, there were bound to be people seeking succour within the keep.

They were the soldiers of Aubrey de Vere, Earl of Oxford, Catrin was told by a weeping village woman, who had watched them take her cow and her pig and set fire to her cottage.

'One of 'em says to me, "tell your lord that the Earl of Oxford's come to call."' She stared round the great hall, her body rocking back and forth in a rhythm of grief. 'He said that they'd cut the right hand off every man in the village.'

'Soldiers often make empty boasts. He said it to frighten you.' Catrin set her arm around the woman's shoulders and tried to ignore her own misgivings.

'Even if he did, they'll still burn it all to the ground and leave us nothing. My animals gone, my home a heap of ashes!' The woman rocked harder and wailed. 'I'll starve!'

'Of course you won't, Lord Louis will see that you do not.'

'He ain't done nothing but take from us since he came,' she answered and turned her head away, refusing all Catrin's efforts to comfort.

Leaving her in the care of another village woman, Catrin went to the large iron cauldron set over the hearth and helped to dish out pottage and sympathy but quickly realised that it was a fruitless exercise. The villagers might have been forced to take refuge in the keep, but they had closed ranks. It swiftly became obvious to Catrin that they hated Louis and had much preferred their previous, irascible, wine-swilling lord. At least he had not dwelt in luxury while they strove to eke a living from their fields. Catrin discovered that they blamed her too. Old Lord Humphrey had not been married and he had never shown a desire for fancy hangings or glass in the windows.

Unable to bear the sidelong hostile glances any more, Catrin left the baby with Amfrid and went up to the battlements to speak with Louis.

The wind bore the acrid stink of smoke, and beneath their walls the soldiers were setting up camp and preparing to roast a yearling calf. Loaded on baggage wains were shaped sections of wood and lengths of rope which would be assembled into siege machinery.

Louis's complexion was greenish-white as he peered out of one of the wooden crossbow towers jutting out from the wall walk. 'The whoresons,' he spat. 'The stinking whoresons.'

'We were always going to come under threat of attack.' Catrin watched the busy purpose of the men below and contrasted it with the stunned shock of the troops within the keep. 'They look as if they know their business,' she murmured.

Louis stiffened and threw her a narrow look. 'Since when have you been so knowledgeable on military matters?'

She felt the anger in him, his need to bolster his confidence by striking out. 'I don't need vast experience to believe the proof of my eyes.'

He made a curt gesture of dismissal. 'Your place isn't up here. You should be with the other women tending your sewing and rocking your precious cradle.'

Catrin tightened her lips. 'With all the villagers taking refuge within these walls, my place is everywhere,' she pointed out. 'You read meaning into my words that does not exist. I came to look, nothing more.'

'Then if you have seen enough, you can go.' His gaze flickered sidelong as a soldier approached.

Catrin lowered her eyes. She had sense enough not to continue the argument in front of others, especially when every ounce of morale was required. Besides, he was sure to find ways of twisting whatever she said.

'Yes, my lord,' she said sweetly, dipping him a curtsey, which she never did, and left the battlements, her head high and her spine as stiff as a spear.

Louis watched her for a moment, a frown on his face, then he turned to the soldier. It was the Welshman, Ewan, his red hair standing on end in the breeze, his features impassive.

'She's right,' he said in his lilting accent. 'They do know their business.'

Louis gnawed on his thumbnail, chewing away at the quick. 'Meaning?'

Ewan shrugged. 'I've always been the hunter, never the prey.'

Louis stared at the gathering soldiers, not one of them within crossbow range. The walls gave him no sense of security, but made him feel as if he had been brought to bay. Trapped. 'Neither have I,' he said as blood welled in the bed of his thumbnail. 'And I don't like it.'

CHAPTER 23

There had been a sharp frost overnight and when Oliver stepped out of the alehouse door, he was confronted by a glittering silver dawn. The first breath he drew almost cut his lungs. On the horizon, the rising sun was a hazy orange disc.

Blowing on his hands, he ducked back within the dwelling where Godard was stacking the two straw pallets they had used as beds against the wall of the room. The ale-wife put a jug of hot rosehip tisane on the trestle and two bowls of steaming gruel, each sweetened with a dollop of honey.

'Cold morning,' she said. 'You'll not want to ride far without stoking your braziers.' Although she addressed both men, her glance was reserved for Godard, to whom she had taken a fancy. Godard, in his turn, seemed quite smitten by the ale-wife – ale-widow to be precise. She was perhaps in her thirtieth summer, with a sheaf of tawny hair bound in a green kerchief, and large bones well-fleshed and buxom. Her name was Edith, in honour of the old King's wife.

'Any more of this fare, mistress, and we'll not want to ride at all,' he said gallantly, as he sat down and dipped his spoon.

Oliver watched the exchanges between them and smiled bleakly to himself. Hope sprang eternal. Godard was popular with the keep women in Bristol. Despite his brusque manner, he had a knack of being at ease with his feet beneath a trestle, and he was always willing to hew wood and draw water.

'Do you ride far?' she ventured.

Oliver sat down in front of his bowl. 'Ashbury.'

She took a besom from the corner and started to sweep

the beaten earth floor. 'You're going to hire out as soldiers then?'

Oliver shook his head and spooned the thick oat porridge into his mouth. It was by far the best he had tasted, better even than Ethel's. 'No, I was born there. It's a sort of pilgrimage.' If he could not possess then at least he could look, and there were graves to be visited.

Edith gave two vigorous sweeps of the birch broom, then rested on the handle to look at him. 'I've lived here all my life,' she said. 'This alehouse belonged to my mother before it came to me, so I know everything that goes on hereabouts. If you were born at Ashbury then you must be an Osmundsson.'

Godard blinked and gazed at his lord.

Oliver continued to eat his porridge and said nothing.

'You even look like Lord Simon, except your hair is paler and you don't wear a beard. He often stopped here on the road home from Malmesbury,' she added.

Sighing, Oliver pushed his bowl aside. 'I am known as Oliver Pascal in Norman company,' he said, 'but you are right. Simon was my brother, God rest his soul.'

She nodded and narrowed her eyes. 'You're the younger son, the one whose wife died in child-bed.'

Oliver inclined his head stiffly. He was wounded enough already without having her curiosity probe at his emotional flesh.

'The rumour is that you were killed on pilgrimage.'

'A good reason never to listen to rumour or indulge in gossip,' Oliver said curtly and stood up. 'I am whole and alive as you can see.'

Edith clutched the broom and put her other hand on her hip. 'If the two of you ride into Ashbury, you won't remain whole and alive for long,' she warned. 'Odinel the Fleming will nail your hides to the keep wall.'

'Only one of us will be risking his hide,' Oliver said. 'I am going alone.'

'But my lord, I . . .' Godard began, but was silenced by Oliver's raised hand. 'I need no company for what I have to do. Besides, your very size will mark you out for comment. I am taller than most men but you stand a full handspan above me. Word will fly quickly enough to the keep as it is. You will stay here and wait for me. I'll be back by dusk.'

'And if you are not?'

Oliver shrugged. 'Ride on. Take the spare horse with my blessing and find another master.'

Godard clamped his jaw and looked affronted but he said nothing, or at least not until Oliver had gone to saddle Hero.

'If there is one thing I regret in my life,' he said to Edith, 'it is not wringing Louis de Grosmont's good-for-nothing neck when I had the opportunity at Rochester. He has nigh on ruined a man of ten times his own piddling value, and the lives of countless others into the bargain.'

Leaving her justifiably bewildered, he stumped off to the privy beside the midden pit.

The sun melted the frost from the open places, but in the hollows it lingered like white, leprous fingers. Oliver rode along the track that had once been familiar territory. Now, although it looked the same, it had changed, for its welfare lay in a stranger's hand; every twig and thorn on every wayside bush, every clod of soil in the ploughed fields. As he rode, Oliver began to wonder if it had been a mistake to make this pilgrimage. The feeling of love and possession for the land was so strong that it filled his eyes. The Welsh had a word for it; *hiraeth*. There was no parallel term in English or Norman . . . or Flemish.

Twice he almost turned the grey and headed back to the alehouse, but sheer doggedness kept his hand steady on the bridle. He had come this far; he would honour the graves of his family. At the back of his mind, pretending not to exist, was the treacherous thought that if he made a good enough reconnaissance of the site, Earl Robert might yet be persuaded to give him the troops to regain Ashbury.

The sun climbed a shallow arc in the sky, shedding light but little warmth. It was mid-December, the time when folk remained at their hearths, making, mending, telling stories. Hero's shadow lengthened on the track as man and horse approached Ashbury village. There were other settlements attached to the keep but mainly in the form of hamlets and outlying farms, spread over a distance of fifteen miles. Ashbury itself boasted a population of four hundred inhabitants. A market was held outside the church every other Wednesday, and there were two water mills on the river, one for fulling cloth and the other for grinding corn. There were fisheries too, and the river was wide enough to permit trade by barge. The honour of Ashbury might be small, but it was prosperous – a treasure worth stealing.

The village road was deserted, but dogs soon ran out from the tofts to yap at Hero's heels. A woman came to her door, a cooking ladle in her hand, and watched Oliver ride past. A little girl of about three years peeped out at him from the safety of her mother's skirts. At the village well, more women stood gossiping over their water jars. He recognised a couple of them and pulled the hood of his cloak further forward. While he would have liked nothing better than to draw rein and speak with them, it was too dangerous. He felt their eyes upon his progress and knew that what had been idle chatter as they drew their water would now become serious speculation.

Another hundred yards and a frozen duck pond brought him to the boundary of the old Saxon church, with its solid timber walls and low, square tower. Smoke twirled from the hole in the thatched roof of the priest's house, but no one emerged as Oliver tethered Hero to one of the stockade posts and entered the churchyard.

The grass was grazed short and scattered with sheep droppings. At the far boundary, the green turf was wounded by the scars of three recent graves. Winter was the dying time. The old, the weak, the sick succumbed.

Stamping his cold feet, Oliver entered the church. The nave was flagged with heavy squares of stone, some marking burial places. It was deemed a privilege to be laid to rest in the presence of God. To the people who came to pray, walking upon the tombs of the dead was a reminder to prepare their own souls for the afterlife.

Oliver knelt and genuflected to the altar. Two mutton-fat candles sputtered and gave off the aroma of roasting, rancid lamb, by which sign Oliver knew that Father Alberic still had the living here. He made his own altar candles, only allowing the grand beeswax ones for Holy days. It was more economical, he said, and it gave the people a greater sense of occasion when they were used.

Oliver remained on his knees. The stone beneath him was cold and the bones beneath it probably colder still. His wife, his tiny daughter, and beside them his parents, grandparents and great-grandparents; the passage of time marked by the increasing smoothness of the heavy tomb slabs. All of his line was buried here, saving himself and his brother. Simon had fallen in battle, the last ruling Osmundsson at Ashbury, and Oliver did not know what had become of his mortal remains.

'I swear you are not forgotten,' Oliver said, his breath clouding the chapel's wintry greyness. 'While I live, your memory lives too.' The forlorn statement echoed off the walls at him. When he was gone there would be no one to remember either him or them. Perhaps he ought to accept Prince Henry's offer of a wealthy heiress, settle down, raise sons and daughters to carry his line and burden another generation with expectations handed down from the past.

He grimaced at the thought and, rubbing his stone-bruised knees, eased to his feet. It was a pilgrimage that he had needed to make, but he felt weary and relieved at a duty performed rather than uplifted and refreshed.

'Lord William?' A voice spoke behind him, filled with fear and question.

Oliver spun round and found himself facing the diminutive form of Father Alberic. The elderly village priest boasted almost as many years as Ethel had done. Peering and squinting in his dark brown habit, he resembled a mole. He was quivering like a small animal too.

'No, it is Oliver. Don't you recognise me, Father? Have I changed so much?'

The old priest stared for a moment longer, then the tension sighed out of him and his wizened features wrinkled into a smile. 'Master Oliver, by all that is Holy! I thought you were your father returned to life!'

Oliver embraced Father Alberic, his nostrils filling with the familiar scent of musty wool and old incense. 'Would that it were so,' he said. 'Would that we were all still here.'

They parted, although the old man remained close to Oliver, his brow furrowed with the concentration of focusing. 'My eyes are not reliable these days,' he said. 'It won't be long before they send a replacement from the abbey and retire me to a corner of the infirmary to mumble my gums. Not that I'll be sorry. It has been difficult of late, very difficult indeed.' His folded his hands within his habit sleeves and gave Oliver a troubled look. 'What brings you here? You put yourself in great danger.'

Oliver lifted his shoulders. 'I had to come.' He lifted his eyes and stared around the bare little church, its one glory a small stained glass window above the altar. It had been presented by his father in celebration of Simon's birth. When the sun shone, it painted the floor with lozenges of jewel-coloured light. 'Do you remember the last time I stood in this place?'

Alberic scrubbed the side of his bulbous nose. 'It would be the day you left for the Holy Land, my lord. We had the wax candles then.'

Oliver smiled, but the expression was fleeting. Alberic's remark only added poignancy to the pain. 'Simon embraced me and wished me Godspeed. I can still feel his grip on my arm.' He looked at the stained window. 'When I returned to England, it was to learn that he was dead and Ashbury in the hands of Stephen's Flemings. I have come to visit his grave, if he has one, and to look again on what is mine by right. Great danger it might be, but like a swallow I return.'

The old man pursed his lips, his expression revealing that he understood the sentiment whilst being concerned at its outcome. 'Then you do well to come alone and quietly,' he said. 'Lord Odinel is reasonable enough for a Flemish mercenary, but the captain of his garrison is a devil.' He made the sign of the cross, his right hand trembling. 'There has been no peace since he came to the keep at Michaelmas.' His old voice was suddenly gritty with loathing. 'Come, I sully the church by even speaking of him within these holy walls. Lord Simon does indeed have a grave. I will show you where he is buried.'

Stiff with rheumatism, the priest led Oliver out of the church and into the large, oval enclosure. At the far end, near the fresh graves, were three yew trees, and in their shade stood an arched marker of carved yellow sandstone. 'The Fleming would not let him lie in the church with the others, but he did grant him the ground beneath this tree. Young Watkin, the shepherd's lad, was serving his stone-carver's apprenticeship at the abbey and he made the stone. We held a proper funeral for him, did what we could.'

'For which I thank you.' Again Oliver knelt, this time feeling cold turf under his knees. Father Alberic stood a little to one side, waiting in respectful silence. His face in repose bore a strong resemblance to Etheldreda's.

Bowing his head, Oliver paid homage to his dead brother. They had never been particularly close but neither had they been rivals, the boundaries of their relationship clearly defined and understood by them both. If not for his pilgrimage, Oliver would have fought for Ashbury at Simon's side and this would have been his grave too.

Crossing himself, he stood up and twitched his cloak into place. 'Say masses for my soul and those of my family,' he requested, and gave the old priest a small pouch of coins. 'Including Etheldreda of Ashbury.'

'She is dead then?' Alberic looked at the bag in the palm of his hand.

'It was her time and she was at peace,' Oliver said, and thought that he sounded more like a priest than Alberic. 'It was only at the end that I found out about the blood-bond we shared.'

Alberic smiled and shook his head. 'My sister was a law, or perhaps a lore, unto herself, God rest her soul. We all knew she was different, but we only loved her the more.' He hung the pouch on his belt, his hands trembling slightly. 'Nine children our mother bore, Ethel the eighth, me the ninth, and I'm the only one left to bear witness.'

Oliver made a wry face, for he knew exactly how the priest felt. Needing to move, he walked out of the shadows cast by the yews. The fresh graves confronted him, three of them neatly dug in a row.

'You said there had been no peace since Michaelmas. Are these a part of it?'

Father Alberic wrinkled his brow. 'Not as such,' he said. 'Lambert of the brook was five years older than me with not a tooth in his head.' He indicated the first grave as he spoke. 'Winter cold took him in his sleep. Second grave's for Martha, mother of Jeb the swineherd. She turned blue and took with a seizure end of last month.'

'She used to work in the hall, scrubbing the trestles. I remember her well.' Oliver's mind filled with the vision of a robust woman with a red, shiny face. 'She was young to have a seizure.'

'Aye, well, it was because of this.' Alberic pointed to the third mound of earth. 'Jeb's daughter, Gifu, her grandchild and only ten years old.'

'What happened?' Oliver crouched by the grave. It was late in the season, no flowers to be had, but someone had laid a cluster of sweet briar on the soil, the berries a bright blood-red. He knew from Ethel that they were purported to protect the dead and ensure them a peaceful rest.

'No one knows, but everyone suspects,' the old man said, kneading his hands together. 'The little lass went into the woods to gather kindling and met with her death. Her father found her drowned in the stream that runs down to the river, but it was no accident and her body had been violated. The entire village raised the hue and cry and soldiers went out from the castle too, but no one has yet been brought to account.' He shook his head. 'It was too much for Martha. We buried her three days after we buried Gifu.'

'You say everyone suspects?' Oliver gave him a sharp look.

The priest sighed. 'Lord Odinel has been absent of late in King Stephen's service, but he has left a strong garrison here. At Michaelmas they came, a dozen soldiers seeking winter quarters. They are war-hardened mercenaries with respect for neither God nor man. Lord Odinel uses them to show that he can rule with an iron fist if necessary.' A look of sadness and anger crossed the old man's face. 'He thinks that we will be grateful to him for curbing their worst excesses, but I have yet to see gratitude grow out of fear and loathing.'

Oliver rose from the grave side. 'And you think that one of these men killed the girl?'

Father Alberic shrugged. 'We have no proof, but most of us are sure of it. The week before Gifu died, one of the keep women who sells her favours to the men was raped by six of them and beaten senseless. I have heard similar tales in the confessional – from witnesses and victims, not the soldiers. I have yet to shrive any one of them.' He spread his arms in a helpless gesture. 'But what can we do?'

'If I had the men, I would come and put an end to this,' Oliver said with cold fury, his fists opening and closing.

'Ah no, my son, it would only be the beginning of a time far worse.' A spark of alarm kindled in Father Alberic's eyes. 'When war comes to a territory, it is the ordinary people who suffer. Their crops are trampled, their homes burned. Pestilence and starvation follow.'

'So you would rather live beneath the fear and tyranny that you have now?' Oliver demanded incredulously.

'What choice do we have? Even if you did come with an army, they would destroy as they retreated so as to leave you with nothing. I beg you, let it be.' He took hold of Oliver's arm. 'The wind blows chill in the open. Come and break bread with me and sup a bowl of pottage before you go on your way.'

From which statement Oliver understood that the subject was closed and that his presence in Ashbury was perceived as dangerous to its occupants. For a moment he was tempted to thrust Alberic's offer aside and ride off in bitter anger, but he curbed the impulse. Setting fire to the river bank was not the way to build a bridge.

'One day I will return,' he said, 'but I swear that not a single ear of corn shall burn or a villager suffer because of it. That time will come, I promise.'

Father Alberic walked towards his dwelling. 'Folk hereabouts don't set much store by the Empress Mathilda,' he remarked by way of warning without actually saying that he doubted the fulfilment of Oliver's promise.

'I know that. I have no expectations on that score myself, but she does have a son and he bids fair to rival his grandfather and his great-grandfather in stature.'

'But a small child as I remember?'

'Growing swiftly. I can bide my time.' He grimaced. 'It's all I have these days.'

Oliver brought Hero into Alberic's compound and gave him hay and water. Then he sat down to dine at the priest's trestle, one eye on the lengthening shadows. He would have to leave soon.

'Tell me about your pilgrimage,' Alberic said. 'What was Jerusalem like?' Obviously the priest was determined to keep the conversation away from troubles in the village and the entire, distressing business of the war.

'Hot enough to roast a man inside his chain-mail, and thick with the dust of ages,' Oliver replied. 'Beauty and squalor such as you could not imagine. There are places that have not changed since before the time of Our Lord Jesus.'

The priest was enthralled and leaned across the table. 'Did you see the temple of . . .' He broke off as the sound of approaching hoofbeats joined the homely crackle of his hearth fire. For an instant the men stared at each other in silence, and then Alberic began urging Oliver to his feet.

'Like as not it's the soldiers from the keep,' he said. 'Someone must have reported your presence. They're wary of strangers just now because of poor little Gifu. Best not be caught. They seize first and ask questions later.'

Oliver spun from the trestle, grabbed his swordbelt and was already buckling it on as he strode to the door. He had no intention of being trapped inside a one-roomed cot by a band of mercenaries, and he knew if they caught him he was unlikely to live. He would be 'legitimately' executed as the Empress's spy or made a scapegoat for the girl's murder.

'God be with you, my son!' cried Father Alberic, as Oliver snatched his shield from beside the door and ran out to the shelter for his horse.

'He has need to be,' Oliver said grimly as he freed the

reins and scrambled into the saddle. Hero gave a grunt of surprise and indignation as Oliver's heels slammed into his flanks. The stallion sprang forward, but the opening on to the village road was already blocked by four mounted soldiers.

The deep tones of late sunlight brightened the hide of the leading horse from bay to red and the rider's shield bore a device of crimson chevrons on a background of brilliant blue. The colours were sharp enough to cut and score themselves indelibly on the brain. Oliver and Randal de Mohun stared at each other in mutual shock, the moment stretching out as each man strove to recover his balance.

De Mohun affected to do so first, crossing his hands on the pommel of his saddle and grinning wolfishly. 'Our paths seem destined to cross, don't they?' he said. 'Have you come seeking employment from me this time?'

'You are on my land,' Oliver snarled as shock gave way to the enormity of rage.

'Your land?' De Mohun continued to grin. 'Passing strange, for I thought that this place belonged to Odinel the Fleming?' He looked round at his men, inviting them to share in the mockery. 'If you have not come as a recruit, I can only assume that you are trespassing.' He drew his sword, the low sun gilding the blade. 'Lord Odinel does not tolerate trespassers.'

'Wait, Sir Randal, wait!' cried Father Alberic, who had been watching the exchange with growing dismay. He hastened forward, tripping on the folds of his habit. 'I can vouch for this man. He has only come to pay his respects at his brother's grave.'

'You can vouch for him, can you?' de Mohun said silkily, and turned the sword in his hand.

'Go within your house, Father,' Oliver said quietly without taking his eyes off de Mohun. 'This is no concern of yours and I would not see any harm come to you because of me.'

The priest dithered.

'Go!' Oliver spat.

Chewing his lip, Father Alberic backed away and with great reluctance returned to his dwelling.

'Touching,' said de Mohun. 'But you give orders as if you are lord of this place, which you are not.'

'Then that puts me on a footing high above yours,' Oliver retorted, drawing his own sword. 'I would not even grace you with the title of "scum".'

De Mohun spurred his mount at Oliver, who quickly turned side-on and parried the blow on his shield. At least, blocking the opening as he was, the other three could not push in and surround him, but neither could he win free without overcoming all four men.

One of them rode his horse up to the sharpened stockade fence, stood on his saddle and leaped over to Oliver's side, a dagger in his hand. Oliver saw the danger and, slashing a blow at de Mohun, pivoted Hero and rode straight at the man on foot. The sword swung and chopped, and the mercenary fell without time to scream, his dagger flying from his hands.

In leaving the entrance, Oliver had opened himself to attack by the other three men, but there had been no other choice. There was a way out if his speed and timing were right but both had gone spinning awry in the frantic game of kill or be killed. De Mohun came at him head-on and his companions went left and right. As Oliver struck and parried, he knew that he faced certain death unless he could diminish the odds.

The soldier on his shield side was wearing a padded gambeson but no mail. Oliver wrenched on the bridle and, as Hero pivoted, he slashed at the garment. The linen burst, disgorging its lining of felted wool. Oliver's sword bit deeper, opening up the man's ribs to the bone.

The soldier screamed and pulled back, clutching at the wound in his side. But in taking his man, Oliver had left himself dangerously open to the weapons of de Mohun and the other mercenary. Even as he turned to face them, he too was struck in the ribs. Unlike his victim, he was wearing a mail hauberk. De Mohun's blade skidded on the steel rings but, although it failed to cut, the blow was made with bone-shattering force. Pain that was both numb and agonising tore through Oliver's chest. A second blow followed the first, then a third and a fourth as the other mercenary joined in with gusto. Oliver warded the assault on his shield, but it quickly became splintered and battered, and his arm began to tire.

'I should have killed you on the Jerusalem road years ago!' panted de Mohun. He was incandescent with the fury and joy of battle. Oliver had no breath to answer. All he knew was that it was now or accept the grave. For all that he had contemplated the oblivion of death, he had no desire to embrace it at the hands of Randal de Mohun.

His shield high, he spurred Hero at the other soldier's chestnut and cut low, aiming at the man's unprotected legs. The sword bit flesh down to bone, and the man bellowed with rage and pain. A space opened up between the mercenaries and Oliver urged Hero through it. Then he slapped the reins down on the stallion's neck.

At a dead gallop, the grey shot out of the priest's yard, through the church gate, and on to the greensward in front of the bell tower. De Mohun's bay ploughed after them at break-neck speed, caught up and confronted. The horses pushed together, hooves flailing, teeth snapping. The men hacked at each other. De Mohun had the advantage of being fresher and without injury. Oliver's shield wavered as he grew increasingly tired, and de Mohun launched a vicious, overarm blow. Oliver felt, rather than heard, his collar-bone crack, and in that same instant lost all strength in his shield arm. De Mohun came in again like a wolf. His sword point lodged in the bend of Oliver's elbow and he began to prise the bones apart.

Through blinding pain, Oliver chopped across and down. De Mohun snatched his hand away to avoid losing his fingers, and once again Oliver turned Hero and dug in his heels. He had no coherent idea of where he was going. All that was left was the hazy instinct to flee.

Showering turf, Hero spun round the side of the church and galloped towards the graves beneath the yew trees. Oliver could not determine whether the roaring in his ears was the sound of de Mohun's pursuit or his own heartbeat. One was as close as the other. The gravestone flashed past and the stockade fence loomed. Oliver lashed the reins down on Hero's neck. The stallion took a short, choppy stride, bunched his muscles and, ears back, took a flying leap.

The horse sailed over the posts, landed on the slope of the bank with a jarring thud, and stumbled and pecked all the way down to the ditch at the bottom. But he kept his feet and, with a tremendous surge, lunged up and out on to the far side.

Barely conscious, Oliver clung to mane and bridle. Through blurring vision, he watched de Mohun's bay take the stockade, drag a hindleg and come down hard on the bank. Man and horse somersaulted over and over, finishing in a tangled heap in the ditch. The bay threshed to its feet but, in the act, rolled and trampled upon its rider, mashing the chain mail into his body. The horse stood trembling and shuddering, bloody froth blowing from one nostril.

'Jesu,' Oliver whispered and, despite his agony, rode Hero over to look at de Mohun. He was face down in the ditch. If not dead, then he soon would be, for his nose and mouth were immersed in the churned, muddy water, but Oliver suspected that his soul was already on its way to hell.

Turning Hero, he headed towards the road and felt the wetness of blood sliding down his arm and webbing his hand.

The day that Godard passed at the alehouse was one of the most pleasant he could remember. It was not that he did anything out of the ordinary. He spent the morning hewing wood for Edith and, after a substantial midday meal of bacon stew and savoury griddle cakes, occupied the afternoon by mending her spade and her wooden rake. The delight was in living as he had lived before the war had torn the land apart; the delight was in looking at Edith as she went about her chores with quiet efficiency. She looked a good, buxom armful; a comfort when a man needed comfort, but she had strength too, and beautiful butter-coloured braids beneath her kerchief.

'Suppose you and your lord will be moving on tomorrow,' she said, and looked at him from her eye corner while preparing a broth with chicken dumplings.

Godard sighed and rose from his stool. 'Like as not,' he said, and went moodily to look out of the door, his arms folded, his massive frame propped against the opening. The light was shifting and slanting as the sun dipped westwards and a chill perked the air.

He heard the slosh of water as she stirred the cauldron. ''Tis a pity,' she said after a moment. 'I did not realise how much I missed male company until I had one to myself again.'

Godard unfolded his arms and looked round. 'What about your customers?'

'Oh, them.' She sniffed and waved her ladle. 'They all have wives waiting at home, and those that don't are only worth a skillet round the head to send them away before bedtime.'

'I've never been married,' Godard said. 'When you're the youngest of eight, you don't expect to.'

Their eyes held for a moment longer. Then Edith made a show of bustle and Godard cleared his throat. 'Mind you, that's not saying I wouldn't like to be.'

She was silent, but he was strongly aware of her presence. One more step, one more push was all it would take. Being a cautious man he held back. Equally cautious, she avoided his gaze and went studiously about her business until the moment had passed.

Godard resumed watching the road. A child came with a quart pitcher and a request from his mother that it be filled with ale. He was followed by two men, thirsty after a day's toil in the fields. Godard drank a mug with them, then went to check on his horse. Shadows lengthened and dusk began to soften the world with shades of blue. The moon rose, luminous and cream-silver. The smell of chicken broth floated on the air in delicious wafts. Godard gnawed his thumb knuckle and willed Oliver to appear on the road, but except for villagers beating a path to the alehouse, it remained empty.

The stars twinkled out and the final strands of sunset vanished over the horizon. Finally Godard strode inside and swept on his cloak and hood. It was one matter for Oliver to tell him to ride on and seek another master, a different one for him to do it.

'I am going in search of my lord,' he said to Edith, who was busy ladling broth and dumplings into a bowl for a customer.

She nodded briskly, adding, 'Have a care,' and gave him a quick look in which there was unspoken concern.

Godard smiled and plucked his quarterstaff from the corner. 'You need not worry about that,' he said in a gruff voice, but he was pleased that she was anxious for his welfare.

Once on the road, he made such haste as the moonlight would allow. He did not want to risk foundering his horse, but neither did he want to waste time. Godard was not afraid of the dark, but he was not particularly fond of being out in it either. Beyond the village, the road dwindled to a rutted cart track with smaller tracks branching off into the fields. Silence descended, the only sounds to break it being the clop of his mount's hooves and the champ of its breath. Godard began to sing to himself, then changed his mind. The darkness was too vast, too wide and full of hidden, listening ears.

He came to a wooded stretch where the road dipped down into a black hollow. Godard drew rein and seriously contemplated turning back for the warmth and welcome of the alehouse. He imagined a steaming bowl of broth, feather-light dumplings and Edith's welcoming smile. The pity was that without discovering what had happened to Oliver, he would be unable to enjoy any of it. 'Hah,' he said with irritation, and kicked the gelding's flanks.

Man and horse descended into darkness. There was a boggy stream at the foot of the hollow which Godard heard, rather than saw, as the horse splashed through it. Emerging on the other side into a lacing of darkness and moonlight, he did not see the dappled horse on the track in front until it nickered and came trotting to greet him. Breath steamed from its nostrils. The reins were knotted around the saddle pommel and there were dark stains on its pale coat.

'Steady lad, steady,' Godard crooned and caught Hero's bridle. He secured the destrier to his gelding and wondered what in Christ's name had happened to Oliver. The stains on Hero's coat looked like blood, and probably Oliver's to judge from their position.

He clicked his tongue and urged the gelding forward, and almost immediately saw the flash of chain-mail near the place where the grey had been standing. Godard flung down from the saddle, tossed a loop of bridle over a tree branch to secure the horses and ran to the fallen man.

'Lord Oliver?'

There was a groan and Oliver tried to raise his head. 'Godard, you purblind fool, I told you to go.'

'My hearing's not what it used to be. Where are you hurt?' With gentle hands for one so huge, Godard tried to make an examination.

'Everywhere. There's not a whole bone in my body. Let me die.' Oliver closed his eyes.

Godard tapped the side of his master's face with rigid fingers. 'I've not made this journey just to bring back your corpse. Where there's life there's hope,' he said sternly.

'Where there's life there's pain,' Oliver responded, but opened his eyes.

Godard tightened his lips. He knew that unless he got Oliver back to the alehouse in short order, he would die. If his wounds did not kill him, the cold would.

'You have to mount up, sir,' he said. 'I will ride behind you and hold you in the saddle.'

Oliver laughed, the sound choking off on a wheeze of agony. 'You're gullible enough to believe in miracles, then,' he gasped.

'Yes, sir,' Godard said stoutly. 'It's no more than two miles to the village. Seems a pity to lie here in the frost, even if you are dying,' he added in a practical tone. Rising to his feet, he fetched the horses. There was a flask of usquebaugh in his saddle bag and he took a swallow for himself and gave the rest to Oliver. 'Drink this down. It'll put fire in your blood.'

'It will take more than fire,' Oliver said, but set the flask to his lips and drank grimly.

'Just get yourself on to the horse, sir, I will do the rest,' Godard said.

The usquebaugh tore through Oliver's veins, infusing a false sense of heat and well-being, taking the edge off his suffering. But it was still agony to stand up. The pain in his ribs was so violent that he could scarcely breathe and his left arm was totally useless. The blood had ceased to flow from the wound when he had fallen from the horse, but now, as he strove to rise, he felt the hot trickle begin again. Gritting his teeth, fighting a nauseous wave of blackness, he set his foot in the stirrup and Godard boosted him across the big gelding's back. He almost fell off the other side and only saved himself by clutching convulsively at the reins with his half-good right hand.

Godard swiftly mounted up behind him and took his weight.

'Jesu, it would be easier to die,' Oliver groaned as the gelding paced forward.

'But better to live,' Godard said. Darkness engulfed them as the horses clopped through the hollow, and then emerged into the moon-dappled woods. 'How came you by your wounds?'

Oliver spoke slowly with effort. 'Randal de Mohun was captain of Ashbury's garrison . . . When he heard there was a stranger in the village he came to investigate.'

'Randal de Mohun, God's teeth!' Godard had asked the question in order to keep Oliver talking and prevent him from slipping into unconsciousness. Now his eyes widened and he paid full attention. 'How did he come to be at Ashbury?'

'Simple . . . He had heard me talk of the place.' Oliver paused to fight the pain and gather strength. 'He knew that it was held by one of Stephen's Flemings . . . small chance of being called to account for his crimes. It killed two birds with one stone . . . gave him employment and a place to keep his head low.'

'The whoreson,' Godard said in hoarse revulsion.

'One girl-child is dead, molested in the forest, but there will be no more,' Oliver said, after another pause. 'We fought, and he is dead.' He closed his eyes and felt the darkness drifting in. Godard's voice prodded at him, asking more questions, making demands. He felt anger and tried to snarl at Godard to leave him be. The sounds he made bore no resemblance to those he had intended. He wanted peace and he could not have it. If he could only achieve the darkness, there would be freedom from pain.

'Not far,' Godard kept saying, but still the lurching stride of the bay gelding continued. He was almost beyond notice when it stopped – too far gone to help himself, but not far enough to diminish the excruciating pain as Godard lifted him bodily from the saddle and carried him into the alehouse. The staring startled faces, the blazing fire, the tearing agony in his body all served to convince him that Godard had plucked him from purgatory and personally deposited him in hell.

CHAPTER 24

Catrin stood with Louis in the keep's undercroft which should have been stuffed to the roof arches with supplies to withstand the siege, but which showed little more than a few barrels of salted fish and meat, some sacks of meal and half a dozen bacon flitches. There was a motley collection of root vegetables, not in the best condition. Hands on hips, Catrin studied the depressing total of their assets. 'There is perhaps enough for another week if we live exclusively on watery stew,' she said. 'Although I suppose we could make it more palatable if we use some of that.' She indicated the casks of red Gascon wine that numbered in total as many as the combined barrels of salt fish and beef.

Louis scowled. Above their heads came the muted clump of one of the siege engines launching a stone at the walls. They were entering the third week and although Wickham's solid stones had stood up well to the pounding, their supplies were in less robust condition.

Louis rubbed one hand over his face. 'I'll have to break out between their lines and fetch help from Simon de Senlis at Northampton,' he said. 'Tonight. There's no moon and it will be easier to slip past their sentries.'

Catrin stared at him in tight-lipped silence. 'You think that is wise?'

He spread his hands. 'What choice do we have? Another week and there will be nothing to eat.'

'They do not know that. Another week and they might go away.'

'Yes, but if I can return with an army, I'll be able to trap them like a grain between two millstones.'

Catrin let out her breath on a sigh of exasperation and paced the length of the half-empty undercroft. Any trust she had put in Louis had long since flown out of one of his precious glass windows. Their supplies were low because he had not bothered to replenish them, preferring to put Gascon wine and colourful wall hangings before the basic daily staples. His excuse was that he had been using the old before buying the new but it was a threadbare lie.

'Like a grain between two millstones,' she repeated, nodding her head. 'And what if Simon de Senlis cannot spare you aid?'

'Don't worry, he will. Wickham's too important to lose.' The words rolled nonchalantly off his tongue but he didn't look at her as he spoke.

So important that they had given it to an untried mercenary? Catrin bit her tongue. Louis's temper was as much in evidence as his charm these days. She wondered what she had ever seen in him, and almost immediately acknowledged that it was his physical presence; the magnetism of a lithe, prowling animal. Now that she had a child to consider, that magnetism did not exert the same irresistible pull. If they argued, they were no longer reconciled in bed.

'Some of the castle folk might see your slipping away as desertion,' she said as neutrally as she could. In truth, she was one of them.

'I do not care what they see,' Louis snapped. 'I am doing this for their hides as much as my own.' His olive complexion darkened beneath her cool stare.

'Of course you are,' she said. 'We'll see the proof of it within the week.' Head carried high, she went to the stairs that led up to the hall.

'Where are you going?'

'To tend to Rosamund. After all, you have no more need of me here, have you?' She looked round and arched her brow. 'You can add me to the tally of salt beef, stockfish and serfs that you leave behind.'

Louis glared at her. 'All I have had from you since that brat was born is piss-vinegar looks and sour words. I am your husband; you will give me respect.'

Catrin reached the top of the stairs and swished round to face him. 'If you return from Northampton within the week and lift this siege, then I will accord you every honour and respect,' she said. 'But if you do not, then I will surrender this keep to de Vere's men, return to Robert of Gloucester at Bristol and seek an annulment of this hell-bound marriage!' Her voice began to rise and crack.

'To Robert of Gloucester, or to that knight of his, Pascal?' Louis snarled. 'I see how much score you set by your marriage oath!'

Catrin was furious. 'Do not talk to me of oaths and fidelity,' she spat. 'I am not the one who has broken faith.' She pushed beyond the thick oak door into the hall. He followed hard on her heels and for a moment she thought that he was going to spin her round and cast her head over heels down the undercroft stairs. She braced herself and drew breath to scream, but instead he swept past her, his stride full of anger.

'You leave and I swear I will brand you a whore before all and sundry and deny that brat up there any claim on me,' he said without stopping, and loud enough for the nearest servants and soldiers to hear. 'It's probably not mine anyway. My loins would have begotten a son.'

Catrin gasped and recoiled as if he had physically slapped her. Tears of rage brimmed and spilled. The very force of her emotion left her incoherent and bereft of defence. She felt the curious eyes of witnesses, the pity, the gleams of salacious speculation. Within the hour it would be all over the keep and grossly distorted. The Lord and Lady had quarrelled. The Lady was accused of whoredom and foisting a cuckoo on her husband. They already blamed her for wasting money on tapestries and fine glass windows.

She swiped the back of her hand across her face and glared after her husband's retreating form. 'Oliver made just as many promises as you,' she said in a shaking, tear-blocked voice, 'and he kept them all.'

As once before, Catrin bid her husband farewell with a turned back and cold lips. She did not go down to the hall to watch him and half a dozen of his best men go out into the bailey on silent feet, their clothing dark and their faces smeared with earth. She did not lie awake in bed, listening for the cry to go up that they had been captured sneaking through the lines, for she knew that they would escape. Like a thief, Louis could move like a wraith. Like a thief, he took everything and gave nothing back.

That was not strictly true, she admitted to herself as she lay in the great bed, her body curled protectively around her tiny daughter. Whatever rumours he strewed abroad concerning the child's paternity, he had given her Rosamund and he had given her heart-sickness and grief.

Perhaps he would return within the week with a force to relieve the siege, but she knew in her heart that he would not. As always he had left others to pay his price, including a defenceless infant. She pressed her lips against Rosamund's brow and vowed to keep the baby safe whatever the cost.

The promised week came and went with no sign of a relieving force. Once their gates were almost breached and only a timely deluge of boiling water and the splitting of the ram log saved Wickham from being overrun. Their supplies dwindled and the stew became progressively less nourishing. The last bundles of arrows were brought from the undercroft and the soldiers muttered behind their hands.

Apart from the time she spent in her chamber suckling and tending Rosamund, Catrin made herself conspicuous around the keep. She took all of her meals in the hall and made a point of mingling with all the castle folk, from the ageing knight left in command of the garrison to the youngest laundry maid, and even Wulfhild, her husband's young mistress. His former mistress now, Catrin thought, as the ninth day dawned without sight or sign of help.

'He promised me a silk dress,' Wulfhild sniffed, knuckling her eyes. Her hair fell in snarled blond tangles and had clearly not been combed or tended for several days, and her face had the gaunt, hollow look that came from lack of food and sleep. A mound of laundry gave off a sweaty smell beside a cauldron that had yet to be kindled. 'He promised me a house of my own with hens and geese and a cow.'

'If that is all he promised, then you are fortunate,' Catrin said grimly. 'You're not the first, and I doubt you'll be the last.' Kneeling down, she set about lighting the fire herself.

'He will come back, won't he?'

Catrin looked at the snuffling young woman, and tried to convince herself that the conversation was real. Louis's mistress asking his wife for sympathy and reassurance. Small licks of flame fluttered beneath the cauldron as the dry twigs caught fire. Standing up, Catrin dusted off her hands. 'If he does, then I will not be here, and if you had the tiniest morsel of sense, you would not cry another tear.'

'What do you mean, you won't be here?' The girl's eyes widened.

Catrin rubbed her thumb on her forefinger. 'We cannot hold out for many more days, and why should we?' She tightened her lips. 'I won't let people starve for my husband's selfishness.'

'But . . . but what about the soldiers out there? What will they do to us if we let them in?' Wulfhild put her hand to her throat.

'We're not just going to "let them in",' Catrin said. 'We'll bargain with them first.' She clicked her fingers at the laundry tub. 'You do what you are paid for and see to that mound of linen. It's not as if we're going to run out of water, is it?'

Leaving the laundry, she went to her chamber and made swift preparations. Her actions had been brewing in her mind for some while. Time and again she had imagined them, so now each movement was clear. What she had not imagined was the overwhelming sense of impatience and urgency. She had to go, and immediately. If not, Louis might just appear on the horizon and blight her entire future.

She donned her two best dresses, one over the other, two pairs of hose, two loin-cloths, two braided girdles. After Penfoss, she was wary of possessing only one set of clothes. Besides, the weather was bitterly cold and she needed all the protection she could get. Her cloak came next, its lining made of fleece, and she pulled her brown hood over the top of her wimple.

Gently and tenderly, she lifted Rosamund from her cradle and wrapped the baby in her blankets until all that could be seen was a tiny triangle of eyes, nose and mouth. Placid as ever, Rosamund gurgled and blew bubbles at her mother. For the briefest moment, Catrin was distracted from her purpose and cooed at her daughter, but urgency was swift to return.

Without a backward glance at the rich hangings, the silk bedcover and tear-grey window glass, she swept from the room to find Berold, the captain of the garrison.

He gazed at her askance when she ordered him to ride out with her under a flag of truce to parley with the enemy commander. 'Lord Louis said that we were to hold out until his return,' he said, and put his hand on his sword hilt in a gesture both defensive and aggressive.

'Judgement day will come before that happens,' Catrin answered with asperity. 'Within the week, he said, but since when has a week lasted ten days?' She looked at the balding, middle-aged knight and, amidst her irritation, felt a softening of compassion. Louis had promoted Berold beyond his competence. He was a good follower, but had no flair for leading men. 'You served old Lord Humphrey, didn't you?'

'Aye, for nigh on twenty years.' He bristled his sparse silver beard at her. 'What of it? Are you saying that I'm not fit to serve Lord Louis?'

'No,' she soothed quickly. 'I commend your experience. What I am saying is that Lord Louis is not fit to be your master.'

He gave her a suspicious look and fingered the hilt of his sword.

Catrin struggled to swallow her impatience. 'Tell me, in all honesty, do you believe that Lord Louis will return with more troops?'

He chewed his lower lip. 'He entrusted me with the defence of this keep. I would not want to pay him in false coin.'

'It is you who is being paid in false coin,' Catrin said sharply. 'To my husband, loyalty is just another side of a die, and if fortune throws it face down he will try his luck at another game.'

The knight rubbed a slick, white scar on his cheek. 'I do not know . . .' he prevaricated. 'What if he arrives on the morrow and discovers that we have yielded the keep?'

Catrin gritted her teeth. 'He is not returning, Berold. I doubt that we can hold out until the morrow anyway. I have to do my best for these people, my daughter and myself.'

Grudgingly the old man nodded. 'But what if their terms are not lenient?'

'They will be,' she said, with far more confidence than she felt. 'I am not without influence of my own.'

Berold pinched his scar and frowned. 'Aye, but I had heard that it was influence with King Stephen. These men are all for the Empress.'

'You heard but only half the tale.' She started towards the hall door, knowing that if she did not move she would scream. 'And that is the problem with listening to my husband. I cannot pull victory out of defeat but I hope I can lessen the damage.'

The leader of the attacking troops was a hard-bitten Welshman called Madoc. He was somewhat surprised, not to say indignant, at being asked to parley with a woman, a swaddled infant and a small, scarred knight with about as much presence as a dead chicken.

'Is this a mark of Wickham's respect or the best you can do?' he scoffed.

'You should not mock our best, since it has held you at bay for longer than you wish,' Catrin replied with spirit. 'The snow will come soon and it will be difficult to keep your men in the field.'

'Oh, I intend to be within Wickham's walls long before the first flakes fall.' Fists clenched in his swordbelt, the soldier studied her. 'But you have come to parley, not to bandy words. What is it you want?'

Catrin shifted Rosamund's sleepy weight on her arm. Beside her she could feel Berold's tension. He was far from happy with the situation but could see that they had small choice. 'In return for a guarantee of safety for everyone in Wickham from the richest to poorest, I will yield the castle to you.'

The Welshman considered her. He had coppery hair and eyes of a narrow, flint-grey. No battle scars marred his face but it was pitted by the old marks of spotted fever. 'You will yield the castle?' He raised his brows. 'Is yours then the sole authority? What of the lord of this place?'

'He is not here,' she said, and met his gaze steadily.

'Ah.' He looked thoughtful. 'Now we come to the meat of the matter. Does that mean that he has not been here at all for the duration of the siege, or that he has seen fit to make himself scarce in consideration of his own hide?'

'It would not be seemly for me to answer that question,' Catrin said. 'You may draw your own conclusions. All that concerns me is the safety of these people and my daughter.'

The Welshman pursed his lips. 'I would have to think about that,' he said. 'The lads are owed some compensation for freezing their balls off these past three weeks.'

Catrin shrugged indifferently. 'There is plunder enough in the keep to pay a hundred ransoms,' she said, 'although I would counsel you against harming anyone within.'

Madoc gave a disbelieving snort. 'You would, eh?'

Catrin drew herself up. 'It is true that my husband is one of Stephen's knights, but in the recent past I have been a chamber lady to the Countess of Gloucester and I am known personally to Earl Robert. For a time I was nurse to his youngest half-brother, one of the old King's sons. I have powerful connections.'

She watched him consider whether to believe her. Catrin knew that she had slightly overstated her case concerning her influence, but all the rest was true.

A soldier who had been standing in the background came forward and whispered in his commander's ear, his eyes upon her.

Madoc listened and nodded. A glint of wintry humour entered his eyes. 'Ascelin here was at Bristol too,' he said to her. 'He remembers you well, and kindly so it seems.'

Catrin did not recognise the man, but then so many of them looked the same in their mail and helms.

'You were at my wife's lying in,' the soldier said. 'You and the old woman delivered our son. He's going on two years old now and sturdy as a young oak.'

Catrin smiled whilst panicking about what else he was going to reveal. 'I'm glad to hear it,' she murmured.

'You had that shelter in the bailey.' He frowned. 'I thought that you were betrothed to that hearth knight of the Earl's.'

'I was. It is a long tale, and not a happy one. But you can confirm the fact that I was at Bristol and known to the Earl and Countess.'

'Indeed, my lady.'

She looked down at the sleeping baby in her arms and then at Madoc who had been listening to the exchange with interest. 'I care little for either side in this war. All I crave is that my daughter should grow up in peace without constantly having to look over her shoulder or worry that each night might be her last on earth.'

'Then best send her to a nunnery,' Madoc said, but she sensed a softening of his attitude.

'Would she be any safer there?' Catrin retorted, holding her own. 'Wherwell nunnery was razed to the ground at the siege of Winchester.'

He conceded the point with a twitch of his lips and a spread hand. 'Go where you will, my lady, it matters little to me save that I do not have to spend another night under the sky.'

'Then you agree to the bargain? The keys of the castle in exchange for the lives and livelihood of all within?'

He sucked his teeth and pondered, finally granting her a curt nod. 'Let it be done. War is war, but why burn and destroy that which is useful?'

'Why indeed?' Catrin replied, her brow raised in irony.

The *Virgo* creaked and heaved at her moorings, her stirring ever more restless as the incoming tide lapped her sides. Stars sparkled in the frosty night, and on deck the passengers had wrapped themselves in their cloaks for warmth.

A pouch of silver hung in heavy comfort from Louis's belt.

He had sold his horse and the dice had smiled on him in alehouse and tavern. There were better horses to be had in the Holy Land, swift stallions of hot Arab blood. Swift mares too, dark-eyed, slim-flanked and wild for the riding. There were fortunes to be made, hearts to be won and broken.

If he thought of Wickham at all, it was with the relief of a prisoner unfettered from his chains.

As the wind bellied the sails and the Master's shout sent a sailor to free the mooring and the steersman to take the rudder, Louis de Grosmont cast off his name like a snake shedding an outworn skin. From this moment forth, he was Louis le Pelerin – Louis the Pilgrim.

CHAPTER 25

It was a long, cold road from Wickham to Bristol. Although the distance was little more than fifty miles, it took Catrin over a week to cover it. The roads were unsafe for folk of all rank and those who had to travel did so in groups for protection. On the second day, she joined three monks, a wool merchant and two young men with spears heading for Gloucester. The weather was atrocious and progress so slow through a mizzle of sleet and rain that it was not until the fifth day that they arrived in the city. Two more passed before Catrin felt fit enough to set out on the last leg to Bristol.

She arrived at dusk, Rosamund bawling fretfully in her arms, and was frowned at for her tardiness by the soldier preparing to close the gates for the night. In the castle ward, Etheldreda's shelter was occupied by a cowherd and his family, eating their supper over a fire of dried dung. Her back and buttocks aching from the saddle, her eyes gritty with weariness and strain, Catrin paid a groom to take her tired mare and made her way to the hall.

Steward Bardolf still held his position and tyrannical inclinations. Scowling like the guard at her late arrival, but otherwise not giving her a second glance, he directed her to a place on one of the lowlier trestles near the draught from the door. Through the open screens at either side of the hall, servants hurried back and forth with heaped trenchers. The meaty smells of ragout and pottage, the sight of the baskets of flat loaves on the trestle made Catrin feel faint with hunger. Obviously possessed of a similar affliction, Rosamund continued to whimper and grizzle. Catrin discreetly lifted her cloak, unfastened her gown and put her to suckle.

Grace was said and folk started to eat. Although only having one hand free, Catrin still managed to break bread and help herself to a generous bowl of mutton stew. While eating, she glanced around the hall and saw many familiar faces, but not the one she sought. But then, why should Oliver be here? As often as not he was absent on the Earl's business and a year and a half would not have changed the situation. Between courses, she asked her companions for news, but none of them were well acquainted with Oliver and they could not help her.

As supper finished and the servants cleared the trestles, Catrin made her way to the women's chambers on the upper floor. She was challenged once by a guard, but then he recognised her and, after a smile and a word of greeting, let her pass.

Catrin's breath grew short with tension as she entered rooms which were familiar to her but where she no longer had a right to be.

'Hello, lady,' said a very small boy, staring up at her from solemn hazel eyes. He had a mop of curly blond hair and there was a peeled, half-eaten apple in his hand.

'Hello,' Catrin responded. 'Who are you?'

'Effry,' he said, and looked at Rosamund bundled up in Catrin's arms. 'I've got a baby too.' He took a bite out of the apple and then offered it to Catrin.

'Geoffrey, come here, what have I told y . . .' Edon FitzMar stopped in mid-speech and stared in astonishment. 'Catrin? Holy Virgin, I do not believe my eyes!'

'I do mine,' Catrin laughed, and tears blinded her eyes. Foolish, vain, giddy Edon looked like an angel at that moment.

With a cry of delight Edon threw herself at Catrin, stopping the hug short when she saw the baby wrapped in her cloak.

'My daughter, Rosamund,' Catrin said with pride.

'A little girl!' Edon parted the blanket to look into the tiny features. 'Oh, just look at those eyelashes!' she cooed. 'Isn't she pretty!' She stroked Rosamund's petal-soft cheek and looked at Catrin. 'What are you doing in Bristol?'

Catrin shook her head. 'It is a long story. We are here seeking refuge – yet again.'

Edon gave her a look full of blatant curiosity but, to her credit and increased maturity, did not seek to have it satisfied there and then. Instead, she drew Catrin to a cushioned window seat, set the youngest maid to making up a pallet, and brought wine with her own hand. Then she stooped by a cradle and picked up a baby of a similar age to Rosamund. 'My second son, Robert,' she announced. 'I wish you had been here. The midwives weren't as good as you and Ethel. At least he came head first and without difficulty.' She popped the baby back in the cradle. The little boy came to peer and poke at his younger brother.

'I wish I had been here too,' Catrin said with a tired smile. She shed her cloak to reveal the top gown of blue wool with its lavish gold embroidery.

Edon's eyes grew huge. 'Have you been stealing from the Empress's wardrobe?' she gasped.

Catrin sipped the wine and laughed bitterly. 'My husband is a man generous beyond all belief,' she said, and flicked back the hem of the first gown to show Edon the fir-green of the second dress. 'I left three others behind. By now they will be gracing the forms of Flemish whores in return for favours.'

'Your husband . . .' Edon said hesitantly. 'Then it is true.'

'I don't know. What have you heard?' A defensive note entered Catrin's voice.

'That he was not dead, that you had found him again. Geoffrey said that he was a noble man. He treated the prisoners honourably and they liked him. Geoffrey was sorry for Oliver and pleased for you.' She swept to her feet and grabbed her eldest son. 'No, sweetheart, not in his eye, there's a good boy.'

'Louis can make anyone like him if he tries,' Catrin said dully. 'He swore to me that he had changed but he hadn't, and I was still too blind to see through his charm. He demanded all my attention like a greedy child, but once he had it, he lost interest. He wanted a son and I disappointed him with a daughter, for which he has not forgiven me – not that I care for such things.' She shook her head. 'It was the same with Wickham. First the passion and desire, then the desertion.'

'He deserted you?' Edon wrestled with her struggling son and looked perplexed.

Catrin shrugged. 'Yes, he did, but this time I did not spend a year in grief before I took up the threads of my life.' Briefly, and against the background of a thwarted, screaming two-year-old, she told Edon about the siege and how she came to be at Bristol. 'So,' she defended herself with a vulnerable half-smile, 'I have come to find Oliver and beg his forgiveness on bended knees.'

The youngest maid had finished making up the pallet and offered to show Edon's son the caged finches in the adjoining chamber. As she led him away and peace was restored, Edon readjusted her skewed wimple. 'He doesn't take after me,' she said with firm denial, and then she sighed. 'It nearly broke Oliver when he lost you. It was all my Geoffrey could do to prevent him from drinking himself stupid every night or seeking his own death in battle.'

Her words deepened Catrin's feeling of guilt and renewed her apprehension. Perhaps Oliver would not forgive her, or even want to see her. 'I had to choose,' she said. 'And I would not wish that kind of choosing on any woman.' She bit her lip. 'In the event, I made the wrong decision.'

There was a brief silence. Catrin glanced at Edon and said, 'Do you think it too late to make amends?'

Edon wrinkled her nose and looked perplexed. 'I do not know. Oliver has not taken up with any other women, but he never speaks of you. Geoffrey says that in the summer Oliver received a message to say that you were very happy with your husband and that you were with child. I think until then he had started to recover, but that news disturbed him greatly.'

Catrin whitened. 'I knew nothing of it,' she said, 'but I would not put it past my husband's malice.'

'Why choose such a man above Oliver?' Edon asked in total bewilderment. 'Why throw away gold for dross?'

'Sometimes your eyes are too dazzled by old shine to know the difference.' Catrin shook her head and wiped at a tear. 'I thought that Louis had the right. Now I know that he had no right at all.' She gazed pensively at Edon. 'I looked for Oliver in the hall at dinner but I did not see him. Is he here?'

Edon wrinkled her brow in thought. 'No,' she said at length. 'I think not. But we do not see so much of Oliver these days since he has been seconded to Prince Henry's household.'

'Prince Henry?'

'If you were in the hall at dinner you would have seen him at the high table. The boy with red hair and a severe dose of the fidgets.'

'Vaguely,' Catrin said. 'We had heard that he was in England, but I never put the two together.'

'Well, he's adopted Oliver as his "pet Saxon",' Edon said. 'When he returns to his father in Anjou, Oliver will be going with him as part of his retinue.'

Catrin absorbed this information with surprise and a frisson of dismay. She mentally scolded herself for the latter. Time and people did not stand still. It was selfish to expect Oliver to remain in the same place, solid as a rock for her convenience. But right or wrong, it was how she had imagined him and now she was thrown off balance.

'And you do not know where he is now?'

'No.' Eden screwed up her eyes in thought. 'I seem to remember Geoffrey mentioning that Oliver had business of his own to attend to – another pilgrimage or something – that he wanted to perform before he committed himself entirely to Prince Henry's service. He'll probably be here by the end of the week, and you know you'll be more than welcome to stay among the women. The Countess was only saying the other day how much she missed your green ointment for sore hands.'

Catrin responded with a wan smile. Impatience and apprehension churned inside her. She wanted to see Oliver now, not at the end of the week. Waiting was impossible, but she had no other course. 'Then I'll be pleased to make her some and whatever else she wishes. Edon, if I do not have something to occupy my time, I swear I will go mad.'

Godard and Edith laid Oliver down on a pallet arranged

near the fire. Curious drinkers gathered round until Edith sent them off to their homes with a communal flea in the ear and barred the door.

Together she and Godard gently stripped Oliver's hauberk and gambeson. He drifted in and out of consciousness, making a continuous low moaning sound. Blood had saturated his left arm, and when Godard slit open the shirt and tunic with Edith's shears, both of them winced at the mess that de Mohun's sword had made.

'Have you needle and thread?' Godard asked. 'It'll have to be stitched.'

She bit her lip and unfastened her small leather needle case from her belt. 'It's more than a flesh wound,' she said doubtfully. 'There's displaced bone too.'

'I know. I'll just have to do my best.'

She looked at him curiously. 'Can you knit bone and sew flesh then?'

Godard nodded, but with more confidence than he felt and there was a waxy sheen to his skin. 'Done it on sheep a hundred times,' he exaggerated. Actually it was more like two or three.

'There must be other damage too. Look at all the swelling and bruises.'

Godard grunted. 'Nothing I can do about that,' he said as he threaded the needle. 'I once knew two women who could, but one's dead and the other's long gone.' He grimaced. 'He cannot remain here. It's too close to Ashbury and they will come looking for him. As soon as I've stitched this wound, we'll have to leave.'

'We?' Edith arched her brows.

'Myself and Lord Oliver.'

'I see.' She gave him a look sidelong, but it was totally lost on Godard who was steeling himself to stitch Oliver's wound.

'The state he's in, he may well die before you have gone more than a mile,' she said.

'He will die of a certainty if they find him here. It will be dangerous for you too. I have seen what soldiers do with very little provocation.'

'I suppose you are right,' she said thoughtfully. 'The men

ride out from Ashbury on occasion to drink and whore. My brew ensures their goodwill, but they would not turn a blind eye to such as this.' She gestured at Oliver's prone form. 'How far do you intend taking him?'

'Bristol. There are chirurgeons there, and he is deeply regarded by young Prince Henry himself.'

Edith put her hands on her hips. 'You did not tell me you were the servants of a prince!'

'A future king,' Godard said in a preoccupied way, as he brought out the flask of usquebaugh and removed the stopper. 'Does it make a difference?'

She cocked her head. 'It does to the hearth tales that people come to tell and have told over their ale,' she answered, then continued in a brisk, practical tone, 'You will never get him to Bristol on horseback. I'll lend you my cart, providing you promise to return it within the week.'

Godard nodded acceptance and, for a while, all conversation ceased as he poured the raw usquebaugh over Oliver's wound, and the injured man screamed and went rigid. 'Hold him for me,' Godard commanded, his own teeth gritted.

Edith moved into position, although it was difficult to know where to grip since there was scarcely a part of the knight's upper torso that was not damaged. His muscles bunched against her for an instant and then slackened as once again he sank into the mercy of oblivion.

'Lady Catrin used to say that it helped to clean out the badness,' Godard said, as he began to stitch. 'But I reckon as the cure's almost as bad as the wounding.'

'Who's Lady Catrin?'

'A healer. My lord was once betrothed to her, but they were parted before they could wed.'

'She belonged to him then, not to you,' Edith said slowly and clearly.

'No, not to me,' said Godard, with a masculine lack of comprehension.

Edith nodded, a gleam in her eyes. When she saw that the lord would not require further holding, she went to harness Godard's gelding to her cart, tethering the grey stallion behind.

Godard did what he could for Oliver, which was not much beyond stitching and binding the gashed arm, and then wrapping him tightly in two blankets like a swaddled infant to keep his limbs immobile for the journey ahead.

Edith backed the horse and cart up to the alehouse door and Godard tenderly bore Oliver out and placed him on the piled bed of straw which she had made in the back.

'God speed you and bring you safely to Bristol.' She presented Godard with a pig's bladder full of ale, some bread and two hard-boiled eggs wrapped in a kerchief.

Godard took them from her, and cleared his throat. 'I do not know how to thank you,' he said gruffly. 'If I offered you silver, I know you would be insulted.'

'Indeed I would,' she sniffed and folded her arms. 'It will be thanks enough if you return the cart to me yourself when you can.'

Godard cleared his throat again. 'Assuredly I will, mistress,' he said and, with sudden bravado, leaned forward and kissed the soft expanse of her cheek.

She stood in the road and watched until the darkness swallowed up the sight of the pale horse attached to the back of the cart, and the rumbling noise of the wheels on the track had faded. Then, touching her cheek, she went slowly back to the alehouse and barred the door.

In some ways, Catrin thought, it was as if she had never left Bristol. If not for Rosamund and a collection of fevered memories, the time she had spent with Louis might never have existed. Countess Mabile accepted her back amongst her women with the minimum of questions, admired Rosamund, and then set Catrin to work making a batch of Ethel's famous green hand salve.

Catrin did not particularly like sleeping in the bower. As always, she felt stifled by its atmosphere, but it was a haven until she could find her feet and speak with Oliver. So much depended on their meeting and his response. She chewed her lip and tried to avoid the treadmill of imagining the encounter. She had lived it so often in her mind, had conjured every scenario from falling into his arms to being totally rejected and ignored, that there was no new ground, no wisdom to be gleaned.

She pounded lily of the valley, lemon balm, sage and plantain in a mortar, and when it was sufficiently macerated, added it to a blend of goose grease and almond oil. It worked better if the herbs were fresh, but in mid-winter the dried substitutes had to suffice.

Chin propped on her hands, Edon watched her work. She was supposed to be weaving a length of braid, but had reached no further than the first six inches before putting the wooden tablets aside.

'Did you really have glass in the windows?' she asked, with a shivering glance at the oiled linen that let scanty light and a deal of cold into the bower.

Catrin smiled and sighed at the same time. 'Yes, we had glass. Yes, it was a luxury and one that I miss, but I hated it too. Louis thought people would admire him for it, that they would look up to him, but instead it made them jealous and contemptuous. They blamed me for being a demanding wife, not him for his delusions of rank and grandeur.'

'What will happen to him now?'

Catrin shrugged. 'I have no doubt that he will make his way in the world. Losing Wickham will set him back, but not for long. He will change his name, his allegiance, whatever is necessary to secure his own comfort.' Her eyelids tensed. 'Edon, I do not care, except with anger.' She used a horn spoon to scoop a dollop of the unguent into a small clay pot, her movements jerky. 'I want to forget.'

'If it was me . . .' Edon began, but broke off as one of the other women entered the bower and hurried directly over to them.

'Oliver Pascal is back,' she announced breathlessly. 'His manservant's just brought him in on a cart, sore-wounded!'

Edon put her hand to her throat. 'Sore-wounded?'

The woman nodded. 'Leastways he wasn't in his senses.'

Catrin had whitened at the news. Wiping her hands on a scrap of linen, she grabbed the maid's arm. 'Where is he?'

'Down in the bailey when I left. They had gone looking for a stretcher and a priest.'

'A priest!' Edon looked at Catrin with stricken eyes. 'Jesu forfend!'

'Look after Rosamund for me,' Catrin said, and with compressed lips grabbed her satchel and sped from the room. Such was her haste that she stumbled on the stairs, wrenched her ankle and burned her hand on the support rope, injuries that she was not to notice until much later. The only thought in her mind was reaching Oliver and protecting him from death.

By the time she burst into the great hall, Godard and another man were bearing Oliver in on a stretcher of laced ropes. They carried him to a side aisle where the roof supports formed a natural alcove and gently set him down.

'Godard, what has happened to him?' Catrin demanded on the same breath as she arrived.

The servant turned to look at her out of eyes that were dark-ringed with exhaustion. 'Sword fight,' he said succinctly. 'Broken bones and a mangled shield arm. I don't know how bad.'

Catrin dropped to her knees at Oliver's side. His face was flushed and he was running a slight fever. Very carefully she began to peel away the blankets. He twitched and moaned but his eyes remained shut.

'I do not know what you are doing here, mistress,' Godard said, 'but I'm right glad. If anyone can help him, it is you.'

'It's not a tale for the telling now,' Catrin said without looking round, all her attention for the wounded man. 'Were you with him when it happened?'

'No, mistress.' Briefly Godard gave her the gist as he knew it.

'I hope Randal de Mohun fries in hell for ever,' she said viciously, and with extreme gentleness unfastened the final binding of the blanket. Beneath it, Oliver still wore his gambeson, tunic and shirt, although all three had been cut away on his left arm. She gasped at the sight of the wound that had scored and torn his flesh.

'I had to stitch his arm,' Godard said with a worried frown. 'I know it's badly cobbled, but I poured usquebaugh over the wound like you and Ethel showed me.'

'You did your best,' Catrin said unsteadily. She wanted to cry but bit back the tears, knowing that she needed clear vision and a steady hand. Later she would weep. For now she had to be strong. 'I need hot water and a strong pair of shears.'

Godard disappeared to fetch them. Catrin laid her hand against Oliver's brow and felt the heat of fever. Knowing that this would probably never have happened if she had stayed at Bristol filled her with guilt. It was not fair that one wrong choice could have such far-reaching consequences. But when had life ever been fair?

Beneath her palm, she felt his skin twitch. He opened his eyes. For a moment they were opaque, as blind as stones, then they cleared and showed a sea-grey spark of life.

'Catrin?' he said hoarsely, and a mirthless smile twisted his lips. 'Holy Christ, now I know that I am truly out of my wits.'

'No, I'm here.' She touched his hand. 'Never mind why. That can be told when you have recovered.'

'You think I'm going to recover?'

'Of course!' Catrin cried with indignation and a touch of fear. 'I will not deny that you have made a mess of yourself, but nothing that time cannot heal. I have treated worse injuries.'

'Ah, time the healer.' He grimaced at her. 'First Godard, then you. Have you not done enough already? Is there no mercy in you to let me die in peace?'

Catrin bit her lip. A single tear rolled down her cheek. 'No, there isn't,' she said brutally. 'Not when you have so much left to live for. Not when I need you. Not when your worst enemy is your own self-pity!'

His eyes sparked again and colour flooded across the sharpness of his cheekbones. 'My worst enemy is my tender heart,' he said. 'Ripped out and impaled for the "needs" of others. Small wonder if my body desires to follow it into death . . . my lady.' He turned his head from her and closed his eyes.

Catrin tightened her grip on his hand. 'The gulf between us is already too wide,' she said desperately. 'I do not want death to stretch that distance for ever. Oliver, please!'

His eyes remained shut.

'I'm not with Louis any more,' she ventured. 'I came to find you. I thought that if you . . . if you still . . .' She could not continue as her throat closed and she choked on tears.

Oliver gave no sign that he had heard. He was waxen pale, the last flare of emotion having drained his strength. Catrin dashed at the tears spilling down her cheeks and swallowed hard. If she was going to nurse him back to health then she had to detach herself. A few more exchanges like the last one and he likely would die, but she had to give him the will to live.

Godard returned with the hot water and shears and Catrin set about cutting the garments from Oliver's body. The gambeson was the worst, for it was made of two layers of thick linen packed with felted fleece and quilted with heavy stitches. Her thumb was throbbing by the time she had slit it up the middle. Oliver lay silent and unresponding throughout the operation and she did not know if he was aware or not.

When finally she exposed his torso to the air, she sat back with a gasp of horrified pity. There was no torn flesh, no wounds to be stitched, but his entire chest and ribs were covered in purplish-red impact bruises. From the shallowness of his breathing and the way he groaned as she gently laid her hand on him, she could tell that he had sustained broken ribs. Beneath her fingers she felt the swellings of damaged bone. The pattern of the bruising led her to inspect his collar-bone and discover that it too was broken on the shield arm side.

'Regular injury,' Godard said, watching her examination. 'If you can disable a man in the shoulder so that he cannot hold his shield, then you can move in closer and do what you like with him.'

Catrin winced. It was not a detail that she particularly wanted to know. 'The ribs will need to be bound in swaddling bands for support and a sling will deal with both the shoulder and the arm,' she said briskly.

'He is going to live then?'

Catrin looked at Oliver. She could not be sure if his closed eyes meant that he was shunning her, or that he was just out of his senses with exhaustion and pain. The latter she thought, but in case he could hear said, 'Yes, I think so, although it is as much a matter of his spirit as his body. The arm wound is the thing that bothers me the most. It will have to be opened and stitched again, and from the damage done I do not know how much use will remain in it.'

'I did my best, mistress,' Godard said anxiously.

She nodded and found a wan smile. 'I know you did. Like as not you saved his life at the time.'

'Is there anything else I can do?'

'Pray,' she said grimly. 'Pray as you have never done before.'

Steeling herself, she set about the task of cutting open and restitching his arm wound. The pain revived the injured man and Godard had to hold him down. Catrin bit her lip and concentrated upon keeping her hand steady while Oliver railed at her and cursed.

'At least he still has the will and the strength to fight,' Godard said wryly.

Catrin looked dubiously at the wound she had just re-stitched. Oliver was insensible again and breathing swiftly. 'Then let us pray he keeps it,' she murmured. 'You will have to raise him up so that I can bind his ribs. If we do this all at once then we can leave him to rest.' She blinked fiercely.

Mistaking her emotion, Godard said brusquely, 'He does not mean the things he says. They are only the ramblings of a man with wound-sickness.'

'Oh he means them at the moment, I am sure.' Catrin smiled through a new welling of tears. 'If I am weeping, it is for the pain I have to inflict in the name of healing. Come, the sooner done, the sooner finished.' She picked up the yards of swaddling band.

Binding Oliver's broken ribs was swiftly accomplished. The closeness, the pungency of his body, the terrible bruis-ing made Catrin feel nauseous and faint. Nursing was easier with a detached mind. Once she had run her hands over his lean, unblemished skin in the act of love, had been as close to him as now, touching with pleasure instead of anxious pity.

'Mistress, are you all right?' Godard asked in concern

as they gently lowered Oliver back down on to the rope stretcher.

Catrin shook her head. 'No, but I can manage.' Raising her head she gave him a fierce stare. 'I would not have anyone else take my place. He is mine now.'

Godard nodded gravely and reached to the pouch at his waist. 'He was before,' he said. 'You'll be wanting this.' He gave her the knot of hair that Ethel had woven in what now seemed like another life.

Catrin took it from him and noticed the charring on one edge.

'It fell in the fire,' Godard said with a dismissive shrug. 'My lord was not disposed to keep it, but I thought that one day he would regret its loss, so I took it upon myself to be a guardian.'

She rubbed her thumb over the intertwined pattern. 'You see a great deal, don't you?'

Godard shrugged again and looked uncomfortable. 'I'm a simple man, mistress. I only see what's in front of my nose.'

Catrin flashed him a sad smile. 'That's what I mean. I . . .' She broke off and turned, her words curtailed by the peremptory arrival of a stocky child with flaming red hair and brilliant, pale grey eyes. He wore a somewhat dusty tunic with a torn hem, but the embroidery on it was of gold thread and his cloak clasp was set with gems.

'Where's Oliver, what's happened to him?' the boy demanded imperiously. He pushed forward to the side of the stretcher and gazed at the wounded knight.

'He was attacked by mercenaries – sire,' Catrin said, adding the last word with the diplomacy of guesswork. This could be none other than the precocious Prince Henry. 'He's sore-wounded, but not unto death.'

The boy grunted and put his hands on his hips. They were square with grubby fingernails. Reddish freckles dusted their backs. 'Who are you?'

His stare was as sharp and clear as glass, and Catrin could physically feel the vibration of his personality. 'My name is Catrin of Chepstow, sire. I am a healer and Sir Oliver is known to me.'

The boy frowned. 'I have heard about you.'

'For the good I hope, sire,' Catrin smiled, but her eyes were wary.

Henry shrugged as if the remark was of no consequence. Later she was to learn that having been weaned on gossip and rumour, he was largely immune to it, preferring to make up his own mind. 'When will he be well?'

'It is hard to tell, sire. The broken bones will take several weeks to mend, but they should not prevent him from being up and around within a few days. He has a difficult injury to his left arm, though, which may take a long time to heal, and he may not retain all the use that he had before.'

The boy accepted the information with a nod. The frown remained, creating two deep creases between his brows. 'But he will have recovered enough to leave with me when I go back to my father in Anjou.' It was more of a statement, than a question. The clear grey eyes fixed Catrin with a gimlet stare.

On the stretcher, Oliver stirred. 'I will be well enough, sire,' he said without opening his eyes, his lips barely moving.

'I told you not to go.' Henry stooped over the man. 'I told you that when I am King your lands will be restored.'

The ghost of a smile touched Oliver's lips. 'Honour demanded,' he murmured.

The boy gave a baffled shrug. 'Honour nearly killed you.'

'Better than dishonour, sire.'

Henry shook his head and, stepping back, turned to Catrin. 'Look after him well,' he said brusquely.

'I fully intend to, sire,' she answered, not knowing whether to be amused or irritated by his manner. Ten years old going on four score.

Henry gave her a chin-jutting nod and, as swiftly as he had arrived, swept out.

'Is there no one willing to leave me in peace?' Oliver muttered, the words slurring.

'It seems not.' Catrin was thankful for Henry's visit. It had given her the breathing space that she needed to compose herself and she was able to reply in a lighter, pragmatic manner. 'Or at least not until you're strong enough to get up and walk away.'

To which Oliver said nothing, for he was already asleep.

CHAPTER 26

Oliver's fever climbed and fell, climbed and fell. He slept for most of the time, his mind and body taking refuge in oblivion. Punctuating the peace of deep sleep there were dreams and waking visions, some beautiful, some terrifying, most of them incomprehensible. His brother came and stood over him and told him that he was a fool. Emma was with him, nodding her head in agreement, the baby in her arms. They gave him no reason for their opinion, seeming to think that he should know.

Simon and Emma went away, although he could still hear the baby wailing. That was strange, because he knew that it had been born dead. There was searing pain and Catrin's voice urging him to drink. He tried to fight her off, but his limbs would not work. The brew she made him swallow was hot and sweet with a bitter aftertaste.

Richard's face loomed over him and the stink of wet dog filled his nostrils.

'He's going to live, isn't he?' the boy's voice demanded, an adolescent crack in its tone.

'God willing, of course he is,' he heard Catrin reply, 'The more he sleeps, the swifter he will heal.' Her hand on his brow was cool. The cuff of her gown was bordered with gold braid. He knew that she was here, but he could not understand why – unless she was part of the dreaming nightmare.

'Is it true that he killed Randal de Mohun?'

'Yes.' Her hand smoothed and then Oliver felt her rearrange the sheets over him. The gesture was protective, he thought. He wanted to say that it wasn't true; that Randal de Mohun had taken one risk too many and been killed by misfortune on the edge of victory, but his lips and tongue would not obey his will.

'Can he hear me?'

'Yes, I think so.'

He felt the light pressure of a hand on his shoulder, the one that did not ache. 'I'm glad de Mohun's dead, but I won't be glad if you die too,' the boy addressed him directly. 'You have to get well, Oliver. We're leaving for Anjou soon and you promised Henry you'd be well enough.'

Oliver heard Catrin's admonitory murmur and would have smiled if he could have made his lips move.

'Well, it's true, he did promise,' Richard said. 'And he's never broken one yet.'

Was that what was holding him to life, a promise? His reputation for keeping his word when all around broke theirs? How much simpler it would be to turn his back and walk away into the darkness.

'No,' he heard Catrin say, and there was a wobble in her voice. 'Only his body, mind and heart in the doing.'

He did not need to walk away from the pain. It reared up and was so huge that it brought its own darkness.

When he woke again, it was to a morning of bright winter daylight. He was lying on a pallet in the bailey shelter that had once belonged to Ethel and Catrin. A dung fire burned cleanly in the central hearth, a thin line of blue smoke twirling towards the hole in the thatch. The door curtain was tied back and he could see the bustle of bailey life. He squeezed his lids together for a moment, opened them again, and was reassured to find that the scene did not change. It seemed that for the moment he was anchored in reality.

That belief was put to the test when he heard a baby's gurgle. The sound of an infant had permeated all his dreams. Turning his head, he saw an oval rushwork basket. A small fist waved from its depths and the occupant made cooing sounds. He arrived at the conclusion that the baby was as real as his surroundings, which did not explain what he was doing lying amongst them.

Rashly he tried to sit up. Intense pain and restricted movement caused him to lie back with a gasp. An exploration
with his free right hand revealed bandages from shoulder to
waist, and a left arm that had been immobilised with splints
and couched in a sling. He felt like a fly parcelled up in a
spider's web.

There was a beaker of watered wine beside the pallet and
Oliver was aware of a desperate thirst. But he couldn't drink
whilst flat on his back.

He made another attempt to sit up, this time using his legs
as a lever, and was successful but not without a deal of pain.
The problem now was that he had to lean over and pick
up the beaker. Legs again, he thought, and swung them off
the pallet. In a kneeling position he shuffled to the cup and
managed to pick it up. For the nonce he trusted neither his
strength nor balance to stand. It was victory enough to have
reached the drink. He took a long, triumphant swallow.

The baby's gurgle developed a fretful note and the fist
waved with increased vigour. Oliver lowered his cup and,
inching over to the basket, looked within. The baby stopped
screaming immediately. Oliver quite rightly attributed its
behaviour to shock rather than his way with infants. It had
beautiful dark brown eyes and a few wispy black curls peeped
out from beneath its cap. With its colouring so like Emma's,
it might have been the child he had lost unborn.

'And who might you be?' he enquired.

The baby opened its mouth and bawled its identity for all
it was worth, quite drowning out Oliver's attempt to soothe
it. He finished the wine and tried rocking the basket, but its
occupant was not to be diverted. Oliver wondered if he had
the strength to shuffle to the door and fetch help before his
eardrums burst.

Just as he was about to try, Catrin swept over the threshold,
her face flushed from running. 'Jesu,' she puffed. 'I cannot
even leave to visit the privy!' Stooping with a graceful ease that
filled Oliver with envy, she scooped the baby from the cradle,
hooked up a three-legged stool with her ankle and sat down.
'All right, all right, I know you're hungry.' She unpinned the
neck of her gown and put the furious baby to suck.

Oliver stared. The tiny fist, waving in temper a moment since, now opened like a star and kneaded the creamy globe of her breast. 'Yours?' he said faintly.

'Her name is Rosamund,' Catrin said. 'And yes, she is mine.' There was a powerful emphasis on the last word that gave it the meaning of 'mine alone'. She looked down at the baby with great tenderness, then at him with slightly narrowed eyes which put him in mind of a feral cat defending its kitten. Then the expression was gone, replaced by concern and irritation.

'What are you doing out of bed?'

'I wanted a drink, and then your daughter introduced herself in no uncertain terms.'

'She was hungry.' Catrin captured the kneading hand in hers. Loud sucking sounds filled the room.

'I can see that.' He watched for a moment and felt a twisting sensation of pleasure and pain beneath his heart. She could have been mine too, he wanted to say, but in the light of her protectiveness he held his tongue on the words and concentrated instead on returning to the pallet. Pride forced him to his feet to walk the few steps required, but he was sweating and shaking by the time he sat down on the bed.

Catrin put the baby on the other side to suckle. 'At least you are in your senses now,' she murmured. 'For a full week you had the wound-fever so badly that I feared only a priest could help you. Prince Henry has been to visit you every day. He even arranged for the family living here to move to one of his uncle's manors so that I could have privacy to nurse you and brew my nostrums.'

Oliver shook his head. 'It is so hard to separate the nightmares of fever from the waking reality that I will have to say that I remember nothing,' he said, as the trembling eased and the pain subsided from his ribs and arm. He frowned at her. 'I saw you in my dreams, but I scarce thought you were real. Catrin, what are you doing here?'

She did not answer at first, all her attention given to the baby. 'Is it not obvious?' she said at last, as she took Rosamund from her breast and laid the child over her shoulder.

He eyed her warily. 'No, it is not. You could have a hundred different reasons.'

'I don't.' Gently patting the baby's back, she rose and went to look out of the door at the busy courtyard.

'Where's your husband?'

The baby watched him with sated, sleepy, dark eyes. Catrin stayed where she was, gazing out on the activity in the bailey. 'I do not know,' she said, her voice cold and hard. 'In hell I hope, but I doubt it.'

Oliver's breathing quickened, and with it the pain in his ribs. Or perhaps it was the beating of his cracked heart.

'He abandoned me again,' she said, 'except that this time it was "us" he threw to the wolves, his own flesh and blood.' She nuzzled the baby's head. 'Girls are expendable, especially when you have boasted to all and sundry that your manhood is proved in sons. So are wives when they mock that manhood by bearing a daughter.' She turned round, her eyes aglitter with unshed tears. 'He left us under siege by Oxford's men, swore he would return with a relieving force, but I knew he would not. I waited ten days and then I yielded up the keep with which Stephen had entrusted him and I came here.'

Had he possessed the strength, Oliver would have gone to her, but he was drained. There was so much he needed to know. He would like to have sworn that circumstances and reasons did not matter, but after Rochester they did. 'Your husband abandoned everything?'

She gave a small shrug. 'He reached a point where he decided that the game was not worth the candle. Being lord of a keep was not all that he imagined. It brought more responsibility than his shoulders could bear. In one thing, though, he and I were alike.' Rosamund had fallen asleep. Softly Catrin laid her down in the cradle and tucked in the fleece coverlet.

'And what was that?'

'We were both duped into seeing gold where there was none, him with his keep and me with old dreams.' She drew an impatient sleeve across her eyes. 'It is finished now.'

'But you are still his wife by law.'

'Not my law.' Her face was suddenly tight with anger. 'If

he walked in here now and commanded me to go with him, I would spit in his face. Priests say that it is God's rule that a woman should submit to her husband. All her worldly goods become his. They say that if she transgresses, he has the right to beat her.' She drew a deep breath. 'Well, I tell you that neither my daughter nor I are going to live by such rules. No woman should do so.'

Her pain and rage surged at him, but he did not recoil from its intensity for he could match it. 'I agree,' he said. 'But if you had stayed with me, you need not have suffered.'

'He was my husband; you were his prisoner. What was I supposed to do?' In the basket, Rosamund whimpered and Catrin stooped over her with a soothing murmur.

'You could have looked before you leaped.'

'Hindsight is a wondrous thing,' she snapped. 'It is always easy to have eyes to see after the event.'

'So what now?' he asked, with a swift gesture of his good arm. 'Have you come to Bristol for refuge because it is familiar, because there are people you know – or did you come seeking me?'

Leaving the basket, she began to pace the room, kicking out the full skirt of her blue gown with each step. 'I came for all those reasons,' she said at last, and stopped at his side. 'But the greatest was to find you and somehow right a wrong.'

Oliver turned his head. 'I do not want your pity or the ministrations of your tender conscience. Dear Christ, I need not have suffered either.'

'I'm not ministering to you out of compassion, you fool!' Catrin's eyes flashed. 'Nor out of guilt, although God knows it does burden me. When Godard brought you into the hall last week, you were on your way to death.' Kneeling by the pallet, she touched his bandaged ribs and arm, then took his good right hand in hers. 'If I had any compassion I would have dulled your pain and let you go. But I don't. I have learned from Louis to clothe myself entirely in selfishness. I wanted you to live because I want to live too.' Her tone grew vehement and her grip tightened. 'I want a man at my hearth who is not going to whine like a child or run off futtering other women when the whim dictates. I want a man who keeps his word whatever the cost. I want a man who will love me beyond the first fire and into the embers. I want a father for Rosamund who will teach her how to judge men.'

Oliver swallowed the lump in his throat. 'You don't want much,' he said shakily, and thought that with speeches like that inside her, she should have been a battle commander.

'Only what you can give, if you still have it within you.'

He swallowed and meshed his fingers through hers. 'Mangled and torn like the rest of me, but what remains is yours . . . and Rosamund's.'

The kiss was somewhat clumsy but its importance far outweighed its technique. His good arm pinned her close, while she tried her best to keep her weight from his damaged left side.

'Catrin, Catrin,' he whispered as their lips clung and parted. And then he laughed. 'If this is another wound-fever dream then I don't want to wake up.'

'It's not, it's real, I promise.' She pressed her face against his shirt.

'I thought I was the one to make promises.'

They kissed again. 'It is my turn now.' Catrin pulled away and went to her satchel. 'Do you remember this?' From the bag's depths she produced the singed love knot woven by Ethel before her final illness.

Oliver's eyes widened. 'I do,' he said, 'but by rights it should not exist, since I threw it on the fire.'

'Godard rescued it. He thought you might regret the act in time to come.'

He took the token from her and looked at the intricate detail of the pattern, yellowed and blackened on one side by the fire-damage. 'I owe Godard more than I can repay,' he murmured.

'We both do.' She touched the love knot, then twined her fingers over and around his. 'And Ethel.' As she spoke the name, she glanced around the shelter and a half-smile curved her lips.

Oliver could almost feel the strength flowing back into his body from the token, from the contact of Catrin's fingers. If far from perfect, life was worth living again.

CHAPTER 27

'*Waes Hael!*' The cry resounded around the crowded alehouse and fists thumped the trestles as the wedding guests toasted the laughing bride and her smug groom. Outside a March gale battered at the shutters, but no one cared, least of all Godard and Edith whose nuptial feast this was. Edith wore Oliver's gift of a silver and garnet brooch in her scarlet gown, and on the table stood his present to Godard, a pitcher in the shape of a bear but given Godard's face and quarterstaff.

Edith had surpassed herself with her latest brew of ale and the guests were enthusiastically appreciating her skills.

'I can see why you're leaving me,' Oliver remarked to Godard as he drained his cup. 'I doubt even the best French wine could compete with this.'

'Then perhaps you should stay too, my lord,' Godard answered. His colour was high and his eyes sparkling. Some of his ebullience was the result of his new wife's ale, but the greater part was caused by the pleasure of his new wife herself.

Oliver smiled. 'A certain young prince might have something to say about that,' he said. 'Besides, I've my way to make in the world.' Almost unconsciously he flexed his left hand, testing the damaged sinews. It was three months since his wounding. A week from now, he and Catrin were due to sail across the Narrow Sea as members of Prince Henry's retinue and make his court their home.

Apart from ridges where they should have been smooth, Oliver's ribs had healed remarkably well and gave him little pain. His left shoulder was still weak but much improved from its first stiffness. It was the blow to his forearm that had caused irreparable damage. De Mohun's blade had crushed and cut sinew, tendon and bone. Not even the best chirurgeon in the land could have mended such injuries. He had some feeling and restricted movement, but the only shields he could grip were the small, light ones used to train the youngest squires, and then for no longer than a few minutes at a time. Catrin assured him that he would improve as the weeks went by, but they both knew that he would never have the whole use of that arm again. The way of his making in the world could no longer be the way of a soldier.

'You stay with Prince Henry and your fortune will be made,' Godard said, with a knowing nod. 'Mark me, you'll be a lord high sheriff before you're done.'

Oliver laughed and shook his head. He knew what was and what was not possible.

Squashed against Oliver at the trestle, Catrin observed the humour in his eyes and was relieved to see him in good spirits. There were often difficult days when he became so frustrated and furious with his disability that he was impossible to reach. What had been a sound, strong limb was now disfigured and impaired. She had watched him struggle and fail at the simplest tasks, such as fastening a belt buckle, and had bitten her tongue and stood back. Time would heal and practice would compensate. It was only three months; he expected too much and was impervious to the voice of reason.

She thought perhaps Godard was not so wrong in his light comment about 'lord high sheriff' though. If Oliver's other faculties could be channelled, there was every opportunity for advancement in Prince Henry's household.

Catching her thoughtful stare, he raised his eyebrows. 'Brewing potions in your mind?' he asked.

Catrin pressed lightly against him. 'Several.' She darted him a provocative look through her lashes.

'Such as?' His mouth curved in a smile.

Catrin nibbled her forefinger and pretended to consider. 'Well, some are private,' she said. 'But I will tell you that you should not belittle your abilities. Prince Henry thinks highly of you.'

'His "pet Saxon".' Oliver's smile became wry.

'But you must have done something to earn that title and then keep it,' Catrin said earnestly. 'The Prince bedevilled me every day of your illness demanding to know if you were improving. It is more than a boy's passing whim that commands you across the Narrow Sea in his service; you are a firm part of his household.'

'Every prince needs his fool,' Oliver said.

Catrin clucked her tongue impatiently. 'It is your arm that is damaged, not your wits, or so I hope to think,' she snapped. 'Why do you think Earl Robert gave his support and blessing to your place in Henry's household? If you answer "out of guilt" or "to be rid of me", I will hit you.'

Oliver tilted his head. 'My place in Henry's household was granted before I was wounded. The Earl is honouring a promise and a debt. No!' he added with a grin as her lips tightened and she grabbed a loaf off the table to threaten him, 'hear me out. It also suits him to have one of his own knights in Henry's retinue among all those Angevin lords.'

Catrin shook her head. There was a gleam in his eyes and she had a strong suspicion that she was being tugged along on a string. Perhaps she should still hit him. At least his answer revealed that his wits were indeed still keen and that this was not a 'difficult' day. 'Well then, it behoves you to make the utmost of that position,' she said, replacing the loaf and folding her hands in her lap to avoid temptation.

'I suppose it does,' he agreed gravely, and held out his cup to be refilled as a fresh pitcher of ale was brought round and another toast was raised to the bride and groom. 'But not with a sword.'

'Any noble or knight can use a sword and still be no more than a brigand or a knave,' she said contemptuously. 'I need only to remember Louis to know that.' She watched him raise the cup in his good hand and swallow. The motion of his throat, the taut skin across his cheekbones, the hint of copper at his jawline flooded her with an emotion so strong that it stung her eyes. She laid her hand over his damaged one. 'I have pride in you, and faith that you will not trample on that pride.'

'Did you not have faith in Louis when you went with him?'

There was no hostility in the question, but there was a demand to know and the residue of pain. Her decision at Rochester was a subject they had avoided, but it had neither gone away nor even begun to fade.

'No,' Catrin said slowly and felt the red heat of chagrin creep into her face. 'I was bedazzled by his charm into believing that he had changed. If my faith in him was shaky at the foundations, it was underpinned by my guilt. I did not wait for him or mourn him as I should. I gave myself to another man. I owed him my duty and obedience.'

'After he left you to think that he was dead?' An incredulous note entered Oliver's voice.

'He knew how to twist and turn me inside out,' she said defensively. 'His excuses were never plausible, but the way he told them was convincing. I was still his wife . . . or so I thought,' she added with a grimace. 'I'm tenfold the wiser now.'

Oliver said nothing, his hand passive under hers. She could not tell from his expression what he was thinking, whether her reply had satisfied him or left him doubting and unsure. Her own feelings were certainly of the latter persuasion. 'Oliver, if you . . .' she started to say, but got no further as his attention was claimed by Godard and one of the other guests, a male relative of the bride.

Catrin put a smile on her face for courtesy's sake, but suddenly she could not bear the banter, the red, sweating faces, the smelly, smoky fug. Making the valid excuse that she had to go and check upon Rosamund, she squeezed out of her place on the trestle and left the feast.

Edith's alehouse was built in the traditional style of most village cots, with a framework of thick oak branches supporting a long house of two rooms with a sleeping loft above. The first room, the alehouse, was the larger. The second usually held stores and livestock, but these had been moved out to a daub and wattle shed to make room for guests intending to spend the night. The floor was thickly strewn with hay. Hurdles of woven willow, normally used to separate the animals, made narrow bays which afforded a modicum of privacy.

Catrin had wrapped Rosamund in blankets and placed her near the entrance in a manger full of the fragrant hay. She was awake and rewarded her mother with a smile in which the very edges of two white teeth were starting to show in the gum. The baby crowed and shouted, demanding to be picked up. Catrin sat on the milking stool beside the manger and spent a pleasant moment dandling her daughter on her knee. It would not be long before Rosamund was sitting up. The little hands were constantly reaching for things and the bright, dark eyes focused and followed with tenacity.

Oliver and Rosamund had been wary of each other at first. In the beginning, the baby had shown a marked dislike of any male voice. It was small wonder when her father had spent so much of his time shouting at Catrin; but gradually Rosamund's anxiety had lessened. She would even coo and gurgle for Oliver now and hold up her hands to be picked up. Oliver, in his turn, had needed to overcome a masculine fear of so tiny a being together with the more personal reluctance springing from the death of his first wife and child.

'It was a girl she bore, dark of hair and eye, but cold and still,' he had said, looking down at Rosamund's small form cradled in his good arm. There had been a moist glitter in his eyes. 'It brings the past to breathe on me. She could have been mine.'

'She is,' Catrin had answered, swallowing tears and embracing him.

Since then, Oliver and Rosamund had grown more comfortable with each other. 'As comfortable as men and women ever are with the other's company,' Catrin now said to her daughter, as she unfastened her gown to feed her. 'I don't know what he's thinking unless he tells me, and I'm not even sure that I want to know.'

Rosamund's only response was to cover Catrin's nipple with a hungry gulp. 'Your father could not be still for a moment,' she murmured to the sucking infant. 'If there was silence he had to chatter like a magpie – anything so that he would not have to stop and look within himself.' She stroked

Rosamund's fine cap of silky black hair. 'Your new father broods too much, I think,' she said gently.

'But then you could always cozen me out of a dark mood,' Oliver said from the doorway. He was leaning against one of the supports, watching her.

Catrin gasped and turned round. 'How long have you been standing there?' she asked indignantly.

He smiled. 'Long enough to admire the view.' He sauntered forward, his gaze on her exposed bosom. 'If you cannot tell my thoughts, Catrin love, then there is no hope for you.'

'I can tell the thoughts of your body,' she answered, her colour high. 'It is your mind that eludes me.'

'They are one and the same at the moment,' he said, 'and they are both yours without reserve.'

Catrin laughed. There was a melting warmth at her core. 'Without reserve?' she repeated, as she lifted a drowsy Rosamund from her breast and placed her, milkily content, in the manger.

'And you a wise-woman and a tenfold-wiser woman,' he said lightly, although there was a serious edge to his jesting. 'You should not have to ask.'

'I'm not asking, I'm inviting.'

The hay gave off the sweet fragrance of summer as it was crushed by their bodies. There was urgency and there was restraint, their passion tempered by laughter, snatched kisses and love play. To Catrin it was balm on wounds that were still tender. To Louis she had been a diversion – his prey. He had fed voraciously on her reactions and his play had possessed a dangerous edge. This was innocent and joyful, without calculation. Oliver would not demand that she scream for him.

For Oliver there was reassurance in her obvious delight and enthusiasm. Louis de Grosmont might haunt the back of his mind, mocking him with the fact that Catrin had chosen him at Rochester, that he had fathered her child and that he could have her back for the snapping of his fingers, but Oliver pinned that spectre to the wall. Catrin might have chosen Louis at Rochester, but she had chosen differently now and there was triumph in that.

Behind them a sudden great noise of shouting and laughter swelled and increased. Catrin half sat up, gasping, her wimple askew and her breasts tumbling out of her gown.

'It's the bedding ceremony,' Oliver murmured. 'Godard and Edith are being escorted to their wedding night.' His tunic lay in a crumpled heap on the straw and his shirt was unlaced. 'Do you want to go up with the crowd and wish them well?'

'Will they miss us?' She plucked a straw from his hair with lazy fingers. A snatch of song shot raucously in their direction as the bride and groom were conveyed up the stairs to the sleeping loft. Something about a hand in a bird's nest.

'With pleasure on this occasion,' Oliver said, with a grimace over his shoulder at the noise. Then he turned back to her and cupped her breast in his good hand. 'But we can still wish them well by example.'

Louis met Roxanne at the Baths in Caesarea. Her father had been a crusader and from him she had taken the light green eyes and chestnut copper hair. Her mother was a native Syrian, and it was from her family that she had inherited the bath house between the harbour and the archbishop's dwelling.

She was a widow, wealthy and sure of herself in business, but still vulnerable behind her confident manner, and she had been alone long enough for grief to fade and interest to quicken when she saw the handsome newcomer with his predatory eyes and lithe, slender body. He was lying on a table being oiled by one of the bath maids, his expression drugged with sensual pleasure. Roxanne dismissed the girl with a flick of her wrist and took over the oiling herself.

Within the hour they were lovers; within the week Louis had moved from the common lodging house by the Jaffa Gate and into her apartments. A month later they were married. She had no reason to doubt him when he told her that he was without commitments in his native land.

CHAPTER 28

ROUEN, NORMANDY, SPRING 1149

She was young, frightened and struggling to bear her first child among strangers. Her thick blond hair was dark with sweat at her brow and her blue eyes were glazed with pain. She crouched upon the birthing stool, her thighs splayed apart and the straw beneath her soaked with birthing fluid.

'It won't be long now,' Catrin soothed, setting her arm around the girl's shoulders. 'Drink this to keep up your strength and help your womb to work.'

Obediently the girl raised the cup to her lips, grimacing only a little as the aftertaste lingered on her palate. To say that she was only just sixteen years old, Catrin thought that she was being very brave. Her name was Hikenai, but since no one without English could pronounce it, she was known as Belle. Prince Henry had brought her back from an adolescent escapade in England two years since when they were both fourteen. She had gone from kitchen-wench to royal chambermaid in the whisk of a bed sheet.

There were those who were jealous of Belle's rise in status, who thought it wrong that a common Saxon wench should share the Prince's bed, but Catrin was fond of her. Belle had no airs and graces. Her heart was generous and devoid of malice, and Catrin's own heart went out to the girl because she was so very young and vulnerable.

Outside, the bells of Rouen Cathedral tolled the hour of nones, and golden mid-afternoon light poured through the shutters on to the waiting cradle by the fire and the copper basin in which the new-born would be bathed. A maidservant moved around the room, unobtrusively warming towels and swaddling to greet the arrival of Henry Plantagenet's first child.

In the six years since leaving England, Catrin had overcome the qualms of home-sickness by resuming her trade as a mid-wife and healer. She had the full endorsement of the Ducal household and custom was soon brisk. Oliver said nothing but employed a burley Flemish mercenary to replace Godard. They had a maid as well, to care for Rosamund when Catrin was about her business.

'Push down through your belly,' she encouraged Belle, as a strong contraction tightened the girl's womb. 'Yes, that's it.'

Belle groaned with effort. It was always hard for younger women, Catrin thought. Their taut, firm muscles wanted to hold everything in rather than let it out, and their labours were nearly always twice as long as women bearing second or third offspring.

For the next hour, she continued to cajole and urge her patient, and was rewarded at last by the appearance of the head at the entrance of the birth passage. 'Gently now,' she mur-mured, and eased her hand around the baby's head to untangle the cord that was wrapped around its neck. The hair, slick with birth fluid, was dark auburn, but would dry to a vivid Plantagenet red. At Catrin's command, Belle pushed again and the baby gushed from her body into the waiting towel.

'A boy.' Catrin smiled with delight as she rubbed the infant in the linen and he let out a reedy wail of protest. 'A lusty man-child for you and your lord.'

Sobbing with effort and emotion, Belle held out her arms for her son and cradled him with an expertise that came of being the eldest of eight children. Catrin watched the first meeting with tingling eyes. She had lost count of the number of babies she had delivered during the past years, all belonging to other women. It seemed an age since she had cradled Rosamund in her arms.

There were precautions which lessened the likelihood of pregnancy, and until Rosamund was three Catrin had used pieces of moss or scraps of linen soaked in vinegar. But another three years had passed since then without result. Her flux was a week late this month, but it had happened several times before and on each occasion had been a false prophecy. Her lack of fecundity posed no problem to Oliver, who was quite content for her not to risk the perils of childbirth, but Catrin viewed each monthly bleed with wistful disappointment. Perhaps Belle's baby was a portent; perhaps this time it would be different.

Competently she delivered the afterbirth and made mother and baby comfortable for the inevitable stream of visitors who would begin to arrive the moment that word of the birth spread beyond the bedchamber door.

Henry was the first to appear, blowing into the room like a gale. Unlike his father he was neither tall nor handsome, but he still had so much charisma and energy that he positively blazed. He was a month shy of his sixteenth birthday, but no one thought of him as a raw youth. Prince Henry was a king in the making.

He gave Belle a robust kiss on each cheek and plucked the baby out of her arms to carry him to the candlelight. 'Hah, red like me,' he said with pleasure, and peered into the crumpled infant face with paternal pride. On the bed, his mistress smiled with weary triumph. Whatever the future held, she would always be the mother of his firstborn son.

The child in his arms, Henry turned to Catrin. 'You do know that you have employment for as long as you want it,' he grinned.

'Does that mean you are going to keep me busy, sire?' Catrin replied with a broad smile of her own.

He laughed and bounced the baby back to its mother. 'Man may plan, but heaven executes,' he said. 'Nevertheless, it will be no hardship to endeavour my best.' In high good humour, he paid her fee and gave her a ring of notched gold and garnet from his middle finger.

In high good humour herself, Catrin made her way back across the tower precincts to the small house against the outer wall that she and Oliver shared.As she approached, she heard gales of laughter and, rounding the corner, came upon her six-year-old daughter, blunt spear in hand, attacking young Richard FitzRoy. He was fending her off with his shield, while his dog leaped and barked around the two of them, its tail wagging like a flail. Leaning against the doorpost, Oliver watched the scene, an indulgent grin on his face.

'So this is how you spend your time when I'm not by,' Catrin admonished with mock severity.

Rosamund whirled, her black braid as glossy as a raven's wing in the spring sunshine. 'Richard's teaching me to fight with a spear!' Her voice was sharp with excitement and her cheeks were flushed, making her eyes look darker and brighter than ever. They were her father's legacy, as were her quickness and grace. She had a lethal quantity of his mercurial charm too.

'It's blunt,' Richard said swiftly. 'She'll come to no harm.' He stood head and shoulders above Catrin now. His adult features were developing apace and there was the lightest hint of a beard on his chin. During the last year his voice had deepened and his narrow girth increased. It was becoming very difficult for Catrin to remember the small boy whose nightmares had woken the Countess's women in Bristol after the raid on Penfoss.

'And learning to fight is more exciting than spinning wool or stitching cloth,' Catrin nodded, stifling a smile. She ruffled the dog's thick, tawny fur. 'Richard, you will be pleased to know that Prince Henry has just made you a great-uncle. Belle has borne a fine son.'

The young man pulled a face. 'I congratulate him, but the child can call me "cousin". I don't want to be anyone's "great-uncle" until I'm in my dotage!'

'What's dotage?' Rosamund demanded.

'What happens when you pass twenty,' Oliver said.

Rosamund looked at him narrowly. 'Does that mean you are in your dotage?'

'You'll have to ask your mother.' He grinned at Catrin.

The little girl frowned.

'Pay no heed,' Catrin advised her. 'Your papa's teasing. When you have finished learning how to be an Amazon, I want you to take a jar of throat syrup to Dame Quenhild in the hall.'

Rosamund screwed up her face, considering mutiny, but decided against it and nodded her head. It was fun playing with Richard, but it was also fun to watch all the coming and going in the hall.

Catrin gave her the jar of syrup and watched Rosamund set off, Richard escorting her for he too had business in that direction. The little girl carried her burden carefully, her black braid swinging as she walked. Catrin shook her head and smiled, her vitals gripped by a sharp pang of love.

'She is growing fast,' she murmured to Oliver.

'Too fast for me in my "dotage",' he agreed and sat down on the pallet they shared.

Catrin gave him a sidelong glance. For an instant she contemplated telling him that her flux was late, that there might be another child to watch over as it grew from helpless infancy to sturdy independence, but she dismissed the idea almost immediately. It was too soon to tell. Besides, knowing Oliver's qualms about the entire matter of childbirth, it was probably best to keep him in ignorance until she was thoroughly sure herself, and that might take several months.

The glance she had given him was met by a considering one of his own, as if he too was deciding whether to speak. Catrin saw that he was unconsciously rubbing his left elbow. Six years after his wounding, he had regained reasonable use of the limb and could even hold a full-sized kite shield for short periods, but it still pained him on occasion. Rubbing it was either a sign that the bone was aching or that he had something on his mind. After the way he had looked at her, she thought it was the latter.

'What's wrong?' she asked.

'Nothing.' Oliver shook his head, but his expression did not lighten and he continued to massage his elbow. 'Did Prince Henry say anything when you saw him?'

'Not a great deal; only that he was pleased with the child and that I was granted employment for life. Why?' Moving three of Rosamund's hair ribbons, a distaff with some neatly spun wool and a doll made of fabric stuffed with fleece, she sat down at Oliver's side.

'He said nothing about England?'

'No.' Catrin gave him a sharp look. 'He's not contemplating an escapade like the last one?' Two years ago Henry had taken it into his head to cross the Narrow Sea with a raiding party of friends and mercenaries. It was an ill-planned expedition, funded by youthful high spirits and little else. Oliver had been at his wits' end over the matter, for Henry had viewed all pleas for prudence as nothing more than the procrastination of old men who had outlived their daring. Oliver had felt the criticism keenly. To all intents and purposes he was Henry's quartermaster, responsible for ensuring that there were enough supplies to sustain the soldiers of his household whether at home or on campaign. Two years ago, Henry had overridden Oliver's protests that they were not sufficiently prepared and had set out to claim England as if he were going to play skittles at a summer feast.

The 'invasion' had been an unmitigated disaster with coin and supplies evaporating more rapidly than summer mist. A plea to his mother and Earl Robert for funds to pay his soldiers had been met with stony refusal in order to teach Henry a lesson. In the event, he did not learn the sort of lesson they had hoped, for the fourteen-year-old had gone to his other uncle, King Stephen, to ask for money. Taken aback but amused by Henry's sheer audacity, Stephen had provided the finances on the understanding that Henry leave England immediately. Henry had done so, his mood chastened but not entirely subdued.

'He's two years older and wiser now,' Oliver said drily. 'And sixteen is closer to man than boy. I know he makes me tear out my hair on occasion, but I will say that Henry learns by his mistakes.'

Catrin picked up her daughter's doll and gazed at its slipshod grin. Rosamund had sewn the face herself using scraps of brown wool. It was a good effort for the five-year-old she had been at the time. 'At sixteen there is still too much to learn,' she said, 'often at the expense of others.'

Oliver shrugged. 'He's not travelling under his own sail

this time – or at least, not entirely. It's at the behest of King David of Scotland and Rannulf of Chester. He's to be invested with his knighthood and officially take up arms against Stephen.' He ceased rubbing his arm and leaned on his thighs. 'He's coming of age, Catrin, love, and if he does not succeed in England now, he never will. But, God help me, the time ahead is daunting. Do you know how many quarters of wheat and pecks of oats it takes to keep even a small conroi in the field for a week?'

Catrin shook her head and slipped her arm around his waist. Already she could see that his mind was adrift in calculation, his lips moving silently. 'No, but I know that you do, and that you are full capable of garnering whatever supplies are needed, if Henry gives you the chance,' she said, to boost his confidence and because it was true. 'How long do you have?'

Oliver blinked. 'What? Oh, I don't know yet. Henry was too busy rushing off to look at his son to tell me, but I dare say I'll know by tonight.'

'England,' Catrin murmured, and gazed out of the hut door. In many respects, living in Rouen was not dissimilar to living in Bristol. Both cities were major ports, dependent on the river for their trade. The main language of the nobility was French as it had been in England, but there were still so many things she missed. The softness of a West-wind rain from Wales, yeasty, golden ale tasting of elder-flowers, oatcakes flavoured with honey and sprinkled with poppy seeds. They scarcely grew oats in Normandy, except to give to horses, and viewed anyone who ate them as coarse and rustic.

'Rosamund and I are going with you,' she said firmly. Two years ago the expedition had been sprung without warning by the Prince. There had been no time to garner camp followers – probably a blessing in hindsight – but this was different. If Henry was going to be knighted and then make a serious play for his crown, the absence from Normandy was likely to be a long one.

Oliver's expression was suddenly neutral. 'I am not sure that it is wise.'

'Neither am I, but you will not dissuade me,' Catrin said

quickly, before he could launch into a dozen reasons why she should remain behind. 'I have been content here because you have been content, but Rouen is not my home – or yours. Don't you long to hear English spoken again other than on the wharf sides where the London merchants unload?'

He made a brief, but by no means enthusiastic, gesture of assent.

'I want Rosamund to grow up speaking both tongues, but all she can manage in English is to ask for wine and swear!'

'That's not true!' There was laughter amidst Oliver's indignation.

'Well, no,' Catrin conceded, 'but I miss England. I want to go home.'

Oliver shook his head. 'We will be on the road much of the time, love,' he said. 'And we may be in danger. I do not like to think of you and Rosamund living as camp followers. Here you have your own dwelling and place in the world.'

'Yes,' she nodded slowly. 'Yes, we do, but that's all it is, a dwelling. Home is where the heart lies. I don't want to be parted from you for month upon month.' She frowned at him. 'You want me to stay here because you fear for my safety, but I want to come because I fear for yours.'

'But there's small reason for you to fear,' he said, and rotated his left arm and flexed his hand. 'I am not likely to be thrown into the forefront of battle, am I?'

'Perhaps not, but you know as well as I do how easy it is to become involved by accident. You might be waiting with the baggage wagons, the enemy breaks through, and suddenly you find yourself in the thick of the fray.'

'All the more reason for my wife to stay in safety. If the baggage wagons are attacked then any woman – or child – among them is fair game.'

Absently she noticed that he had referred to her as his wife, a habit of such long-standing now that everyone in Rouen assumed that they were full-wedded in law and that Rosamund was his daughter. But she wasn't his wife and she was free to do as she chose. It was on the tip of her tongue to tell him as much but she held back, for it would have inflicted a wound on flesh that was already too thin and scarred. 'You might frighten me with such tales,' she said, angrily, 'but you will not stop me. When you sail for England, Rosamund and I sail with you.'

Oliver breathed out heavily. 'As stubborn as a mule does not even begin to describe you,' he said with exasperation.

'No, it doesn't.' She saw that she had won. There was resignation in his eyes, and perhaps a spark of pride. But if she had been wary of telling him about the suspected pregnancy before, she knew now that it was impossible. Wife or not, he would have her locked up in the highest room of Rouen's tower for the full nine months. While she would not lie to him, she was not above committing a sin of omission.

'Besides,' she said, as much to herself as to him, 'if the danger becomes too great, I can take Rosamund to Bristol. We'll be safe there, and I know that Edon and Geoffrey will welcome us.'

'I am sure they will,' he said, but it was an unthinking response and his eyes were distant again. She wondered if her mention of Bristol had brought back memories of living there. It had all changed now. Earl Robert had died of clogged lungs a few months after Prince Henry's invasion escapade and his eldest son, Philip, was now earl in his place. Oliver's position in Henry's household had become embedded, his loyalty was to the Prince alone rather than the house of Gloucester. It would be a poignant revisiting.

But Oliver's thoughts were not on Bristol. 'I will not push a boulder uphill and try to stop you,' he said, 'but what if . . .' He chewed his lower lip and looked at her, his grey eyes quenched and dark. 'What if you encounter Louis again?'

The crux of the matter blazed out like dry grass catching fire from a tinder spark and caught her utterly by surprise. It was not his fear of losing her in a raid on the baggage wains that made him protest at her desire to go with him; it was his fear of losing her to Louis.

'He is less than nothing to me,' she said with all the vehemence that she could muster. It was ground they had often trodden before, frequently without words. She turned his face on the palm of her hand and spoke close to his mouth.

'You are the world. Yes, I thought I loved him once, but it was only lust in disguise and I have long outgrown the empty trappings that are all he ever offered.'

He took her hand from his face, closing his fingers around hers, and kissed her. She felt his possession and anxiety and for a moment kissed him back with fervour. Then she broke away. 'You have to trust me, Oliver. If you don't, then our life together has been as nothing.'

He swallowed. 'I do trust you. It is him I do not. Supposing . . . supposing he wants Rosamund. She is his daughter by right.'

'He gave up all right to her long ago,' Catrin said, and then shook her head to remove the dread of the thought. 'Our paths are unlikely to cross and, if they do, I am no lamb to the slaughter this time.' She gazed through the doorway and watched Rosamund returning from her errand, her face bright with sunlight and a spring in her step. 'I will kill him before I yield so much as an inch of ground, let alone my . . . our daughter,' she said softly, but with utter conviction.

In Caesarea, Roxanne lay on her bed and wept bitter tears at the perfidy of men.

Outside the walls of Jerusalem, by the pool of Siloam, Louis let his horse and pack pony drink their fill and smiled at the sloe-eyed woman with gold bracelets clinking on her wrists. She gazed back at him, letting him know that she thought him insolent but that it was not an insurmountable barrier, and then she turned away, snapping her fingers at her servants.

He watched them bear her towards the city in a litter decorated with red and gold silk tassels. The exotic scent of sandalwood and patchouli filled his nostrils and stirred his hunting instincts. The curtains of the litter parted and the woman glanced out to see if he was following.

In his own good time, Louis took his horses and did so.

CHAPTER 29

It was May when Henry Plantagenet set sail for his Uncle David's court in Scotland where he was to receive his knighthood and plan the claiming of a kingdom.

Although the crossing was moderately gentle, Catrin was wretchedly sick throughout. She hung over the wash strake, the cold, green water striking and bursting in silver bubbles mere inches from her face. She had tried sucking ginger root which was usually very effective at stemming nausea, but to no avail. Six years ago she had been seasick on the journey across the Narrow Sea, although not with this appalling ferocity. But then on that occasion, she had not been pregnant.

She was sure now. The time of her second flux had come and gone four days' since without so much as a spot of blood. Her breasts were full and tender, she felt bloated, and the sickness had begun with a vengeance. Fortunately, Oliver thought it was due to the sea-crossing, which in part it was, or else he would never have allowed her on board ship. Catrin endured as best she could, telling herself that it would pass as soon as she quickened.

Rosamund was completely unaffected by the rolling of the ship, and as brightly unsympathetic as only a six-year-old could be. 'It doesn't make me sick, Mama,' she announced, peering over the side, then leaned over the gunwale trying to reach the water and trail a hand. Catrin struggled upright and, with aching stomach, dragged her daughter from harm's way.

'No, but you might drown,' she said crossly.

Rosamund pouted. 'I only want to see if the water's green in my hand.'

'No, it isn't, it's just water-coloured,' Catrin said shortly. Nausea surged. She clutched the side and closed her eyes.

'Then why does it look green?'

'Because of the way the light shines through it, because of the way that darkness is never really black but many different colours,' Oliver said, coming to Catrin's rescue. Sweeping Rosamund up, he tucked her under his right arm so that she squealed. 'I could always throw you overboard to find out,' he teased.

Rosamund pummelled him but to no avail, he had her fast. 'Feeling no better?' he said to Catrin.

She shook her head. It was beyond her to speak. If she opened her mouth she would be sick.

'I came to say that we'll be making landfall in a few hours. The lookout has sighted the Scottish coast in the distance.'

'Where, where, let me see!' Rosamund demanded.

Catrin leaned over the side again and felt the salt spray tingle on her face. Oliver took Rosamund to the prow of the vessel and pointed out the distant smudge of coastline. Other vessels ploughed alongside theirs, each of them bearing a cargo of men and supplies. Prince Henry's ship fluttered a red and gold banner bearing a device of three lions, a blazon adopted from his father. On board with Henry was Roger, Earl of Hereford, who was also to be knighted at the ceremony on Pentecost Sunday. The bright colours of tunics and cloaks glowed against the brown and white of the ship.

Henry had left Belle and baby William in Normandy. For all her earlier determination to follow Oliver, Catrin found herself wishing that at this precise moment she was back in Normandy too, lying on a bed that did not move.

Even when Henry's entourage disembarked from their ships, Catrin's nightmare was not over. The journey by sea had to be continued by land to Carlisle. Riding in a baggage wain meant that she could lie down with a lavender-scented cloth across her forehead, but the lurching of the cart over successive potholes in the road made it almost as bad as being at sea. She sucked more ginger root and fought her rebellious stomach.

Rosamund sat with the driver and chattered nineteen to

the dozen about all the things they saw along their way. The border country was wild and green whereas Normandy's greenness was lush and padded. The Scots lowlands hinted at the bones of rock beneath the soil. Among the fields of corn there were as many fields of oats, and the cows were smaller and tougher than the great slab-sided cattle of Normandy.

Catrin watched all of this from a detached distance. She was aware of Oliver riding beside the wain and peering anxiously inside. She managed to give him a wan smile and, turning on her side, fell into a deep, exhausted sleep.

Carlisle was a grey border town with a fine new keep defending the approach to Galloway and standing proud against Cumbria. To honour its king and greet Prince Henry, his nephew, the castle had been decked with horn lanterns and the barbaric splendour of pine pitch torches. A fanfare of trumpets welcomed the arrival of Henry and his entourage and they were escorted into the castle by King David and his knights in the full splendour of court dress. A great feast was set out in the hall with glistening roasts, whole tender sucking pigs, and pies made with chopped venison and spices. Banners and weapons gilded the walls and a fortune in gold plate was laid out upon an embroidered cloth on the high table.

Catrin ignored all the rich, fatty meat. The sight of it made her ravenous and sick at the same time and she knew that if she ate it, she would only purge it back later. While Rosamund gorged herself, her small face shiny with grease, Catrin made do with plain bread and oatcakes, washed down with a little wine. Luckily Oliver had too many duties to spend much time with her, but Catrin knew that eventually he would notice, and if she continued to be ill she no longer had the excuse of a brisk sea crossing.

Fortunately, by the end of the week Catrin was slightly better. Although she was still being sick, especially in the mornings, she could at least eat plain food during the day without vomiting, and she was still managing to conceal her indisposition from Oliver. He was too preoccupied with Henry's intended strike at Stephen's positions in northern England to notice her lethargy and pallor and she did her best not to call it to his attention. She would pile her trencher in the hall, eat some, leave some for the alms basket and slip the rest to the dogs which always lurked under the tables ready to snap up offerings.

To put more colour in her cheeks, she sat close to the hearth, or dabbed her cheeks with the merest hint of red powder. The latter was the resort of older women trying to recapture their youth and younger ones who were advertising their attractions, so she had to be very careful.

She soon came to the conclusion that she need not have bothered, for all the notice that Oliver took. Henry, now a fully fledged knight, was planning to advance to Lancaster to meet Earl Rannulf of Chester, and from there to march upon York, one of the major strongholds of the north country. Henry's designs had to be supported by supplies and Oliver was kept busy from dawn to dusk securing the wherewithal to march an army.

'There are to be no camp followers,' he said to Catrin on their last evening in Carlisle. They were lying side by side in the hall, Rosamund cocooned in her cloak beside them. 'Henry intends to move with all haste – and that means with the minimum of baggage. Once we reach Lancaster, you must either stay there or continue to Bristol if you prefer familiar territory.'

'You are saying that I cannot go with you?' Catrin half-raised her head. In the grainy light cast by the night candle, she could see the pale gleam of his hair and the thin line of his nose.

'Not to York.' He slipped his arm around her waist, softening the blow. 'Much as I want you by my side, I would find you and Rosamund a hindrance too. I would be fearing for your safety instead of concentrating on the task at hand.'

His fingers moved back and forth at her waist and Catrin sucked in her stomach and wondered if he would notice the thickening there.

'Stay in Carlisle, if you want,' he added. 'As soon as he has the victory, Henry will advance his full household.'

Catrin folded one of her hands over his and stilled his motion. She felt the curve of his knuckles, the length of bone, the shortness of nail. He had argued for her and

Rosamund to stay in Normandy; now he was preventing them from following him to York. But this time she was more disposed to listen. There would be distance between them, but less than the Narrow Sea, and now that her pregnancy was fact, not speculation, she had the baby's welfare to consider. The fight for York was only the beginning. If Henry was successful, his army would push on to the next city and the next. If Henry lost, then he would have to retreat to one of the loyal strongholds – Carlisle, Bristol, Devizes.

The truly logical step was to remain in Carlisle, but the place did not call to her in the way of home. People had been kind, but there was a reserve in them, a cool buffer which they set up between themselves and what they saw as 'Norman' strangers. If Catrin was going to build a nest, then she wanted to build it in Bristol where there was familiarity and a kinder climate.

'No,' she said. 'I will go to Bristol. Although I hate to be parted from you, I can see the sense in what you say.'

'Well, there's a miracle,' he muttered against her hair. She pinched him and he recoiled with a muffled yelp.

'In Bristol,' she said in a firm tone, overriding his sarcasm, 'I know the people and the surroundings. It will be good to see Edon again.'

'And you enjoy your gossip.'

Catrin used her elbow this time. 'Besides, Henry is bound to bring his army to Bristol sooner or later, although why I should cite that as a reason I do not begin to know.' She sniffed at him.

'Of course you do. For the joy and pleasure of having me in your arms.' He tightened his hold to prevent her from attacking him again and pressed his lips over hers. Catrin put up a mock fight and then softened her mouth beneath his.

'Don't let it be too long.'

'I think you need have no fear on that score,' he murmured against her lips.

Catrin arrived in Bristol during the first week of June. The weather was balmy and so saturated with the scent of bursting green growth that it seemed about to split asunder.

Full summer heat had yet to smother the land and the scents and stenches of the city were merely ripe and evocative rather than overpowering. The same fishwife, more wizened and leathery with the passage of years, offered Catrin and Rosamund a basket of eels using the same words: 'Fresh caught, not an hour old!'

Rosamund recoiled, her little face screwing up in disgust as Catrin bought a dozen, a misty smile on her face.

'Mama!' There was a wealth of meaning in the single word and the look that Rosamund cast. She was a hearty eater but she had a marked dislike of fish in any form.

'I bought them in memory,' Catrin said. 'You don't have to eat them.'

'I'm not going to.' Her nose still wrinkled, Rosamund turned where she sat pillion on her mother's small brown mare and pointed to the large white building rising among the houses. 'Is that where we're going?'

'The castle, yes. With good fortune, you'll be sleeping there tonight.' Catrin looked down at the eels writhing in the basket. Her stomach was queasy, but she was not in immediate danger of being sick. She was becoming accustomed to feeling permanently tired and nauseous and, having accepted it as a fact of life, it had less effect on her now. Besides, she was at the end of her third month, and she knew from her experience as a midwife that the sickness would probably abate soon.

It had been a long journey from Lancaster to Bristol. She could have travelled by sea, but even the thought of lurching down the coast on a trading vessel had sent her dashing for the privy. The gentlest way had been on horseback with an escort of two mercenaries and her baggage carried by a pack pony. They had travelled by quiet roads and avoided the major towns unless they were held in Henry's name.

'It's a bit like Rouen,' Rosamund said, as they drew closer to the castle. Gulls wheeled over the estuary and the river glittered like a strip of silver braid. Ships' masts forested the skyline. 'Not as big, though.'

'No, not as big,' Catrin said with a smile. 'But it's home.'

Although Catrin had been away for several years, there were

still people at the castle who recognised her and called out greetings as she dismounted in the bailey. There was Alain the blacksmith, whose wife she and Ethel had delivered of their first son. The lad, now a sturdy nine-year-old, stood pumping the bellows at his father's forge while his two little sisters watched. There was Wulfrune, now a charcoal burner's wife, who had sought love philtres from Ethel to capture her husband's heart. Catrin had always suspected that her wheat-blond hair and bright blue eyes had had more of an effect than a mere tincture of rose petals, the main ingredient in Ethel's philtres. And there was Agatha, the laundry maid, who had been Ethel's particular friend and living proof of the efficacy of the hand lotion that Ethel made from purified goose fat and scented herbs.

Almost toothless now, her skin as weathered and shiny as cowhide, Agatha was still a large, robust woman with enormous forearms developed by a lifetime of pummelling linen sheets, bolster cases, shirts and chemises. She threw her arms around Catrin and gave her a ferocious hug that left Catrin gasping and Rosamund recoiling warily lest the same greeting be meted out to her.

'God bless you, lass, where you been a-wandering this time!' Agatha demanded in her broad, Bristol accent.

'I've been in Normandy with Oliver, mostly in a town called Rouen. It's a port, a bit like Bristol.'

'You're still with him then.' Agatha set her hands on her hips. 'That's good,' she nodded. 'You should never have gone off with that other wastrel like you did. Ethel would have told you that, God bless her soul.'

'She did,' Catrin said ruefully. 'She told me to beware of a man on a bay horse, but I took her to mean someone else.'

Agatha sucked her gums. 'Folks can't always see woods for trees.' Her eyes lit on the little girl. 'And this must be your daughter. By the Virgin, you've grown!' She bent towards her. 'Last I saw you, you was a tiny babe at your mother's breast. Now you're almost a woman!'

Rosamund gave her a severe look from her large, dark eyes. 'I'm six,' she said.

'Then you're sixty years short o' me.' Agatha smiled at

Catrin. 'She bids fair to break some hearts when she's older.'

'Plenty of time for that later,' Catrin said. 'The years are too precious to think them away.'

'Aye, and that they are. Don't seem a moment since I was six years old myself. Mind you, I was never so pretty.' Agatha looked wistfully at the slender black-haired child. 'Where's Lord Oliver?'

Catrin sighed. 'Somewhere between Lancaster and York with Prince Henry. We've come to Bristol for "safekeeping". It's closer than Rouen.' She glanced round at the limewashed stone and the banners fluttering from the square battlements. 'And it's home,' she added with a smile and, reaching down, took Rosamund's hand. 'We're on our way to see Edon. Is she still here?'

Agatha sucked her teeth again and the furrows seaming her brow deepened. 'Aye, she is that, Mistress Catrin, and mighty glad she will be to see you as well.' Her large hands kneaded her apron.

'Is there something wrong?'

'No,' said Agatha slowly, without relinquishing her frown, 'not really. 'Tis just that she's with child again and not carrying it as well as she did the last one. The Earl's death struck Lady Mabile hard, and a household in mourning ain't done much for her spirits either.' She forced a smile. 'They'll all be right glad to see you, especially if you've fresh news. A good cheering is what they need.'

Unsure of what she was going to find, Catrin made her way into the hall and was escorted to the Countess's rooms by a young squire. The steps seemed interminable to her growing body, and she was gasping for breath by the time he led her along a walkway and banged on the heavy oak door.

It was opened by Beatrice, one of the older maids. Her eyes grew round as she stared at Catrin and Rosamund. The little girl quickly hid behind her mother lest another session of hearty embracing was in order but, after the woman had cried out in surprise, she made do with kissing Catrin on both cheeks before ushering her into the room.

Mabile's maids sat at their embroidery. One of them

played a harp and another was reading aloud from a leather-bound book of French tales. The appearance of Catrin and Rosamund was a welcome diversion and the story book was immediately abandoned in favour of news from the outside world. Catrin was viewed by the women as a form of walking tale herself. They spent their lives enclosed within the bower walls, their most daring exploits confined to a day out with the hawks or a visit to the Michaelmas fair. Catrin's nomadic existence, with its tidal sweeps of danger, heartache and fortune, was seized upon and devoured in one hungry gulp.

Rosamund was petted and given sweetmeats from the Countess's own supply, which the little girl considered far more appetising than the basket of eels that her mother had left in the kitchens with one of the cooks. There were other children in the bower too – two boys slightly older than Rosamund and three fair-haired little girls in stepped heights of about a year's difference. All of them proved to be Edon's.

'And my belly's big again,' Edon said later, when Catrin had emptied her budget of news and the excitement of her arrival had calmed down. The women returned to their embroidery and the harp music rippled softly through the room.

Catrin looked at Edon's swollen stomach which made a nothing of her own thickening waistline.

'It will be my seventh,' Edon said. 'I lost one a year and a half ago in my third month.' She gave a little grimace. 'Geoffrey and I try our best, but you can't go without all the time unless you're a monk or a nun.' She looked sidelong. 'How do you and Oliver manage?'

Catrin patted her belly. 'As it happens, I too am with child, although less further along than you,' she confided. 'Oliver would have left me in Rouen if he had known, so it's going to be a surprise when he sees me.' There was sudden apprehension in her voice.

'You mean a shock,' Edon said shrewdly.

'Yes, that too. But as soon as he knows, he will start to fret. The longer I can keep it from him, the better for his well-being, no matter that he will be hurt that I did not tell him before.'

'You know best,' Edon said dubiously, as if she thought the opposite.

Catrin tightened her lips but did not argue because she had a sneaking suspicion Edon was right. 'How many months of carrying have you left?'

'The child is due at Michaelmas,' Edon said.

Catrin stared, unable to equate Edon's words with the evidence of her eyes. Edon was already enormous. Successive pregnancies had slackened her muscles and laid pads of fat upon what had once been the toned, slender body of a girl. Edon could be no more than eight-and-twenty now, but she looked ten years older. There were puffy shadows beneath her eyes and her fingers were so swollen that her rings were half-buried in flesh. Catrin had come across such signs before and knew that the labour often went hard for women who displayed them.

'I'm pleased you're here.' Edon pressed Catrin's arm. 'You'll stay for my confinement, won't you? I will never forget how you and Ethel saved my first one's life.'

Catrin gave a warm smile of response, although her heart dropped. 'If I can, I will,' she said.

Rosamund had settled in a corner with the other three children to play a puzzle game with a loop of wool. Catrin looked at the bent heads, the absorbed faces, the dextrous little hands.

'You should drink plenty of raspberry leaf tea and rest with your feet above the level of your body to adjust the balance of your humours,' she told Edon. 'The birth will go easier then.'

'You are saying it will not be an easy birth?'

'No, no,' Catrin said quickly, knowing Edon's propensity for panic. 'What I mean is that whatever the church says about women bringing forth children in pain to pay for Eve's sin, the less pain involved the better. I suggest these remedies to all women once they have quickened. Indeed, I shall take my own advice.' She was aware of how rapidly she was speaking, rushing with words to make her defence more plausible.

Edon gave her a level stare, then chose to believe her and relaxed with a little sigh. 'I shall tell you the easiest way of all,' she said, 'and that is to be a man. You plant the seed and then go on your way.'

Catrin nodded. 'But men have their own set of dangers too,' she murmured, thinking of Oliver and wondering where he was.

CHAPTER 30

Oliver too was wondering where he was. Certainly not York, as had been the grand plan. That remained securely in King Stephen's hand. News of Henry's approach from Lancaster had flown ahead and the citizens of York had sent for aid. It had arrived far more rapidly than anyone had anticipated, in the form of Stephen himself at the head of a large band of mercenaries.

Faced with a pitched battle which he was not yet ready to fight, Henry had chosen discretion over valour and retreated. At sixteen years old he had all the time that the fifty-three-year-old Stephen did not. He dispersed his army. King David returned to Carlisle, Rannulf of Chester retreated into his marcher heartlands and Henry headed for the Angevin strongholds in the south-west; for Gloucester, Bristol and Devizes.

The journey was a game of catch-as-catch-can, for Stephen had sent out patrols to intercept Henry's troops. Although the ride was not desperate, it still gave Oliver uncomfortable memories of the retreat from Winchester eight years before. He had a recurring nightmare of being apprehended on the road by a smirking, dark-eyed faun of a man wearing the blood-crimson tunic of a noble. In his dream, instead of surrendering Oliver drew his sword and attacked Louis de Grosmont. But at the moment when he struck, the face became Catrin's, her expression bewildered and accusing, and he jerked out of the imagining with thudding heart and clammy palms.

They rode in the dark, kindling their way with pine pitch

flares. When it rained, they rested until daylight within a wood, the rain dripping from the leaves of the great elms and rolling down their necks. Chain-mail shone, slick and silver, patterned with streaks of rust-red. Horse-hide gleamed with damp. The smell of the forest was heavy and green with a combined aroma of growth and rot.

Bearing down the marches, they took the lesser roads, some of them no more than sheep trails, although once they found a stretch of road which Henry said had been built by the Romans and which, even now, was more sound and solid than recently shod surfaces. They swam rivers rather than risk the bridges where Stephen's troops might be waiting, and until they were in the south-west did not attempt to spend the night at any destination more conspicuous than a hamlet or barn.

They took a day's respite at Hereford, which was loyal to the Prince, and then moved on towards Bristol. Henry still had to exercise caution for Stephen's heir, Eustace, had swept into Gloucestershire with an army of Middlesex men, intent on crushing Henry's challenge before it could begin.

Within a day's march of Bristol, Henry stopped to spend the night at Dursley Castle near Stroud. He was red-eyed from lack of sleep, but there was very little evidence that the setbacks had sapped his seemingly bottomless reserve of vitality. All Oliver wanted to do was curl up in a corner and sleep without dreaming for a year at least. His left arm was aching from constantly gripping a bridle, his collar-bone too from the weight of his shield strap.

'My head feels like a gambeson,' he said, as Richard cheerfully thrust a cup of hot wine beneath his nose. 'So stuffed with wool that whatever strikes it is just absorbed without result.'

Richard grinned. 'At least we'll reach Bristol tomorrow,' he said cheerfully.

Oliver took a sip of the steaming wine. It was sour but he didn't care as long as it revived him. 'Then what?' He glanced at Henry who was prowling confidently around the room talking to his commanders, his short, stubby hands gesturing eloquently as he spoke. Even now, at the end of a long, harrowing day, he was still on his feet with a bounce in his stride. In a moment Oliver knew with awful certainty that the Prince was going to ask him a preposterous question about their supplies and expect him to have the answer.

Richard shrugged. 'Then we eat an enormous meal safe behind huge walls where Stephen cannot reach us, and in the morning we start planning again.'

Oliver groaned. Actually the planning did not bother him too much. He was quick and efficient at working out logistics, and supplies were always easier to come by in the summer months. What he disliked were the fits and starts of campaigning, the furtive hiding, sleeping in full mail, a horse beneath him. Although still very young, Henry was a competent commander, but Stephen was competent too and also battle-wise. To best him, Henry needed the luck of the devil, who was said to be his ancestor, and thus far it had not been forthcoming.

'Very soon I will have spent half my life on the battlefield. My bones, including the broken ones, are too weary to do anything now but lie down.'

Richard tilted his head on one side. 'Catrin and Rosamund are in Bristol,' he said. 'We'll reach them tomorrow too, and Geoff FitzMar.'

Oliver nodded to humour the young man and wondered if Richard's resilience was the result of being a full fifteen years younger or whether it was a derangement of the royal bloodline. While Oliver was indeed looking forward to seeing Catrin and Rosamund, he was too bone-weary to make the effort of conversation. The last decent night's sleep he remembered was in Carlisle before setting out for Lancaster, and even that had been marred by Henry's propensity for rising three hours before the lark. He had never known anyone need so little rest.

Giving up on Oliver's tepid response, Richard drifted away to join Thomas FitzRainald who was spreading his saddle-roll near the hearth to air out the damp. With a quick glance in Henry's direction, Oliver took his own saddle-roll outside, deciding to find a quiet, sheltered spot in the bailey where he could sleep in peace. The Prince needed to know nothing from him at the moment. Let him bedevil some other poor individual for his intellectual stimulation.

It was a quiet night, thick with stars. Sentries paced the wall-walks, their boots scraping softly on the wooden planks. Sheep bleated to each other in the fields beyond the walls and danger seemed so far away that it had no meaning. Oliver found an animal shelter supported on two strong ash poles. It smelt faintly of goat, but there was no sign of an occupant and the straw on the floor was clean and dry. He spread his cloak, lay down upon it and wrapped it over like a blanket. Within moments he was sound asleep.

It seemed only seconds later, but was more than three hours judging from the position of the stars, when he was woken by the sound of someone crying for admittance at the keep gates. There was urgency in the voice and as Oliver threw off his cloak and sat up, he saw guards hastening by torchlight to raise the bar and admit a rider. As the horse clattered into the bailey, Oliver recognised one of Henry's Welsh scouts.

The man tethered his blowing mount to a ring in the wall and headed towards the darkened keep. Starlight glittered, casting blue light beyond the red of the guards' torches.

'Math?' Oliver called.

The Welshman turned, his hand by instinct already on his dagger, then he relaxed. 'Oh, it's you, the pet *Saeson*,' he said in his broad, sing-song accent. 'What are you doing out here?'

'Trying to sleep without being disturbed,' Oliver said with a shrug. 'I should have known it was a lost cause.'

'Aye, well, the entire cause of yon lad will be lost if you don't put spurs to your mounts and ride for Bristol,' Math said. 'Eustace has an army not twenty miles away and he's headed straight here. He knows that Henry's inside.' Math gazed around at the walls, his mouth turned down at the corners. 'Not fit for a siege, this one. I'd sooner be attacking it from without than hiding within, see.'

Oliver followed Math into the keep to raise the alarm and bade farewell to sleep.

The next hour was complete hell as men were roused from their slumber and forced to don armour and weapons which they had but recently removed. The horses were tired. Some just hung their heads and patiently allowed themselves to be saddled – which did not bode well for swiftness on the road. Others, with more spirit, kicked and snapped as the harassed grooms and squires tried to harness them by the poor light of guttering pitch flares.

The Prince was one of the first to leave Dursley, riding on a fresh horse borrowed from the castellan. His capture could not be risked with Eustace and his army so close. Stephen's eldest son was neither generous nor amenable and Henry was his bitter rival.

Oliver rode out with Henry's rearguard. Hero was seventeen years old and beginning to show his age. He did not have the kick or spark of the younger mounts, nor their stamina any more. Still, he responded gamely to Oliver's urgency and broke into a trot. Only a madman or someone completely desperate would have galloped his mount in the dark, and so Oliver was able to keep pace with the rest of the troop.

There was a prickling between his shoulder blades as he rode, and his sleep-starved imagination fed him a waking dream of being pursued not by Eustace but by Louis de Grosmont. Closer and closer the spectre came, his sword raised and his dark eyes reflecting the glow from the travelling torches like hell-fire. No matter how much Oliver spurred Hero, Grosmont continued to close on them.

'She's mine!' Grosmont snarled at Oliver. 'Mine until death!'

'You can't have her!' Oliver sobbed and drew his sword. The sound shivered the night and brought him awake with a huge surge of breath like a man too long submerged. His sword was in his hand, braced and ready.

'What is it?' Beside him, Richard's own sword was half out of the scabbard. 'Have you seen something?' The youngster's eye whites gleamed with fear.

'No.' Oliver passed his hand across his eyes. 'I was saddle-sleeping,' he admitted sheepishly. 'I thought we were being hard-pursued.'

Richard glanced over his shoulder into the darkness, his expression intent. Then, with a sigh, he slotted his weapon home. 'Nothing,' he said. 'Jesu, you frightened me yelling like that and drawing your blade.' Despite himself, he looked over his shoulder again. There was silence except for the thud of their own horses on the baked mud road, and the soft creak and clink of leather and harness.

'Sorry. I'll try and stay awake.'

'Be light soon.' Richard cast a glance at the sky. There was a milky opacity in the east and the stars no longer burned as brightly. 'Eustace won't dare pursue us as far as Bristol.'

Oliver shrugged. 'You never can tell with Eustace. He's half wolf at least.'

'Was he in your dream?' Richard asked curiously.

Oliver shook his head. 'No, but another wolf was – one in sheep's clothing.'

The milkiness in the east took on an opalescent quality. A dawn chorus of birds filled the air from every coppice and field; trees and grass turned from grey to summer-green as the daylight brightened. The men doused their torches and began to speak in less hushed tones as the strengthening light and the rising sun increased their confidence.

It was just after daybreak when Oliver felt the change in Hero's gait. The smooth lope had given way a while back to a shorter stride as the horse grew tired, but now there was a definite lurch. With a soft curse, Oliver dismounted and ran his hand down the stallion's foreleg. There was a hot, tender swelling on the knee, puffy to the touch, and the horse stamped and tossed his head at the pressure of Oliver's hand.

Richard circled his mount and returned to Oliver and Hero, his blue eyes troubled. 'Do you want to ride double with me?'

Oliver gazed round. The landmarks were familiar now. Although they still wanted several miles to Bristol and safety, there was another haven closer to hand. 'No, lad, go on with the others. Godard and Edith live close by. I'll rest Hero with them and borrow a horse, if they have one. Tell Catrin for me.'

'Are you sure?' Richard glanced behind at the powdery dust settling in the troop's wake as if expecting to see an army of vengeful mercenaries bearing down on them at full gallop.

'It's all right. Eustace isn't that close. Go on with you.'

With reluctance, Richard rode away to rejoin the rest of the rearguard, by now a furlong in front of him.

The silence of summer birdsong and the hissing of the wind in the grass filled Oliver's ears with its tranquil immensity. He wrapped his hand around the bridle and led a limping Hero through the army's dust until they came to the branch in the road that led to Ashbury.

'By all the saints, Lord Oliver!' Godard put down the curry comb he had been using on the old brown cob and strode to greet his former master. A grin broke across his face, parting the luxuriant beard. ''Tis right good to see you!'

''Tis right good to see you too,' Oliver responded, as they clasped hands. 'Hero went lame a mile back and the troop couldn't afford to wait. I need rest and shelter . . . and a place to hide.'

Godard's dark gaze sharpened. 'They are all yours, you know that,' he said. 'Bring the horse into the barn and we'll see him comfortable.'

Oliver clicked his tongue, encouraging Hero to take a few more steps on his swollen foreleg, and followed Godard, noting as he did that a transformation had taken place. What had been a cosy village alehouse and a couple of storage sheds had been enlarged to the status of a hostelry, with a small barn and substantial stores.

'You have prospered,' Oliver said, with a nod at all the alterations.

'Aye. I built most of it myself with a little help from the village carpenter and his sons. We're used by folk heading for Bristol who get caught out by the dusk, although trade really became brisk when a hermit settled over by Three Oak Hill. We get pilgrims and wisdom seekers coming through all spring and summer, war or no war.' He rubbed the side of his nose. 'Of course, some folk come out of their way especially to sample Edith's brew. She's taken to making bread and cheese too.'

'I'm pleased for you.'

Godard cleared his throat. 'I'm indebted to you, my lord.

If you had not gone to Ashbury on that day, I would never have met my Edith and found a place to settle down.'

'It's an ill wind,' Oliver agreed as Godard led him into the barn and indicated a couple of stalls partitioned off from the main portion of the building by withy fences.

'You said a place to hide?' Godard raised his brows. 'I could put you in the understore, but who is it you are hiding from and how urgent is your need?'

Oliver told him about Prince Henry's army and how it was probable, but not certain, that Eustace was in pursuit. 'He'll stop long before the gates of Bristol, but here might be as likely a place as any to take refreshment before he turns back.' Oliver stroked the grey's sweaty flank. 'I could have ridden double with Richard and cut Hero loose, but I owe the old lad better than that. Besides, two men to one horse makes for slow progress. Eustace will be on the lookout for stragglers, but I would rather hide my armour and weapons in the understore than myself.'

Godard gave a considering frown, then nodded. 'Best unarm then,' he said, 'and I'll lend you one of my tunics.' Humour creased his eye corners. 'You speak English. If anyone comes, you're my Saxon labourer and the horse was left by a pilgrim when it went badly lame.'

Oliver unhitched his swordbelt. He still felt bone-weary but, despite the danger, his mood was lighter than it had been for several weeks. He was among true friends and Godard's twinkle imbued the whole situation with a sense of adventure. The heir to the throne was safely on his way to Bristol. For the nonce, Oliver's only responsibility was to himself.

Edith greeted him with open arms and smacking kisses on both cheeks. She was as round and ruddy as ever and obviously flourishing on their increased custom. The evergreen ale-stake, which traditionally signified to customers that a fresh brew was available, had been replaced by a smart, permanent board that swung on wrought-iron fixings from the gable end. On it, in bold colours, was painted an exuberant green bush. There were new trestles in the main room, and the old byre, where Oliver and Catrin had spent the night of Godard's wedding, had been converted into a dormitory for travellers.

Oliver found himself envying Godard and Edith their settled prosperity. No stumbling about in the middle of the night for them with enemy troops on their tail. No parting from loved ones. No uncertainty. Hard work and simple routine. Oliver felt a great yearning within him.

Edith sat him at one of the trestles and brought a huge bowl of chicken stew and half a freshly baked loaf. Then she stood over him and watched him eat like a mother with a finicky child. She need not have bothered for Oliver was ravenous. The pickings of the last few days had been unappetising to say the least, and Edith was as good a cook as any who served the Prince.

'So Mistress Catrin and the lass are in Bristol,' she said, as she removed his scraped bowl and set down another one containing an apple dumpling. A jug of thick yellow cream and a pot of honey joined it on the side.

Nodding, Oliver picked up his spoon and prepared to tackle the dish. 'I saw them off from Lancaster with an escort. Catrin didn't want to stay in the north, and I did not want her with me on the road to York lest anything happened.' He grimaced. 'As you can see, I was wise. I'll join them on the morrow, God willing.'

Edith watched him in silence for a while. 'How's your arm?' she asked at length.

Oliver stopped eating and pushed up the loose left sleeve of Godard's tunic to show her the knotted white scar. 'It aches in the winter,' he said, 'and it tires more swiftly than my right, but there are days when I do not think of it even once.'

'When I first saw you, I thought you would die.'

'I thought it too.' He smiled at her. 'Catrin wouldn't let me, and I'm glad now, although I cursed her for it at the time.'

'Do you think that . . .' Edith broke off and looked round as Godard flung open the door.

'Soldiers,' he said without preamble. 'It will look suspicious if you hide. Go out and be ready to take the leaders' horses if they decide to stay.'

Oliver spooned up a last mouthful of the apple dumpling and Edith whisked away his bowl. 'My name's Osmund,' he said to Godard. 'I've been working here for the past two years ever since my village was destroyed. I'm your second cousin, so you felt a duty to give me house room.'

Godard nodded brusquely. 'That should satisfy them, although I doubt they'll ask.'

Oliver went out into the road. Other folk from the hamlet were poking their noses out of doors to watch the troops ride through. While people were wary, there were no signs of panic. Their settlement owed its rents and dues to the Abbey at Malmesbury and although church lands were not immune from attack, soldiers tended to think twice before jeopardising their souls.

Godard shaded his eyes against the sun and watched their approach. Oliver stood a little way back, his expression calm, almost bovine, but his heart thumping like a drum. In the alehouse, he could hear Edith singing as she tipped fresh water in the cauldron and filled the jugs with new ale.

As the soldiers came closer, Oliver recognised the man who led them. 'It's Prince Eustace,' he muttered from the side of his mouth. 'Have a care with him. His nature's as sour as spoiled wine.'

Prince Eustace drew rein under the sign of The Bush. His complexion was almost purple with frustration and heat. 'God's arse, is there no one here who can do anything but stare like a half-wit!' he snarled. He was wearing a very fine hauberk of lammelar-mail, the kind favoured by the Byzantines. Each overlapping scale collected the heat and Eustace was literally cooking inside his armour. His horse was creamed with sweat and blowing hard, its nostrils distended and its sides heaving like smithy bellows.

'Surely, my lord,' Godard answered in French, his manner polite but not servile. 'But we're more used to pilgrims for the hermitage than soldiers.' He snapped his fingers at Oliver, who moved forward to act the part of groom. 'You're welcome to water your mounts and yourselves if you've a mind.' Turning to Oliver, he told him in English to take the horses round to the trough. 'He speaks no French, sir,' Godard added, as he translated the instruction for Eustace's benefit.

Eustace grunted. 'I wouldn't expect him to. He looks a brainless dolt.'

Oliver lowered his head and cultivated a vapid expression. Eustace decided not to trust him with his horse and gave it to his squire instead. Oliver showed the soldiers the trough and the haystore, then, on the receiving end of several cuffs and kicks, returned to the alehouse to help Edith and Godard serve.

'So you have seen neither hide nor hair of an army pass this way?' Eustace demanded as he drank down the first cup of Edith's ale in several fast swallows. He had complained loudly about the lack of wine but was embracing the alternative with gusto.

'No, my lord,' Edith replied, refilling Eustace's cup. 'There's only pilgrims that come through here, and sometimes the troops from Ashbury. Odinel the Fleming holds the village there,' she added, without looking at Oliver. 'He's a man loyal to your father.'

Oliver spoke rapidly in English.

Eustace glowered at him. 'What does he say?' he demanded. 'Jesu, it's small wonder that they were defeated on Hastings field.'

Godard cleared his throat. 'Sire, he says that he saw troops riding on the Bristol road before dawn this morning when he was out bird-nesting. Says that they rode right past our fork in the road, going swift with torches to light the way. He wonders if you belong to them.'

'Before dawn?' Eustace repeated with a scowl.

'Aye, my lord.' He spoke over his shoulder to Oliver who grunted a reply, one forefinger held up. 'About an hour before, so Osmund says.'

'How far is Bristol from here?'

'Four hours' ride, my lord, on horses like yours. Takes me five on my old horses and half a day with my cart.'

Eustace calculated and threw back his second cup of ale with an angry tilt of his head. 'Then we've lost them,' he growled. 'I'd give my soul for just one fingernail of that bastard Angevin's luck.' He slammed the cup down on the trestle. 'So close,' he said bitterly, and held up his forefinger and thumb. 'I might as well be a hundred miles away!' He made a sound of pure disgust and glared at Godard. 'Let him skulk in Bristol. He'll have to emerge at some time, and when he does I'll crack him open like a flea.' He closed his finger and thumb, clicking the nails together.

'Yes, sir,' Godard said diplomatically. 'Would you like to try a bite of my wife's chicken stew?'

Eustace declined. 'We have work to do.' He thrust to his feet. 'The Angevin whoreson might have escaped by the skin of his teeth, but I can yet singe his tail.' He tossed two silver pennies from his pouch on to the trestle. 'Fortunate for you that you entertained the right army,' he said, and strode out.

The troop mounted up and rode away. A hot silence descended on the village as the dust began to settle.

'Jesu.' Legs suddenly weak, Oliver collapsed at one of the trestles and ran his hands through his hair. He poured himself some of Edith's ale, took a long drink and then laughed with relief and dark amusement.

'What's so funny?' Edith's tone was waspish. She had half-expected the alehouse to go up in flames.

'I told him that Henry had gone through three hours since, but it's much nearer to one. If Eustace ran his horses ragged, he might just catch him.'

'Well, what was all that about singeing Henry's tail?' Godard asked. He took the ale jug from Oliver and poured himself a cup.

The laughter died from Oliver's eyes. 'I wager that he intends to burn and ravage villages beholden to the Earldom of Gloucester. He's fuming with choler and desperate to strike out. He'll loot and torch and then retreat to Oxford to await his next opportunity.'

Edith tightened her lips and busied herself clearing the trestles. 'Who cares who rules the country as long as all this wanton waste and destruction stops,' she snapped. 'Time and again it is the innocent who suffer for the ambitions of men who dare to call themselves "noble".'

Godard cleared his throat and looked uncomfortable.

'I agree,' Oliver said, 'but I am caught up in it for good or ill. What would you do if another ale-wife appeared and took your home for herself? Would you just walk away with a shrug?'

Edith wrinkled her nose and took his point, but she was still none too happy. 'Well, I still say they should compromise their differences. Let Stephen keep the throne, let Henry have it after him and let everyone have the land which was theirs at the time when old King Henry died.'

'And beggars might ride,' Godard snorted.

'They well might,' Oliver said less sceptically. 'Henry has spoken of such a move before. He wants his grandfather's crown but, if necessary, he's willing to outlive Stephen to get it.'

'And what about Eustace?'

'If you saw Henry and Eustace together, you would know that there is no comparison. Eustace may have blood as royal as Henry's but the similarity ends there. I'd give my life for Henry Plantagenet, but I'd not even consider giving my oath of loyalty to such as Eustace. Neither would most of the barons in the country if the truth were known. Men who are loyal to Stephen will not remain loyal to his son.'

'Well, as long as it doesn't touch us here, I'm not bothered.' Edith hitched her vast bosom. 'Can't say as I liked him much myself, but with good fortune he won't happen this way again.' She stumped off to continue with her tasks.

'Women,' Godard said, a trifle uneasily.

Oliver could see him wondering if offence had been taken. He smiled to set him at ease. 'They live by different codes,' he said, 'and who can blame them. Often as not when a pot is broken, they are the ones who are left to either mend or sweep up the shards.'

'Often as not the pot was thrown at a man's head in the first place,' Godard said with a roll of his eyes.

Grinning, very pleased with themselves at having outwitted Eustace, and bonded together in masculine camaraderie, the men went off to inspect the state of Hero's foreleg.

Although improved a little, it was obvious that the stallion would not be fit to be ridden for several days, if not a full week, and then but lightly. Godard offered Oliver the use of his brown cob to reach Bristol and Oliver accepted, intending to set out on the morrow when Eustace would be well out of the vicinity.

He was cleaning his hauberk with a mixture of sand and vinegar and inspecting the rivets for any weak or broken links, when he heard the thud of horse hooves and the jingle of harness. It was too late to bundle up his equipment and thrust it back into the understore. He grabbed an armful of hay, tossed it over the hauberk and went swiftly outside, adopting a crabwise, servile gait, his back slightly stooped.

Catrin stared at him in astonishment from the back of her brown mare. Beside her, Geoffrey FitzMar stared too.

'God's bones, Oliver, what in Christ's name are you doing!'

Equally astonished, Oliver straightened and gaped at Catrin and Geoffrey. 'Lying low and keeping my hide intact,' he responded, when he could find his voice. 'But I might ask you what in Christ's name you are doing!'

Catrin flushed. 'Richard told us Hero was lame and you had taken refuge with Godard. Prince Henry's sent you a re-mount.' She indicated the handsome blue-roan stallion that Geoffrey was holding on a lead-rein and, kicking her feet from the stirrups, jumped down from the mare.

Oliver clenched and unclenched his fists, the colour draining from his face to leave him ashen with rage. 'Don't you know how foolish it is to be abroad just now – a lone woman, a single knight and three good horses?' he choked. 'You could have been set upon and killed!'

She shook her head. 'We saw no one on the road, our worry was for you.'

'But you knew I'd be safe with Godard.' He jerked his arm in an angry gesture.

'I knew no such thing!' Running to him, she set her arms around his neck. Her nails dug into the flesh at his nape. 'You don't understand. I had to know that you were whole.'

'Of course I'm whole,' he snapped. He was still furious, but the fierceness of her embrace and the tears in her eyes compelled him to put his own arms around her.

She buried her face in the old, hay-burred tunic. 'Twice Louis rode away and left me,' she said, her voice muffled by the scratchy wool. 'Then when I sought you in Bristol, you were brought to me at death's door. I don't want to be told by others that you are safe, I need to see it for myself.'

She raised her face, uncaring that they were in full public view, and kissed him. Oliver kissed her back, hard, with considerable exasperation, but was aware of a treacherous tenderness overtaking his anger.

'That "seeing for yourself" could have meant your own life,' he said, giving her a little shake. 'Eustace and his mercenaries are ravaging and burning hereabouts. If they had come upon you and Geoffrey, you'd be butchered corpses by now!'

'But they didn't and we're not,' she said practically. 'You cannot live your life by the code of "what if". Besides, Eustace would not harm someone who has tended his own father's sickbed.'

Oliver shook his head. 'You do not know Eustace.' He scowled at Geoffrey. 'Could you not have stopped her?'

'Short of binding her hand and foot and bolting her in the cells, no,' the knight snorted. 'I tried to reason her out of it, but it was as if I was talking a different language.' He gave Oliver a sudden shrewd look from his light blue eyes. 'It was like the time at Wareham when we assaulted the town. Do you remember? You did not care whether I was at your side or not, you were determined to plunge into the thick of the fray?'

Oliver glowered but had the grace to nod in acceptance of the point. 'I remember,' he said tersely, 'although I would rather forget.'

'Are you not pleased to see me and a fine new horse?' Catrin gave a little sniff and forced a smile.

'Of course I am,' he growled, and gave her another little shake. 'But I'm terrified too. You do not want to lose me, love, but by the same code I do not want to lose you.'

They embraced again, this time with more gentleness. He stopped short of asking her to promise that she would not do the like of pursuing him again, for he knew that she would refuse, they would quarrel and both of them would lose. Breaking the embrace, he went to look at the horse that Henry had given to him.

'Where's Rosamund?' he asked, as he ran his hands down the animal's sound young legs.

'I left her in Edon's care. She's struck up quite a friendship with her brood.'

'Her brood?' There was something in Catrin's tone which suggested there were more than the two boys Oliver recalled.

'She's got five, and another one due in the autumn,' Catrin said neutrally.

Geoffrey grinned and shrugged. 'I never was much good at pulling up before the finishing line.'

'Then you should practise,' Catrin said.

'I do, all the time.' Another grin.

Catrin tightened her lips and turning her shoulder on him gave her attention to Oliver. 'What do you think of him?'

'He's a fine animal. What I cannot understand is why Henry should give him to me.

'His name is Lucifer,' Geoffrey said drily. 'All the journey he has been as docile as a lamb, but I seem to remember one of the grooms muttering something about him becoming frisky under a saddle.'

Oliver nodded without surprise. He had learned literally never to look gift horses in the mouth when Henry was the benefactor. The Prince liked to appear generous but would not spend good money unless forced. Still, if the stallion was saddle-shy he could be schooled and Oliver was no impatient novice with horses, to be thrown at the first obstacle.

'What's he like without a saddle?' Answering his own question, Oliver grabbed the headstall and swung smoothly astride. Lucifer back-kicked and plunged a few times, but once the reins were drawn in tight he settled down. Oliver trotted him around the open space in front of the alehouse. An interested crowd of villagers collected to watch.

Catrin watched too for a while, then quietly disappeared.

Going out to toss scraps into the pig-pen, Edith found her retching into the midden pit, her complexion a gaunt, greenish-white. With an exclamation of concern, Edith put a maternal arm around Catrin's quivering shoulders. 'What's the matter, lass?'

'I'm all right, I'm not ill,' Catrin gasped, clutching her stomach. 'It's passing now.' Tentatively she straightened.

'You're not ill,' Edith repeated with scepticism, and placed her large, firm palm on Catrin's brow. 'A mite clammy, but there's no fever,' she said with cautious optimism. 'Shall

I fetch that man of yours from his love affair with his new horse?'

'No!' Catrin said, more sharply than she had intended.

Edith eyed her curiously.

'No,' she said in a calmer voice. 'I am not ill, but if he thinks I am he will worry. God knows, he was ready to burst because I rode out to find him instead of staying in Bristol.'

'Well, it was foolish, you must admit.' Taking her arm, Edith drew her towards the alehouse. 'Lord Eustace and his troops wouldn't have stopped to ask questions if they had come across you, and they're not the only brigands on the road by any manner of means. Here, sit you down.' She pushed Catrin gently on to a wall-bench and fetched her a small cup of strong, sweet mead. 'Drink this; it will settle your belly.'

Catrin took the mead and gratefully sipped. The sweetness was what she needed now. Not only would it settle her stomach, it would help the sudden feeling of weariness in her limbs. She stifled a huge yawn.

Edith studied her thoughtfully. Her shrewd gaze dropped to the hand that Catrin had tucked against her belly. The gesture in itself was protective and the outline showed a slight roundness.

'You are with child!' Edith said like an accusation.

Catrin immediately lifted her hand and smoothed her gown so that the gentle swell of her womb was not so obvious. 'I think I might be,' she prevaricated, 'but nothing is certain yet.'

'And you a midwife!' Edith snorted. 'I know only as much as the next woman about child-bearing, but I can see that you're beyond the "might be" stage.'

Catrin reddened beneath Edith's forthright stare. 'You are right.' She shook her head. 'Fortunately it is much easier to conceal from men than it is from women. I am due to bear a child at Christmastide.'

Edith's lips moved in silent calculation. 'Then you're almost four months along,' she said, and then frowned. 'Do I understand from what you have just said that Oliver doesn't yet know?'

'I don't intend telling him until I must.' Catrin sat upright and squared her shoulders.

'Why ever not?'

'His first wife died in childbirth after a prolonged labour. My anxiety for his well-being on campaign will be as nothing compared with his anxiety for me once he finds out.'

Edith gave her a troubled look. 'But you cannot just leave it. Sooner or later he is bound to notice, and he will be wounded that you have not trusted him enough to tell him.'

Catrin gave her a wry and weary smile. 'Yes, but the real enemy is that neither one trusts the other to keep on living against the daily odds.'

CHAPTER 31

The water in the bath-tub was a scummy dark grey, but at least the man dozing in its heat was now flesh-coloured and the lank, grimy hair had turned wheat-blond. He smelled much more presentable too.

It was Oliver's hauberk that caused it, Catrin thought as she warmed towels on the spit bar near the hearth. The mail had to be greased to keep out the elements; the grease picked up minute filaments of steel and these blackened whatever the hauberk touched. For the past month, Oliver had been on campaign with Henry and that meant living in the garment. The padded gambeson worn under the hauberk to act as a cushion against both the chafing of the rivets and enemy sword blows could have stood up on its own. She had rammed a broomstick pole through the sleeves and hooked it up outside the shelter to try to air out the pungent stink of sweat and smoke, but with little hope of success.

At least her stomach was not quite so swift to turn these days and there had only been a couple of mild nausea pangs as she dealt with the gambeson. She was almost into her fifth month of pregnancy. While carrying Rosamund, her belly had been scarcely noticeable until well into the seventh month, but this time she was showing much earlier. Oliver could not help but notice once the time came to undress for bed. He had been absent for four weeks; now the reckoning was at hand. But first she would let him rest.

She knew that she did not have him for long. Henry was being harried hither and yon throughout the West Country by Eustace and although the young prince always kept one step ahead of his enemy, and even managed to make some small gains, he was effectively pinned down and suffering. Oliver's arrival in Bristol was only to muster supplies for the garrisons at Marlborough and Devizes. The latter was Henry's base for the nonce. Catrin would have been there herself had it not been for Edon insisting that she stay for her lying-in. It was more obligation than willingness which caused Catrin to agree, but she would not have dreamed of refusing.

In the meantime, she did her best to control her fears for Oliver by keeping herself occupied. The bower was now very well supplied with unguents for plumping and softening the skin. There was enough cough syrup to cure an epidemic and so much staves-acre salve that no one in the keep had any excuse for being lousy.

Oliver slept on in the tub, his breathing becoming slow and deep. Catrin hated to wake him, but knew if she did not he would lie there until the water was stone cold. Taking a towel from the spit bar, she went to the tub and gently touched his shoulder.

He awoke with a jerk and a gasp of breath. Then his eyes slowly cleared from the smokiness of sleep and he reached for the towel. 'I don't know what a bed feels like any more,' he said. 'The times we are not running from Eustace, we are running to targets of our own, and when we do manage to sleep, it isn't for long. Henry thinks that sleep is a waste of time. He doesn't even sit down to eat but prowls round the hall with his food in his hand attending to business.'

'I thought you admired him for his energy,' Catrin murmured.

'I do. But sometimes I wish it was from a distance.' He stepped from the tub and glanced in distaste at the colour of the water.

'You're at a distance now.'

'For a day and a night.'

Taking the towel from him, she patted the droplets from his back, then lightly ran her fingertips over his skin. She was relieved to see that dirt and exhaustion were the only consequences of Prince Henry's regime. There were no new wounds over which to trouble. 'I've missed you,' she said.

'Dear God, that's the worst of it, being parted.' Turning, he caught her in his arms and kissed her. 'I was tired of fighting before, but now I am sick to the back teeth.'

Catrin kissed him back, her fingers in his sleek, damp hair. 'I am sick of it too,' she said, adding only half in jest; 'we could run away and open an alehouse like Godard and Edith.'

'Don't tempt me.'

They kissed again. His arm circled her waist and Catrin had to make a deliberate effort not to draw away. It was her guilt that made her think he would immediately detect her growing belly. 'As soon as Edon is delivered of her child, I will come to you at Devizes,' she said '. . . Under proper escort of course. And do not say that Devizes is no place for a woman because I will not listen.'

Oliver laughed ruefully. 'Do you remember when I first brought you to Bristol? You clung to my belt and stared around with frightened eyes? Now you think nothing of walking straight into the lion's mouth.'

'I have learned there are fates far worse.' She rubbed her face against his damp shoulder. Beneath her lips she felt the hard protrusion where the broken bone had healed. 'Listen, there is something I have to . . .'

With equal feelings of relief and disappointment, she stopped speaking as Rosamund skipped through the door. The little girl was carrying the flask of wine that Catrin had asked her to fetch. Rosamund pulled a face at the colour of the bath water and, having handed over the wine, sat down on the bed to play with her straw doll, cradling it like a baby.

'You were saying?' Oliver broke away to finish drying himself.

Catrin shook her head. 'I'll tell you later.'

Oliver glanced at the child and his lips twitched. 'Oh,' he said. 'Hardened gossip not fit for big ears.'

'My ears aren't big,' Rosamund piped up immediately, her eyes flashing with indignation.

Oliver leaned over and lightly pinched one between his forefinger and thumb. 'They are when it comes to listening!

If Prince Henry had you among his troops, we'd know when Stephen was blowing his nose up in York!'

'You wouldn't. It's not true. Mama, tell him!'

Laughing despite herself, Catrin intervened. 'Your papa means that you sit very quietly and listen very hard. That's a good thing to do, but sometimes people have things to say to each other that are private.'

Rosamund nodded, a serious frown between her eyes. She was a well-behaved child, easy to reason with but, by the same code, always needing a reason when sometimes there wasn't one. 'What's hardened gossip?' she asked.

Oliver choked and busied himself putting on his clothes.

'Something that grown people talk about when they shouldn't,' Catrin said, her face suffusing. 'And your papa is wrong. It's not gossip that I want to discuss with him.'

Oliver looked at her. Catrin gave him a tight smile and a little shake of her head.

To his credit, he did not pursue the matter but finished dressing and swung Rosamund up in his arms. 'Do you want to go into the town and see the market? Perhaps find some ribbons for your hair and a new brooch for your mother?'

Rosamund squealed with delight. Catrin smiled with pleasure, although there was a certain reserve in her expression. 'Do you not want to rest awhile? You fell sound asleep in the tub.'

Oliver sighed. 'There is nothing I would like better, but I do not have the time. I'm not going into the town just for the purgatory of escorting my womenfolk around the stalls. There are things I have to do for Henry; people to see, supplies to secure. Don't worry, I'll rest well tonight.'

With the news she had to give him, Catrin was not so sure of that, but she nodded and fetched her cloak.

The market place was heaving with people. As usual, the eel woman was crying her wares and, because it had become a kind of homecoming tradition, Oliver and Catrin bought a dozen while Rosamund looked on and pulled faces. Oliver went off to conduct his business leaving Catrin and Rosamund to browse among the stalls. Catrin bought some new needles and two wimple pins. For Rosamund there were some scarlet silk hair ribbons and a delicate little belt of silk braid woven with a traditional lozenge pattern. The sun beat down, but there was a fresh breeze off the river and everyone was in high good spirits. Rosamund danced from booth to booth with the eagle eye and indefatigable energy of a born bargain hunter. Catrin made a mental note to seek a man with a bottomless purse when the time came to find a mate for her daughter.

Oliver returned from his own excursion and bought Catrin a new cloak brooch of intricate Irish silver work, strong, but still delicate enough to be worn on a winter dress as well as a cloak. With much fluttering of her eyelashes, Rosamund managed to cozen a string of polished wooden beads out of him.

'I'm glad I won't be a languishing young man when you reach womanhood!' he said ruefully. 'You'd empty my pouch and cut my heartstrings in very short order!'

Rosamund gave him one of her grave, puzzled looks, but Catrin laughed and took his arm. 'I know exactly what you mean.'

The three of them wandered among the booths until they came to a cook stall that Ethel had always favoured. Here they bought spicy lamb pasties and little cakes made with honey and figs. To wash it down there was cider bought from a nearby stall and buttermilk for Rosamund.

Catrin was licking the last sticky crumbs from her fingers and sighing with satisfaction at the pleasure of the day thus far, when Geoffrey came thrusting through the crowd, his expression agitated.

'Found you at last,' he panted. 'Edon's in travail and calling for you. You must come quickly. The women say she's in much pain. There's a midwife with her, but it's you she wants.'

Catrin wiped her hands together and nodded. The idyll was at an end sooner than she had thought. She could not refuse Geoffrey. Indeed, he looked as much in need of a soothing tisane as his wife.

'Go,' Oliver said. 'I'll bring Rosamund home.'

Catrin kissed him, stooped to hug Rosamund and then hurried away with Geoffrey.

Rosamund gazed up at Oliver, her top lip beaded with cake crumbs. 'Can we go and look at the stalls over there?' she asked, pointing to the spice booths. 'Mama always lets me smell the things when we come to the market.'

Thankful that she had not asked him what 'travail' meant or why Edon was in pain, Oliver let her lead him like a lamb to the slaughter.

Catrin arrived at Edon's bedside to find her being comforted by two of Mabile's women while the midwife gently examined her.

'Edon, I'm here,' Catrin panted, out of breath from her dash. The women stood aside and Catrin stooped to take her friend's imploring outstretched hand. The fingers gripped with talon intensity. Edon's face was contorted with pain. She lay on a bed of birthing straw, her blond hair lank and wet, her belly a taut, distended mound.

The midwife already in attendance, Dame Sibell, was a thin, good-natured woman in early middle age with competent hands and humorous green eyes. Just now they were devoid of all sparkle. 'The afterbirth wants to come before the babe,' she said, wiping blood and oil from her hands.

Her gaze met Catrin's and she gave an infinitesimal shake of the head. When an afterbirth came first, the chances for mother and child were poor, and there was nothing that even the most skilled midwife could do.

'Send for the priest,' Catrin mouthed silently.

Dame Sibell signalled that it had already been done.

Catrin smoothed Edon's brow. Beneath her fingers the other woman's skin was clammy and grey.

'I'm glad you're here,' Edon whispered, trying to smile. 'I'll be all right now.'

'Yes, you'll be all right.' Catrin's voice almost cracked.

'There's something wrong, isn't there?'

Catrin swallowed. How could she tell Edon that her time was likely upon her? 'It is going to be a little difficult,' she said. 'The baby's lying awkwardly.'

Edon nodded. 'Like my first,' she said with a gritted smile. 'He came out feet first, remember? You and Ethel saved us both.' Her womb tightened and she arched with a cry of pain, her nails digging bloody little half moons into the back of Catrin's hand. Catrin bit her lip and prayed for God to be merciful and not let Edon suffer.

The contraction lessened, but Edon's womb remained hard. 'Thirsty,' she muttered.

Catrin gave Edon a sip of watered wine from the cup by the bedside and, as she helped to raise her, felt the racing, thready pulse against her palm.

'How long before it's born?' Edon asked.

'Not long.' Catrin compressed her lips, but still her chin wobbled.

Edon gave her a pain-glazed smile. 'Are you thinking that you have all this to endure when your own time comes?'

Catrin shook her head, too choked to speak. If the labour had been normal, she would have laughed and retorted that she had no intention of enduring any such thing, that Edon's labour was not hers. But how could she jest with a dying woman? She felt so helpless.

The priest arrived as another contraction shook Edon's body. Edon tried to scream as she saw him and realised what his presence meant, but she had no breath. Her blood gushed into the bedstraw. Dame Sibell exclaimed and grabbed a towel to stanch the flow, but it grew red and sodden in moments.

The priest flinched away in horror, but Catrin seized his wrist and dragged him forward to the bedside. 'Shrive her,' she commanded, her voice biting with anger and grief. 'Shrive her now while her soul is still in her body.'

His face contorted with shock and distaste, the priest set about his grim duty and, to his credit, did not linger over the rituals. '*Ego te absolvo ab omnibus censuris, et peccatis tuis, in nomine Patris et Filii et Spiritus Sancti,*' he gabbled, imprinting Edon's brow with holy oil. She rose against him, her teeth clenched, her eyes staring, and every muscle in her body rigid. There was another surge of blood from between her thighs and she shuddered violently in Catrin's arms. Then her body slumped. Her head fell against Catrin's shoulder and the slightest breath whispered past Catrin's ear. When Catrin lowered her gently to the bed, Edon's eyes were half-open and blind.

'The child,' Dame Sibell said. There was a sharp gutting knife in her hand.

Catrin glanced over her shoulder. 'Do what you must.' She had to swallow her gorge to speak. Edon, finicky, fussy Edon with her love of French romance tales and pretty fripperies, had died in her own blood and was now about to be opened up like an ox in the town shambles.

It was a midwife's obligation to save a child if she could, even after the mother had died. There was always the chance, albeit a remote one, that the infant was still alive. Catrin had seen Ethel do it twice. Both times the child had been dead and Catrin had a sure knowledge that Dame Sibell's efforts would be in vain too. She turned her head and looked at the wall as the woman made her incision.

'A little girl,' Dame Sibell announced, as she set aside the bloody knife and lifted the limp, bluish infant from Edon's torn body. 'There is no life in her.' She rubbed the baby clean in a towel and placed her beside her mother.

Catrin stared numbly at Edon's still, grey face and thought of their friendship. It had been sporadic and filled with flaws, but nonetheless genuine and she was going to miss her terribly. Earlier, Catrin had been on the verge of tears, but now they refused to flow, remaining behind her eyes as a hot and tingling pressure.

'What about the husband?' said Sibell. 'Who is going to tell him?'

Catrin swallowed. 'I will,' she said with a brief gesture.

'We'd best clean her up then. He can't see her like this.'

Catrin almost asked why not. In part it was Geoffrey's fault that she was dead. Appalled at the bitterness of the thought, she took herself to task. It was only Geoffrey's fault as much as it was Edon's. Blame nature; blame God. She had seen what the burden of guilt could do to a man whose wife had died in childbirth. Some husbands were unlikely to care less, but others were scarred for life. It was that very reason which had prevented her from telling Oliver about her own pregnancy. Now how much more difficult was it going to be?

Together, she and Dame Sibell disposed of the bloody bedstraw and washed and composed Edon's body. It wasn't just Geoffrey who had to be told, Catrin thought, a cold lump in the pit of her belly; it was their children too. She combed and braided Edon's hair. Once thick and heavy with a curl in its depth, it was like old straw and threaded with silver. Exhausted at eight-and-twenty. There but for the grace of God and Holy Saint Margaret.

Catrin gently kissed Edon's moist, cold brow and went to find Geoffrey.

It was worse than she could have imagined. At first he refused to believe her, as if denying her words would make them untrue. Then he insisted on seeing Edon.

'She's just asleep,' he said, his voice tight with precarious control as he looked at her on the bed, her hands clasped on her breast and her lids closed and smooth.

'I'm sorry, Geoffrey. The afterbirth came before the child. There was nothing we could do.' Catrin laid a tentative hand on his sleeve. Although she and Sibell had cleaned and composed Edon as best they could, no one in their right wits would have mistaken the grey-white tones of death for those of normal slumber. One of Mabile's other women had taken charge of the children, and she was glad for Geoffrey could not cope with himself at the moment, let alone five offspring.

'She's still warm.' He shook Edon's shoulder. 'Edon, wake up!'

Edon's head flopped on the bolster like a child's badly stuffed straw doll. One arm lost its position and dangled awry, sprawling across the dead baby. Appalled, Catrin tried to pull him away, but he thrust her aside and, when she renewed her efforts, he gave an almighty shove that flung her to the ground. 'Leave us alone!' he bellowed. 'What use is a midwife who doesn't know her trade!'

Catrin landed hard, but fortunately her hip and flank took the brunt of the fall. She was bruised and winded but otherwise uninjured.

Geoffrey shook his wife again and, when she did not respond, dragged her up against him, commanding her to rouse. 'Edon!' he howled.

'Geoffrey, for God's love she's dead!' Catrin wept from the floor.

He turned on her such a look of grief-torn loathing that she flinched. 'She trusted you and you betrayed her,' he said hoarsely. 'She thought no harm could come to her if you were at the birth.' His hand cupped the back of his wife's head; his other arm was banded around her limp spine.

'I cannot work miracles!' Catrin answered in a voice that shook with the effort of controlling her anger and grief. 'Her fate was sealed from the start; you're not being fair.'

'Fair? What has fairness got to do with anything!' he raged. 'Go away, leave us alone. We don't want you, we don't want anyone!' He buried his face in Edon's lank blond hair.

Catrin struggled to her feet. Her hip was numb and her ribs sore. She looked at Geoffrey. Silent tremors were ripping through him. His hands grasped and flexed on Edon's unresponsive flesh. He did not want anyone, but certainly he needed someone. And yet, for her own safety she feared to approach him. For one so gentle of nature, the violence in him was wild and unstable. One wrong touch or word and he would strike out again, perhaps with his sword.

Without a word, she left the room. The priest was waiting outside and some of Mabile's women, their eyes red and swollen. She warned everyone but the priest to keep their distance – after all, it was his duty to comfort the bereaved – and rubbing her hip, limped down to the hall to discover if Oliver had returned. He at least had weathered the storm once. The timing could not be worse to ask him to guide Geoffrey through the turbulence to calmer waters, but there was no help for it.

It was so late when Oliver came to bed that the castle folk who worked in the bakehouse and kitchens were stirring to begin the day's work and the summer dawn was paling the eastern sky.

'Christ in heaven, may I never spend such a night again,' Oliver murmured, as he sat down by the hearth and rubbed his face in his cupped hands. 'Is there any wine?'

Catrin had slept very little herself. The threat of one of her headaches probed the back of her eyes and her stomach was tied in knots. 'Just what's left in the jug.'

He reached across the hearth and picked up the small, glazed pitcher.

'How's Geoffrey?' Keeping her voice low, mindful of Rosamund asleep on the bed-bench, she wrapped her cloak over her shift and sat beside him.

'Asleep. No, that's not right. You can't call a wine-stupor sleep. I left him lying in the hall covered by his cloak – put him on his side so that he won't choke if he vomits. My brother did as much for me when Emma died.' He upended the pitcher to the dregs into a round-bellied cup and glanced at her in the dim dawn light. 'The only wisdom I had for him tonight was that of wine. What could I say? That after years of suffering it gradually eases? That he has their children? That I know how he feels? Where is the comfort in any of that?'

Catrin shook her head. 'There isn't any.'

'No, there isn't.' He swallowed the wine straight down and then grimaced at the cup. 'It brings it all back,' he said softly. 'I look at him and I see myself all those years ago. And I know that there is nothing I can do for him except ply him with drink and stop him from going out and picking a fight to ease his rage. Tomorrow it will be the same, and the day after that and the day after that. He will watch the soil drop on to her coffin and he will think about killing the grave diggers and dragging her out to try and waken her one final time.' As he spoke, his expression grew progressively more bleak.

'Don't,' Catrin said, a tremor in her voice. She brushed at her eyes.

'Friends and companions will surround him and he will curse them for keeping him away from her,' Oliver continued, as if he had not heard. 'He will hate her for dying; he will hate his children for looking like her and, most of all, he will hate himself for sowing the seed that killed her.' Very gently he put the cup down at the side of the hearth, but Catrin could tell that he had wanted desperately to throw it.

'One day he will begin to heal,' Oliver added, looking down at his hands, 'but it will not be for a long time, and he will carry the scars until his dying day.'

Catrin could bear the understated emotion and grief no more; she threw her arms around his neck and sat in his lap to be comforted. Oliver's arm tightened around her waist and he buried his face against her throat.

'Ah God, Catrin, why is it always so hard?'

To which she had no answer for she was about to make it harder yet. For a moment she remained quiet on his knee, summoning up the courage and fighting several quite plausible procrastinations.

'Oliver, there is something I have to tell you.' She cleared her throat. 'I have been trying to find the right moment. Indeed, I was going to tell you last night . . .'

'What?' He blinked. 'Oh yes, "the hardened gossip".' His voice was dull. 'Can it not wait?'

'I wish it could because now is not the time, but delay will only make things more difficult yet.'

She felt him tense. 'Is it about Louis?'

'No. Jesu, I don't even want to think of him, let alone talk.' Licking her lips, she drew a deep breath. 'Oliver, I am with child.'

He sat very still and the silence was deep, punctuated only by the soft sound of Rosamund's breathing.

'I was going to tell you sooner, but you were away with Prince Henry and I wanted to be sure that the signs were not false.'

'When will you be brought to bed?' he asked tightly.

The way he phrased the words was telling to Catrin. He did not mention the child, as most men would, but spoke instead in terms of the labour. 'I am not quite sure,' she said. 'Some time in December I think.'

There was another silence while he counted and then it was broken by his voice, fierce with anger but low-pitched to avoid waking the child. 'Then you are half-way through the carrying. Are you going to tell me that as a midwife you did not know?'

'We have been apart for almost four weeks,' she said defensively.

He pushed her off his lap and jerked to his feet. 'But still you must have known long before that.'

'Not enough to be sure,' she lied, but he turned round and outstared her.

'How much do you need to be sure?' he demanded. 'I thought that you did not travel well from Rouen to Carlisle. It wasn't just seasickness, was it?'

'I thought it was.'

He made a disgusted sound and went to stare out of the shelter entrance. 'You thought I would force you to stay in Rouen if you told me.'

'I swear on God's Holy Cross that I did not know for sure I was with child then. One missed flux does not make for a definite pregnancy, and there had been other times when my bleed was late.' Catrin bit her lip. She had been dreading telling him and now that she had, it was as bad as she had imagined. 'I did not want to trouble you too soon.'

'So you trouble me half-way through your term on the night that my friend's wife dies in childbirth,' he said roughly.

She heard the grit in his voice and saw how stiffly he was holding himself, the outline of his body blocking the light that was growing outside.

'Should I have left it longer?'

'Christ, you should have told me at the outset!' He whirled round and faced her with tear-glittered eyes and an anguished expression. 'It's time I could have had that has been time squandered!' Grabbing her arm, he drew her outside the shelter and stood her in the grey morning to look her up and down.

Instead of drawing herself up and sucking her stomach in, Catrin leaned back a little so that her belly showed against the folds of her gown. 'Not every woman dies in childbirth, else there would be few people in the world,' she said forcefully. 'It's as much a hazard as going to war. Edon died because her body was worn out. If a woman bears one baby after another, year in, year out, she is bound to suffer. Your wife died because her hips were too narrow to allow the child's passage.' She raised her palm to his face. 'I have neither of those difficulties; I am young and strong. You must have faith.'

'Even when it has been betrayed?' he said bitterly.

'What else is there to do?'

He shook his head. 'You could have taken . . .' He bit down on the end of the sentence and stared across the bailey.

But Catrin knew what he had been going to say. 'I could have taken a potion to bring on my flux?' She suppressed the urge to slap him across the face. 'Yes, I could, and it would have been as dangerous as childbirth itself. I would have been sick until I vomited blood; I would have purged my bowels and while losing the child I would have bled heavily from my womb.' Taking his hand, she pressed it against the mound of her belly. 'Yesterday I felt the first movement. This is our child, Oliver. It will live, I swear to you, and so will I.'

She felt his fingers tense as if he would draw away, but she held him there a moment longer so that word and sight and touch were inextricably combined. 'I swear,' she repeated firmly, fixing his gaze with her own.

With an inarticulate groan, Oliver pulled her into his arms and held her in a tight embrace. 'Then keep your oath,' he said, his voice rough with emotion, 'for if you do not, I will follow you into the afterlife and neither of us will ever have peace.'

'I will keep it, you'll see,' she said and, with soothing murmurs, led him inside and lay down with him on the narrow bed. For what little remained of the night, they lay in each other's arms and neither of them slept.

CHAPTER 32

Catrin gradually grew accustomed to Devizes. She missed Bristol for the river, the salt tang of the sea and the great array of trading vessels which had made purchase of every conceivable commodity a simple matter of going down to the wharves. She missed the familiarity of place and people, but she was not sorry to have left.

The women's bower in the castle had become a dolorous place since Edon's death, everyone cast into shocked mourning. Since the household was still grieving Earl Robert's death, the atmosphere had been unbearable.

Devizes was completely different. Here there was vast energy and bustle created by the red-haired young man in search of a crown. Henry was never still. Even if he physically stopped, his mind was whirling like a top. Those who surrounded him became charged with his vigour. They needed to be for Stephen and Eustace were like terriers after a rat, determined to seize Henry by the back of the neck and shake him until he was dead. They chased him hither and yon across the south-west, burning the harvests in the fields and slaughtering the livestock as they went.

Fortunately for Henry, if not the suffering people, allies such as Rannulf of Chester and Hugh of Norfolk created various diversions to draw Stephen and Eustace away when they came too close to their goal. Stephen turned north to Lincolnshire; Eustace to East Anglia. But the feeling of danger still crackled around Devizes like the air in a thunderstorm.

'Devon,' Oliver announced to Catrin, with a bemused shake of his head. 'In two days' time.' He sat on the bench that ran along the sidewall of their dwelling. They were renting a house owned by the monks at Reading. It had belonged to a merchant who, feeling his years, had exchanged it for a pension and care at the abbey.

'Henry is going to Devon?' Catrin turned from the cauldron, a ladle of stew poised over a bowl. She saw his eyes flicker over her body and then determinedly look away.

Despite the looseness of her robe, her pregnancy was unmistakable now. Privately, Catrin thought that if she grew any larger she would burst, but did not say as much to Oliver. He was so ridden by his fear that one word out of place was enough to tip him over the edge. She was not unduly bothered by her size for she felt healthy and strong. There was only a slight swelling of her ankles at the end of the day and the baby's kicks were so vigorous that she had no qualms about its well-being. Securing a good midwife was proving difficult, but she was not going to mention that to Oliver either. With Henry's army based in Devizes and so many camp followers and wives in the town, midwives were in great demand and short supply. Until she grew too large, Catrin had attended at several births herself and was still receiving enquiries which she had been forced to turn away.

'With Stephen and Eustace out of the way, Henry has plans of his own; while the terriers are away, the rat intends making some inroads of his own,' Oliver said. 'We're going to make a sally against Bridport.'

Catrin ladled the stew into the bowl and set it down in front of him. His gambeson, once cream, was a dirty charcoal grey from the constant wearing of his steel hauberk. A summer in the saddle had left him wire-thin. His hair was almost white and his skin was so sun-bronzed that the greyness of fatigue was undetectable. Nevertheless she knew that it was there. Prince Henry drove men so hard that the path behind him was littered with their broken debris.

'Is that wise?'

Oliver shrugged. 'We can likely take it, and there's a useful harbour. If matters go well, then we'll look to take other places.' He rubbed his eyes. 'But provisioning the men is hard. The grass has almost stopped growing in the fields so we have to transport fodder for the horses or commandeer it from the nearest friendly castle. Half the time they haven't got enough for themselves because of the wrecked harvests.' He dipped his spoon, stared at the stew, then ate it, but without relish. 'It's not going to win us a kingdom.'

'Then what is it going to do?'

'Prove to Stephen and Eustace that Henry's a thorn who refuses to be plucked from their sides. Prove to all witnesses that he can command men and go on the offensive even in the throes of being the underdog – and you know how much popular opinion loves an underdog. Henry milks that one for all it is worth.'

Catrin nodded. 'I can see the sense in that. But if it still is not going to win him a kingdom, what is the point?'

'It's laying the ground. It does not take a seer to foretell that we'll have to return to Normandy sooner or later. Henry needs more troops, more backing, more maturity.'

She went to the door and looked out on the narrow street. A group of children, Rosamund among them, were floating twigs in a puddle, thoroughly absorbed in their game. She called her daughter to come and eat, and as she watched Rosamund come skipping felt a lump in her throat. Six years old. In another six she would be growing into a woman and the baby in Catrin's womb would be the child that Rosamund was now. She could not bear to think that they might still be at war when that time came.

'I wish I did not have to leave you,' Oliver said, as she turned back into the room to ladle out a smaller bowl of stew for her daughter.

'And I wish you did not have to go, but there's no profit to be had in wishing.' She forced herself to smile. 'Perhaps it is for the best. If you stay, you will only spend your time worrying and demanding to know if I'm all right. With Prince Henry's supplies to look after, you'll have no leisure for anxiety.'

He echoed her smile but with less success. 'I don't need leisure for anxiety,' he said. 'It will hound me whether I am occupied or not.'

'I swear on Ethel's love knot that no harm will come to

me,' Catrin said steadily. 'I promised you a strong child and a healthy wife and mother to care for it, did I not? Just look to yourself. It will need a father too.'

Rosamund danced into the room, her gown soaked, her face and hands muddy. Her arrival ended the conversation as Catrin attended to her and Oliver resumed eating, but Catrin could still sense the currents of fear and anxiety as a tangible presence within the room. It didn't matter how many assurances each gave the other, the feeling of naked vulnerability remained.

'Twins, no doubt about it,' said Dame Sibell. 'I can feel a head here and here.' She laid her hand on Catrin's mountainous belly. 'Won't be long before your time either.'

The midwife was travelling to her niece's wedding in Ludgershall and was spending a week with her sister in Devizes before the two of them went to join the celebrations.

Catrin thought of her promise to Oliver. Bearing twins would make it more difficult to keep, but not impossible. Most women who bore two babies survived the experience, but there was a significant minority who did not. 'I am not surprised,' she said. 'I knew I was too large for my time just to be carrying the one, unless it was a giant.' Indeed, in a way she was relieved. She looked at Sibell. 'Can you stay for my confinement?'

The midwife pursed her lips, causing the fine spider lines surrounding them to deepen and pucker. 'I can be back here in a three-week,' she said, 'but I don't know as you'll last that long.'

'But will you come?'

'Aye, lass, if that's what you want.'

'It is.' Catrin struggled off the pallet. Her belly began under her breasts and was as round as a full moon. She had to lean over it to view her feet, and putting on shoes was a nightmare. She offered the midwife a cup of mead and listened politely to Dame Sibell's recounting of the family business that brought her away from Bristol. Then she asked after Geoffrey and his children.

'He's bearing it well to the world, but not within himself,'

Sibell said sombrely. 'The children have gone to stay with his cousin in Gloucester and he visits them when he can, but I think he finds more solace in the bottom of a cup just now.'

'Will it pass, do you think?'

'Only time and God can say.' Sibell crossed herself. 'At least he isn't hiding the grief away like some men. I keep thinking about the poor lass. There was nothing any of us could have done.'

'No.' Catrin laid her hand upon her belly and told herself fiercely that she was going to keep her promise to Oliver. For her sake, for his and Rosamund's. And Edon's memory.

Sibell finished the mead and took her leave, promising to return from Ludgershall as soon as she could.

The thought of twins in her mind, Catrin began sorting through her swaddling bands and linens to decide how much more she was going to need.

There was a sea-mist at dawn. Coughing, Oliver rose from sleep and found the entire camp bedewed in hoar. Soldiers faded in and out of the cloud like wraiths. The fires were damp and reluctant to burn, and everything had an other-worldly aspect. They were, after all, on the verge of King Arthur's old kingdom. Southwards lay Cornwall and the ruins of Tintagel that some said was once called Camelot.

Oliver was grateful for the fleece lining to his cloak for there was a biting chill in the air. Although full winter had yet to arrive, campaigning on its threshold was far from pleasant. His left arm ached and his fingertips were numb. Everything made of steel was streaked with rust.

For their pains they had taken Bridport as Henry had hoped, but other success had been elusive. Stephen's commander, de Tracy, had retreated behind his castle walls at Barnstaple, refusing to be drawn into open battle. Henry had pursued him doggedly but did not have the resources to crack open such a stronghold at one attempt. In retreating, de Tracy had burned everything in his path, leaving nothing for Henry's army to forage.

All that the cooking pot contained for breakfast was thin gruel. Being in command of supplies, Oliver was acutely sensitive about not taking more than his due. If there was no abuse, there could be no crime. He ladled some of the unappetising mixture into his bowl and thought with longing of Catrin's hearty stews, of hot hearth bricks, glowing logs, and the pleasure of a warm, dry bed.

The wistful pleasure of his thoughts was curtailed by a vision of Catrin stretched upon the rack of childbirth, her body arched, her belly mountainous with the child that she was unable to bear. The image was so vivid that he hissed through his teeth and, bowl in hand, went to kick awake the other men at his fire so that he was not alone with his fears.

After breaking his fast, he tended to Lucifer and went to find Henry. The mist was slowly clearing and men were gathered around the fires, warming their hands, spitting and coughing the winter damp from their lungs.

Henry was breaking his own fast with his cousin, Philip of Gloucester, and Roger, Earl of Hereford. Gruel was their fare too, but enriched with milk and sweetened with honey. To one side, a pretty young woman was daintily dipping a spoon into a bowl. She had silvery hair and a pink and cream complexion. Henry's cloak was wrapped around her body, keeping out the morning chill. Oliver marvelled anew at the Prince's ability to find attractive bed mates even in the middle of nowhere. A pity he could not conjure up oats, stockfish and wine while he was about it.

Oliver swept them a bow but before he could open his mouth, Henry pre-empted him with a wave of his horn spoon. 'Yes, Pascal, I know. We're short of everything but mist and rain; there are no friendly keeps within foraging distance, and nothing left to take from the land because de Tracy has burned it all.' He gestured Oliver to sit down. Henry himself remained standing, his shoulder pushed against the tent post. 'If we could take Barnstaple of course . . .' His grey eyes gleamed.

For one dreadful moment, Oliver thought that Henry might seriously be intending such a move, but the Prince gave a regretful shrug of his shoulders and sighed.

'Unfortunately, I don't have the force to do it – not this time at least. But I've sunk my teeth in and I will do so again.'

'So we're turning back?' Oliver asked, with a feeling of relief.

'Aye,' said Philip of Gloucester, and gave Henry a wry look. 'Although not without due consideration.' Despite being cousins there was no family resemblance. Philip had inherited Mabile's cow-brown eyes and he had Earl Robert's fine, dark hair and receding hair-line. He was an accomplished soldier but, like his father before him, not inclined to take risks unless pushed. His experience informed and balanced Henry's opinions and decisions. Roger of Hereford said nothing, but that was usual. His character was dour and quiet. Getting him to say anything at all was like prising open the jaws of a bull-baiting dog with a wooden spoon.

Henry set his bowl aside. 'You could obtain supplies if I wanted to keep up the campaign, couldn't you?' he asked Oliver.

'Only by sending to Bristol by coastal trader, sire. There is nothing here except what we carry. You could put the men on half rations and hope to find a few farms that have escaped the torch, but it makes for poor morale.'

'So you agree with the decision to turn back?'

'Yes, sire, I do.'

'Then you can escort the vanguard. Move out as soon as you can strike camp.' Henry ran his tongue around the inside of his mouth. 'I need not tell you that it falls to your duty as the commander of the van to find us a safe place to rest for the night and provender for man and beast.'

'No, sire,' Oliver said, managing to keep a blank expression. 'You need not tell me.'

Catrin winced at the amount that the cloth-trader was demanding for a loom length of plain, unbleached linen with which to make swaddling bands.

'Bad harvest,' he said, spreading his hands. 'Too much sun and rain at the wrong time. Add that to the burning of war and it don't leave a sight for weaving.' He rubbed the side of his nose and looked at her. 'Tell you what, since you're in need, mistress, I'll cut my own wrists and offer you the length for two shillings.'

Catrin shook her head. 'We have to eat,' she said, with a gesture at Rosamund who was wearing her oldest gown – one that was almost too short and had a patched hem. It was her playing gown, she had two others that were far better, but Catrin knew that traders always based their amount of profit on the customer's personal appearance. Of course, she did not want him to think that she was not worth the bother, so she had dressed herself neatly but plainly; a respectable townswoman who was prepared to buy but not to be fleeced.

'Can't sell it to you for less, but what about this bolt end?' He produced a fine piece of tawny wool with a thread of darker weave running through it. 'Make a dress for the little lass. Colour suits her a treat. I'll give it to you free of charge.'

Catrin pondered. It was his first offer and she could probably improve on it if she was prepared to bargain hard. Seeing a sale in the offing, the trader gave her his stool to rest upon. 'Take the weight off your feet,' he said with a kindly wink.

Catrin thanked him and offered him one and a half shillings. He shook his head and sucked his teeth, finally declaring that she was robbing him but he would accept one shilling and nine pennies.

'With the tawny wool thrown in?' Catrin said.

He laughed and scratched his head beneath his woollen hood. 'With the tawny wool thrown in,' he said. 'It's a good thing not all my customers drive such hard bargains. I have to eat too.'

Catrin took his complaint with a very large pinch of salt. Traders might have different ways of selling and their own line of banter, but some phrases were common to all. She paid over the coins and waited while he tied the linen and the wool into a bundle with a length of hemp twine. Rosamund was looking at the silks on the end of his stall and wistfully fingering a length of shimmering sea-green.

'Good taste for one so young,' the trader commented with a nod.

'Expensive tastes,' Catrin said, thinking that Rosamund had more than a touch of her father's love of luxury. Louis, whatever his failings, had also possessed an excellent sense of style and Rosamund had inherited this too.

'May she marry a rich husband and revisit my stall often,' the trader said, clasping his hands as if in prayer. There was a twinkle in his small brown eyes.

Catrin smiled in reply and went to drag Rosamund away from the silks. Now that she had her linen, she wanted to go home and rest her aching feet.

It was then that they heard the commotion and turned to see an agitated horseman riding among the market crowds, shouting at the top of his voice. His mount was lathered and its nostrils showed a crimson lining.

'Eustace!' the man bellowed, his voice raw and hoarse. 'Eustace is coming, save yourselves!'

Catrin and the cloth-trader looked at each other in stunned shock. 'Eustace is putting down a rising in East Anglia,' Catrin said faintly.

'He ain't if he's here.' The trader began to pack up his stall with rapid efficiency. 'Be a regular feather in his cap if he takes this place.'

The horseman rode closer to the cloth stall, still bellowing the alarm. 'Eustace and his army, not five miles away, hide while you can!'

'Not five miles means closer to three,' the trader said grimly. 'He's almost killed his horse getting here to warn us, but Eustace won't be travelling slow either.' He looked at Catrin. 'Where's your home and husband, mistress?'

'My home's near the castle, my husband's with Prince Henry,' Catrin answered in a distracted voice, and grabbed hold of Rosamund's hand.

'Do you want a ride there on my cart? You'll not be wanting to run anywhere.' He indicated her swollen belly.

Catrin thanked him gratefully and set about helping to pack up his bales. All around them other traders were hastily throwing their wares on to carts and across pack ponies, while the townspeople fled towards the safety of church and castle.

'God curse this damned war,' the trader muttered, as he backed his old cob up to the cart. 'My father was a cloth merchant in the days of old King Henry. You could travel from one end of the country to the other and know that you were not in danger. I've a son of my own at home – twelve years old. I dare not bring him into the towns for fear of happenings like this.'

Catrin lifted Rosamund on to the cart. Her belly felt tight and there was a low ache in the small of her spine. She pushed the sensations to the back of her mind. They might be a warning of the onset of labour, but by her reckoning she was not due for two more weeks at least and her first priority was getting herself and Rosamund to safety.

She clambered up beside Rosamund on to the bales of fabric. The trader sat on the front board and shook the reins. The cob took the weight and the cart rumbled forward on the road. The bumping of the wheels sent a squeezing sensation through Catrin's belly. She put her hand across it and found that her womb was as tight as a drum. The pain niggled in the small of her back. All around there were people running, stumbling, crying out in fear.

Rosamund was stroking one of the fabric bolts as if taking comfort from the slippery feel of silk beneath her small fingers. 'Prince Eustace won't catch us, will he, Mama?'

'No, of course not,' Catrin said rather too brightly. 'We'll be safe at the castle.'

'If they let us in,' the trader muttered under his breath.

Reaching the keep, however, was their first problem; every other citizen had had the same idea, and the way was blocked by carts, by people running with armfuls of belongings, by panicking horses and their frantic owners. The trader cursed and laid around with his whip, but to no avail.

Catrin picked up her bundle and beckoned to Rosamund. 'It's quicker to walk.' Laboriously, she clambered down off the cart. 'I wish you luck,' she said to the trader.

He shook his head grimly. ''Tis either my life, or my livelihood. One's no use without the other.'

Catrin left him struggling to inch his cart through the tide and joined the smaller flotsam of running people. They were jostled, bumped and buffeted. Rosamund began to cry. The dull ache in the small of Catrin's spine grew sharper and the tightness across her belly became pain. Despite her anxiety, her need to reach the haven of the castle, she had to rest against a house wall to wait out the contraction.

'Mama, what's wrong?' Rosamund's voice was high and frightened. 'I don't like it. I don't want Prince Eustace to come and get me!' She clutched Catrin's hand and began to wail.

Catrin bit her lip to stifle her gasp of pain. 'It's all right, no one's going to hurt you,' she panted when she could speak. 'I won't let anything happen, I promise.' She forced herself away from the wall and rejoined the crowd of running townspeople.

As they approached the castle's outer works, another contraction seized her in its grip and brought her up short with a bitten-off cry.

'Mama!' Rosamund screamed, her dark eyes wild with fear.

Catrin struggled with the pain. When she had borne Rosamund she had been in labour for a full day and the first spasms had been far apart and irregular. These assaulting her now were close together and much stronger. The labour looked as if it was going to be vigorous and short.

With relief, she saw a neighbour making her way towards the keep, her three children clinging to her skirts. The two boys and a girl were Rosamund's playmates and their father was a cook at the castle. Goda, their mother, wove braid and sold it to make belts and straps.

Catrin called out and Goda turned. A deeper look of concern crossed the woman's already anxious features.

'Catrin?'

'Will you take Rosamund with you?' Catrin panted 'I cannot run and I want her to be safe if anything should happen.'

The woman looked at the way Catrin's hand was pressed against her belly. 'God save you, mistress,' she said, 'of course I will.'

Catrin gave Rosamund a kiss and a swift hug. 'Go with Goda,' she commanded. 'I'll find you later.'

Rosamund's lower lip quivered, but she was an obedient child and had no reason to doubt her mother's word. Besides, Goda's daughter Alfreda was her best friend.

'You will be all right?' Goda asked, lingering but wanting to be gone.

Catrin made a small gesture and nodded. She could feel another contraction gathering and tightening. 'Yes, go. I'll follow you up.'

Goda told Rosamund to hold Alfreda's hand, and set off, tugging the children at a pace that was a half-run. Rosamund looked back over her shoulder and waved. Returning the wave, Catrin looked at the sweet oval of her daughter's face, the black hair curling round her cheeks where it had escaped its braid, and wondered if it was the last time she was ever going to see her.

Taking herself to task for such a negative thought, she forced her legs to move. When the contraction grew too fierce, she stopped to try and breathe through it. As the pain eased, she heard the first scream and, turning round, saw the plumes of smoke rising from the houses behind her.

There were more people running and screaming now. Those who had been in their homes, those who had not heard the warnings, now fled before the looters and the flames.

Catrin swallowed, tasting smoke as the wind drove the stink of burning thatch into her face. The castle was less than two furlongs away but unless she reached the safety of its walls, she would die. Terror drove her onwards step by staggering step, while behind her the sounds of destruction grew.

There was a sudden hot gush of liquid between her thighs as her waters broke, drenching her undergown and shoes. The contractions sharpened, growing hard and deep, doubling her over as she reached the outer ditch. As she screamed with the pain and dropped to her knees, the first soldiers rode up to the outerworks, their weapons red in their hands.

People scattered, wailing and screaming. Some fell beneath the chop of sword and mace. The contraction passed, but instead of struggling to her feet and trying to run, Catrin slumped to the ground and closed her eyes. It was freezing and wet, it was dangerous, but still safer than attempting to outrun the savagery of Eustace's troops. Her mind's eye filled with a vision of Penfoss burning under a lazy summer sky;

the rape and butchery; the stench of blood and eyes blank of mercy. Amice miscarrying. Oliver.

Another spasm hit her and she dug her fingernails into her palms and stifled her scream against the moist ground. The taste of mud was in her mouth, the crackle of flame and the brutal, metallic thud of warfare filled her ears. She was part of it, her body seared and torn by shattering pain. The roar of battle grew with the intensity of the contraction. A horse thundered past so close that mud sprayed from its hooves and spattered her face. She lifted her lids and saw feathered black hocks and heavy steel shoes. Swords clashed. There were grunts of effort, and then a dull thump followed by a gasp of pain. She raised her eyes and saw spurs dig into the black's flanks as the man astride wheeled him and rode out of her vision.

For a far too brief and grateful moment, Catrin was free of labour pains. She dared not move for fear of being struck down, so her vision was limited and what she saw confused her. The mounted soldiers had ceased to attack the fleeing townspeople and were fighting among themselves. She was so dazed that even when one of the men yelled 'Le Roi Henri!' at the top of his lungs, she did not understand at first.

It was only when she saw the distinctive brown and white patches of Richard FitzRoy's skewbald destrier and the red shield with its gold lion blazon that she realised their own troops had returned. Richard was staring round, his sword in his hand, his jaw with its edging of new black beard clenched and grim.

Catrin forced herself to her feet and screamed his name, but he didn't hear her. He was seeking Eustace's mercenaries, not a hysterical woman dripping with mud.

'Richard, for God's love help me!' she shrieked, but he was gone, spurring along the top of the ditch.

The next contraction hit, and an uncontrollable urge to push swelled down through Catrin's loins.

She lurched towards the outer wall, needing to brace herself. Another wave of mounted men ploughed into those already fighting amongst the outer works. There were more belligerent shouts of 'Le Roi Henri!' If she had not been in so much pain,

Catrin would have laughed. At least she had a guard while she gave birth.

Another red shield flashed, this one emblazoned with a gold cross. It was smaller and lighter than the great kite shields of his companions and he held it at a tilted angle as if his arm was tired. The horse was a steel grey, its coat made light silver by a thickening of winter hair.

'Oliver!' she screamed, putting the last of her voice and all of her will into the cry.

He turned his head. His eyes wandered as if he had heard something but was not sure what or from where. Then he saw her. His fist came up on the bridle and he tore the horse out of line. In one movement, scarcely before the animal had stopped, he was out of the saddle, shield and sword discarded as he gathered her in his arms.

'Christ, Catrin, what are you doing here?'

Her fingers dug into the cold, steel hauberk rivets. 'Bearing a child!' she panted.

'What!'

'No, that's a lie. Bearing two!' Grasping him for support, she rode out the next contraction. 'Oliver, I'm in travail!'

He stared frantically round. 'We'll get you inside the keep.' He started to lift her but she thrust him off.

'No time. Too late. Spread your horse blanket on the ground.'

'Christ, Catrin, you can't!' He gaped at her in sheer horror.

'Tell that to your offspring!' she gasped. 'Quickly, you'll have to help me, there's no one else!'

'I don't know what to do!' His voice rose and cracked.

'I'll show you.' She curled her fingers in his hauberk and pressed her forehead into his chest. The urge to push was unbearable.

With a gasp like a drowning man, Oliver left her to run to his horse and tug the blanket off the crupper. At the same time he yelled at the wide-eyed Richard to go and find some female help.

He spread the blanket against the palisade fence lining the ditch. Catrin propped herself against the stakes, her legs drawn high and wide and her skirts soaked with mud and birthing fluid.

'Jesu,' Oliver said hoarsely. His face was ashen.

'Tell me when the head is there. You will need to support it as it is born.'

Oliver swallowed. He felt sick. He wanted to run and hide. The nearest he had been to a birth was pacing up and down outside a closed bedchamber door while behind it Emma died. Now Catrin was demanding that he play midwife. He glanced over his shoulder in the forlorn hope that help might be at hand, but there were only more soldiers going brutally about the business of securing the keep's outerworks and driving Eustace's troops from the town. Smoke billowed and there was a sting of rain in the wind.

'Oliver!' she screamed, her spine rammed up against the wood of the palisade.

Her cry brought him reeling to his senses. With no one else to help them, he had no choice.

'It's all right, I'm here,' he said, in what he hoped was a reassuring voice, and knew that he would rather face heavy battle with his injured hand a hundred times over than crouch here now and watch Catrin suffer.

She grunted and strained, putting all her breath, all her will and effort, into pushing the baby into the world. Wet and dark, the head crowned at the birth entrance.

'It's here,' Oliver said and reached out. Catrin was biting her lip and her face was flushed with exertion, but her eyes were lucid and fierce on his, demanding his attention.

'Is the cord clear?'

'It's not around the neck. Sweet Christ, its eyes are open!'

'Wouldn't yours be?' Catrin panted. 'Now the shoulders, take the shoulders. Don't pull on the cord.'

Once the shoulders were out, the rest of the baby followed in a slippery rush and Oliver only just kept hold of his off-spring. 'A boy,' he said, on a note full of stunned surprise at the swiftness with which matters had progressed. The baby regarded him, a similar, if more myopic, expression on its face, then yelled lustily and waved its tiny arms. Removing his cloak, he wrapped it around the infant and laid it beside

Catrin. The cord still pulsed between her thighs. Her belly looked little smaller than it had done before. Blood smeared her flesh and welled around the birth passage but the flow was not copious.

'You see, I promised you,' she said, with a tremulous smile.

'Jesu God, I don't want any more promises in this fashion!' Oliver retorted, a quiver in his voice. His eyes went from her to the crying baby. He could feel his limbs weakening. In a moment he was going to collapse.

'Wait, it's not finished yet,' she said sharply as she saw him waver. 'Did you not hear me say that there were two of them?'

Oliver licked his lips. 'Two?' he said hoarsely.

She nodded, unable to speak, and braced herself against the palisade. 'Pull gently on the cord, the first afterbirth's coming.'

By the time two women from the castle finally arrived, so had Oliver and Catrin's second son. He was a little smaller than his older brother but just as loud. Hands trembling with shock and relief, Oliver wrapped him with the first one and gazed at their two crumpled little faces side by side.

'Twins,' he said numbly. 'Jesu, Catrin. Even to deliver one would have been a baptism by fire.'

'So now you are thoroughly scoured.' Through the weariness, her voice held a note of triumph. 'You need never fear again.'

He rubbed his hands over his face. 'I wouldn't say that. I tell you, if men had to bear children the human race would quickly come to an end.' But there was a gleam of satisfaction in his grey eyes. The very fact that he had been able to do something, instead of standing helplessly outside a locked door, had been a catharsis.

Crying and exclaiming over Catrin's state, the women bundled her into warm blankets and gave her wine to drink. Richard had possessed the foresight to send out two men with a rope stretcher and, in no time, Catrin was lifted up and borne with her new sons into the keep.

Prince Henry, still in his mail, his red hair rumpled from

wearing a coif, came striding across the hall to look as mother and babies were carried through. 'Born against the palisade wall in the pouring rain and delivered by their father; that marks them out as unusual from the beginning.' He smiled at Oliver. 'Name the eldest Henry, and I'll stand godfather to them both.'

It was not an offer that Oliver was about to refuse. A royal godfather was a giant step up fortune's ladder. 'I was going to do as much, sire,' he said gracefully, and bowed.

'Just as long as you don't name the second one Eustace.' Henry's smile became a grin, although there was a hint of a snarl at its edges. Eustace had almost seized Devizes. Although he had been thwarted and his mercenaries had taken a battering from Henry's troops, houses and livelihoods had been destroyed and Eustace had proved that he could strike right at the heart of Henry's defences.

'My wife has the gift of his naming, sire,' Oliver replied, with a tender look at Catrin.

'Then what say you, mistress?'

'Simon,' Catrin said immediately. 'For Oliver's brother, killed in the first years of the strife.'

Henry nodded and looked pleased. Across the hall Roger of Hereford beckoned his attention and, with a parting murmur of congratulation, he strode off.

Catrin was conducted to a small wall-chamber where she was cleaned, tended and left to rest with her new-born sons.

On his way out to find Rosamund and bring her to see her new brothers, Oliver paused on the threshold and gazed at Catrin and the babies, one either side of her on the pallet.

'What?' She raised heavy lids to look at him.

Oliver shook his head and smiled. 'I was just thinking that once I had nothing but dregs in my cup and now it's full to the brim.'

She smiled back at him. 'So is mine,' she said.

CHAPTER 33

APRIL 1153

Chicken stew bubbled gently in the cauldron, the steam enriched by the scent of cider and herbs. Outside the alehouse, a rainy April dusk was settling over the land. Inside it was cosy, the main room glowing with warm red light from the lantern and the fire.

Catrin gave a small sigh of contentment. 'It is good to be back in England,' she told Edith, and cast her glance around the cosy room. 'And I always feel at home here.'

'So you should,' Edith replied. 'You know there's always a welcome for you and Lord Oliver at our hearth.' Her hands were floury as she rolled herb dumplings to add to the stew.

Catrin smiled her gratitude and for a while just sat and gazed into the fire, absorbing the warmth and comfort. Outside Oliver, Godard and the children were looking at a mare and her new-born foal. Catrin savoured her moment of peace. Not that she would be without Rosamund and the boys, but it was pleasant to have a respite.

Edith plopped the dumplings into the stew and wiped her hands on a linen cloth. 'So, where have you been?' she asked with genuine curiosity. She had no desire to travel beyond her own backyard, but she had a lively interest in the experiences of those daring enough to venture further afield.

Catrin clasped her hands around her raised knees. 'You know that the twins were born at the fight for Devizes?'

Edith clucked her tongue. 'Aye, in a ditch, so Godard heard when he went to Bristol for news.'

Catrin laughed. 'Not quite – on the outer palisade with Oliver acting as midwife, the houses burning and rain pelting down.'

Edith folded her arms and hitched her vast bosom. 'The wonder is that you all survived,' she said, with a shake of her head. 'You'd never think to look at those two little lads that they had such a start in life.'

'A start that made Prince Henry their godfather and brought them more christening gifts than we could stow in our baggage. They've become a sort of talisman – proof of success against the odds. It's an ill wind, Edith.'

'Aye, I suppose it is.' Edith sucked her teeth and nodded as she absorbed the words. Then she cast a bright glance at Catrin. 'Well, where did you go after Devizes?'

Catrin frowned in thought. 'As I remember, they were less than three weeks old when we crossed the Narrow Sea to Normandy. Henry needed more resources. We were too small in number to have a hope of defeating Stephen.' She gave a little shiver of remembrance and hugged herself. 'It was the middle of winter, freezing, raining and rough. The sea crossing alone made what happened in Devizes seem like a summer picnic.'

'And you only three weeks out of childbed? Girl, you must have been mad,' Edith snorted.

Catrin smiled. 'I thought that myself by the time we reached dry land.' She slipped another piece of split wood beneath the cauldron and watched the flames explore its sides. 'I was so sick that I would have paid a fortune to anyone willing to throw me overboard.'

Edith clucked her tongue, tut-tutting at the detail whilst relishing it all the same. 'I suppose you lived in Rouen like before?'

Catrin shrugged. 'For a time. Mostly we followed the court through Normandy and Anjou.' Her eyes gleamed. 'I saw Henry's father, the man they called Geoffrey le Bel because of his great beauty.'

'And was he beautiful?'

'As an angel,' Catrin sighed. 'Not that he acted like one. He had a cutting wit and he used it without mercy, but that was part of his glamour. He died of a chill after bathing in the river Seine on his way back from Paris.'

'You went to Paris too?' Edith's eyes widened.

Catrin nodded. 'We went with Henry and his father to the court of King Louis.' She pulled a face. 'I would not like to live there.'

'Why not?'

Catrin pursed her lips and considered. 'At first it took your breath – all the colour and richness,' she said, exploring her reasons as she spoke. 'King Louis had a book and the cover was inlaid with jewels as big as pigeon eggs and his tunic was embroidered all over with clusters of pearl. But after a while, it became stifling. We had to stand on ceremony all the time, and what lay under the silks and jewels was not so fine. With Henry there is no show, no sham. He can face the world in an old hunting tunic; he doesn't need a silk robe to make him royal.'

'Did you see Eleanor of Aquitaine?' Edith's voice was eager.

Catrin smiled. 'Yes, I saw her.'

'Don't tease, what is she like?'

Eleanor of Aquitaine had until recently been the Queen of France. King Louis had divorced her because she had given him two daughters when he was desperate for a son. He was serious of demeanour with no leavening of humour to brighten his nature. Eleanor, a great heiress, was his opposite. Glamour, scandal and mystery followed her like an exotic perfume. Prince Henry had seized his opportunity and married the newly divorced Eleanor, thus acquiring for himself vast areas of south-west France. He was nineteen years old and she was thirty. Everyone knew about the match. It was the stuff of rumours and ballads and the news had filtered to every corner of the realm.

'Well,' Catrin pursed her lips in consideration. 'She has black hair and greenish-brown eyes set on a slant. She's tall and slim and she has a voice that sounds as if she's been inhaling smoke for a week.'

Edith sniffed. 'That doesn't sound promising. I'd heard that she was the most beautiful woman in Christendom.'

'Not if you are judging beauty by silky yellow hair, blue eyes and rosebud lips,' Catrin said bluntly. 'But she has something more enduring than beauty – a sort of allure that will still be with her when she's an old, old woman and all the ordinary "beauties" have long since lost their attraction. You would have to see her to understand it. All the men are besotted with her, and the women try to copy her mannerisms and style of dress.'

'Is Oliver smitten then?' Edith asked mischievously.

Catrin laughed. 'He won't go near enough to find out. He watches her from a distance the way he would watch a lioness. And I think he's right. She can snarl as well as purr.'

Edith gently stirred the dumplings in the stew. 'Like you then,' she said.

'Oh, no, I don't have her glamour,' Catrin denied. 'And no desire to wrap any man around my little finger.'

'Not even Oliver?' Edith gave her a sceptical look.

Catrin frowned. 'I hope that whatever Oliver does is of his own free will. To manipulate him would be dishonest.'

'So you think Eleanor's dishonest?'

'No. But what suits her, does not suit me.'

Silence fell again while Edith continued to gently stir the dumplings and prevent them from sticking to the bottom of the cauldron.

'All this travelling hither and yon,' she said after a while. 'Do you not wish that you could stop and settle?'

'With all my heart,' Catrin said wistfully. 'It is true that I could live in Bristol or Rouen, but how often would I see Oliver then? His sons would grow up hardly knowing their father. I know it is the way that many women live, but it would not do for me.'

'Yes, I can understand that,' Edith murmured. 'Godard and I work side by side and share all our tasks. I ran this alehouse alone for five years after my first husband died, but I cannot imagine being without Godard now.'

Catrin pursed her lips. 'If Henry prevails, then Oliver might regain his lands, but nothing is certain. We live each day as it comes.'

'You think Henry will prevail this time, on his third attempt?'

'I think that neither will prevail unless they come to a truce,' Catrin said thoughtfully. 'Stephen's barons cleave to him out of friendship and loyalty, but they do not cleave to Eustace in the same way. They want Henry to be our next king, so it is my guess that they will keep from outright confrontation. There will be little fights and skirmishes – grapples for position – but in the end the barons will decide, and they will decide for Henry.'

'Then I pray sooner rather than later,' Edith said.

Catrin crossed herself. 'Amen to that.'

The women's moment of peace was ended by the sound of excited voices. The door flung open and two small boys burst into the room like dervishes, Rosamund chasing close behind. In their wake, Godard and Oliver strolled together, talking.

'Mama, we seed the foal!' announced Henry, and climbed on to Catrin, forcing her to lower her knees and pull him into her lap. Not only did he possess his royal godfather's name, he also seemed to have more than his share of the Prince's ebullient personality. His hair was a light copper-blond and his eyes were Catrin's hazel.

'Did you, sweetheart?'

Henry nodded vigorously and launched into a spate of description which his vocabulary could not quite encompass. Simon, black-haired and grey-eyed, tried to help him. The little voices rose in a crescendo. Rosamund grimaced and stuck her fingers in her ears.

'Quiet!' Oliver bellowed, his own voice rising above all others.

A deathly silence fell, but it was a telling one. The boys neither cried nor cowered but looked at their father with round, reproachful eyes.

'Better,' Oliver said with a stern look and a stiff nod, although a twitch of his lips almost betrayed him. 'What will our hosts think of your manners?'

Edith's eyes crinkled as she smiled. 'Oh, we're accustomed to it,' she said, 'although our clients have usually consumed a jug of ale before they become as loud. Don't come down on the mites too hard. It's good to hear them.'

'Mites about sums them up,' Oliver said, but tugged Rosamund's braid to show that he was jesting and swept Simon up in his arms. 'Noisy mites.'

'Would you rather be without them and have silence?' Edith said.

Oliver kissed his son. 'Even at their loudest they hold me to sanity. I would rather they sat as good as gold for more than one minute, but when you're three years old that is just too much to expect.'

They all sat down to dine on Edith's chicken stew. Henry and Simon tucked in with a will and did not make too much mess. They were robust children, large for their age and taking after Oliver in bone and build. Rosamund, dainty and dark, mopped up what mess they did make and behaved with a ladylike grace that filled Catrin with pride – and Oliver too. She could see it in his grey glance. Despite the conflict life was good, she told herself, and in time it would be better yet.

That night she and Oliver bedded down in the room where they had lain before, in the days when the dormitory had been a barn. The boys slept entwined on a heap of straw, protected from its prickle by a sheepskin fleece. Rosamund slumbered beside them, the sound of her breathing mingling in soft counterpoint with theirs.

'Bristol on the morrow,' Oliver murmured against Catrin's hair.

She smiled and snuggled against him. 'Eel stew,' she answered, and felt the silent laughter in his chest. He wrapped her in his arms and they pressed hip to hip, mouth to mouth. Since the children had grown, they had become experts at making love in silence and taking opportunities when they arose.

It was ironic, Catrin thought as Oliver pushed into her and she clasped her legs around him, that Louis had demanded she cry and moan for him, and that now she was constrained to utter silence. She clutched Oliver and bucked, her teeth clenched, her throat tight and her loins dissolving. It had been too long between opportunities. His mouth covered hers in a frantic kiss and they shuddered together, each absorbing the other's pleasure with every surge until they were spent.

He raised on his elbows and nibbled the salt sweat from the hollow of her throat. Catrin closed her eyes and arched her neck. The feel of him still within her sent small after-quivers of pleasure through her flesh.

'Bristol tomorrow,' Oliver repeated.

'Eel stew,' she said, stifling a giggle.

'Henry will not be there above a week, but he'll be using it as one of his bases. I want you and the children to stay there while I'm gone.'

Catrin opened her eyes and studied his face in the strip of moonlight filtering through the window space. 'For safety's sake?' she said neutrally.

'Until we are sure that Stephen is well and truly muzzled by his barons. I would not want another Devizes to happen.'

She rubbed her leg along his and adopted the purring tone that she had heard Eleanor of Aquitaine use when flirting with men. 'Fortunate then that you are bribing me with old haunts, else I might not stay.'

His teeth closed gently on the skin of her throat. 'I know that you're safe there – that nothing can happen.'

'So you would rather that I had the worry than you?'

'If there is fighting, I won't be involved,' he said, a trifle impatiently. 'I'll be with the baggage carts. If Stephen gets that far in a battle, we're all lost anyway.'

'Is that supposed to reassure me?'

'Of course it is.' His lips returned to hers, silky and persuasive. 'I won't be in any danger, I just don't know how quickly Henry might need to move. We cannot afford a large baggage train.'

'Ah, then you don't want me.'

'Catrin!' he whispered with exasperation.

Laughing, she curled her arms around his neck. 'First you have your will, then you have your way.'

He pinched her. She stifled a yelp. Rosamund made a little sound in her sleep and turned over with a sigh.

Catrin held her breath. Oliver withdrew and rolled on to his back. Rosamund's breathing resumed its regular pattern.

To make amends, Catrin snuggled up to Oliver and laid her arm over him.

He reached down for her hand and tucked it against his breast with a drowsy murmur of contentment.

Catrin was tired too, but she lay awake for a while longer savouring the peace, the sweet scent of herbs and new hay, the sense of security and well-being. She wanted to hold the moment, to fix it in her memory, to bind it in a charm.

As she fell asleep, her other hand clutched Ethel's woven knot on its leather cord around her neck.

CHAPTER 34

BRISTOL, APRIL 1153

Louis sat in a corner of The Mermaid nursing his wine and watching the clientele. For the most part they were sailors, or men with the scarred, weather-beaten countenances of soldiers. Men like himself, except for the fickle roll of fortune's dice.

Louis was still handsome. The Holy Land had whittled the boyishness from his smile and salted his hair with grey, but it had enhanced rather than diminished his looks. Playful had become dangerous and, as always, he attracted women like a magnetic stone attracted iron.

He looked down at his hands, at the clipped nails and tanned brown fingers. These days he examined them often to reassure himself that there was nothing to see, that no one but himself knew of the legacy he had brought home from the Holy Land, although he had come to the conclusion that there was nothing in the least holy about it. To the contrary, it was the domain of the Devil.

His descent into hell had been the bequeathing of the woman he had met by the pool of Siloam. He had taken her body, her silk robe clinging, diaphanous with the sweat of lust. He had dwelt in her house, luxuriated in every pleasure and vice imaginable; gorged himself upon the wealth she earned from other men. She was a courtesan, the midnight consort of the wealthy officials and prelates who served the King of Jerusalem. She had almond-shaped dark eyes outlined in kohl, honey-golden skin and a lithe, sinuous body that could wrap and tighten around a man like a snake. Now she was nothing but dust and bones. Her name was

Jasmine. She had given him everything – including his own slow death.

He clenched his hands into fists, but that made his knuckle bones gleam beneath the skin, reminding him all too potently of his fate. He snatched his cup and gulped down the wine. As a matter of habit he had ordered the best that The Mermaid had to offer, but he would not have noticed had it been vinegar.

The door swung open and Ewan thrust into the crowded alehouse, ushering before him a nondescript man of middle years with sandy hair and a sparse yellow beard.

'About time,' Louis hissed beneath his breath, and signalled one of the serving maids to bring another jug of wine.

Ewan brought the man to Louis's trestle and was dismissed by a flick of the lean brown fingers.

'You are Adam the apothecary?'

The maid set a fresh jug on the trestle and a second drinking cup. Louis paid her with a glance and a smile from habit.

'Aye,' the man nodded cautiously. 'What's your business with me?'

'A remedy.' Louis poured the rich red wine and pushed the new cup across to his guest. 'I have heard that you are skilled in making medicines.'

'That I am.' Adam took a drink from his cup and pinched his upper lip to remove drops from his moustache. His light blue eyes were wary. 'A remedy for what?'

'I need to have your oath of secrecy first.'

Adam blinked several times rapidly. 'That will add to the cost of my services.'

'I can pay.' Louis fished in his pouch. Whereas before he had brought out a common silver halfpenny for the girl now, under cover of his cupped palm so that only the apothecary should see, he displayed a bezant of solid gold.

The lids fluttered like a butterfly beating at a window.

'One of these now, one when you've made the potion.'

Adam reached out. Louis snatched his hand away and closed his fist over the gold. 'But only if you swear to hold your tongue.'

'I would be mad not to swear,' Adam said with a breathless laugh.

'Aye, you would, because the alternative to you holding your tongue is me cutting it out on the edge of my sword.' Louis tapped his hilt for emphasis.

The apothecary paled and swallowed, but greed overcame caution. 'I swear,' he said, and held out his hand.

Louis palmed him the coin, a fierce look in his dark eyes. 'Then you are committed,' he said, and took another long drink of his wine as if it was red lifeblood. Then he banged the cup down on the trestle. 'It's not for me, you understand, I'm acting on behalf of a friend.'

'Of course.' Adam inclined his head and stroked his pouch where the gold now rested.

Still reluctant at giving his fate into another's hand, Louis produced a scrap of vellum from his pouch. 'These are the ingredients,' he said with a frown. He had no idea what they were for he could neither read nor write. He had purchased the remedy from a fellow traveller on the ship home, who had assured him that the mixture worked on a whole range of diseases.

'As a remedy for what?'

'Scrofula.' Louis forced himself not to rub his wrist where there was a patch of lichen-like white skin, frilled with red at its edges. Scrofula was acceptable. Leprosy was not. Leprosy would make him an outcast, dependent on charity for his existence. It would eat away his good looks and there would be no one but other lepers to see. When they rolled him unceremoniously in his grave, perhaps many suffering years from now, it would not be as Louis le Loup, leader of men, or Louis le Colps, lover of women. It would not be as Louis de Grosmont, confidant of kings, or even Lewis of Chepstow, grandson of a groom. It would be as Louis the Leper, despised outcast.

'Ah, scrofula,' the apothecary repeated, with an exaggerated nod to show that he was playing along but not in the least fooled. He scanned the list of ingredients, murmuring to himself and nodding. 'Pennywort, sorrel, St John's wort, grey lichen . . . yes, I have all those.' His voice fell to a mumble as he took in the other ingredients, nodding at each one. But then suddenly he stopped and a look of utter revulsion crossed his face.

'This I do not have and I cannot obtain it for you,' he said.

'Why not, what is it?' Louis leaned forward, panic tightening in his chest.

'The fat from a stillborn infant, rendered down and used to carry the rest of the ingredients.'

Louis felt a brief queasiness in his gut, but a gulp of wine and his desperate need quelled his own sensibilities. 'And if I obtain it for you?'

The apothecary swallowed and shook his head. 'It is against all Christian law. If either of us was discovered, we would be hanged from the nearest gibbet.'

'We won't be discovered. You need have no fear. I will get the ingredient – all you will have to do is mix it with the others. The risk will be all mine, and you will be handsomely paid.'

'I . . . I do not know.'

'Then give me back the gold and I will find someone else who is willing.'

Adam touched his pouch and frowned and twitched. But he could not bring his hand to reach inside and throw the money back. 'It is wrong,' he said.

'Why?' Louis shrugged. 'The infant doesn't need its fat if it is dead.'

'Where are you going to find a midwife willing to risk herself too?'

'God in heaven, man, have you seen it out there?' Louis threw his arm wide. 'Prince Henry's army, Gloucester's army, all their allies. Where there are fighting men there are whores, and where there are whores there are midwives. I'll find one.' He held out his hand. 'Now, my gold returned, or your final agreement.'

The apothecary gnawed his lower lip and finally clasped Louis's hand for the briefest of moments. 'Agreed,' he said stiffly. 'Bring me the ingredient when you have it.' Looking sick, he rose to his feet, surreptitiously wiping his palm on his thigh.

When he had gone, Ewan came and sat at the trestle to finish the jug of wine with his master. Louis had told him nothing about his ailment and Ewan had never sought to probe, on the principle that thinking beyond orders caused nothing but worry and moral dilemmas.

'Where do we go after this?' he asked. 'Are you still planning to hire out with Prince Henry?'

Louis raised the cup to his lips, drank and swallowed. 'Tomorrow,' he said. 'I'll not get further than a hurling in the dust if I go to recruit smelling of wine. The first impression is the one that lingers. Go, do what you want with the rest of the day.'

Ewan grinned wolfishly. 'If it's all the same, I'll stay here.'

'As you please.' Louis tossed a silver penny on the table and, leaving The Mermaid, went out to wander Bristol's bustling heart, a place in which he had not set foot since he was a young garrison soldier of one-and-twenty, bringing his bride to buy fripperies and small items for their home.

Jesu, it was so long ago. A lifetime. A lifetime of wandering and squandering. What would it have been like if he could only have set his will to the grindstone at Wickham? Would it have rewarded him with satisfaction and even greater honours, or would he have grown to hate it? The latter, he thought. Wealth and status he enjoyed, but not the responsibilities which came with them. He had spent most of his life cultivating the former and shedding the latter.

He made his way to the wharves to watch the vessels loading and unloading their cargoes – wines from Gascony and Burgundy, bundles of Irish flax and five Irish mares – and trading barges from upriver with cargoes of iron from the forges in the forest. He inhaled the sharp, salt air and savoured the textures of life, an overwhelming anger growing within him.

He was a part of the great flow and he had no intention of being stranded above the tideline and left to rot by the disease consuming him.

'Do you think ill of me?' Geoffrey FitzMar looked sidelong at Catrin.

'Why should I?' They were sitting on a bench facing the herb garden that lay at the side of the dwelling. Philip of Gloucester had given Geoffrey the house to live in and an income of rents from three others in recognition of his services.

It was pleasant and sunny, sheltered from the wind. Eight children ranging in age from twelve to three years old, her own among them, romped in the orchard at the foot of the garth. With them was a young woman, neatly dressed, plain of feature, but with a lovely smile brightening her face as she threw a ball for one of the girls to catch. Her laugh rang out, clear and happy.

'It is not so long since Edon died. Perhaps you think that I do not respect her memory by marrying again so soon.'

Catrin watched her small sons twinkle in and out of the trees. 'It is three years,' she murmured. 'What you do is your own business. And no, I think that you honour her memory by doing as you have.'

'Truly?' He looked at her anxiously.

'Truly.' She gave his hand a squeeze and smiled. Most men would not care what others thought. Most men had hides so tough that it took a spear to pierce them, but not Geoffrey. It was probably the reason why he and Oliver were friends. There were times when each irritated the other beyond bearing, but there were bonds of similarity too. 'Look at all the years that Oliver wasted in recrimination and mourning. Better to grieve and then to move on.'

He nodded. 'I try, but I still do grieve for Edon, you know, even though I have Miriel – and it hurts.'

'I miss her too,' Catrin murmured. 'She was always part of my return to Bristol, and now she's not here.'

'It was my fault that she died,' Geoffrey said bleakly.

'It was the will of God.'

His smile was grim. 'I tried telling myself that, but it led me down the path to heresy. I asked a priest why it was God's will, and he said that it was ours not to reason why. So are we not to think for ourselves but to follow in blind faith?' He shook his head. 'It's easier to blame myself for lust than God for failing.'

'Geoffrey . . .' She touched his arm, unsure what to say.

'I can live with it,' he said. 'When it becomes too dark for me to bear alone, Miriel is there, and I have my children.'

Catrin bit her lip. 'And supposing Miriel quickens with child. How long have you been wed?'

'A six-month,' he replied. 'She looks young, does she not, but she's eight-and-twenty. Since the age of fifteen she has been widowed once and cast aside once.'

'Cast aside?' Catrin regarded Geoffrey's new wife with a spark of sympathy having herself been abandoned twice by the same man. 'Whatever for?'

'Being barren,' Geoffrey said expressionlessly. 'Her first, widowed, marriage lasted five years without children and her second match bore no fruit either. Barren soil rather than barren seed. Whatever I sow cannot grow and destroy the place where it was planted.'

Catrin felt both sorry for him and relieved. 'I wish you both well,' she murmured. 'With all my heart I do.'

The sunset was a striking silver-streaked pink, overlaid by streamers of charcoal and rust. Oliver paused in his examination of a pack horse to watch it and thought about stopping to eat. Henry was preparing to ride on to Gloucester to hold his Easter court. There was so much to do and so little time to accomplish it all.

'Fine evening,' greeted Humfrey de Glanville, pausing on his way across the bailey. He was one of Henry's recruiting masters, and Oliver knew and liked him well. They had frequently worked together, their respective positions in Henry's household making them allies and fellow sufferers.

Oliver nodded agreement and for a moment the two men watched the sunset flame and darken over the estuary. Oliver told his companion that he was inspecting the pack ponies before he sent them off to an outlying manor to collect supplies.

'It's like feeding a bottomless pit,' he said with a grimace.

The weather creases at Humfrey's eye corners deepened. 'Aye, I know what you mean.'

'Hire any new men worth their salt today?' Oliver asked.

Having recruited in the past, he knew how difficult the task was. The dross came anyway, lured by the promise of plunder and pay. Finding steady soldiers of good calibre, who would not break at the first testing, was somewhat more difficult.

Humfrey shrugged and rubbed his grey-salted beard. 'Most were of the usual sort. Welsh youngsters in search of adventure and scarce old enough to grow a beard between them. Men with mouths to feed and no other way of doing it. Others who think that Prince Henry's footsteps are printed in gold.'

Oliver grunted in sympathy.

'There were a couple who intrigued me though.' Humfrey scratched his nose. 'Adventurers I'd say, after plunder and prestige, but they'd got a sharper edge than the others. A knight and his servant.'

'Oh?'

'Claimed to be returned crusaders and it's likely true. The knight had a red cross sewn on his cloak and they were both as brown as nuts.'

Oliver raised his brows with interest. 'Did they say for whom they fought before their crusade?'

Humfrey grinned and shook his head. 'No, they avoided that one with more agility than a pair of maypole dancers. I suspect that they've always sold their swords where it has been to their best advantage. No shame in that I know, but I am not entirely sure that they will honour their part of the bargain with loyalty. It could be that if it comes to a fight, they will break as easily as a couple of raw Welsh lads.'

'But you hired them anyway?'

'Yes, I hired them, but if you asked me why, I could not tell you.' A puzzled, slightly irritated, look crossed Humfrey's face. 'This is the first time in my life that I've been persuaded to ignore my doubts by a silver tongue. Louis le Pelerin will bear watching.'

Oliver took his eyes off the sunset. 'Louis le Pelerin?' he repeated, feeling the familiar wrench in his gut as he heard the first name.

'That was what he said.' Humfrey looked at him curiously. 'Why, do you know him?'

Oliver shook his head. 'I hope not. Describe him to me – and his companion too.'

'Not above average height, lean and wiry,' Humfrey said in the manner of someone accustomed to summing up the points of men and horses both. 'Black hair, black eyes, scar on the cheekbone. Dresses like an earl – far better garments than either you or I possess. No common soldier could afford to wear a tunic of dark blue wool beneath his armour.'

Oliver began to feel sick. He clenched his fists. 'And the other one? Let me guess. Is he a red-haired Welshman called Ewan?'

Humfrey's eyes widened. 'You know them?'

Oliver swallowed jerkily. 'Yes, I know them. Christ Jesu, Humfrey, do not take them into the Prince's employ. Louis le Pelerin as he calls himself is worth only six feet of fresh soil to bury his perfidious corpse.'

Humfrey continued to stare.

Oliver cleared his throat and spat. 'His true name is Lewis of Chepstow, and if he comes within range of my blade, I will kill him.' His voice quivered with rage, but beneath that rage was a terrible fear made all the more potent for the length of time it had been brewing. At some dark, unconscious level of his mind, he had always known that Louis would return and try to claim what was his by law even though he had no right.

'What has he done?'

Oliver shut his eyes and forced control upon himself. When he opened them on Humfrey, they were expressionless storm-grey. 'It is a personal matter,' he said woodenly. 'Of honour and common decency. Suffice to say that he is faithless. You would do better to put your trust in quicksand.'

Humfrey stirred his toe in the dust and sucked his teeth. 'Very well, I will dismiss him on the morrow, and the Welsh-man too, but I would still like to know your reason. It is not enough to say that he is faithless when we are so short of men.'

Oliver drew a deep breath. 'He was one of Stephen's mercenaries at the time of the battle of Winchester.'

'So much he told me,' Humfrey nodded. 'He said that he

had grown sick of the war and joined the crusade instead because it had more point.'

'He joined the crusade,' Oliver bit out, 'because Stephen had entrusted him with a keep that he did not have the backbone to hold. He abandoned it under siege – rode out and left his wife and baby daughter to face the consequences. When he left he told them he was going for aid, but he had no intention of returning.'

Humfrey eyed him keenly. 'You know a great deal of the matter.'

'That is because his wife and daughter are now with me.'

Humfrey's jaw dropped. 'Catrin and Rosamund. I thought that they belonged to y—'

'Everyone thinks that,' Oliver cut across him savagely. 'Even those who know the truth have almost forgotten. They think us husband and wife, as close as this!' He raised two crossed fingers before Humfrey's startled eyes. 'If you only knew the heartache and suffering he has caused. So help me God, I will run a sword through his heart rather than march at his side.'

'All right, I have said I will dismiss him. Calm yourself.' Humfrey held up a placatory hand. 'Come, we'll go to the hall and eat.'

Oliver breathed out hard and scooped his hands through his hair. He was no longer ravenous. All he felt was sick and angry and afraid. 'No, I have to go home to Catrin and Rosamund.'

Humfrey nodded reluctantly. 'Do you want me to come with you?'

'No,' Oliver said tersely, then, with an effort, forced himself to be civil. 'My thanks, Humfrey, but you attend to your concerns and I will attend to mine.'

'Don't do anything rash,' the knight warned with troubled eyes. 'A sword through this man's heart will be as much your death as his.'

'You think so?' Oliver raised his brows. 'He put a sword through mine ten years ago. Wouldn't you say that the reckoning is long overdue?'

'Oliver . . .'

'But if I seek him out and kill him, his dishonour will become mine.' His mouth was bitter. 'Either way, I pay the price.'

Agatha the laundress deposited the basket of fresh linen on the trestle. 'All done,' she declared. 'Since you've returned to Bristol, you've been one of my best customers.'

Catrin gave her a rueful smile as she paid Agatha for her work. 'Some would say that I'm a dreadful spendthrift for washing chemises and shirts more than twice a year.'

'Not me,' Agatha chuckled, putting the coins in her pouch. 'And I'll tell you something else. The knights who pay me to wash their shirts and drawers the most often are the ones who have the success where women are concerned. Who wants to get close to someone who smells like a gong farmer?' She glanced around the room. 'Fine house,' she nodded. 'Ethel would have liked it here.'

'We've rented it from Geoffrey FitzMar,' Catrin said, joining Agatha in her admiration of the spacious proportions afforded by the cruck frame. 'Oliver's riding on soon, but I'm staying here with the children until the army returns.' She offered Agatha a cup of wine. The laundress's eyes gleamed and she plumped down on a stool.

'Just a cup,' she said, 'else I won't be fit to do my work. After all the sadness that Geoffrey FitzMar's had, it's good to see him back on his feet again.'

They sat and talked for a while. Of Geoffrey, of the war, of women's things. Rosamund proudly showed Agatha her braid weaving and a scrap of wool embroidery she had been doing. The boys clamoured to be jiggled on her ample lap.

There was a knock at the door. Cup in hand, a smile on her lips, Catrin opened it upon a townsman – one of the poorer citizens who earned his living from holding horses, carrying baggage and running errands. She knew him vaguely, for on a couple of occasions he had been sent to fetch her to a childbirth.

'Eldred, isn't it?' she said.

'Aye, mistress, that it is.' His teeth were yellow and little more than worn-down stumps in the gum. He poked his head round the door. 'Morning, Mistress Agatha.'

'Morning, Eldred,' she replied, with obvious irritation.

'What can I do for you?' Catrin asked.

Eldred eyed the wine but was not so foolish as to chance his luck. 'I been asked to find a midwife, one as knows her trade. I knew you was back in Bristol, word gets around. I said as I'd bring you straight away if I could.' He sleeved a drip from his nose and sniffed loudly. An overpowering stink of midden heaps wafted from his garments. Another of his occupations was sorting through the town's rubbish for items still of use and Catrin suspected that his clothes were some of the finds. Her nose told her for a fact that he had never paid a laundress in his life.

'Now? The woman is labouring now?' Catrin lifted her cloak from the peg in the wall.

Eldred shrugged and spread his grimy hands. 'I reckon so. Didn't see her, only the husband, but he were trembling like a leaf. He pays well – be worth your while.'

'Agatha, will you look after Rosamund and the boys until myself or Oliver returns?'

'Aye, mistress, go on with you.' The older woman waved her hand. 'Where be you going in case we have to find you?'

'Wharf Alley,' Eldred said. 'In the middle, atween the cookshop and the bathhouse.'

With that they were gone. Agatha frowned after the closed door and pursed her lips.

While Wharf Alley was not the worst area in Bristol, neither was it the most salubrious. In between the houses of the merchants and craftworkers, there were bakeries and cookshops. There were also taverns and bathhouses. A man could have a meal, get drunk and find a whore all without walking more than thirty yards. He could be robbed and tossed in the river within the same distance too.

'This house,' said Eldred, halting before a dwelling that was squeezed in the middle of two larger establishments. Its daub and wattle walls had recently been limewashed and the thatch was also new.

'Belongs to the folk at the bathhouse,' Eldred confided. 'They bought it off the widow who used to live there. Rent it out now, they do.'

Catrin eyed the house as Eldred banged on the door. It was the sort of place that men used for assignations with their mistresses, rather than renting as a domestic home. Perhaps the mistress was in labour.

Eldred's knock was answered by the red-haired Welshman.

'I brought the midwife like your master wanted,' he announced.

Catrin did not recognise Ewan at first, except to know that she had seen him somewhere before. By the time she did, she was over the threshold and putting down the hood of her cloak.

'Ewan?' Her eyes widened.

So did the soldier's before he rounded on Eldred. 'What trickery is this?' he snarled.

Eldred stared in bewilderment. 'No trickery,' he said. 'You asked for a midwife, I said I could find you one and here she is. You owe me my fee.' He extended his hand.

'You're owed nothing,' Ewan growled.

Catrin felt weak and disoriented with shock. Ewan's master could only be Louis. Mother of God, after all these years. He flitted in and out of her life like a destructive spirit; wreaking havoc and leaving her to pick up the pieces, only to reappear and dash them to the ground again in ever more fragile shards. She laid her hand on Eldred's indignant sleeve.

'Escort me home, Eldred,' she said, with as much calm as she could muster. 'I myself will pay your fee.' She turned to the door.

'That will not be necessary,' Louis said quietly, and barred her way. 'Master Eldred, I thank you.' He gave the messenger a silver halfpenny and, setting his hand on Catrin's shoulder to detain her, stood aside to let the man depart. Then he closed the door.

But for the thought of the woman she had been brought to aid, Catrin would have thrust him off and hastened after Eldred. She glared at her husband. 'I was summoned to attend at a childbirth,' she said. 'I suppose some other unfortunate woman has fallen victim to your charm.'

Louis looked hurt. 'Why do you always think the worst of me, Catty?'

'Because I know now that there is no better,' she retorted. 'And my name is Catrin. What are you doing in Bristol, Lewis?'

He shrugged and smiled, familiar gestures which had once sent a pang through her, but now filled her with distaste. They were affected, not charming. 'The same as everyone else. Paying court to Prince Henry, our future King.'

'Why, do you think he might give you a castle to ruin?'

A scowl marred his brow. 'You've still got the claws, I see.'

'I don't suffer fools gladly. Show me to the woman in travail or else let me go.' She set her hand on the door latch.

'There isn't a woman in travail,' Louis said. 'The need for a midwife is my own. I did not know that the old beggar would bring you.'

'What?' Catrin gazed at him and wondered if he had lost his wits. 'Why should you want a midwife?'

Louis flicked a glance at Ewan. 'Go next door and amuse yourself,' he said, flipping the soldier a coin. 'I want to talk privately with my wife.'

'I am not your wife,' Catrin said coldly. 'You gave up that right when you rode out of Wickham and left me and a tiny baby to face the siege.'

'You are mine in the eyes of the Church.'

'But not in my own and that is all that matters.'

Eyes lowered, Ewan opened the door and stepped out into the street. Catrin started after him, but Louis was quicker and leaped in front of her, his extended arm barring her way.

Filled with loathing and a spark of fear, Catrin drew herself up. 'Let me go,' she hissed. 'For whatever purpose you want a midwife, find someone else. I owe you neither loyalty nor service.'

'Then what about pity, Catrin?' His voice softened and filled with pathos. 'Can you not find it within you to pity me?'

'No, I can't,' she answered savagely, but was aware of a betraying spark of uncertainty.

Louis perceived and sprang upon it immediately. 'I do not believe that. Your heart was always tender even if the shell was of steel.' He bowed his head. 'I'm dying. That's why I sent Ewan away; he doesn't know. You'll be rid of me sooner than you know.'

'Dying?' Catrin did not know whether to laugh or be appalled, to believe or to doubt. 'I can see nothing wrong with you.' She couldn't. He was lean and tanned, with all the vibrancy she remembered.

'Then look again.'

She followed his gaze along the outstretched arm barring her from freedom and saw on the bare skin of his wrist a raw patch about the size of a brooch.

'Leprosy,' he said, lowering his arm and turning it to show her the sore in more detail. 'The crusader's plague. I took the cross to atone for my sins and it took my life. Pity me, Catrin. Lie in your warm, adulterous bed and think of me at the roadside in beggar's rags with a clapper bell for my bedmate and the cry of "Unclean!" on my lips.'

She shook her head and swallowed, her gaze drawn in fascination to the raw skin with its scummy, grey edges. She had often seen lepers before, had thrown them quarter and halfpennies for charity's sake, but always from a distance. They clothed themselves in voluminous robes to conceal the desecration wrought on their bodies by the disease, but she had seen enough sores to know the signs.

'Go if you want.' He stood aside, leaving her way free to the wet street outside. 'Go back to your life and pretend that we were ships that passed in the night, that we never had this collision.'

'I'm sorry, I'm so sorry,' she whispered. Handsome, vain Louis with his need for adulation, his delight in all things sensual. It was the cruellest end that fate could have devised. Although the doorway yawned, she found it impossible to walk out.

'So am I.' He pulled his sleeve down over the sore. 'I understand that it creeps slowly; that it will be a while before it reaches my fingers and causes them to rot. For the present, at least, I can hide the sore, live among other men and make my way in the world. But soon enough that will change.' He gave her a mocking look. 'Now do you pity me?'

Catrin clenched her fists. She felt compassion and loathing in equal proportions. It was typical of Louis that he would rather infect others with the disease than sacrifice his own way of living. 'What good would it be to you if I did?'

The mocking expression vanished and in its place came a pleading look through which calculation glimmered. 'For pity's sake you might help me to live.'

'Why should I do that when it would be of more benefit to me to have you dead?'

His smile was more than half grimace as he shut the open door. 'Conscience, Catty, your bleeding conscience. I don't have one, but you always had enough for both of us. That's why you didn't walk out when I gave you the chance.'

She bit her lip, knowing that he was right and as always he had found a weakness and exploited it. 'I know of no cure for leprosy,' she said. 'There is nothing I can do for you.'

'But there is. The physicians in the Holy Land are more learned than any here. They know of all manner of remedies that we have not even begun to comprehend.' His eyes gleamed.

'I know that there is a great healing tradition among the peoples of Araby,' Catrin answered. 'Ethel taught me many of their ways. But I know of none for leprosy.' She wondered what his intention was. Why did he need a midwife when a physician was the more obvious choice? A niggling suspicion began to grow in her mind, but it was so preposterous that she did not allow it to surface.

'Then the wise-woman did not teach you everything; she

was not as wise as she thought.' Louis smiled and folded his arms, but she could see that it was a façade, that he was trembling with suppressed fear or excitement.

'What do you want?' she demanded, suddenly impatient. 'Bleeding conscience or not, I swear I will leave. I have my man and my children waiting at home.'

'Then you are fortunate. All I have is Ewan and my rotting flesh,' he replied with a curl of his lip. 'How is my daughter?'

'If you had stayed, you would know,' Catrin said contemptuously. 'You can lay as little claim to her as you lay to me, and that is nothing.'

He snorted, and looked away. 'I do not blame you for being bitter, Catty, but at least have a little charity.'

'I'm not bitter; I'm happy,' she retorted. 'Rosamund is flourishing and bids fair to be a beauty, and I have two fine sons. Oliver and I are greatly content. As to charity . . . If all you have is Ewan and your rotting flesh, then you have only yourself to blame. Now tell me what it is you want from me and let me go.' She took a step towards the door to emphasise her point. From outside came the sound of hurrying footsteps in the rain. They faded away down the street. Next door the cook-stall owner was riddling out his brick oven.

'The cure for leprosy is an ointment made up of several ingredients,' Louis said against the backdrop of the muted, familiar sound. 'All of them but one can be obtained by an apothecary . . .'

'All but one?' Catrin repeated, and the hair began to rise on the nape of her neck.

He unfolded his arms and braced them on the trestle. 'I need the fat rendered from a stillborn infant,' he said. 'Only a midwife can obtain it for me.'

'Jesu God!' Catrin stared at him in utter revulsion. 'I knew that you loved yourself, but I did not realise that it was to the perdition of your very soul! The answer is no!'

'I need it, Catty, I have to have it and I can pay – in gold.' He waved his hand. 'Christ, don't look at me like that. What does it matter if the child's dead? It doesn't need its fat. Even if it's buried intact, the worms will feast on the flesh and leave only bones.'

Catrin struggled not to retch, but it was no use. She staggered over to a corner and heaved. She had dwelt with the dark side of Louis's personality at Wickham, but never had she guessed its true depths. It was sacrilege but he gave it no more importance than the butchering of an animal. A lamb to the slaughter. She swallowed and swallowed again, her mind filled with the images of children she had delivered. Of Rosamund and the twins, red and bawling from her womb. Of Edon's slashed body and the grey, dead baby.

'I thought your stomach was stronger than that,' he said behind her. 'All I am asking is that you procure me a dead new-born. Bring it to me and I will do the rest.'

Catrin thought that she was going to faint. For a moment the world whirled and blackened. She clutched the wall and drew slow, deep breaths. 'Even to ask such a thing puts you on the road to hell,' she said, hearing her own voice as if from a distance.

'If I do not find a cure, I will be in hell,' he answered desperately. 'I will pay you in gold bezants, Catty.'

'Not all the coin in the world would buy my services for such a deed.'

There was a long silence behind her, then he said, 'What if I give you an annulment to our marriage so that you can wed Pascal? What if I obtained a dispensation from the Church?'

There was an instant, the tiniest flash when, to her utter revulsion, Catrin felt herself respond, and because of that her abhorrence redoubled. He offered her what she wanted at a cost beyond paying. 'Perhaps you don't have leprosy,' she said, gritting her teeth. 'Perhaps it is just your rotten soul bursting through your skin.' She turned and faced him, her complexion ashen. 'I want neither your money nor your bribes nor any part of you.'

They stared at each other. Then he lowered his eyes and shrugged. 'I thought you would have more compassion, but I see I was wrong. I can expect more from a stranger.' His mouth twitched in a bitter smile. 'Never fret, Catty, I'll find someone less self-righteous who can be bought.'

Catrin stepped to the door and set her hand on the latch. Although she was trembling inside, her movements were decisive. 'Not here,' she said, 'not in Bristol. I will tell every other midwife about you, and then I will go and tell the sheriff. By that time you will be on board an Irish galley or as far away from here as your horse can gallop.' Her gaze was cold and bright. 'If you are not, then you will hang.'

'You wouldn't do that.' His voice was uncertain.

'Watch me,' she said, jerked the door open, and banged out into the rainy street.

Louis stared at the door and listened to the echoes of its slamming. His first emotion was disbelief that she had threatened him and then walked out, leaving him no time for the final word. Hard on the heels of disbelief came anger and then, because he was Louis, outrage. She was his wife, she had no right to gainsay his will. He should have forced her to her knees and beaten her into submission rather than offering her rewards and reason. He had not liked the way she said that she was going to warn the other midwives in the city and then seek out the sheriff. If she did that he would become a fugitive, no longer the hunter but the hunted, as much for the disease as his request for a cure. No one would tolerate a leper in their community.

'Bitch,' Louis swore. He grabbed his sword belt from against the wall and flung open the door. She had to be stopped.

Catrin ran, uncaring of the puddles which soaked her feet and splashed the hem of her gown. Raindrops and tears mingled on her face. The wind was cold, but the chills that shook her body were of shock. To have encountered Louis under ordinary circumstances would have been difficult enough, but this last meeting had been hellish. Again and again she heard him describe what he wanted in that smiling, reasonable voice that suggested she was the one at fault. The details rolled around in her head. If she stopped running, she knew she would begin retching again.

'Catrin, wait!'

She turned round, narrowing her eyes against the needle

slant of the rain. Louis was waving at her and running up the thoroughfare. He wore no cloak, his dark head was bare but, despite having no time to dress for the weather, he had put on his sword belt.

That was enough warning. If she waited, she would be dead. Whirling, she began to run, at the same time drawing her satchel forward and groping inside it for the knife Oliver had given her. If he caught up with her, she would use it. Memories of Randal de Mohun swept through her mind. She saw herself cornered again, and felt the wind of the blade and then the fiery pain in her side. Louis would not kill her in full view of witnesses. He would catch her, drag her into some Shambles alley and silence her there. It was easily done. She had almost been a victim once before. She was not going to be a victim now.

Running in skirts was difficult. Heavy and wet, the hem slapped against her legs. People looked at her curiously. Even in these parts of the city, a running woman was a sight to be remarked upon. Behind her she could hear Louis panting in her wake and knew without looking round that he was gaining on her. He had always been fleet of foot and her own neighbourhood and the castle seemed impossibly far away. Before her, the church of Saint Nicholas rose against the fortified city wall and she redoubled her effort. If she could reach the sanctuary of its interior, she would be safe.

'Stop her, stop the whore!' Louis's shout pursued her, nipping at her heels. 'Thieving bitch has stolen my pouch, stop her!'

A man stepped out in front of Catrin, his arms outspread to do just that. Catrin sobbed and ducked. His fingers closed on her wimple and for a choking moment he yanked her back. Then the fabric gave, her black braids tumbled down, and she was free and running. But the check had given Louis precious yards and she knew that she was not going to reach the precincts of the church.

'She's gone to a birth in Wharf Alley,' Agatha replied to Oliver's enquiry. 'Don't know how long she'll be. Eldred fetched her 'bout an hour ago.' She tilted her head to one side and eyed him anxiously. 'Is there something amiss, my lord?'

Oliver looked at the plump old woman, at his sons sharing her lap. Henry with Catrin's hazel eyes, Simon with grey like him. Rosamund sat at their feet, absorbed in braiding five loops of wool. She was dark and bright like Louis and Oliver had no intention of giving her up to him. Catrin neither. And he did not care what it cost. 'Yes, there is,' he said. 'I need to see Catrin now. Will you stay and tend the children a while longer?'

'Of course, my lord.' There was naked curiosity in her gaze, and then fear as he took his sword from the coffer and laced it on to his belt.

'Wharf Alley you said?'

Agatha swallowed. 'Yes, my lord. Halfway down next to the bathhouse.'

With a last glance at the laundress and his children, Oliver went out. The rain whispered in the wind, soft as cobwebs, and the sky was a clinging grey. He turned down Corn Street and headed towards the river. As he strode, he rehearsed what he was going to say to Catrin. His initial impulse was born of instinct not reason. He only knew that Louis's presence was dangerous and that he needed to have Catrin at his side, as close as Adam's rib. He had to see her, hold and touch her and know that Louis was powerless.

Although he was sure of Catrin, he had a supernatural dread that Louis would still find some way of winning her back. The thought made him quicken his pace and swear softly under his breath. As he reached St Nicholas Street and turned right, his hand was on his sword hilt, and those who encountered him stepped rapidly out of his way.

'Stop her, stop the whore!'

The cry pierced his concentration. His eyes flickered to the left and he saw a woman running, her stride desperate with no space for decorum. In the same instant, he realised it was Catrin and that she was being run down by Louis like a wolf after a doe. A man stepped out to bar her way, and her wimple tore off in his hand. Catrin's black braids streamed down her back. She ran, and then she whirled to face her pursuers, her knife at the ready.

Oliver drew his sword from his scabbard as he sprinted. 'Halt in the name of Prince Henry!' he bellowed.

The citizen who had grabbed Catrin's wimple splashed to a halt just out of her knife range. His face was congested with excitement and exertion. 'It's this whore, sir, she's stole the man's pouch!'

'Oliver!' Catrin sobbed in relief, but kept her knife tilted. Louis jammed to a halt and looked at Oliver with feverish, glittering eyes. Oliver returned the stare implacably. His rage and fear had burned beyond heat and become a flame, ice-cold and steady.

'The lady is no whore but a gentlewoman held in great esteem by the Prince himself,' he said, without taking his gaze from Louis. 'The man who makes the claim is faithless, mercenary scum.'

'So says the adulterer, the stealer of another man's wife and child!' Louis sneered.

'Do not prate to me of stealing,' Oliver said tight-lipped. 'You have compromised your own honour so many times that not even a miracle would unstain its tarnish . . . or perhaps you were honourless to begin.' The sword flickered suggestively.

Louis looked at the gesture and a sour smile crossed his face. He raised his own weapon.

'No!' Catrin clutched Oliver's sleeve. 'He's not worth it. Let him go!'

'To haunt us again and again?' Oliver said grimly. 'In my esteem, he is definitely worth a shroud and six feet of earth.'

'It doesn't matter, he's dying anyway, that's why he . . .'

Before she could finish, Louis spun on his heel, pushed through the crowd which had gathered and ran back down the narrow street.

'It matters to me,' Oliver said with soft intensity. 'When I have touched his corpse with my own hand then I will be content.' Unlocking her grip from his arm, he sprinted after Louis.

'Oh, Jesus Christ in Heaven!' Catrin snatched her wimple from the townsman and chased after the men. Whatever Louis had done; whatever he was, she did not want his blood on Oliver's hands.

Louis was fast. He had always been fleet of foot and possessed excellent stamina, but Oliver was fit and fast too. He was taller with a longer stride and he had not already run half-way through town. As they reached the bridge leading across to the open suburbs on the other side of the Avon, Oliver finally caught up with Louis and brought him crashing down.

The men rolled in the mud and dung. Louis was as fast and slippery as a Severn eel and, although Oliver had landed on top, succeeded in wriggling free.

'She'll always be mine,' he panted, as he lunged to his feet. 'You can't change it whatever you do.' He lashed out viciously with his boot.

Oliver ducked the blow and brought him down again by snatching his ankle. This time his knife was out of his belt.

Louis's eyes widened, not with fear but with feral excitement. 'Go on, kill me,' he panted, daring Oliver with a broad, white grin. 'Have your will and then watch her cry for me.'

Oliver gazed down into the hot brown eyes and revulsion burned his gullet. For a moment, he imagined the satisfaction of slitting Louis's throat. The triumph would be intense but last only as long as it took spilled blood to cool. In death, Louis would have won far more convincingly than in life.

Withdrawing the knife, he sat back on his heels. 'No,' he said softly. 'You're not worth it. A clean, quick death is too easy for you.'

The exultation died in Louis's eyes and, incongruously, Oliver saw a flicker of the fear that had been absent before.

'Perhaps I will just follow you, as you have followed me,' Oliver murmured, turning the knife over in his hand. 'Dark corners, black winter nights will never be safe again.'

Louis laughed with bitter humour. 'Such a threat might frighten a child, but not the damned,' he mocked, still taunting, his eyes on the knife like a drunkard's on a fresh flagon of wine.

A crowd had started to gather. Catrin elbowed her way through and reached the scene. There was shouting now. A trader with a cart wanted to pass over the bridge before the gates closed for nightfall, and soldiers were strolling up from the other end, spears at the ready.

'Ask her,' Louis said. 'Ask her what she wants.' Backing away from the knife, he pulled himself up and smiled at Catrin. 'What should he do, Catty? Rip out my heart or set me free?' He spread his hands. 'The choice is yours.'

Catrin clenched her fists. She looked at her husband and then at Oliver, who was breathing swiftly. While her eyes were on him, Oliver sheathed the knife.

'The choice was mine.' Going to Catrin's side, he slipped his arm around her waist. Then, turning to Louis, he said, 'I intended to kill you. Perhaps if you hadn't demanded it quite so hard I would have done it. Now it doesn't matter. There are always dark nights and quiet corners, Louis – for the damned as well as the innocent.' He glanced towards the advancing guards. Louis did too, and then at the crowd blocking the town end of the bridge.

'Go on, Lewis of Chepstow, take your freedom. I won't stop you.'

Louis swallowed. He opened and closed his fists. Catrin began to speak, but Oliver silenced her with a nudge.

'What's the trouble?' one of the guards demanded, then touched his helmet to Oliver as he recognised him through the mud and the gathering gloom of dusk. 'Sir,' he acknowledged.

'Nothing,' Oliver replied, his gaze upon Catrin's husband. 'A confusion over name and identity.'

The rain whispered down and the cart driver yelled at Louis to get out of his way.

Louis turned in a slow circle meeting the gaze of everyone, lingering upon Oliver with derision and finally closing on Catrin as if they were alone in a bedchamber. 'Do you remember Chepstow, Catty?' he asked huskily, 'That first year?'

She said nothing, but bit her lip and leaned into Oliver's

body for protection, her knuckle-bones showing white where she clutched his mantle.

'Or Christmas at Rochester – that game of hunt-the-slipper? It wasn't all bad, was it?'

Catrin's throat worked. 'It was false,' she whispered.

His lips stretched in a mirthless smile. 'Was it? Then we were both duped. True or false, for what it is worth, I did love you, Catty. Remember that if you forget all else.' Turning, he walked with light step to the side of the bridge, and just as lightly leaped off into the murky water of the Frome before anyone could move to stop him.

Catrin's cry of denial was swallowed up in the rush of the crowd to the side. There was nothing to see but churning brown water, flowing fast in spring spate. No head broke the surface, no string of bubbles showed where he had gone down.

Catrin covered her face with her hands and pressed herself into Oliver's cold, muddied breast. Expression grim, Oliver set his arm around her shoulders.

'Be washed up on the strand next tide,' observed the cart driver with grim cheer. 'Last one did after the winter storms.'

'Unless he survives,' Oliver said. It was not logical that Louis could live – he had jumped in the water wearing his sword and a heavy quilted gambeson – but Oliver still had a nightmare vision of Louis crawling out of the water on to the riverbank and grinning at him like a demon while he wrung out his clothes.

'No.' Catrin sniffed and raised her face, dabbing at her eyes with the edge of her wimple. 'Living would mean a slow death as an outcast, and I know that his vanity could not bear it.'

Oliver touched her wet cheek, his eyes questioning.

'He had leprosy.' She swallowed, struggling again with nausea. 'He . . . he asked me for an ingredient for the cure, and when I refused because it involved a stillborn child, he lost his temper. The rest you know.'

Oliver wrapped his arms around her, encompassing her in love and comfort, sharing her anger, absorbing her grief. Around them the crowd dispersed and the cart rumbled through on its way into the town. One guard returned to his post. The other went to report the incident and instigate a search.

'Home,' Catrin said, clinging to Oliver. 'Take me home.'

'You are home,' he said, burying his face in her half-exposed hair. 'For ever.'

On the eve before Henry's army marched out of Gloucester, the body of Lewis of Chepstow washed up on the estuary shore. Three days it had been in the water and now it was bloated, the skin heavy grey-white. There were tears and contusions where it had struck stones and driftwood. The brave blue colour had washed out of the tunic and one shoe was missing in parody of the time before when he had pretended death by drowning.

Oliver crouched by the corpse, his nostrils filled with the scent of the sea and the taint of decaying flesh. As the sheriff's men looked on, he made identification and then gently turned the right wrist. The lesion was where Catrin had said it would be; pale as the body was pale, but still evident.

'Poor bastard,' one of the men muttered.

Oliver stood up and looked down at the remains. Gulls wheeled and cried. The sun slanted, filling his eyes with light. 'Bury him deep,' he said. 'And let God be his judge.'

CHAPTER 36

SPRING 1155

There was sunshine in the hollow this morning, bright liquid gold filled with a heart of green dapple and birdsong. Oliver drew rein to inhale the heavy aroma of the April forest and turned to look at the troop of soldiers riding two abreast behind him.

Spear points glittered, armour and harness were burnished. Shields were carried on their long straps, slung round to the back. For all the array, there was no danger of battle. King Stephen had been in his grave since autumn's end. Eustace was dead and Henry sat upon the throne of a relieved and peaceful kingdom.

The land bore scars of the conflict, some that were healing, others that were still raw wounds. Oliver opened and closed his left hand, feeling the strength and the weakness against the leather brace encircling his forearm. He looked at the ploughlands, tipped with new green, and his spirit rose to meet them.

Half-turning, he smiled at Catrin. 'I once rode this way despairing that it would ever be mine again,' he said. 'And if not for Godard, I would have died in this hollow here without ever knowing that a day like this could exist.' His glance swivelled further to the huge man sitting on a tall bay gelding, two small boys perched up with him, one copper, one dark.

'I couldn't leave you, my lord. Besides, you saved my life once on the road.' Godard waved dismissively but Oliver could tell that he was touched and pleased at the acknowledgement. The hostel-keeper was wearing his best tunic for

the occasion and his dark beard had been severely barbered by
Edith, who was riding in the baggage wain with a consignment
of her famous ale for the feast to come.

'Why have we stopped?' Simon demanded, craning round
at Godard and then looking at his father. 'Are we nearly
there?'

'Almost,' Oliver replied, with a fond glance at his sons.
'Twenty years is a long time to be gone. The moment can
ripen a little longer.' He drew a deep breath of the air in the
hollow which marked the boundary of Ashbury land.

Simon wrinkled his nose, the concept of twenty years being
completely outside his grasp. Henry yawned and sucked his
thumb. Rosamund sat her pony demurely, but the way the
small animal sidled and swished was a sign of its rider's
suppressed excitement.

Fond pride and amusement in her eyes, Catrin eyed her
daughter and smiled. She knew how Rosamund felt. There
was a pleasant churning in her own vitals as she thought of
what the day was to hold, and she was filled with joy for
Oliver. At last he was returning to the lands that had been
his family's, time out of mind. Not only that, but he was
bringing the future with him.

There had been no encounter with Odinel the Fleming.
He had died of a septic wound in the same month that Henry
became king. His wife and daughter had gone to London to
live with a distant relative whose lands were not in dispute.

Catrin was glad that it had not come to a fight. From what
they heard, Odinel had been a decent man for a mercenary,
honourable by his code. Apart from the few months when
Randal de Mohun had been captain of the garrison, the people
had not suffered unduly from a foreigner's rule.

Oliver gathered up the reins and heeled Lucifer's flank.
The grey paced forward on the path. For a moment Catrin
admired the sight of man and horse in fluid motion before
riding up to join them. There was a glow about Oliver today,
as well there should be. The planes of his face were relaxed and
there was a curve to his lips. Nothing could mar the pleasure
of the day.

It was almost two years since Louis had died. At first the

memory of that day, the ghost of his presence, had cast a long shadow. There were times when even in death it would have been all too easy for Louis to have sundered the bond between Catrin and Oliver. And because it would have been too easy, because neither of them wanted Louis to win, they had fought – with each other and then side by side; emerging from the fray strong and polished. Louis's shadow still lingered, but it was small now and insignificant. They could turn their backs on it and walk in the sunshine. Husband and wife. She touched the talisman of the woven love knot around her neck.

Oliver must have caught the movement for he glanced at her, a question in his eyes.

'I was thinking of our wedding day,' she said with a smile.

Oliver returned it. 'It is not every couple who have England's King and the heir to the throne as groomsmen and the Archbishop of Canterbury to perform the rites.'

'I wasn't thinking of the splendour.' They had been married during the negotiations for the peace treaty at Winchester, which meant that almost the entire baronage of England and the borders had been present to witness the ceremony.

'Then what?'

Catrin looked at him through her lashes. 'I was thinking that that day was and this day is perfect and how much I love you.' Conscious of the men behind him, she spoke quietly. Soft, bedchamber talk was not appropriate for the moment, but he had asked her.

Without bothering to look over his shoulder to see how many were watching, Oliver reached out and briefly squeezed his hand over hers. 'And set to become more perfect yet,' he said. 'I love you too, wife.'

They rode into Ashbury and the people gathered outside their houses to watch the troop ride past. Everywhere there were flashes of colour. Best garments had been donned. Hands and faces had been scrubbed and hair tidied. It was a mark of welcome and respect, but it was also anticipation. They knew that a feast of grand proportions was coming their way. Oliver grinned with pleasure and greeted many by name, reverting with ease to the English tongue. Rosamund stared on wide-eyed. Henry clapped and shouted. Simon hid his face in Godard's tunic.

Instead of riding on to the keep, Oliver led the troop towards the small stone and timber church at the end of the main street and here dismounted. The villagers crowded behind, laughing, chattering, arguing.

Oliver lifted Catrin from her mare and led her to the church door. Then he turned her on his arm to face his troop and the people. 'I know we are already wed,' he murmured, 'but would you consider tying the knot again at the church door in front of Father Alberic?'

Catrin tilted her head to one side. 'Why?' From the corner of her eye she saw an elderly man in dusty priest's robes hurrying from the direction of his cottage and almost tripping over his robe in his haste.

'It would mean a great deal to the old man,' Oliver said. 'He wed my parents here and my brother. He's Ethel's half-brother, you know. My great-grandfather sent him to be educated for the priesthood at Malmesbury.'

Catrin stared. She was lost for words by the turn events had taken.

'It would mean a great deal to me too,' Oliver added softly, and took her hand, his thumb gently rubbing her knuckles. 'I want to set the seal on our new beginning.'

The priest arrived and for a moment leaned against the church wall to regain his breath. His tonsure was in need of a trim and his habit looked as if it had been used as a dog bed, but his careworn face was kindly and Catrin could see a distinct resemblance to Ethel in his blunt features. He was clutching a wedding chaplet fashioned out of daffodils and primroses.

'Welcome, my lord, my lady,' he wheezed.

Catrin eyed the chaplet narrowly. It had taken more than five minutes to make. 'You planned all this beforehand, didn't you?' she asked Oliver, with a gesture at the grinning villagers in their best feast-day clothes.

'Was I wrong?' His hand tightened over hers and his grey eyes were alight with love and humour . . . and perhaps the faintest trace of anxiety. Louis's shadow sulking in its corner.

Catrin gently took the chaplet from the recovering priest, removed her wimple and set the crown of flowers upon her braids. 'No,' she murmured, 'and in any case, I forgive you.'

They kissed to the accompaniment of cheers. As they entered the church, the scent of the flowers was joined by a poignant, herbal aroma and Catrin knew that this moment was special for Ethel too.

AUTHOR'S NOTE

The author's note at the end of my novels is the place where I like to explain the threads of my research which have had an important bearing on the telling of the tale. I think this is because quite often the truth is stranger than fiction and I want to show that while the main characters in *The Love Knot* have come from my imagination, the roots from which they sprang are firmly grounded in fact.

The period of the civil war in England between Stephen and Mathilda is a complicated one with families and loyalties strained and sundered, sides swapped at the flick of a sword, and sudden shifts in the balance of power. I have tried to simplify the politics as much as possible so that they do not hold up the drive of Oliver and Catrin's story. Indeed, to have covered every switch and turn of the conflict would have made *The Love Knot* longer than *The Lord of the Rings*, more complicated than a tangled ball of knitting wool, and given my editor a nervous breakdown! Having said that, all the broad brushstrokes of the turbulence are in place.

Since leprosy made a sufferer an outcast from society, there were those prepared to take desperate measures to find a cure. It was while researching the midwife's art in the Middle Ages that I came across the true case of a Frenchman stricken with leprosy who had inveigled an unscrupulous midwife into procuring a stillborn child for him in the belief that its fat was a certain cure for the disease.

It was also while researching the role of the herb-wife in more general terms that I turned up a wealth of information on knot magic, a lore which had been practised from the time of the Ancient Greeks. Even today, when people marry they are said to be 'tying the knot', a saying that goes back to the binding of two life threads by the Goddess Aphrodite. For anyone wanting to read further, I recommend the utterly fascinating *Woman's Encyclopedia of Myths and Secrets* by Barbara G. Walker.

Although I have used the name Chepstow in the novel, during Stephen's time it was known by the earlier Welsh title of Striguil. As this is a name unfamiliar to the modern reader, I have changed it to the later rendition by which it is now known.